The Emma Caites Way

The Emma Caites Way
A.V. Walters

Two Rock Press

Cedar, Michigan

This novel is entirely fictional, with no intent to depict actual persons or events other than those within a few historical allusions.

Copyright © 2011 A.V. Walters

Published by Two Rock Press
P.O. Box 209, Cedar MI 49621
TwoRockPress.com

Book and Cover Design by Rick Edwards

ISBN: 978-0-9832172-0-6

Library of Congress Control Number: 2011925333

Printed in the USA

In loving memory of the very best of my

Dear Old Dad

Fiona sighed, and wiped her hands again on the damp, germ-free wipe. She was running out of them and was reaching back into the wad of sodden, smudged towelettes in the bottom of her purse. This was not her idea of a fun Saturday. She glanced over at Amanda, who was running her fingers across the tops of the racks of vintage clothing. Amanda was totally engaged. Fiona was bored and impatient. Fiona knew that Amanda was convinced she needed a hobby. When Amanda wasn't teaching special-ed, she was a bottom feeder. She shopped the flea markets and thrift stores, then sold her finds on eBay. It was hard to argue against such an endeavor, when last year Amanda brought in an extra $27,000, under the table. And she loved it.

Fiona was not impressed. While she credited herself with having a good eye, all she saw here was dirt and dust. The merchandise in this little antiques/consignment store was shopworn and filthy. Fiona was asthmatic. Two dogs wandered the cluttered aisles of the store. Fiona sneezed. Where Amanda saw potential, Fiona saw grime. She reached into her purse, and pulled out her inhaler, for the fourth time, since they'd come in the door. In an effort to minimize her exposure, Fiona had parked herself in a corner by a rack of old paintings, and was idly flipping though them, killing time, waiting for Amanda. She'd glance down from time to time—another moonlight seascape, another lighthouse. These paintings must have been sold by the gross at Kresge's. If a painting was unframed, well-framed or clearly on a stretched canvas, Fiona'd give it extra consideration, but those were far and few in this collection of dreck.

Amanda had accumulated quite an armload of goods. Every now and then she'd mutter, "Oh my" under her breath, or shout out, "Geez, Fio, remember these?" while waving some God-awful plaid jumper at her. The killer was that Amanda really could find the gems. Even if they didn't specifically appeal to her, she knew what would sell. Fiona had no such insight into the second-hand market.

She absently flipped to another filthy painting, and then tipped it back in recognition. Fiona stepped closer. It was a small oil painting of a well-tended, 1920s Mediterranean courtyard-style apartment building, viewed from inside one of the apartments. Fiona pulled it out for a closer look. It was a painting of her own apartment complex, viewed from an odd angle. Painted, maybe even exactly, from her upstairs window. Through the years of neglect, Fiona could see its soft pinks and yellows, the colors of the stucco when the night's grays faded into the early morning. It wasn't big, only about ten inches by fourteen, but the picture captured the feeling of Fiona's familiar morning view. It was muddied but charming. Fiona brought the canvas over to the light. Surely that painting was done from the window of her very own apartment in Oakland. Fiona knew that view, the undulations of the terracotta tiles, the warmth of the stucco, and the familiar metal-framed windows. She had to have it. Fiona fought back her natural shyness, and approached the counter.

"How much for this old painting?" she asked the shopkeeper. He was grizzled and as unkempt as the store itself, so his alert response surprised her.

"What ya got there, an Emma Caites study?"

Fiona looked down and studied the squared capital letters of the signature, sure enough, it read, "EMMA CAITES '38."

"Yes, I guess it is. I picked it because it looks like my building."

"You live over on Wayne Street, by the lake?"

"Yeah, do you know it?"

"Not been by for years, but when I was a kid, my uncle used to take me there when Ms. Caites lived there. He was her framer, and we'd pick up her paintings regular, for framing."

"So this really *is* my building?"

"Yeah, she lived there on Wayne for most of her life."

"How much for the painting?"

The shopkeeper came over, and looked at it over Fiona's

shoulder. "It's a nice one, kinda dirty but once it's cleaned up, she'll shine. I have a couple of her paintings myself. I tell you what. I'll let you have it for one twenty-five."

Fiona was taken aback. She'd been thinking fifty. Amanda stepped over to look. Her face reflected her natural disdain for a seller's price, and she added her own two cents worth.

"That frame on it is junk, plus you'll have to get it cleaned, that's not cheap." She paused, and looking at the shopkeeper added, fishing, "It's not like she's famous or anything."

He paused and jutted out his lower lip, "No, more like talented local color. She painted all her adult life, here in Oakland. I think she earned her living with it but there'd always been rumors she came from money."

Amanda turned to Fiona. "It needs a lot of work. Offer him seventy."

Fiona was mortified. Never in her life had she bargained in a store. She looked down at the painting in her hands. She really wanted it, but couldn't speak. The shop was silent.

"I'll give it to you for ninety, and I'll throw in some chemicals and cleaning instructions."

Now both the shopkeeper and Amanda were looking at her. Fiona flushed with embarrassment but still could not find her voice. She reached out to hand the painting back to the shopkeeper. It wasn't clear, even to her, whether this was a purchase or a resigned shrug at the price. She just couldn't get her mouth to work. The painting hung in the air, from her extended grasp.

The shopkeeper let a moment pass, then looking at the stack in Amanda's arms added, "Okay, same deal, but for eighty dollars. But that's my last offer. It *is* an original oil painting."

Fiona nodded, placed the painting on the counter and reached for her purse. It was hers. She sighed with relief, and wrote the check, her hands shaking a little.

Amanda piled her goods on the counter and proceeded to dicker sternly for every piece, item by item. Fiona was dumbstruck. She'd seen this at flea markets, but she would never have imagined Amanda fighting for pennies on chipped ceramic salt and pepper shakers. Amanda was a pit bull. This revealed a new wrinkle in her friend's hobby.

They made an odd pair—Amanda, tall, thin to the point of gaunt, with flaming red hair and kooky clothes and Fiona, plump,

3

conservatively dressed, with every hair in place, nails polished and precision make-up. Thus they'd been for forty years of friendship, Catholic school refugees bonded by teenage misery. Indeed, it was a good pairing. Amanda needed grounding and Fiona needed spunk. Between them they shared particularly sick senses of humor, one Fiona would never indulge with anyone but Amanda.

After Amanda's goods were bagged, the shopkeeper turned back to Fiona, "I'm going to give you two solvents. You clean with the creamy one, and neutralize with the clear. Don't do it inside, and don't saturate the canvas or push on it too hard. Some people use Q-tips. I like a soft rag." He smiled, "My name's Norm. Here's my card if you have any questions."

Outside with their treasures, Amanda lost her bargain-hunter's edge, and reverted to her regular bubbly and enthusiastic self. "You were great in there. I thought you were going to roll over and pay full price, but you hung in there. When you handed him back the painting, it was perfect." She smiled, "It's a good deal too. I can hardly wait until we get that home to clean it." Then she went on to describe the deals she'd found, and show off the vintage haul that would distinguish her as a savvy eBay seller.

Fiona was still in shock. She hugged her painting to her chest. She already loved it, and wanted it cleaned and reframed immediately. She was relieved that Amanda thought her tongue-tied silence had been astute bargaining. Fiona was dying to know more about the artist who had once lived in her building.

That evening, Fiona set up in the garage with the painting, some cotton swabs and a small pile of rags. The painting was filthy and smelled of cigarettes. She removed the tacky frame, and began rubbing the canvas with the cleaning solvent, alternating with the neutralizer. In little patches the true painting revealed itself. Slowly the colors brightened, the reflection of sunrise pinks on the stucco walls of the Mediterranean-style building shone, becoming clear and luminous as the grime lifted away, its early morning sky filtering a soft yellow light. Fiona was up almost all night, but by morning the painting was a gem. She brought it upstairs to the east window, and there it was. The painting was clearly painted from exactly that spot in her apartment. It gave Fiona chills. Emma Caites had painted it from her apartment back in 1938. More than that, the painting was beautiful. Broad brushstrokes in the shrubbery gave way to smooth and stippled stucco strokes, capturing exactly the texture of the walls outside her window, its glass in the painting even reflected back the same distorted reflections from the units across the way. Though she'd often stood at the window in the morning with her coffee, Fiona felt now that she'd seen this for the first time, through eyes from almost seventy years ago. She wondered that this artist had taken the time to notice these little details and to record them. For what audience? Who would care enough to note such details in an apartment? Who *was* Emma Caites?

After catching a couple hours sleep, she invited Amanda over for brunch to see the transformation. Ever since her daughter had married and moved out of town, Fiona could tell that Amanda had been trying to lure her into something new to grab her flagging interest. For twenty-six years the center of Fiona's life had been her daughter, so much so that when her husband left the day of Denise's fifth birthday party, Fiona didn't notice his absence until the next day and, after the initial shock of it, not much after that. Even when Denise went off to college, and then started a career of her own, they'd talked every day. Fiona orchestrated their life together with Denise in tow.

That spring, after a year of planning and spending, Fiona had thrown Denise a lovely wedding with everything she might need to start off her new life. For her part, and to Fiona's shock, Denise did just that, almost immediately relocating to Houston for her new husband's job. For the first time in her adult life, Fiona found herself entirely alone and without focus. She hardly felt comfortable alone in her apartment in the evening. Fiona's closest friends understood, but could do little to make up for this sudden emptiness.

In the face of Fiona's obvious enthusiasm over the painting, Amanda was smug. She tried to get Fiona to list the painting for sale by auction, but Fiona wouldn't hear of it. This little painting was for her.

Amanda laughed, "You'll never make any money collecting. You have to *sell* stuff."

Fiona didn't see herself as a second-hand dealer. She was a professional in an orderly, tiny world of numbers and things. Fiona did accounting on estates and trusts. In her world, only the values changed. She tidied up after the mess of life, arranging the affairs of the dead, and placing the appropriate numbers in the right boxes. Her own world did not include much mystery or mess.

Later that day Fiona tried to return to the thrift shop on Piedmont for more information but it was closed Sundays. Instead, she found a frame store and spent several hours picking the perfect frame for her little gem. She was determined to learn more about Emma Caites, her work as a painter and her association with the Wayne Street apartments. Fiona Googled "Emma Caites" but found no listings. How could a painter, who'd lived and painted in Oakland her whole life, not be listed? From her work doing probate accounting, Fiona knew some art appraisers, and she decided to see what they knew.

Chapter Two

Frustrated. That's how Fiona felt. Nothing was working in the right direction. She had several work projects, each of which needed minor input from others before she could finish. With no return calls on any of them, she was spinning her wheels. What she really wanted to do was find out more about Emma Caites. There, too, she'd been hitting brick walls. Her landlord thought she was crazy to inquire about former tenants—going back to the thirties no less! She'd called her contacts at the Oakland Museum, who had no references to Caites at all. She'd called several local art dealers, some of whom had heard of Emma Caites, vaguely, but could give no specifics. Emma Caites was low on the radar of the art world. Fiona was disappointed. Not that she expected to have unearthed a Rembrandt but she so loved her little painting, that she found it hard to believe the artist wasn't more renowned.

She'd tried calling Norm, the shopkeeper on Piedmont, but could only leave messages. And when she dropped by, the gum-snapping teenager watching the store said that Norm was in the hospital, nothing too serious, something about legs and clots. Fiona was troubled by that. It occurred to her for the first time that Emma was from a time that was fast losing any survivors to remember her. Fiona could almost feel the sand slipping through the hourglass. On a long shot, Fiona had submitted a Request for a Death Certificate at the Alameda County offices. Since she didn't have a date of death, the clerk told her the search couldn't be done on the microfiche, and she'd have to pay and wait. Leave a self-addressed stamped envelope with your application form, please. Fiona was almost ready to visit Norm at the hospital but that seemed alarmingly forward. In the meantime, the painting was still at the framer and Fiona felt like she was chasing shadows, without even the company of the quiet painting that had started all this.

With Saturday approaching, Fiona was eager to resume the search of junk stores and estate sales with Amanda. But then Amanda informed her that she didn't shop every weekend. Acquisition was only one phase of the hobby. She also had to launder, mend, refurbish, market, auction and ship goods in an endless rotation of vintage restoration and recycling. Fiona was intimidated by the idea of trekking alone, from one grimy shop to another, in search of clues on Emma Caites.

On Friday morning, Fiona almost had a meltdown trying to decide what to do about the weekend. She clung obsessively to the idea of pursuing Emma Caites, but didn't know how or where to start. She had almost settled on visiting Norm in the hospital when the framing store called to tell her the painting was ready. Fiona was so excited, she blew off the work day and went directly to retrieve her painting. It was hanging in the window at the framers. It was stunning. The clerk seemed disappointed that Fiona had returned so quickly to get it. Fiona had forgotten how lovely the piece was, and now framed, it took her breath away. Why wasn't this woman famous? Fiona had selected a gilded flat frame with carved corners. The rose and peach tones glowed like a sunrise against the gilding. With that satisfaction, Fiona's professional resolve returned, and she headed directly to Clar's Auction Gallery to have it appraised. They were local. Surely they'd have some insight into Emma's Oakland history.

"There's not much that's official on her," the appraiser intoned. He was a large florid gentleman with pink cheeks and round, silver framed eyeglasses. "She was very prolific. We used to see her work all the time. It's lovely, but she never broke into the top tier. Seems she never really tried. She was just as talented as many of the artists of her time, and her plein air work is incredible, but she mostly stuck with private commission work and teaching classes. There's not much of a secondary market for portraits and home paintings. Yours is a lovely study. She did literally dozens of these, from all angles of the apartment complex. We see some of her work each year on the auction side." He stopped and pulled out a black ledger, and flipped through it.

"We used to see more, mostly through estates, but there's a turnover on such things. We liquidate them when the original owners die, and the new owners hang onto them for a while before they come around again." He turned a few more pages and looked up, "It's a bit of a lull these days. As for value, she's a bargain. Right now the California plein air stuff is really hot, but collectors are looking for listed artists, known names. Even the smaller, insignificant paintings, start at about $6,000."

He leaned back in his chair, pulled a handkerchief out of his pocket and started cleaning his glasses thoughtfully. "Since Caites is not listed, a little study like this goes for about $1,200 to $1,800. Framed up nice like yours an Emma Caites could bring $2,200 at auction on a good day, mostly to the decorator crowd. It's a lovely little study but from a value perspective, she doesn't touch a Xavier Martinez or a Seldon Giles. I think she was disabled or something, that's the reason she did so little outdoor work. You have a lovely picture here, and if it's of your apartment you have that extra satisfaction. But it's not tremendously valuable as a California piece goes. You should just enjoy it." He smiled broadly, "Did you need that written up for insurance?"

Fiona should have been delighted. Her eighty dollar painting and two hundred dollar frame had just jumped to a possible $2,200 value. Amanda would be really impressed, but Fiona felt cheated, mostly on Emma's behalf. Why didn't her work rate with other artists? Disability? How crippled was she? Was it the fact that she was female? Maybe Fiona needed to see more paintings to solve the mystery. Maybe hers was a fluke.

"Do you know where I could find out more about her?"

The appraiser wrinkled his face, "You might check out the History Room at the Oakland Library. Put in a card here too so you'll be called if any Caites paintings go on the block, and then just scout around like you are."

"Thank you, I'll do that. If you hear anything, would you give me a call?"

"Sure." He made a notation on the computer screen. "But don't hold your breath. You're more likely to track this down than I am. You seem pretty motivated."

9

Chapter Three

Fidgeting nervously in the elevator, Fiona stood, bouquet in hand, punching the third floor button awkwardly. She had the painting, wrapped in butcher paper, under her other arm. It'd been so difficult selecting flowers. How do you choose hospital flowers for a man you don't know? Ultimately she'd gone with a combination of blue irises and sunflowers, not too frilly, colorful, cheery but not intimate. She sighed and wondered if maybe sometimes she just thought too much. Fiona wasn't sure why she felt compelled to show Norm the painting. There was the risk that he'd feel cheated, now that the eighty dollar painting was cleaned up and looked so good. Yet, it was the only association she had with him, and now, visiting the man in the hospital, she felt she needed the painting connection, even if just as a prop. This early Sunday morning, she hoped he didn't have any other visitors. It would be hard to explain why she was there.

Fiona needn't have worried. Norm lay quietly in bed with the television blaring, tethered to his hospital bed by tubes in and out of every limb. He looked very small. There were no flowers in the room, or magazines, or any other personal touches showing he'd been there all week. Fiona barely recognized him, but then reminded herself she really didn't know him anyway, so that wasn't surprising.

"Norm? Norm Gilbert?" He looked up, confused, not recognizing her either.

"Norm, I know you don't know me, but…"

"Are you religious?" he demanded. "I don't need'ny Sunday visitors, thank you."

Fiona realized Norm thought she was proselytizing. "No, no, no, I'm from your shop. I kept coming by to thank you but you weren't there."

Norm squinted up at her, still no recognition. Fiona couldn't blame him; she was entirely out of any context and they really didn't know each other. She just stood there nervously holding the flowers. This had been a mistake.

"I am the one who bought the Emma Caites painting. You told me how to clean it." She spoke a little too loudly, as if he was deaf.

"You bought a painting? At my shop?" Norm struggled to sit up, "The apartment building?"

"Yes, yes and you gave me the cleaning fluids."

"Hell yeah, I remember you. You came with that wacky vintage clothing lady, the redhead. She drives me nuts."

Fiona wasn't quite sure how to respond. "Yes, I came with Amanda. I guess she's a regular."

"Nothing regular about her, that woman's just weird. Imagine her jumping in to talk down the price on your purchase like that. You just looked shocked. No sense of decorum in some folks. So, what are you doing here?" Just like in the store, Norm was quick once he knew the score.

"I wanted to thank you. I did what you said, with the cleaners, and the painting turned out beautifully."

"Glad it worked out." He paused and nodded at the flowers, "Them for me?"

"Oh, yes." Flustered, Fiona had forgotten the bouquet in her hand.

"Well, best get'em in some water. No point in wasting flowers." Fiona rushed to arrange the blooms in the plastic water pitcher on the tray-table.

"So, what else you got there?"

Hands freed, Fiona began unwrapping the canvas, "It's the painting. I brought it so you could see it cleaned up." She pulled it out and held it for his approval.

"Yeah, looks great. Nice frame too. I'm glad you went with a traditional Arts and Crafts. That painting wouldn't work in a modern frame. She did a lot of those, the studies of the apartment building."

"I wanted to ask you more about her. I can't seem to find anything."

"She was a beautiful woman, crippled up a bit but with the face of an angel. I always had a crush on her. I was only pint sized, mind you, but my uncle and I went to her apartment, probably twice a month. She couldn't fit the larger canvases into her car, or really handle them well, so we'd pick them up and the customers would come in and would pick out the frame."

"What did she look like?"

"She was slim, with dark hair, a little wavy like yours, and parted in the middle, to here," he gestured to his shoulders, "Curled

11

under at the ends." He tipped his head back, and closed his eyes. "She had an oval face and almond-shaped brown eyes, perfect skin, and she had the most beautiful rounded eyebrows. She could look at you and laugh with just her eyebrows. She liked me, used to give me treats, oranges and stuff. This was during the Depression, so that was really special."

"What else did she paint?"

Norm looked up. "Well, in the thirties, she did some portraits, lots of the apartment paintings for herself, and some landscapes, when she could get out. Later she did more commissioned portraits and the house paintings."

"House paintings?"

"Yeah, folks'd hire her to do a portrait of their house. Lots of folks in Trestle Glen would do that. One guy even had her paint a portrait of his car!"

"Were her other paintings as good as mine?"

"Sure, mostly better. She was really good. You should've seen her landscapes, she made those men artists look silly. Trained in France you know, she was the real deal. I have two of her paintings at home. One wasn't ever picked up at the frame shop and the other little one she gave me for helping to carry her canvases."

"I'd love to see them, when you get better, if that would be okay with you." Fiona shyly realized she was inviting herself to this man's home. "Why wasn't she more recognized?"

"It was hard times. She was crippled, and a woman. I never questioned that until years later, it seemed normal at the time. She gave classes; some women took in laundry. It just seemed that people did what they had to do. Later I lost track of her. There was a falling out in my family and I had to stop working with my uncle."

A nurse came in with Norm's breakfast tray. She checked his vitals and made notations on the chart. "Doctor's orders Mr. Gilbert, you and me have to go for a walk right after breakfast."

Norm looked at Fiona, and shrugged.

"Norm, I'm imposing. I'd love to talk to you more on this and see your paintings. Is there a good time for me to visit again?"

"I think I'll be home in a couple of days, I'll give you a call, got your number still, on the check. In the meantime, you might want to try looking up the boy."

"The *boy*?"

"Yeah, Ms. Caites had a son, spitting image of her right down to those eyebrows, cutest little guy. Maybe you should try to find him. His name was Thomas."

Fiona's heart leaped. Maybe there was a living son, someone who would know her story. "I didn't know, a son," she said thinking aloud, "I wonder how I could find him."

"Well, I'm not one of these computer types. If it was me, I'd try the phone book for starters."

Fiona thumped herself on the forehead. "Of course, how stupid of me. Caites is not a common name. Thank you Norm, you've been tremendous."

"I'll give you a call when I'm out of here. Good luck on your search." He pulled the tray of food over to the bed, and removed the cover.

He grimaced, then smiled at her, "Thanks for the flowers. Next time, bring food."

Chapter Four

"Can I offer you some tea?" Norm Gilbert seemed much more formal here in his home. Fiona hoped he'd relax back to his regular self. The breakfast nook, and attached kitchen, looked like a perfect late 1940s museum piece. She was seated at white enameled table with green trim around the edge, set on dark green wood painted legs. The green chairs matched the table base. The wallpaper was a print in soft tones, yellow, green, rose and rust with a repeating little farm scene. Flanking the window were two built-in corner china cabinets, painted to match the creamy yellow trim that ran throughout the nook and the kitchen. A colorful ceramic rooster perched on top of one of the corner cabinets. The kitchen had the original off-white tile counters with tiled yellow edge trim. Even the appliances on the countertop were forties vintage, a mint-condition Mixmaster with a green milk glass bowl and an old KitchenAid coffee grinder. A worn green and yellow apron hung on a hook on the back of the kitchen door. Amanda would go nuts in here. Given his business, Norm had to know that his kitchen was Smithsonian-grade, vintage Americana. Except that this was all original, in a cheery mid-century unpretentious way. It was clear that this was the Gilberts' first and only effort at kitchen décor. It was in impeccable shape. The only sign of age was where the paint had worn thin around the cabinet knobs and edges. Fiona felt a pang of tenderness for them, frozen in time. The kitchen was neat, except that Fiona noted a slight film on the enamel table as if it had been wiped with a dingy sponge. *Elderly housekeeping.* Fiona remembered how her own mother's cleaning had slipped as her eyesight failed. Norm noticed her looking around the kitchen.

"It's old-fashioned, but it's good enough for me. Besides, I couldn't possibly change it. This was my wife's kitchen, and she loved it."

"I do too," countered Fiona, "It feels like home. I'd love some tea, thank you."

Fiona watched as Norm boiled the water, pre-heated the green ceramic teapot and set the cups on a wooden tray. He dropped in two Lipton teabags, and poured the water. Finally, just before carrying the tray to the table, he placed a crocheted cozy over the teapot. It was obviously a well-practiced ritual.

"When my wife died, I tried to keep everything just as she did. I really haven't kept up the shop but the house is still pretty much as she loved it."

"I can see why, this is such a warm and friendly kitchen. You must have been very happy here."

"We had our good times and bad, like most folks. We hung in there." Norm sat quietly for a moment, lifted the cozy, and poured two cups of tea. Fiona sipped her tea, and Norm continued, "So, any luck reaching Thomas?"

She set her cup down gently on the enamel. "Good luck and bad, I think. There were only four Caites in the residential book. At least one of them was a relative, a nasty woman who either didn't know or like Emma well. I actually found Thomas in the business section. Apparently he's an architect, and still working. I found an office number in North Berkeley but no home listing for him."

"And?"

"I called, but it did not go well. Mr. Caites did not appreciate unsolicited contact. He really didn't like questions about his mother."

"What did you say?"

"I introduced myself and said that I'd purchased a painting done by Emma Caites, and was looking for more information about the artist. Then I asked if he was any relation."

"Did you tell him you lived in the apartment in the painting?"

"I never got that far. He said that Emma Caites was his mother, but that she'd been dead since 1958. He said he hoped I enjoyed my painting but that he was a busy man and not inclined to reminisce with amateur art enthusiasts. He wished me luck, and then hung up on me."

"How rude."

"Not rude exactly, but crisp. I was hoping you might be able to suggest some better strategy for reaching out to him."

"It's not like we really know each other. I worked at the frame shop from the mid thirties through the end of the war, first as a kid, and then more regular when I was a teen. My uncle always brought me along because Ms. Caites kinda liked me. I used to play with Thomas when we went there. But I don't know if he would remember me. Maybe he would. When I got older he used to ask me questions about cars. I think he was looking for information to help

15

his mom buy a new car." Norm poured more tea.

"Is there anyone else that she knew, that you knew?

"She continued to deal with the frame shop into the fifties, so my cousin, Murray, might remember stuff. You'll have to make that inquiry directly to him without naming me. I think I mentioned there was some bad blood there. Murray will probably be listed in the Oakland phone book, Murray Gilbert."

"Is the frame shop still there?"

"I don't know, don't go by there much. It was, up into the mid-nineties. Murray's daughter was running it then. Murray is easily impressed. Tell him you're considering writing a biography of Emma Caites, that way he'll be more likely to help."

"Maybe I should tell Thomas I'm writing a biography?"

"Not till you have more information on her. Maybe then."

Fiona sighed. She set her cup down in its saucer. "It feels all uphill. Could I please see her paintings?"

"Oh yeah, of course." Norm stood weakly, and led the way to the living room. Fiona reminded herself not to overstay her welcome; Norm had just spent ten days in the hospital. The living room was comfortable but sparely furnished. She wondered at the contrast between the cluttered shop and the simple furnishings here. She followed him to a large painting of a Tudor-style home, with English style gardens on a suburban looking street. It was well painted, slightly impressionistic, a clearly recognizable rendition of a house with a car in the driveway out front. The controlled brush strokes were even and the colors accurate, but a little muted. The same squared letters marked the signature, "EMMA CAITES, 39."

"Here's one of those house portraits I told you about. The family that commissioned it never came to pick it up. I never understood why, whether or not Emma got paid for it, but after a year or so, my uncle let me have it. I know it's odd to hang a painting of someone else's house, but I always liked it. When I got it, I rode my bike all over Trestle Glen till I found the right house. Ms. Caites used to laugh and say that she was a house-painter."

"You don't get much of a feel for her as a painter from this. It's not like my painting; mine just glows."

"Well, she was pretty attached to that apartment. Like I said, she painted it over and over again. I asked her why she painted it so often. She said, 'Because it's there. Because in its own way, it's beautiful.' She told me that some artists painted haystacks or lily

16

ponds, she just painted the Wayne Street apartments. Then she threw back her head, and laughed out loud. Much later I learned that those were references to famous French painters. At the time all I cared about was the way she laughed so loud and enjoyed the joke so much. It was years before I got the punch line." He paused, reflecting. "Let me show you the other one."

Norm led her to the bedroom where a small landscape hung over the dresser. Norm reached over to open the curtain for more light. The painting was stunning. It showed a line of eucalyptus trees hugging the curve of a golden summer hill. In the foreground, neat rows of field crops angled up to that procession of trees, and in the open, steeper pasture above three cows grazed. At first glance the colors seemed accurate, but a closer inspection showed burgundy in the foreground and turquoise edging the amber summer grasses. The green and silver foliage were punctuated with a deep claret, which reminded you in the moment that that was the color of the eucalyptus blooms. The trunks captured the light in their peeling sage and sienna bark. The angle of the planted furrows, in deep greens and ochres, led the eye to the trees, then up the line of the hill to the open field. The painting sang. Its brushstrokes mirrored the textures of the subjects, choppy short strokes for the row crops, wild curving strokes for the foliage and smooth hill hugging strokes for the golden, late summer grass. The cows were merely suggested, with a few quick dashes of brown and white, but were clearly round and solid cows. In the right lower corner was the now familiar signature, and the date, 1940. Fiona could see that the appraiser was right. Emma Caites could capture a landscape.

"Norm, this is really beautiful."

"I know. I've always loved it. She gave it to me when I was sixteen. I'd admired the fresh canvas on the easel where it was drying, and Ms. Caites just up and handed it to me. I was stunned, tried to give it back, but she refused. After that I was always afraid to comment on any of the paintings. When we married, Lily used to joke that she married me for that painting. Once, she told me she knew it was okay to love me because I loved that painting so, and loving something so beautiful was a good sign. We always kept it here, in our bedroom because it was our private painting." There were tears in the old man's eyes.

"I think I understand. It gives me the same feeling as mine does." Now Fiona had tears in her eyes. She was touched that the old man

17

from the junky store was so moved by the beauty of that small canvas.

"Norm, why did you sell me my painting? You could have kept it for yourself."

"I thought about it, but you know, I have trouble making any changes in the house. When that painting came in, I thought I'd let it sit awhile, maybe clean it and get a good price. But when you picked up that and only that, I knew you really saw it. Then when you said you lived in the building, I knew you had to have it. Hell, I would have given it to you. I thought of all those other tenants who bought Emma's paintings of the apartments. It was so nice that regular renting people could have house paintings, too. Even nicer than those new Trestle Glen homes."

"Norm, we have to find out more about her. She's too good to be lost without her story being known."

"I never thought so until you visited me in the hospital. I'm glad I sold you that picture, happy to help. So, I guess you really will have to be a writer then."

"I guess so." Fiona flushed with the realization that she had to do this.

Chapter Five

"Well, it's not really like that," Fiona had the phone jammed between her ear and her shoulder as she fried eggs. She could hear Denise sigh.

"Mother, it's exactly like that, you went alone into the home of a strange man. If I'd done that, you'd be all over me."

"But I was invited in to see the paintings."

"Yeah, right, *Come in and see my etchings.* Mom, it doesn't change that you weren't being wise or safe. I can't believe I have to say this to you."

"You don't, Denise, I'm an adult. I *am* able to assess the risks. Was it completely lost on you that the gentleman in question is over eighty *and* frail? Don't worry babe, if push comes to shove I think I can take him." Fiona whirled around with the skillet, slid her eggs onto the plate next to the toast and bacon, without missing a beat. For a woman of her size, Fiona moved with grace and precision. Not that she was fat but the years had settled on her, and lately she sometimes didn't recognize her reflection if it came on her unexpectedly. With the phone still sandwiched on her shoulder she picked up the plate and walked to the table.

"He's that old? I didn't realize…"

"Then you haven't been listening. She painted the landscape in 1940, and she gave it, still wet, to Norm when he was sixteen. That's sixty-seven years ago. Do the math."

"That's your department, Mom. It's just that since you bought that painting you've been acting a little weird."

Between bites, Fiona kicked it right back, "How so, because I have an interest in something and I'm pursuing it?"

"*No.* You're taking this wrong on purpose. Are you eating?"

"Yes, sorry. I'm trying to get out of here early. Amanda and I are going to take the day and hit the estate sales."

"See, that's exactly my point. Since when do you traipse around town digging through dead people's junk?"

"Wow, just a month ago you were encouraging me to join Amanda on her forays. What happened to *getting out and having some fun?*"

"It doesn't sound like fun, it sounds like an obsession."

19

"Well, I *am* having fun. I'm learning, and I've discovered a world of Arts and Crafts era paintings that I didn't even know about before. I've been reading up on the period, particularly the Plein Air Movement in Northern California. I tell you, Emma Caites' work was really good. The estate sales aren't just me digging around in things, I'll get to meet dealers and ask questions. There could be leads in this."

"See what I mean, mom? It comes right back to this artist. It's like you've turned into some kind of detective."

"Well, I have a little, and I'm enjoying it, so bear with me. I've really got to run, so we'll talk later." Dropping the phone back onto its base, Fiona picked up the plate, carried it to the sink, and washed the pan and the breakfast dishes. She wiped them before any spots could form, and then wiped and dried the countertop.

The doorbell rang, and Fiona greeted Amanda at the front door. Amanda's enthusiasm bubbled over.

"I've picked our route to maximize the chances of Caites paintings or contacts," she announced. "These are also really good spots for my purposes. I tell you, this new interest of yours could really pay off. I'll be frequenting a better class of junk. Today we'll focus on the areas around and just north of the lake. Lake Park, Trestle Glen, Crocker Highlands and Piedmont. Be chatty, talk to the other dealers, especially if they appear interested in art, and especially if they're older."

Fiona rolled her eyes. Today it seemed everyone wanted to tell her what to do. But Amanda had a point, and Fiona knew she had to fight her own first inclination towards shyness.

Most estate sales are pretty boring. There's the same collection of used, chipped and partial sets of dishes, dinged pots and pans, tacky glassware, ironing boards, barbecues, LP collections, gardening tools, old clothes and furnishings that have seen better days. Even in wealthier communities, estate bottom feeders realize that the truly old have long since stopped acquiring. Amanda explained that savvy buyers sometimes reviewed the obits, in addition to the estate sale ads, trying to hit those sales where the decedents were a bit younger. The "downsizing sales" were becoming more popular too, as even the upper-crust geriatric set scaled back to accommodate senior housing. Amanda was accustomed to moving through such sales, quick to spot indications of quality that would make a good buyer linger, and look harder.

Fiona had no such shielding. The first several stops yielded typical stuff, with Amanda making only a few purchases. There was nothing of note for Fiona, and the endless deluge of knickknacks and junk depressed her. She vowed to go home and clear out her own closets. On the fourth stop though, the deceased had been a recognized artist. There were some lovely pieces. Fiona picked up a small bronze sculpture of a nude. As she walked around the house, she noticed she was being followed. The man appeared to be flamingly gay, his hair dyed a brash blond with dark roots, set off by a colorful ascot tied loosely around his neck. His movements through the house mirrored hers, but each step seemed precise, even choreographed.

Finally, gesturing at the sculpture, he asked, "Dear, have you decided on keeping that?" He had a deep and smooth FM voice. It didn't quite match his appearance.

"Yes, it's a nice piece, isn't it?"

"She wasn't a great talent," he replied, "but like many artists, she had a good eye. Often artists are the best collectors. That little bronze isn't hers, but it's certainly well worth the listed price."

"Oh, did you know the woman?"

"No, but I knew her work. Actually, I thought she'd died years ago. I'm a dealer, arts and antiques." He reached out to shake her hand, "Marvin, Marvin Rivard."

"Fiona Hedge," she replied taking his hand in hers. "Do you know much about Oakland's artistic history?"

"Some, though Oakland wasn't exactly a pinnacle of culture. Was there something of interest to you in particular? I do have a finder's service." He flashed a set of perfect teeth. There was something genuine about him, despite the hair and affected mannerisms; he was direct and looked her straight in the eye when he addressed her.

"I'm interested in paintings by Emma Caites, and any information about her."

He raised an eyebrow at that. "Ah, Caites. Yes, she was a talent. Prolific too, but that cuts against value sometimes. She didn't participate in any of the shows or competitions, so she's not well-listed. What makes you interested in her?"

"I bought one of her paintings. It's actually of my apartment, so I'd like to know more about her."

Marvin rolled his eyes back, and pursed his lips. "That's a tough

21

one. Asking around at sales like these has potential but it's a bit of a long shot. Hmmm," he rubbed his hand along the edge of his jaw, "She was a Mills graduate, so you may want to check with them. If you give me your card, I'll keep my eyes open."

Fiona dug through her purse and pulled out a card. Marvin took it, and wrote, "Emma Caites," on the back. He glanced up and nodded, "You'll be hearing from me." He handed her his card.

Fiona hoped so. She thanked him. There was something flip and funny in his approach that she liked.

By the end of the day, Fiona had made no further connections, but still was elated. Marvin had given her enough leads that she'd be busy for awhile. She was especially delighted about the Mills angle because Denise had attended Mills, so Fiona had contacts and was comfortable there. That shouldn't have mattered, she told herself, but she was pleased that Emma had a college education. A degree from an elite women's college must have been quite a distinction back then. Perhaps there was something to Norm's comment that Emma came from money. She wondered if the Mills connection would help her with Denise. Honestly, she didn't understand why Denise had such an edge about her Emma Caites pursuit. As an added bonus for the day, Fiona really liked her bronze sculpture. She was still hesitant about her tastes in this world of turn-of-the-century art, so she'd been reassured that Marvin was also interested in the bronze. She grinned at the cliché, but Marvin's opinion, as a gay art dealer, did carry more weight. Fiona imagined that Norm wouldn't see much in him. Amanda, as usual, had armloads of stuff, more grist for the eBay mill.

"Girl, this is great stuff. I should have started being more picky years ago. Thank God for Emma Caites."

Fiona looked over at Amanda's odd assortment, and nodded, "I'm glad the upgrade is working for you." Really, Fiona couldn't see any difference at all between Amanda's earlier picks and what she was now loading into the trunk.

Chapter Six

"Amanda, it's amazing. Suddenly she's a real person, there are photos and everything."

"Where the hell are you? You were supposed to be here twenty-five minutes ago." It wasn't like Fiona to be late, for anything. *Ever.* Fiona had agreed to help Amanda in cleaning her last batch of treasures from the estate sales. Amanda said it was a necessary part of Fiona's apprenticeship in the world of secondary property.

"Oh jeez, I'm sorry. I'm on my way but I got caught up in the archives at Mills. I'll be there in minutes. Do you want me to pick anything up on the way?" Fiona knew her friend all too well, and intended to buy forgiveness with a stop for goodies at Neldham's Bakery or La Farine. That girl could inhale sweets without ever adding an extra ounce.

"You whore. Yeah, some éclairs will buy you absolution. I hate being such a pushover, but there you go." Fiona stopped to pick up two éclairs, both for Amanda. She let herself in downstairs and, checking to see the upstairs hall was empty, rang the bell, then knelt at Amanda's apartment door, holding the white bakery bag up as an offering.

"Get in here, you fool, ahh," Amanda said, taking the bag from Fiona's hands, "This will do nicely. We have a lot to do. You can talk once we get going."

"Just tell me what to do."

"Well, you have some choices. These linens need to be hand washed and then ironed dry. Hand washing for the cotton dresses too, though they'll hang dry on the balcony, or if you prefer, there's silver polishing to do."

Fiona looked down at the basket stacked high with vintage linen napkins and embroidered handkerchiefs. The next basket was filled with 1950s cotton summer dresses. The table was heaped with metal things, sterling serving pieces, napkin rings, salt and peppers, souvenir spoons and a pile that looked like silver and colored chain mail.

"What's this?" Fiona said, gesturing at the pile.

"They're mesh handbags, mostly from the twenties. They need cleaning and/or polishing, depending on what they're made of."

"I'll do that."

"Really? I thought you'd go for the world of hand wash. Branching out are we, Clean-Queen?"

"Let's just say I'm intrigued, and you've picked the right era for me. What do I do?"

"Okay." Amanda showed her the work stations already set up on the table. "Solid silver pieces that aren't too tarnished you clean with the silver buffing cloth. If really dark, we drop them in the ultrasound vat for a few minutes first. The handbags are fragile. We start all of them in the ultrasound, one or two at a time. When they come out, gently pat them dry with these diapers, then lightly with the silver buff cloth. If there are stains after the ultrasound, use the soft brush and toothpaste, or Q-tips—*gently*, then rinse and back to the ultrasound. Then, for the silver bags, a final gentle rub with the silver polish buff cloth. Got it?" Amanda needn't have asked. Fiona's auditory memory was inescapable. Moreover, cleaning was as natural to her as breathing. Fiona rolled up her sleeves and set to work.

"What do you clean the linens with?

"Lightly soiled, Woolite. Soiled or grayed, I soak in Dreft but you have to be careful, it will eat the fibers if you leave them in too long."

"Dreft, like for baby clothes?"

"Same stuff. Don't let the pastels on the box fool you. Just because it's for kids doesn't mean it's gentle. Infants and toddlers are filthy little people, and Dreft is the only way to get the stains out."

"Yeah, I remember." Of the two of them, Fiona was the only to have had a child. Amanda had never had the inclination, but Fiona always thought she'd have made a great mom. Unconventional, but great. Motherhood had been defining for Fiona, her mission. But, as a working single mom, it hadn't left room or time for much else.

They set to work, and as soon as they'd hit a working rhythm, Amanda commanded, "Okay, spit it out."

"What can I say, it's like she's there, at Mills, waiting to be found. You know, because of Denise's scholarship I did a ton of volunteer work at Mills. I felt I owed them. So, I know everyone and boy, that opens doors. There are records on records. The place is a gold mine. Because the school and faculty were deeply committed to the Mills' objective of honing brilliant, cultured young women, they documented everything. So for school records, grades, class schedules, and correspondence, it's all there. But then there's so much more, records, photos, student writings and artwork reflecting extracurricular activities, clubs and competitions. The extra stuff is not well organized, and there are boxes and boxes of it. It's like dropping into another century."

"And they gave you access?"

"Without question. Mind you, I can't take anything but I can go anytime. When I said I was contemplating writing on the life of a Mills' graduate, an unsung artist, they practically gave me the keys. I'll be going back for weeks. But Amanda, look at this," Fiona reached for her purse, and pulled out a photocopy of a photograph. "Check it out, she's the one sitting."

Amanda wiped her hands dry, and took the picture from Fiona. In it, four girls in draping, toga-like costumes posed for a promotional photo for a dramatic production. One was seated in a chair, flanked by two girls kneeling with laurel branches, with the fourth girl standing behind the chair back with a harp in her arms. They were lovely, young and lithe. The seated girl was particularly stunning, her oval olive face framed by thick dark hair. Her dark almond-shaped eyes looked directly into the camera, almost challenging, and she alone smiled. The other girls were just as lovely, but demure. Their eyes were cast aside, and faces wistful. On the back of the chair, hung a black cane with a silver top.

"So that's her. Wow. She gives me goose-bumps. My God Fiona, she's perfect, but she's in the wrong century. Look at her."

"I know. The hours and the dusty files were worth it, just for the photo. I can hardly stand it."

"Hey," Amanda laughed, "This is no party, girl. Get back to work, yak whilst you polish!" Fiona picked up another spoon, and rubbed it to sparkling. She laid it in the line of the other gleaming spoons and serving pieces. Two of the purses hummed in the ultrasound cleaner as Fiona worked in silence, reflecting on the impact of the photo.

"That can go on the book jacket," Amanda purred, "It's such a telling photo."

"I don't want to admit that in my head, I'd already put my painting on the cover. I'm designing the cover of a book that's just an idea." She shook her head and paused, "But I'm only just beginning to discover this woman. What made her step back, what

25

made her lose the poise, the challenge?"

"That's not fair," Amanda shot back, "By all counts she painted till she died. She was prolific, talented. You're suggesting, without ever knowing her burdens, that she wasn't successful. You're basing it on public measures of success. So, she's not in the Oakland Museum, what of it?"

"But she was good enough. I've been through the collection there. I've looked at all the books of the period. She was good enough. What happened?"

"Based on what? On all of three paintings you've seen? Besides, she was a female artist in the 1920s and after. It's not like that was easy. And she had a kid to raise."

Fiona sighed, and took the last of the mesh handbags out of the ultrasound and gently wrapped them in the diapers. She polished a lovely sterling ladle. "Were these things at the sales last Saturday?"

Amanda looked up, "Everything except the cotton dresses."

"This is some really nice stuff. I didn't see any of it at the sales."

"Well you had other things to look for. Besides," Amanda tapped her temple, "I have the trained eye." She laughed, and twirled a freshly ironed, embroidered napkin. "It's why I'm so rich!"

"I like these handbags, but they're so fragile." Fiona was gently polishing a sterling chain mesh purse.

"They were the elegant consumer items of their time, designed for beauty in the moment and planned obsolescence. Though they made them by the thousands, most didn't last long. It's a factor in their value today. Think about it, granted they're evening bags, but really, what could you put in a tiny delicate bag like that?" Amanda picked up one of the handbags, and held it as though she were a fashionable date from 1923. "These are particularly nice items. Some of the enameled ones are even more valuable though, because the enamel chips and fades."

"Sort of like the upper class women of the day, I suppose, fragile and for show."

Amanda nodded, "Sure, yet there's always women who do their own thing. That's the cool thing about Emma Caites. I think there's more story there than you know. Keep digging, you've found a perfect Fiona project."

Fiona glanced up to see a small pile of lustrous silver spoons, napkin rings and utensils in front of her. "I feel like a pirate, piles of silver." Handbags hung from all the doorknobs in the apartment.

26

Amanda waved towards the living room where the furniture was covered with crisp linens.

"I think we're about done for the night." Fiona stood up, and stretched her legs.

"If you want, Fi, you know I'll come and wade through that stuff at Mills with you."

"I may just take you up on that, but for tonight, I'm done in."

"Me, too." Amanda stood, and reviewed their progress, "Not bad for two old ladies, eh?"

Chapter Seven

Fiona glanced at the clock—4:50. She checked traffic in her rearview mirror, and changed lanes, deciding to get off the freeway a few exits early; at this time of day the surface streets were faster. She'd be lucky to get in any time at Mills at all. Generally, she really liked her work but recently she'd had a series of deadlines and pressures that pulled her away from the research on Emma Caites. She couldn't tell if her schedule was really any different, or whether she truly just wanted to be doing something else. One of the downsides of self-employment was that she lacked any framework for comparison. The Mills staff had been enormously helpful with the files, but the deep files, the unorganized material, was inaccessible after six o'clock. Fiona would have to satisfy herself with the official records. So far she had been avoiding them because she expected they'd be dull.

The guard in the security booth recognized her, and waved her through. She parked by the library and walked through long shadows, thinking for just a moment how the walled and gated campus gave a sense of security within its bounds, even in the urban wilds of East Oakland. The evenings were getting shorter and the crisp air was scented heavily with eucalyptus. When Denise had been accepted to Mills, with a full scholarship, Fiona had been elated. As a single mother, she could only have afforded UC, or even the Cal State schools.

Mills was a small, prestigious women's university tucked at the edge of the Oakland hills. It was as close to Ivy League as California had to offer, except perhaps Stanford, which lacked the intimacy and local history of Mills. The school was started in Berkeley in 1852 by Susan and Cyrus Mills, and moved to its permanent home in Oakland in 1871. The campus was an oasis, an island of green trees and ivy covered halls in an otherwise blighted area of town. As a volunteer there, Fiona had come to love the camaraderie and warmth of the small institution. She'd completely revised her modern ideas on segregated education as she watched Denise bloom and grow into a confident young woman under the guidance of truly dedicated and progressive instruction. Mills had been a gift to her, too. She'd almost dreaded Denise's graduation, since it meant a slowing of her involvement with the school. She still volunteered occasionally, but the Emma Caites project had brought her back with a sense of mission.

Fiona checked in with the librarian on duty, as instructed. The archived student files were kept deep in the bowels of the library's basement. Nonetheless, records this old didn't merit scanning for computerized retrieval. Despite the dust and asthma factor, Fiona liked the old archives, and wondered if future researchers would end up slaving over cold, soulless keyboards. It seemed to take the heart out of the endeavor. She took a quick puff on her inhaler, and bent to the task. From the extracurricular files Fiona knew that Emma had attended Mills from 1919 through 1923. She already had stacks of copied papers and notes with questions written throughout the margins in her tight backhanded cursive scrawl. Fiona's handwriting was the only part of her that didn't match the rest of the tidy package. She figured it was the result of left-handedness, a stubborn spirit-thread that refused to comply with the rest of the program.

It took her some time to locate the date range. The old files had an organizational structure that defied easy analysis. There was a direct correlation between Fiona's frustration level and her asthmatic symptoms, and she reached for the inhaler repeatedly in the dim light of the basement. Once she found the right years though, her fingers flew through the dusty files without much wheezing.

Fiona was also on the lookout for anything on a student whose first name was Henrietta. Henrietta appeared regularly next to Emma in many of the Drama Club photos, and Fiona figured that that was a likely indication of friendship. She wasn't sure it that could translate into any real information though, since all these women would surely be dead by now, anyway. With as much difficulty as she'd had with Emma, Fiona wasn't hopeful that she'd be able to trace her college pals too.

She found Emma's academic file, and while thick, it contained few surprises. There were pages of transcripts. Emma's education included art, but was also steeply dedicated to the classics. She took Advanced Greek Literature, Ancient Greek (language) Advanced French, French Literature (a class that appeared to have been taught in French by the notations), Anatomy, Painting, Sculpture, Life Drawing, Illustration, Landscape Expression, Introduction to Photography, Printmaking and various Art History classes. All normal selections for the budding artist. But Emma also had an academic and practical bent. In her years as an upperclassman she pursued Economics, Introduction to Business, Political Theory, Philosophy, History of Western Civilization and an oddly titled class called Religious Significance. The file was filled with letters permitting enrollment in advanced classes without pre-requisites and records reflecting Emma's success in meeting academic requirements by "testing out," that is, by passing the final examination without actually taking the class. Fiona wondered what elementary education had led Emma to have such eclectic and irregularly elevated levels of knowledge upon entering college. Her grades ran from very good to exceptional.

Her file contained annual waiver letters, permitting Emma to skip mandatory physical education classes because of her medical condition. In the last two years the waiver was conditional on Emma's continued participation in independent swimming and riding activities "as appropriate," whatever that meant. The letters identified her condition as *Legg Calve Perthe* syndrome, and specifically indicated skeletal weakness and deformity of the left leg. Fiona furiously took notes. She already knew about the cane, but was determined to understand the extent to which physical problems imposed Emma's limits.

Late in the file, some dated well after her graduation, were copies of letters of recommendation, many in French, to art schools and institutes in France. The letters candidly discussed Emma's ample talent in painting and her academic successes at Mills. In several cases the letter's authors went to some lengths to indicate that Ms. Caites proficiency in conversational French, combined with her artistic talents made her an excellent candidate for admission. Fiona was a little offended that every such letter (at least the ones in English) referenced Emma's physical limitations along with opinions that the candidate's health would not be a negative factor in her performance as an artist. One letter went further to suggest that if there were any concerns, that the limitations of her gender would be of larger import than any physical problems. Fiona was livid. Even here, at a progressive women's college, Emma's potential was minimized by gender, even while recommending her. She bit her tongue, and remembered that the letter was written in 1924.

At the end of each year's records was a separate file reflecting the application and admissions documentation for the successful applicants to Mills. But reviewing each of the relevant years, Fiona found no information on Emma Caites. Perplexed, she cross-referenced the names to the records in each file. Finally she understood that the admittees' application materials invariably were located in the files for the year before actual admission. Fiona realized she might be getting tired; she'd missed the obvious. She glanced at her watch, and realized that the library would be closing in twenty minutes. Quickly she shuffled through the 1918 Admissions file till she found Emma's folder. She flipped through the pages of recommendations and comments looking for Emma's Admissions essay. There, on yellowed paper in the squared, bold printing she'd come to recognize in Emma's signature, was her application essay.

Dear Members of the Admissions Committee,

I realize that mine is not the usual application for admission. I am not the usual applicant. My formal education was disrupted at ten, when I was stricken with a terrible and disabling condition that changed the course of my life. It sounds pretentious to contemplate "the course of life" of a ten year old; that tender age does not normally lend itself to personal analysis. However, I was reduced from a normal, active, happy girl to a child imprisoned by pain and physical debilitation. I was confined to a plaster body cast for fourteen months, and spent the next two years recovering from the physical and emotional ravages of disability and atrophy.

The reason that I am an excellent candidate for Mills is that this horrible but transformative period was undoubtedly the best gift that could have been bestowed on me. During that time I was blessed and challenged. Since my care was burdensome to my family, I was abandoned to my maternal grandparents, whose love rebuilt and created the me that is worthy of Mills admission. Impressed by the very real possibility that my illness might result in my being reduced to an invalid, my grandparents sought to open to me the world of the mind, the world of art, culture and ideas. As I was unable to attend regular classes, my grandfather undertook my education with the vigor of Zeus. I read every book in his extensive library of over 3,000 volumes. My governess covered the usual curriculum, but my grandparents extended that to teach me philosophy, history, political theory, French, Greek, mathematics,

31

music and theater. I was trapped in my body, but with my grandparents' love, my mind was trained to soar.

When the cast was removed, my grandmother undertook to rebuild my broken body and spirit. She taught me to savor the gifts of nature, to see beauty and light, to smell the air, the earth and its flora, essentially to find the good in all circumstances. When I demonstrated a small talent in painting, my grandparents seized the opportunity to develop my aesthetic appreciations, and I was immersed in art. Painting combined the appreciation and imitation of nature and beauty with the positive health aspects of being outdoors, breathing fresh air and the healing rays of the sun. I could tell you that I am an accomplished artist, but that is a story best told in its own language, so I have submitted a sampling of my canvases with this application so you can see for yourselves whether my efforts are worth developing at Mills.

At the end of my recovery I had to accept that physically I will never be whole. By then the benefits of my education were clear, and if there was ever a fair exchange, this was one I would repeat in a heartbeat. I had completed all the requirements for regular secondary school early, and my grandparents argued fervently for higher education. My parents would have none of it. I was returned to my familial home in San Francisco, where my parents sought to wrap me tightly in the domestic values of middle class life. My mother believed (and still believes) that the solution to my limitations is the world of high society, fashion and charm. I was never so imprisoned and crippled as I was when I tried to fit into a life that denied the strength of my mind and my talents. While I knew immediately that further education was my salvation, my parents resisted because their world view does not include a place for a crippled, bright, artistic daughter. But you cannot hold back truth. I am an artist, and I intend to pursue the arts with every ounce of my energies.

I lost my beloved grandmother to influenza earlier this year. It was her dying wish that I attend university, and prepare for a life large enough to encompass my deficits as well as my talents. In the face of that, my parents have relented. I am seizing the opportunity, and I choose Mills as the institution best suited to my mix of educational needs. Since I lack the usual educational accreditation, I request that you review the accompanying letters of recommendation and my artwork portfolio, and thus base your

32

decision on proven results. I look forward to a fruitful and productive association with Mills College.
Respectfully,
Emma Caites

Fiona set down the yellowed pages, and wept.

Chapter Eight

"This is Marvin Rivard. I met you at an estate sale, recently. You indicated an interest in Emma Caites' work. I have some items that might be of interest to you, so give me a call at the gallery or at the cell number on my card. Thanks, and I look forward to hearing from you."

Fiona played the message again, and then rifled through her purse till she found Marvin's card. She glanced at her watch and then chanced a call to the gallery. He answered.

"Marvin?" Even though that voice was unmistakable.

"Is this Fiona? I was hoping to reach you. I've picked up some Caites canvases I thought you might like to see. Any luck in *your* search, yet?"

"The Mills tip was good." Fiona decided to play her cards a little close to her chest here, "So far, nothing definitive."

"Sorry to hear that, I was hoping you'd have more to report. I'm counting on you, dear."

Though the last remark was strange, Fiona felt oddly warm about him. "So what have you got?"

"Well dear, I've picked up three canvases, two of which are definitively hers, and another questionable. I thought you'd like to see them. How's this week?"

"Absolutely, I'm pretty open."

"For me, Saturday morning is good. It's short notice but I'm here till eight o'clock this evening, or we can work something out for early next week."

"I can come tonight. Shall I come right now?"

"Great." Fiona could hear his smile through the phone, "Do you need directions?"

"No. I know the area, Thanks."

The gallery was located in an 'up and coming' neighborhood, one with cheaper rents but not without location credibility.

Marvin greeted her warmly, first taking her hand, and then escalating to a welcoming hug. Fiona couldn't tell if this was an affectation or salesmanship, but she felt comfortable with the social intimacy. The two just clicked. She relaxed into the camaraderie.

"Can I get you tea? Or perhaps a glass of wine?"

"I'd love a cup of tea."

Marvin left her to peruse the gallery while he disappeared into the back. It was comfortable, the walls well-appointed with contemporary and antique paintings. The furnishings were new, but were all handcrafted, modernized versions of the clean lines and warm oak finish of traditional Arts and Crafts furniture. There were three main rooms for display. Instead of the usual reception desk, the center of the room had a good sized round oak table with matching mission chairs. Fiona wandered the gallery, taking in the art, and the prices. A stack of price lists graced the central table, printed on a heavy laid ivory paper. She noted, with a smirk, that some of the lesser pieces, prints, watercolors or just less than attractive paintings, were lavishly framed. Fiona and Amanda had just been discussing this.

"It's a decorator trick," Amanda had said, "like staging a house. Many buyers care more if it matches the sofa than about the actual artwork." Fiona had thought she was being cynical.

Marvin stuck his head out of the little kitchen in the back, "Herbal or green?"

"Herbal's good, thank you."

"Honey?"

"No, just plain is fine."

Marvin reappeared with a tray with two china cups of tea. He set the tray on the table and took a seat, gesturing for her to join him. Again, Fiona noted his graciousness but again couldn't help wondering if this was a sales tactic. So far, no Caites paintings were in sight. She sat and sipped her tea, waiting for his presentation.

"The other day, I got the feeling you're really serious about researching Emma Caites."

"Well, it certainly has turned into a bit of an obsession. Why?"

"I've always liked her work and thought of her as an undiscovered talent. I have two of her paintings at home."

"Is that what you planned on showing me?" Fiona was beginning to question the vibe. She'd certainly been under the impression that Marvin was gay, up till now. A sideways invitation to his home hadn't occurred to her.

Marvin caught her doubts, "No, no, I picked up three canvases earlier today. I'm the scrounge partner here. The other two cultivate new artists, and I do the antique angle. I'm expected to work miracles on a very limited budget."

35

"So," Fiona leaned forward, "Do I get to see them?"

"Certainly, but let's sit and talk a bit first."

She sipped her tea, and let Marvin explain.

"Here's the thing, I've always liked her work. My partners, however, are more interested in living, name talent. Today, when I brought these pieces in, it was made very clear they didn't want to invest in some unknown dead woman."

"Are they any good?"

"I'll let you judge. They'll need some repair and cleaning, but my partners don't want to put in any additional money. They so much as told me not to buy any more of Caites' work," he sighed, "With a live artist, you don't need to purchase every piece. It's a percentage deal. Obviously with antiques, you need to front the transaction."

"Feeling stung?"

"More than you know. I've been here, as partner, eight years. But there's a disparity in how the business runs. Let's just say my contributions are not always appreciated."

Fiona felt awkward. She shifted in her seat.

"Let me show you the paintings." He pushed back his chair and stood up, "I'm dying to see what you think of them." Marvin came back with two smaller canvases stacked on his hip and the third dangling from his left hand, all were unframed. He leaned them in a line facing against the wall. Using his chair as an easel, he propped the largest canvas on the chair in front of Fiona.

"Yes, I've seen her house portraits before, but while technically good, they don't capture my interest." Fiona leaned back. It was another house painting, like Norm's, about the same size. It featured a large, low-slung California bungalow nestled under a spreading oak tree on a sun-dappled tree lined street. This one was livelier than Norm's. Still, Fiona found this genre dull, even when well painted. She said so. Marvin nodded.

He tipped the next painting into place. This was a small self-portrait. In it, Emma sat in a Morris chair with a book propped in one hand, while the other hand held her paintbrush, the give-away as to the identity of the subject. This was an attractive, but somber Emma Caites, who, by the dated signature, was thirty-one. There was a window to her side, providing the only illumination. The silver banded top of her cane gleamed, leaning against the chair arm. The light caught her oval face, illuminating one side, leaving

36

most of the features on the other side obscured in semi-darkness. Her hair was worn up, loosely pinned in a French twist. Loose strands of hair fell on the lighted side, sharply defining the edges of the negative and positive space. She wore a burgundy dress, with a modest, squared neckline, creamy white skin visible at the neck. She gazed directly at the viewer. The effect was alarmingly present. This Emma was still young, elegantly beautiful in a direct, almost confrontational way. The painting was grimy, and desperately needed a cleaning. Fiona wondered if restoration would strip away the atmospheric feeling. She sighed. "Lovely."

"I thought so too. Is this what she looked like?"

"That, and more."

Without another word, Marvin placed the last painting. It was in dire need of restoration. One of the stretcher bars was broken and where the bottom corner had been crushed, the surface paint was scraped away, obscuring most of the signature. Still, what was there, sang. The painting depicted a sunny kitchen with a table sitting in the nook just to the right of the kitchen entry. A dark-haired little boy with arching eyebrows knelt on one of the chairs, himself painting on large sheets of paper on the table. The boy was positioned in the middle of the center, looking up at the viewer, obviously interrupted in his task, with his paint brush suspended in air. The late afternoon sunshine slanted in from the windows, cutting light and dark stripes across the field of the painting. It was an intimate, happy, domestic moment.

Fiona gasped, recognizing her kitchen in the painting. "That's Thomas. This takes my breath away."

"I think I have a pretty good eye. When you snapped up that little bronze the other day, I thought maybe you did, too."

"What do you want for the last two?"

"That's what we need to discuss. I have a proposal."

Marvin explained that he needed to recover what he'd paid for the three pieces, plus a little for the gallery's trouble. He wasn't going to invest gallery funds for the needed cleaning and restoration. What he proposed was a sharing arrangement where the two of them would work together to purchase Caites paintings. Once purchased, they could decide who'd take which painting, with an agreement to alternate picks if they couldn't otherwise agree. As they learned each other's tastes, they'd get more selective. If he'd known how she felt about the house paintings, he wouldn't have made that purchase, since they left him cold, too.

"Why include me?"

Marvin looked her squarely in the eye, "I don't really know. I've liked you since the estate sale. I like that you found Emma Caites on your own, and that she speaks to you. I also think that you may make her famous, and that will make both of our paintings more valuable."

"Wow, that's a lot of pressure."

Marvin continued, "I have a good feeling about this. And if I'm wrong, the worst that can happen is that we collect paintings at a bargain, by a woman whose work we admire."

"What about your partners, the gallery?"

"Ah, they've told me not to buy Caites' paintings. So I'll buy on my own, on our own account."

"How much for these three?" she paused, "And for the restoration?"

"I spent $670 for the three. The gallery should see $800. Normally they'd want a lot more, but they just want their investment out on this one. Cleaning, another $200 per, the repairs are going to run about $350.

"I can clean them, I did mine."

"Okay. So that puts us at, what?"

"Eleven fifty for the three." Fiona was always quick with the numbers.

"Okay, we'll each pick one, and then hold the third for a future allocation or sale." Marvin moved the painting, and sat down.

"Which one do you want?" Fiona held her breath.

"The self-portrait."

"Good, because I could go either way, but I love that kid with the paintbrush." Fiona smiled.

"Then it's a deal?" Marvin looked surprised.

"Done."

"Fiona, I'd still like to see your first painting."

"Sure," she grinned, "I'll show you mine if you show me yours."

Marvin laughed. "And we'll need to coordinate on the research. You'll have to do the legwork, but I may be able to help with suggestions. Partly, like you, I just want to know who she was."

Fiona was suddenly exhausted. She pulled out her checkbook, and looked up at Marvin. "I'll write you a check for half. You'll have to arrange the repairs."

"Cleaning first."

"Okay. And, we each cover our own framing costs." She handed him the check.

"Sure, but you may want to coordinate with me on that. I can get some great deals through the gallery contacts."

Fiona walked out that night with three paintings to clean and a partner. At the door they hugged again, but this time both knew it was genuine.

Chapter Nine

Flush with several successes, Fiona was feeling pretty smug. Her skills at cleaning oil paintings were improving at a rate that impressed even her own critical judgment. She'd converted the garage into a workshop with an old slant-top draftsman's desk, now arrayed with rags, Q-tips, paintbrushes and bottles of various solvents. In addition to the open garage door, and the existing overhead light, Fiona had positioned two work lamps over the desk for optimal lighting. It was near blinding. Given her endeavor with Marvin, Fiona was taking the restoration business very seriously. To top it off, the results were amazingly satisfying. Like her original painting, each of the new acquisitions had, in turn, been an amazing journey, a treasure hunt as the decades of dirt daubed away, revealing the glow of Emma's original intent in place. The two completed paintings hung above the desk. From time to time, when she needed to stretch her back, or rest her eyes, Fiona stood rocking in front of her finished work marveling at how vibrant the colors had become, revealing the quiet beauty of a former era.

The painting on the desktop now, Emma's self-portrait, was coming alive under her careful ministrations. It wasn't a dark piece after all. She'd found that on the smoother brush strokes she could apply the cleaning solvent with a paintbrush in an even coat in one or two inch squares. After just a few minutes, she could use a Q-tip to carefully roll against the surface of the paint, blotting up the crud. Norm's advice echoed in her ears, "Roll, don't scrub. Don't push on the canvas." Pressed and rolled gently, the cotton tip absorbed the wet solvent, and pulled up a layer of grime, revealing a surprisingly different, brighter painting below. Sometimes it took three, even four applications to be able to see the painting without its accumulated armor of dirt.

Fiona was careful not to rework an area too soon. Norm had warned against saturating the surface with solvent. She worked in a grid pattern careful not to apply more cleaner than she could manage in the emulsion's drying time. In those areas where the texture of the brushstrokes held more crevices, Fiona gently worked the solvent into the creases with short, delicate, stippled strokes using a regular oil painting brush. The dirt, flushed out with the solution, came up with the same careful daubing of the cotton swab. Fiona liked the work. She even liked the smell of the solvents, the metallic tang of the cleaner and the strange orangey-mint sting of the neutralizer.

It was tedious. Letting the cleaner do its magic, Fiona worked, neck craned, simultaneously rotating between two or three areas of the canvas. In badly soiled or heavily textured areas, Fiona caught herself biting her bottom lip as she worked, her mantra: restraint, patience, aah, see the colors come through, and shine. Every now and then she'd turn the canvas ninety degrees on the desk, so that the angle of attack didn't create a shadow of neglect on the painting's surface. On one turn, she noticed that the painted plane extended beyond the face of the painting, overlapping on two sides. She lifted it up and tipped it to examine. Sure enough, someone had re-stretched the canvas in a slightly smaller configuration, probably to fit a frame. She shook her head disapprovingly. That kind of short-term thinking altered the artist's vision by cropping the design.

This painting presented a particular challenge because the canvas already hung a little slack on the stretcher bars. Over-saturating or putting pressure on the canvas could only make that worse. The first two paintings had been stretched with small carpet nails but this one used the kind of power staples that Fiona had used back in art school. Judging by the slack, whoever had re-stretched it was an amateur, and hadn't done the best job of it. Fiona considered prying up the staples to tighten it up, but her inspection of the edges showed that the paint had cracked along the redefined edge lines, and she didn't want to contribute any more to the existing damage. Worse yet, the vandal had trimmed away the canvas 'excess.' There wasn't enough material left to undo the damage.

Fiona was working the background and saving the figure, and especially Emma's face, for last. It let her practice her skills, and set aside the sweetest reward for the end, like dessert. Still, it caught her breath when the richness of the detail suddenly appeared from behind the decades of dirt. She took particular delight in cleaning the area where Emma's cane leaned up against the chair. After two passes, the cane suddenly came into view, round and real, clearly captured with that silver banding at the top. Fiona was awed when she saw how a few deft brushstrokes and highlight dabs fleshed out what the viewer perceived as a fully rendered cane. Restoration

41

forced the close look. The close look forced the full understanding of Impressionism. It made Fiona want to paint.

Painting had been her biggest challenge in Fiona's brief art school adventure. Now revealing Emma's details, almost forensically, Fiona could see that in her own efforts she'd tried to paint what she knew to be there, rather than what she actually saw. It was a beginner's error. Having struggled with it only made Fiona appreciate Emma's talent that much more. Her admiration grew as she peeled away the darkness, revealing Emma's handling of the rich tapestry upholstery of the chair behind the cane.

During her frequent breaks Fiona dashed up to the computer to scour the internet for clues to cleaning and restoration techniques. It was slow work, but that was what all the experts said. Slow and steady. Fiona's early successes built her confidence. They hung above her for inspiration.

Already it was looking good. After four evenings of painstaking work Fiona was ready to finish up with the face, arms and torso of the self-portrait. It was a smaller area than she'd done in previous nights, but critical. Fiona made herself a cup of tea, and headed down to the garage to unveil Emma. She was careful to work in the direction of the original brushstrokes. She rolled her Q-tips carefully, in the direction of their manufacture, so that the cotton stayed tight on the tip and didn't leave fibers on the canvas surface. Revealed, Emma's hands were small and elegant, one resting lightly on the arm of the chair, and the other aloft holding her paintbrush. Her own brush in hand, Fiona intimately felt connected to the original artist, uncovering her inch by inch. Fiona turned the canvas, and started in on the face. As she melted away the gray and yellow of old varnish and grime, Emma's quiet expression shone through. The steady gaze from her almond shaped eyes gave the impression of an understanding beyond her years. The painting was exquisite.

Finally Fiona was satisfied. She gave it one final pass with the neutralizer, and propped it against the wall. Standing back, Fiona was mesmerized by its beauty and quiet strength. Save for the sag in the canvas, the painting and her cleaning efforts were perfect. Fiona was tempted to call Marvin but remembered that he had headed out of town for the weekend. This one was, after all, one of his picks. Checking her watch she realized that she'd just missed him. Fiona picked up the painting and re-examined the misaligned staples, wishing she had the confidence to dive in and fix the flaw. Setting the work back against the wall, she sighed. Perhaps the framer could suggest a solution. It would be a shame to frame it this way.

Strewn across her work surface were the soiled remains of the effort; sodden cotton swabs, rags and paper towels. She grabbed a trash bag and swept it all away, walking the entire mess off to the outdoor Dumpster for her apartment complex. It was still early. Her task complete, she surveyed her work one last time, gulped back the last of her tea, and headed upstairs to make a light supper.

Fiona was in the habit of having dinner at her desk with the company of her computer. Between bites she'd check email, keep up with the news or surf the net. This night, with a celebratory glass of wine and a cheese and mushroom omelet, she was scouring the art restoration and conservation sites for tips on tightening aging canvas. She easily rejected the idiotic suggestions—the Windex solution and the lady who claimed that the way to clean old paintings was to rub them brusquely with soft white bread! But the image of the lovely Emma sagging in her frame kept Fiona at the task. One site suggested that a minor canvas face-lift could be achieved by lightly spraying the back of the canvas with water and drying it in the sun or under strong lights.

Fiona was intrigued. The theory was that the cotton fibers would naturally shrink when dried warm. Fiona shrugged, and kept looking. She tightened her search terms, and found another site referencing that method. Then, on the third page of largely inapt search results, she found a footnote to an actual conservation article, describing the shrink method as an 'old-timer's cheat.' The article warned that the technique should be used with great caution, emphasizing that no canvas should ever be saturated, and noting that the best results required even distribution of any applied water. Uneven distribution could result in the canvas buckling or twisting. Too much moisture was disastrous. Fiona printed up the page and read it repeatedly. She carried her dishes into the kitchen, and tidied up. Under the sink she found an empty spray bottle which she filled with bottled water.

Back down in the garage, Fiona turned on all the lights. She flipped the canvas back-side out, and trained the two desk lamps at the raw canvas side. In just a few moments the lamps warmed the fabric. Breathing deeply, Fiona sprayed the backside, ever so lightly with the atomizer. Changing to her reading glasses, she peered closely at the fabric and saw a very fine mist dispersed across the weave. She left it there, leaning against the wall under the lights. Heart thumping, Fiona climbed the stairs up into her kitchen to set a timer.

She needn't have. She spent the entire forty-five minutes pacing. Finally she pulled out the vacuum, just to take her mind off the experiment below. Even with that distraction, Fiona checked the time three times before the ringer released her to go inspect. It was a qualified success. The painting had tightened considerably, though some of the sag remained. Fiona was impressed. The back was nearly dry, and the improvement was noticeable from the front. With just a little more progress she'd have no qualms about framing it without the risks of re-stretching. She breathed a sigh of relief and satisfaction. Carefully she pumped the plunger, checking again to be sure the spray was evenly spread before she put the painting back under the lights. This time she went upstairs with a measured confidence in her old timer's cheat. To wait she flipped on the television.

Fiona woke up past midnight confused by the flickering blue light of a late night pledge drive. It took a minute but then she remembered the painting. Awake, she bounded downstairs. From the back the canvas looked taut under the lights. Eagerly, Fiona flipped it around to confirm the results.

Emma gazed back through the decades, tight and lovely. But something was wrong, horribly wrong. Across the bottom edge of the painting the paint had curled and separated from the canvas. At the signature, the paint was bubbled. Indeed, all along the upper edge of the bottom stretcher bar the paint was pulling away. Fiona's mouth dropped. Her stomach heaved. This was Marvin's painting! She'd ruined it! Carefully, carefully she laid the piece flat on the desk and tried to understand what had happened. Obviously, too much moisture was disastrous. The water had wicked down the surface, and pooled along the edge of wooden stretcher bar. *Saturation.* Fiona could barely breathe.

She ached to call Marvin, to confess this horror. But he was away, and it was the middle of the night. Oh, this lovely painting—a triumph just hours ago, now reduced to a flaking, peeling disaster. She couldn't look. She needed it fixed. Surely someone could undo what she'd done. Fiona slunk up to her bedroom and climbed into bed, without even undressing. She didn't sleep though. She couldn't even cry.

She lay there, tossing, distraught, stewing in the realization that she'd destroyed Emma's self-portrait. *Marvin's painting.*

Chapter Ten

Fiona watched and waited as her room grew light. She hadn't slept since her discovery. Now, charged with this horror, she was committed to finding a way to put it to rights. Giving up on the night, she rolled out of bed, and went downstairs to make coffee. With Marvin out of town she had no idea where to find a reliable restorer. It was Saturday. Internally she settled into a deep grim silence.

She found a large shallow box. Gently, she lowered the painting into it and loosely closed the flaps. Even that careful movement had those curls of paint wafting in the faintest puffs of air. She groaned. Fiona filled her commuter mug, and loaded the box into the back seat of her car. Her sighs punctuated the gray morning as she drove to Clar's Auction Gallery, and parked out front, waiting for them to open. The coffee soured her already churning stomach.

Finally, someone opened the accordion security gate across the entry. Fiona was the only customer, and she made her way to the desk of the gentleman who'd helped her before with the appraisal. He was sipping a latte and shuffling papers on his desk. He looked up at her without a trace of recognition.

"I need a painting restorer." Her voice was barely a hoarse whisper. "It's an emergency."

"A painting *emergency*?" He smiled.

She didn't appreciate levity in this. "Really, it's no joke. I need a referral to someone good."

"I'm sorry, didn't mean to make light. What kind of damage?"

"It's… it's in my car, out front. Can you come and look?"

He followed her out to the car and watched over her shoulder as she gently turned back the flaps on the box.

"Oh my, I see. Close it up, out of the breeze." Fiona resealed the box. "Come back inside, I think I have just the man for you."

Inside she sat on the chair by his desk while he fiddled with a Rol-A-Dex. He copied the information on an index card and handed it to her. Just then, as he peered over the top of his glasses, there was a flicker of recognition, "Aren't you the Emma Caites lady?"

Fiona cringed. Given that she'd ruined a Caites painting, she was embarrassed. "Yes, we talked a while back."

"I'm so sorry about your painting. In the future you should stick with professional restorers." He nodded at the card, "If anybody can help you this guy can. Wait just a minute. Let *me* give him a call." He reclaimed the card and, leaning back in his chair, dialed the number. Fiona was mortified, but resolved. After a brief conversation, the appraiser swiveled back to her and returned the contact card. "Go right on over. He'll see you. I explained about the damage."

Fiona was so relieved, she didn't know what to say. She stood stammering, "I... I," she lowered her head, "Thank you, *so much*."

"Don't worry about it. Get going. He doesn't let just anyone come by, so don't keep him waiting."

Fiona bowed and hurried back to her car.

The address on the card was in the warehouse district of Emeryville. Fiona wound around the back way through North Oakland, scanning the street signs. It was a low, brick shop/warehouse with a huge roll up door and a little office tucked up front. There was no sign. Cradling her precious box she went to the office door and rang the bell. A small man in camouflage fatigues answered the door.

"Amir?"

He acknowledged her with a nod and gestured her in. He was soft-spoken and well-mannered, with a slight Persian accent. He invited her to take a seat and reached for the box, which he placed on his desk. Fiona looked around. In the office, and the open space beyond, the place was a veritable circus—an emporium of retro paraphernalia, especially juke boxes and pin ball machines.

"Wow!" Was all she could manage.

He looked up. "Thanks. Shall we talk about your painting?"

Fiona joined him at the desk.

"Sprayed it too heavily, did you?"

She nodded, thankful that she didn't need to explain.

"As they say, *oil and water don't mix*. That's true for oil paint, as well. It'll need re-lining. That may reseal the paint. I use the old ways, you know, bees wax and heat. Sometimes that's enough to reattach the original paint. Good that you kept it flat. It looks like it's all there." He looked at her squarely. "It can get expensive if I have to completely repaint the damaged areas. That's time-consuming."

She nodded, "I don't really have much choice."

"So you know, any repair will affect value, but then…" He glanced down at the painting. "I'll try to retain the signature and date from the original. You don't by any chance have a picture of what it was like before?"

"I might, but I have others of her paintings, does that help?"

"Absolutely. Can you email me photos?" He reached into his back pocket, and handed her his card.

"Sure."

"It's a lovely self-portrait. I can see why you're upset."

"It's worse. It's not mine."

He winced. "Cleaning it for a friend?"

"Yes."

"No good deed…" he didn't finish the expression. "I know this may sound lame but except for the damage, it's a good cleaning job."

"Thank you. It's nice of you, but given its condition, I'm not exactly taking a bow."

Amir gently lifted the canvas from the box and tilted it one way, then the other. "I suppose you noticed that it's been re-sized?"

"Yeah, I did. And trimmed too, unfortunately."

"Well, as long as I'm re-lining, I try to return it to its original condition as much as possible."

Fiona squinted, "But they cut the edges."

He explained, "When I re-line, I essentially float this painting onto a new linen canvas. They adhere with the wax. It lets me extend the edges back out to their original dimensions."

"Well, there's a silver lining. Thanks. Do you have an estimate?"

"I won't know till I see how much fill-painting is needed." He focused on the loose paint bits of bubbled paint, "Not less than $500, not likely more than a thousand."

Fiona tugged her purse strap off her shoulder.

"Not yet. I don't like to bother with deposits."

She reached into the outer pocket, and fished out a business card. "Is this what you do, restore paintings?"

"Paintings, paper items, art, antiques and antiquities." He bowed his head.

"How did you get into that?"

"Back home," he gestured with his head, "in Persia I trained as a child."

"And the juke boxes?"

"My special collection, from the fifties. I love it."

Fiona smiled, and handed him her card. "Thank you, this means a lot to me."

"I'll give you a call. Probably it'll be a week, ten days at the most."

Fiona could feel some of the tension draining away. She prayed that he could repair the painting. She drew in a deep breath, "Thank you, Amir. I feel much better."

He glanced down at her card, "Thank *you*, Fiona."

Chapter Eleven

Finally, a Saturday that Fiona felt she could devote to loose ends. She was up with the dawn, anxious to get going. As much as the painting collaboration with Marvin had made the bond with Emma Caites tangible, it had also diverted her energies from her research. After they met at the gallery that night, Fiona had devoted several weeks to cleaning the paintings. Her grievous efforts on the self-portrait had been humbling and she'd learned a lot, not the least of which was to ask when in doubt. She'd been on the phone constantly with Norm, who'd come over to give her additional instruction in conservation and restoration. Norm fell in love with the painting of Thomas, and could barely speak when he saw the self-portrait. Fiona was relieved that he didn't know the story of the painting's near miss with disaster. Observing his reaction to Emma's serene countenance, Fiona could see the boy who had had the crush on the beautiful artist.

Norm laughed, and said that when Thomas was about that age, he and his mother walked all over the neighborhood. They were quite a sight, the two dark haired beauties, with matching oval faces and rounded brows. Only Thomas's riveting blue eyes distinguished him from his mother. If Thomas fell behind while they walked, he would naturally fall into the same limping cadence as hers. Norm didn't think Emma ever knew, but the entire neighborhood was in on the joke. Norm sat back, lips pursed, his hands folded together, nodding with the memory.

The first three paintings had cleaned up beautifully, especially the self-portrait, which now glowed from all the professional attention. Now, cleaned, the shaded side of Emma's face was not quite so foreboding. She didn't look unhappy, sitting in the gloom, but content, enjoying a moment of sunshine in an afternoon of reading. The cleaning also revealed more of the room, which was not in Fiona's apartment. Fiona noted that, based on the date of the painting, Emma hadn't moved to Wayne Street until after 1931.

Even the bungalow painting had more of a presence with its layers of grime removed. Fiona was having second thoughts about having rejected it out of hand. Norm even knew the house. He remembered that the lady of the house had taken a class with Emma, and that she and her husband had purchased several of Emma's paintings in the thirties. Norm's story reminded Fiona to ask Marvin where he'd purchased the paintings. It had occurred to her that each purchase could provide additional leads.

Fiona wasn't sure where her cleaning responsibilities ended; so she purchased new stretcher bars, and under Norm's instruction, re-stretched the kitchen painting. Pleased with the result, she re-stretched the bungalow, using her new power stapler to secure the canvases on the back or sides of the stretcher frame, alternating from end to end as she went to keep the tension equal. Now, with the paintings cleaned, re-stretched and the two completed ones varnished, she could deliver them back to Marvin for framing and for repairs to the kitchen painting. She was relieved but hated to give them up.

So today, she'd drop off the canvases with Marvin, get a peek at his two, and then the rest of the day would be devoted to digging at Mills. She hadn't been back to the library since the evening she discovered the application letter. Fiona was determined to try to streamline the process, to copy whole files and then cull at home. Armed with pockets full of change for the Xerox, she loaded the canvases, and headed for Marvin's.

Marvin had made it clear that he didn't want any paintings returning to the gallery, not even as a drop off. While he felt entirely justified in engaging in his own collecting, apparently he was not so comfortable that he wanted his partners at the gallery to see evidence of his project with Fiona. Their future rendezvous would avoid the gallery. Marvin lived in a duplex in Rockridge. It was a small one story double brown shingle bungalow with an odd, back to back configuration, where each unit had its address on a different street. While only a one bedroom, his unit had a large, mostly above-ground basement where he had an office and workshop. Marvin, still looking rumpled, invited Fiona in, and insisted on an immediate showing and critique of her work on the canvases.

Fiona was not surprised that Marvin's tastes in furnishings leaned towards modern, punctuated by occasional and exquisite antique pieces. The total look was light and spare. His antique paintings, and small sculptures stood out like gems, exactly the look Marvin wanted. Marvin set the first canvas, the house painting, on an easel across from the windows.

"Really, Fiona, you've done a wonderful job. None of my

contacts through the gallery could have done better. We may need to train you for repair work, too. I didn't much like this one before, but now it really shines.

Next he put up his favorite, the self-portrait. He squinted at it, oddly. Fiona cringed, waiting, but Marvin didn't seem to notice the repair.

"Wow, the ambience is totally different. It went from twilight to mid-afternoon. I thought I liked the intense chiaroscuro, but this is really much better. It's certainly kinder to Emma." Finally he placed the kitchen painting. The cleaning had made the shafts of sunlight luminous, with Thomas, radiant in the center. The cleaning revealed the bright colors of his artwork on the table and the pattern in his striped shirt. Cleaned and taut on its stretcher frame, the damaged corner looked far less ominous.

"Oh, this will work out fine." He pointed to the remaining paint in the scraped area and added, "There's enough here for the restorer to recreate. You'll never know it was damaged. I'll bring the others so the full signature can be completed. I may come to regret my choice of the self-portrait. You should be very proud of your work, Fiona. It's as good as the pros."

"Thank you." She told him briefly about Norm, and all his assistance. She didn't mention her professional help.

"Do I get to see your paintings?"

Marvin looked up from the easel, "Sure," But then his face clouded over. "Well, maybe next time," he blushed. "They're in the bedroom, and I have company still sleeping there."

Fiona winced and regretted her early hour. How awkward. "No problem, I'm headed to Mills anyway. Next time we'll do another show and tell. Are you headed out to estate sales today?"

"No, I previewed yesterday, and there wasn't much of interest. Let me know how Mills goes."

"Sure." Fiona shouldered her purse, and headed out for East Oakland.

At Mills, Fiona signed in and went straight to the records archives. She quickly culled Emma's transcript file and her application file, and headed out to the library copier. She started copying the files, hoping she could move the process along but an hour and ten minutes later, Fiona was getting discouraged. She didn't want to monopolize the copier, so whenever a student needed to copy, she stepped aside. The old originals were stapled or odd sizes, and the paper was brittle so the copying took special care. She sighed. This was her source material, and she resigned herself that it would be worth it to have the documents on hand at home. At this rate though, she wouldn't even finish this batch today. One of the library assistants approached Fiona, and informed her that the librarian wanted to see her.

Shit, she thought, I'm breaking some rule. Fiona really didn't want to abuse Mills' good graces. "Sure, where?" she responded.

The assistant pointed to the office at the back, and left. Fiona gathered up her things, and headed to take the heat. She knocked lightly at the office door.

"Come in, oh Ms. Hedge, I've been looking for you. When I didn't see you for a few weeks, I was afraid you'd lost heart in your project."

"Not at all, I've just been tied up with living. I'm back at it today."

"Please, have a seat." Fiona sat down nervously.

"I've been asked by the Dean to discuss your project. Is this a serious endeavor for you?"

"Getting more so by the day, why do you ask?"

"Mills has taken a special interest in what you're doing. Apparently Ms. Caites left a substantial sum to the school as a scholarship fund. We know very little about her, Mills usually likes more recognition for its benefactors, especially if they're alumnae."

"I don't see how that affects what I'm doing. How can I help?"

"Just the opposite, Fiona, we'd like to help you. We have plenty of scholarship students or special studies students who are looking for an opportunity to contribute in a meaningful way. I've seen you here late at night poring through the documents. And there you were, just now, stuffing that machine with quarters. Mills would like to give you access to office equipment, and if you'd like, maybe a research assistant, at least someone who could fetch and copy."

Fiona was dumbstruck. "Thank you, but I feel as though you may not understand. I'm not anyone official. I'm just a woman interested in an obscure painter."

"Yes, but she's *our* obscure painter, too."

"Thank you. I'm not sure what to say."

"Just say, yes. And it's Mills that wants to thank *you*. You need to talk to Arthur Bradley in the Art History department. He has some candidates for you. I certainly hope we can make this endeavor fruitful. Mr. Bradley has offered to advise you as well, but we don't want to intrude in your process. Just let us know what we can do. For starters," she reached into her drawer, "Here's the key to the little office down the hall, there's a copier there that won't eat all your parking change." She smiled broadly. Fiona took the key.

"For today, Jennifer can finish up your copying. Then we'll get you set up with someone assigned to you."

"Thank you."

"You're welcome. When you get a chance, during office hours, there's a storage area for old students' artwork. It's really a mess, but you and your assistant may want to check it out." The librarian picked up the phone and spoke to the circulation desk, "Can you spare Jennifer this afternoon for a special project? Okay, I'll be sending someone over for her." She looked back up at Fiona. "She's the redhead at the circulation desk. You can't miss her."

Fiona thanked her again, and headed out to the circulation desk.

Two hours later, as the library was closing, Fiona was headed to her car hugging a completed stack of freshly copied documents to her chest. Jennifer was organized and cheerful. Without the constant quarter feeding, and with Jennifer's help, the copying sped by. She could hardly believe her luck. The universe was conspiring to bring Emma Caites to light. Fiona hoped that she was up to the task.

Chapter Twelve

Fiona and Jennifer groaned with dismay as Arthur Bradley led them to the final storage room containing alumnae art works. This was the third room and, he promised, the last. So far, no luck. Fiona had been tempted to quit, but Arthur was so certain that in the early days, the Mills Art Department always kept a sampling of each student's work. This rule was mandatory if the student was an art major; so Emma should have samples in these storage rooms. Of course, there'd been a fire back in the early 1960s, the soot from which explained how the two women looked now. Regarding each other in the dim light, they both broke out laughing at the sight; like coal miners, they were filthy. Fiona had pretty much given up on the inhaler. If her body didn't revolt at this treatment, something must be wrong. Besides, the two had spent so much time laughing, Fiona's asthma had forgotten to kick in.

In a nutshell, that explained why Jennifer was still on the assignment. While she didn't technically meet the assistant requirements set by Art Bradley, she had a sense of humor that wouldn't quit. That was enough to persuade Fiona to request her. At the same time, Jennifer had actively sought the job, so Art relented. She was bored stiff in the library, and Fiona's project was different.

Arthur Bradley was a very tall, almost emaciated man, who walked with a bit of a stoop. Now he proceeded hesitantly in the shadowy basement hall, rattling the ancient keys as he went. Jennifer started to giggle, so Fiona tagged her with a quick jab of the elbow. Though she wasn't a professional researcher, and since Mills was really stepping up to the plate to help, Fiona thought they should show some level of decorum in front of the Dean of Arts.

"I think this is it," he said, leaning to jiggle the key into the lock of the old door. The door swung open with a Halloween creak. He reached inside and found the old push-button switch, turning on the single bulb. Inside, it looked like the set of a horror film, theater props were stacked in the middle of the room, and row upon row of paintings, leaned against each other in long columns, and portfolios were stacked every which way.

"Good thing we've got flashlights."

Art Bradley turned to them, "Just make sure you turn the light off when you leave. That old wiring makes me nervous. This place is a fire trap."

"Sure thing. Thanks for all the help."

"Actually, I'm really impressed that you're sticking with it. I'd have given up by now."

"We just know a good time," quipped Jenn. Fiona rolled her eyes in the dark, but Art laughed. He excused himself and made his way back down the hall and up the stairs to air and light.

"Alright, we'll do the same drill we worked out at the end of the last room. Your turn to man the flashlight, I'll rack the paintings." Fiona took her station at the end of the row of stacked canvases and waited for Jennifer to get her flashlight trained on the bottom right corner of the first canvas. Once Jennifer was ready, Fiona started flipping the paintings so she could quickly review the signature and date as each flipped by. Fiona was reminded of the first day she found the Caites painting in Norm's shop. She'd been so appalled by a little dust. Now look at her. Fiona almost wished she had a photo, because Amanda would never believe this. Fiona was just glad it was too dark to see spiders or bugs. She wanted to scream every time cobwebs brushed her hair, but restrained herself because of Jennifer. She just hoped Jennifer would think her gasps and grunts were asthmatic.

The women settled into a rhythm, quickly moving through the stacks.

Jennifer slowed up and noted, "Heads up. These are older, we may be getting close."

"What year are these?"

"We're in the mid thirties." Jenn wiped the dust from her face.

"I don't know how you can tell, this stuff is so filthy." Fiona's arms were beginning to ache.

They continued, more deliberately.

"Slow down now, they're mixed up by date in here—seeing some twenties in the mix."

"Stop. No, go again." Fiona kept flipping. She had to reach further down to catch the edge of a small canvas when Jenn cried out, *"Bingo!"*

"What, *this*?" Fiona asked, lifting the tiny framed piece, no bigger than eight-by-ten inches, with its gilded frame. Jennifer trained the light on the canvas. There, in small block letters, was Emma's signature followed by the date, 1921.

"Shit, I'd about given up."

"Me too, what's it look like?" Suddenly the flashlight felt inadequate. After all their efforts, the two women really wanted to see this little painting. But it was dark, and the painting was filthy. They could barely make out the subject matter.

"Looks like a little boat," murmured Fiona.

"Yeah, but we'll have to get out of here to see more. Let's set it aside and keep going. At least there's something for our efforts. Ready to switch?"

"Sure," groaned Fiona, standing to stretch her aching arms and back.

After some shuffling, they rearranged themselves, and settled back to the task with renewed interest.

Then, they hit a rich vein. Almost one right after another, they pulled four more canvases from the stack. They could barely stand it.

"We should take a break, and head up to the light," said Jenn, impatient to view the loot.

"No, we'll never come back down here. Let's stick with it. This row looks to be before her time. Once we're solid into the mid-teens we can quit the paintings. Then we need to take a quick look at the portfolios."

They knew from previous rooms that the portfolios were full of class drawings. The good news was that the portfolios were all prominently marked by student name on the outside. They'd be quick.

Fiona hesitated again. Suddenly the basement felt small and creepy. But as much as she wanted out, she wanted to make sure they'd found all this basement had to offer. Thankfully, Jennifer had caught the bug. She'd seen Emma's paintings, and now she had a stake in unearthing this mysterious Mills student. "Okay, let's get to it."

"We've got another one, this big one. Oh Jenn, it's the campus. It's lovely." Jennifer stepped over to better see what lay at the end of the flashlight beam.

"It's more built up now, but that's the main hall. Look, is that a pond there?" Jennifer picked it up and set it with the others. They bent back to the task.

Several paintings along they found another, a small nude, dated 1919.

Jennifer turned to Fiona, "Did they have studio life-drawing back then?"

"I don't know. We'll have to ask."

They turned in silence back to the stacked canvases, and methodically continued. After another twenty minutes or so, Jenn asked, "What are the dates now?"

"We're about to quit. I'm showing 1912 now, nothing before 1915 for fifteen or twenty canvases."

Fiona stood, rubbing her back. Jennifer turned to the portfolios. She took the flashlight and perused them quickly for the dates. "If there's anything, it'll be in this area."

Fiona took a quick puff of her inhaler, and squatted next to Jenn. The dim light from the single overhead bulb was enough to see the aged labels on the portfolios. Jennifer was moving with renewed energy. She rifled quickly though the jumbled cardboard and canvas, oversized folders.

"Wait a minute." Fiona pointed at a dark portfolio further back, "Pull that one."

Jennifer looked at her. This was no time to abandon method. "But…"

"Just check it. I have a hunch on this."

Jennifer stood and stooped over to the dark folder. It had a heft that the others lacked. She pulled it aside, and sure enough the yellowed label read, "Emma Caites"

"How'd you know?" she cried out.

"Emma had money. I figured she might have a leather portfolio. That's it, we're out of here. Let's get these up to the light."

It was a struggle moving the paintings up to the air. Once they'd turned off the overhead, they realized it was dark outside. Neither wanted to stay alone down there, but they couldn't carry all the pieces at once. Between them, with the flashlight, they shuttled all seven canvases and the portfolio through the basement halls, and up to the surface.

When they came out into the courtyard it was dark, and threatening rain.

"Now what do we do?" said Jenn.

"What do you mean?"

"What are we supposed to do with these paintings? Where do we take them?"

"Oh." Fiona realized it might be odd to take them to her house.

After all, this stuff belonged to Mills but that was what she'd intended. "These paintings all have to be cleaned and catalogued. I can't do that at the library. Don't worry, you'll keep me honest, but we've got to get them somewhere safe. Stay here, I'll get my car."

Jennifer helped Fiona load the trunk of the car. Then Fiona turned to her, "Where's your dorm? Grab a change of clothes, you're coming to my house."

Jennifer smiled broadly. She wanted to be there when there was enough light to see these things. Jenn hopped in, and directed Fiona to her dorm. Moments later, dodging raindrops, she ran back out to the car, and they headed to Fiona's with Emma's artworks.

Chapter Thirteen

"But, you're qualified, right?" Fiona wrapped her fingers in the phone cord.

"I think so, but I'm not sure what you're asking so I'm not sure how to answer."

"Well, we've got seven paintings and a portfolio of class drawings. We want to make the case to Mills that they are worth restoring, so we need some kind of valuation. We also need a professional opinion as to the probable costs involved in cleaning and restoration."

"Are you expecting *Mills* to pay for restoration?" Marvin sounded dubious.

"No, if it's just cleaning, I can do that, and I want to train Jennifer as a part of her special studies units. But we need to show Mills that there's value here, and at the same time, document the works' existence."

"You just walked away from the campus with them?"

Fiona shrugged, "What can I say. It seemed like a good idea at the time."

"Ooooh, girl, don't tempt me. Are they signed?"

"Yes, at least the paintings, not all the portfolio works."

"Okay, otherwise, we might have a problem with the provenance. When do you want to do this?"

"Anytime, they're in my trunk."

"Well, I don't want them in the gallery. And that also means I won't do this on gallery time or stationery, but I am free this afternoon. Do you have a well lighted place where I can have a look at them?"

"Sure, my basement garage. It's a beautiful day, you'll have natural light."

"Okay, be there about two. I can also see your first painting too. How about the new batch. Any good?"

"Don't know. The expert hasn't seen them yet," Fiona laughed.

Marvin made good time. Seeing his car pull up, Fiona met him downstairs at the garage door.

"How do you want to do this?" Fiona was remembering the suspense of the first time Marvin showed her Emma's paintings.

"Well, since it's a professional review, how about you just line them up in chronological order. Then, we can go through the portfolio and paper goods inside so we can spread out." Marvin reached into the passenger side of his car and pulled out a digital camera and a yellow legal pad. Fiona set about to line up the canvases.

"Jeez, Fiona, these are really filthy. I'm not going to be able to give an accurate assessment in this condition."

"Then just say so, and do your best."

Marvin started with his camera, fully documenting the entire lot, and then each of the paintings individually. He took a tape measure from his belt and measured each piece, making notes on the yellow pad. He pocketed the camera, and pulled out a small voice recorder.

"Mills Paintings, presumed artist, Emma Caites. Group of seven canvases, all dated. Student work from Mills archives: retrieval by Fiona Hedge and Mills assistant, Jennifer Sullivan. All works are discolored and require extensive cleaning. Initial review does not reveal damage, though once cleaned that determination could change. All works are framed, several with high quality and remarkable condition gilded, Arts and Crafts frames. Values, as student works, are based solely on aesthetic and decorator values for similar canvases, as reported by auction results, and gallery sales experience. Artist is NOT listed. Measurements indicated are canvas size. In chronological order:

"One. 1919. Small nude. Nine-by-thirteen inches. This painting shows a young woman, from the hips up, revealed brushing her hair, in the reflection of a vanity mirror. The reflection captures some details of the room behind the subject. Colors obscured. Pending cleaning, this is a lovely canvas, likely to fetch as much as $800 to $1000, even without a known painter. This type of painting moves quickly at auction. Given the subject matter, and date, it is unlikely that this is actually an assigned student piece. Life drawings/paintings in an academic setting in 1919 would not usually be so intimately located. Moreover, nudes would not be a painting subject for a first year student, and records indicate the artist had only enrolled at Mills that year. This painting far exceeds the usual skill levels found in early training.

"Two. 1921. Small rowboat. Six-by-eight. This is a tiny impressionist style painting, on stretched canvas. Note, this piece is framed in a gilded Newcomb Macklin frame, in excellent condition, original label on reverse. Frame alone is worth several hundred dollars. Subject is a small rowboat, oars akimbo, pulled ashore on a sandy beach. While colors are unclear because of layered grime, close inspection shows the piece captures the worn, peeling paint of the boat exquisitely. A dock, shown diagonally from the left mid-ground to back frames the boat for the viewer. Well designed on the small canvas. Cleaned, this piece could be a small gem. Again, the subject matter is not specifically student oriented, though it could well be a plein air class assignment. The value here lies in the deft treatment of the design and subject matter. Decorator or auction value, including frame (as assumed original) approximately $1800, regardless of artist.

"Three is a 1921 portrait. Fourteen-by-eighteen. Medium sized portrait of a young woman at a desk near a window. This appears to be a student work, with the subject not well positioned in space. The subject is well rendered though, with a book on the desk in front of her, and looking up to address the viewer. This work is nicely painted, but, in the absence of context, of limited value. Painted on the reverse of the canvas is the word "Wren," which offers little explanation that would affect value. In an Arts and Crafts era fumed oak frame. Some damage to finish. Frame with restoration valued at $250, with painting. Not likely to exceed $400."

Marvin straightened and rubbed the small of his back. He collected the first three canvasses and stacked them vertically against the wall, and then set the next three in their stead, in the good light. He spent a few minutes measuring and making notes before he resumed his dictation.

"Four. 1922 coffee cup. Fourteen-by-fourteen. Lovely semi-abstract or Expressionist painting of a coffee cup on a table in the corner of a kitchen. The environment is merely suggested with bold broad brushstrokes in muted tones. The spoon in the saucer elegantly indicated with mere wisps of the brush. Again, probably not a student assignment, as it does not reveal typical academic still life subject matter. This canvas breathes life into the solitary cup on the table. Cleaned, this might be another gem. It's a bold venture into the semi-abstract for a student work of this era. Framed in a simple black frame, this painting would have auction or decorator value of up to $2,200.

"Five's also from 1922. Eighteen-by-twenty-two. Here's the more typical student still life. The subject matter an assemblage of vase, flowers, Greek-style plaster bust on draped fabric. While deftly painted, this painting is dull and speaks to class requirements rather than to any artistic merit. Limited value unless the artist has collectable value or is listed. Framed in simple wooden frame of no particular value.

"Six. 1923. Mills. Twenty-four-by-thirty inches. This is a large, lovely painting of the buildings and environment at Mills College. Even filthy, this painting is bright and warm. The landscape and foliage are superbly rendered. It shows a number of halls, set against eucalyptus groves with a pond at one side. The sunlight reflects on the stucco walls and the trees move in the breeze. Note that since this pond does not currently exist, it is not clear whether the artist has manufactured this bucolic scene or whether it reflects a historical scene, long since changed. The painting is like a tender portrait of a loved sanctuary. Despite its excellence, it remains an institutional painting, with limited value on the auction market. Its highest and best value would be for display at Mills. Restored, this will be an impressive student work, worthy of display in the facility's permanent collection. Framed in a large gilded frame in good condition. Minor nicks. No label but of Newcomb Macklin quality. An antique frame of this size and quality, without the painting would auction for $1,200 to $1,800."

Marvin stacked this batch with the first, and pulled out the last painting. He stood in the slanting sunlight in the garage, smiling at this last canvas. He measured it and turned to Fiona, who until now had retreated into the shadows.

"Really, Fiona. These are a find." With that he turned his back to her, and picked up his soliloquy.

"And finally, number seven. 1923. A self portrait. Twenty-by-fourteen. A not unusual assignment for an upper level art student. This self-portrait exhibits an elevated level of self awareness and poise. The artist has created a warm, three-dimensional environment in which she sits and addresses the canvas. She places her palette in the foreground, with loose fluid brush strokes. Here the artist has added the almost humorous touch of the painted brush reaching out to touch up a final, roughly blocked corner of the canvas. She sits in what appears to be a dorm chair, with a black cane leaning against the arm of the chair. The face is revealed as a peaceful, direct and engaged, rendered in what appears to be a completely pastel palette. Cleaning should be very revealing of this otherwise delicately rendered canvas. Value on such a personal depiction is difficult to assess. In a listed artist, this would be a very valuable work. Even with an unknown talent, this piece speaks so directly of the identity of the artist, it may carry a value in excess of $2,500. In a carved, cherry frame with a gilded liner. Frame value exceeds $2,000."

Marvin flicked off the record button, and breathed deeply. Fiona was awed. Marvin spoke the language. He was the real deal art expert. She couldn't resist though. "So, come on, what do you *really* think?"

"Fiona, I even love that there are some oinkers in the mix. She's so human. You've got to get these cleaned. The values will probably be much higher when restored. I can't tell color quality or skill in this condition, but that self-portrait is *stellar*."

"What about the restoration costs?"

"I'll put it in the written report. But you're right, these need to be cleaned. It makes me wonder though Fiona, how did these compare to the other student's work?"

"We didn't even look. I mean I glanced from time to time, but I can't really say."

Marvin leaned forward, "Fiona, Emma Caites needs a retrospective show. We need to find enough work to make it happen. If we can't, we'll have to cull the other works and curate as a lost treasures show."

"Whoa, I think you're a little ahead of the curve…"

"No, Fiona, Mills is just the venue for it, that's the angle here. She needs to get the gallery space she always deserved."

Fiona sucked in her breath, "I'll talk to Art Bradley. But Marv, this is really a long shot."

"Not if I find us more paintings." Both wondered to themselves how likely that would be. They stood in contemplation.

Fiona broke the silence, "Okay, but how about some tea, and a quick portfolio viewing."

"I'd love it." Marvin gathered up his tools, tape measure, camera and recorder, and followed Fiona up to the kitchen.

Fiona set to making tea and spread an artful display of biscotti on a tray. Marvin flipped through the student portfolio, pausing from time to time to take photos of specific pieces. He moved quickly and precisely, cautious with the aging, brittle paper pieces. He had finished by the time Fiona was ready to serve.

"Well?"

"There are a few really nice items, maybe a handful frame-worthy. Mostly the point of a portfolio review is to identify early talent or style trends. We have that, and more, with the paintings. Should we get to a single artist show, the portfolio pieces would be used to flesh out the artist's early directions. In a larger show, it has no real value."

"You've already decided on the retrospective show, haven't you?"

"Well, of course it will depend on whether we can fill it out with quality. If we can, it's a no-brainer... You'll see, Bradley will be onboard for this. What we'll need from you is theme."

"You mean life story, eh?"

"Yeah. Especially if you can get why she didn't go further."

"Marvin, I think you're being harsh. This was the early Twentieth Century, not exactly easy territory for women, and she was disabled."

"I hope that's not the whole story, it'd just be sad."

They made small talk. Fiona described the dark gritty basement, and they laughed at the picture she conjured. They finished up the tea, and Marvin teased, "So do I get to see the painting that started this whole adventure?"

Taking no quarter, Fiona countered, "Sure, there's nobody sleeping up there."

Marvin blushed, "Touché," and followed Fiona upstairs to where her first painting hung next to the window it portrayed.

Marvin took his time examining the canvas. Finally, turning he said, "You did good girl, that's a great piece. It'll look great in the show, especially if we hang it next to a really good photo of the view out the window."

Fiona laughed, "You sound so certain, I'll just go with it."

"Wise woman."

Chapter Fourteen

Amanda sprawled on the loveseat, gimbaling a glass of chardonnay in her left hand. She looked at them sternly, and in her most commanding tone she demanded, "So, what have we got?"

The other two looked at each other and laughed. Jennifer was curled on the floor on pillows, wine by her side and clipboard in her lap. Fiona sat at the table, glass in hand, with the photos of Emma Caites' paintings spread out in front of her, and Marvin's final report on the Mills' cache. She'd just finished reading it to the two redheads, who were duly impressed. The three of them had polished off two pizzas, and with the wine, were settling into a relaxed celebratory Saturday evening. Jennifer in particular was pleased that their thankless grimy efforts in the basement had borne fruit.

Marvin's report, complete with photos, made a strong case for cleaning and restoration. Fiona had requested a meeting with Art Bradley, the librarian and the Dean to pitch the idea of letting her and Jennifer clean the paintings. She was trying to include all the people who'd been involved in helping with the search. Now she'd faxed them advance copies of the report, and was nervously awaiting Tuesday's appointment. For his part, Marvin had geared the report as an initial installment on the concept of "the undiscovered talent," with the idea that additional paintings or information later would build the ultimate case for a retrospective. The main thrust was historical, but a review of his estimates illustrated the financial value of the little collection, especially if restored.

"Marvin has a point," Fiona added, "Mills is Emma's alma mater. It's a prestigious institution with a firm footing in the arts, and California art in particular. A retrospective show at Mills would really put Emma on the map."

Amanda sat up and extended the bottle, "Anyone?" The other two groaned and shook their heads. Amanda emptied the last of the chardonnay into her glass, "Really, where are we on the story part?"

Fiona hesitated. "Well it's still pretty skimpy. What I'd like would be to get enough of a handle on it to approach Thomas again, and prove to him that I'm serious about this endeavor. Maybe then he'd cooperate."

"Fiona, your conversation with him is what was skimpy, and it was on the phone. Are you sure he was really so negative?" Amanda's gaze caught Fiona directly.

Fiona, a little defensive, shot back, "Amanda, I may be shy, but I don't have *any* trouble reading people or situations. As soon as I mentioned his mother, Thomas clammed up. He wasn't nasty or rude but he certainly wasn't warm. There was something particularly chilly, no, officious in his pauses. I got about the same reception that you give the Jehovah's Witnesses at your doorstep."

Amanda giggled. "Okay, so you need more proof to convince him. You always did over-prepare and more digging will really work for you in the long run." She turned her attention to Jennifer, "So, just what have we got on Emma?"

"Mostly we've got boring, biographical stuff." Jennifer was referring to her clipboard with Fiona's notes. "Born in 1900 to a comfortable merchant family. Contracted that Legg Perthe thing in 1910, and moved to the East Bay to her grandparents' home to convalesce, where she remained for several years. Informally but broadly educated there. Learns to paint. Then she moved back to San Francisco, but it doesn't appear she did much there. Applied to Mills in 1918 after the death of her grandmother, and enrolled there in 1919. Despite physical limitations she was active in many clubs and societies. She acted, she debated, she painted. She gets great grades." Jennifer paused here to roll her eyes, "I hate her already. Her best friend at Mills appears to have been Henrietta Simpson, who may be the 'Wren' in the portrait. Less clear is whether Henrietta is also the model for the early nude study. She graduates in 1923. There's some indication she goes to France for further study, but no confirmation. Apparently, money is not an issue for her. We have nothing from Europe, no artwork, no story. Then she resurfaces in the early 1930s with more local paintings. Sometime between 1931 and '38 she moves to Fiona's apartment. She is known to give classes; she does commission work. She has a son. She does not appear to affiliate with other artists of the time, nor is her work represented in any major gallery. She is prolific, but not well known. Her work is beautiful, sensitive and as good as any other local artist. She..."

Fiona cut in, "I'd say you're inserting bias here Jenn. We aren't in a position to judge her artwork in her times."

"No, but Marvin is, and he thinks she's that good."

"Okay, given."

"Besides," Jenn continued, "Then she just fades away. We know she dies in 1958 and we know she leaves a chunk to Mills but that's it."

Amanda interrupted, "What's a chunk, in fifty-eight?"

Fiona jumped in to protect Emma, "Well, she gave the school $250,000 in 1958. That's not chopped liver now, and certainly was a lot in 1958."

"But we already knew she came from money."

"Admittedly, it's not much to go on, and certainly I'd like to have more before I approach Thomas again!"

"Well, you have Marvin's report."

"And that helps a lot, really, it does. But I'm not sure it will convince Thomas to give it up. After all, it's a limited report on Emma's student work."

Jennifer wrinkled her brow, "So what was wrong with her, the leg thing?"

Fiona was ready for this, "I looked it up, it's a weird syndrome where something goes wrong in the cap of the hip bone or end of the leg bone, the blood supply is interrupted. It's painful, but the big problem is that it can stop the bone from growing. If it happens when the person is young, they'll be disabled because of the difference in leg lengths."

"Is it contagious?"

"Probably not. I don't think they know the cause. It tends to run in families."

Amanda chimed in, "So the only thing wrong was that one of her legs was shorter?"

"Well, it's not as simple as that, being unbalanced like that has a whole set of problems, plus if the bone ending dies or is seriously damaged by the initial episode, it can be brittle or fragile for the rest of the person's life. If only part of the bone dies, you can get irregular or crooked growth. We know she walked with a cane, that's clear in the Mills pictures and the later self-portrait."

"It's interesting that she puts the cane in the paintings." Jennifer's head was tipped back, and she was regarding Fiona through the edge of her wine glass, "I mean, what does it say about her, that the cane appears in the self-portraits? We've seen it several times."

Fiona had thought about it, too. Everyone has a feature that is

68

somehow self-defining. In her paintings, Emma had several. Clearly her direct gaze was always there, both in the paintings and in the photos, and those dark almond eyes. But Emma could have glossed over the cane, and yet it was there, leaning on the chair arm in two self-portraits separated by two decades, and in the photo as well. Emma viewed her handicap as central to who she was. She was talented and rich and bright. But at some level, she couldn't escape the fact that she was crippled. It made Fiona a little sad. She wished she could fill in more of the picture.

"Really Amanda, I am a bit stuck. I'm missing something big in Emma's motivation. I wish I had enough material ready to go back to talk to Thomas."

"Why don't you write him, lay out some of what you have…"

"I need more. He was so dismissive. I need to convince him that this is a serious inquiry."

Amanda paused, and her mouth dropped as she turned to Fiona, "Jesus, he's a bastard."

"Well, that's a little harsh. I'm sure he…"

"No, I mean it, Fi. It's been right in front of us the whole time. He's a bastard."

"What are you talking…" Fiona flushed, but never finished the question.

"Get it. She registered at Mills as a teenager…"

Fiona finished the thought, "As Emma Caites! He's Thomas *Caites!* Oh, this has been obvious for weeks. There isn't a Mr. Caites in the picture, it's her maiden name."

"Maybe there's your missing motivation, honey." Amanda looked smug. "Bad enough she was a bohemian artist type, but in the middle of the Depression she bears a son out of wedlock, and then keeps him."

"That just might be enough to explain staying out of the limelight."

"And *his* reluctance to prying eyes."

But Jennifer didn't buy it. She set her wine glass aside, and pulled herself upright. "It shouldn't matter. She was an artist. She was painting nudes in her teens. It's not like she was a prude."

But this time, Amanda stepped in for Emma. "It was a big deal, times were very different then. My father was conceived before his parents married in the 1930s, and his mother falsified his birth certificate to hide it. Even into the 1950s, illegitimacy was a shameful family secret."

"Yeah," Fiona added. "Women risked dangerous back street abortions even into the 1960s. Actually, it might even have been worse that she came from a good family. She had farther to fall."

The three fell into silence, pondering the enormity an unplanned pregnancy at that time.

Fiona looked up, "I think we've got something here, but I'm not sure this will make it any easier to approach Thomas."

Chapter Fifteen

"Doesn't it strike you as a little weird, Mom, that you'd want to approach a complete stranger, in his seventies, to ask him questions about his long-dead mother?" Denise was skipping back to an earlier topic, avoiding Fiona's question about Thanksgiving.

"Whoa. Let's go back to the calendar issue for just a moment. What do you mean you won't be home for Thanksgiving?"

Denise swallowed. "Well, Tom only gets one extra day with the holiday, so, with the connecting flights and all, we wouldn't really have enough time to make flying to Oakland worthwhile."

"So when did you know this?"

"A couple of weeks ago but..."

Fiona sighed, exasperated, "Well," she shifted and swiveled in her chair with a recognizable squeak, "I could come there, but it's a tight time crunch now. You should've told me earlier." Gazing at the computer screen Fiona continued, "I can get a flight out on Wednesday, but I'd have to stay clear through to the next Tuesday. Wait, wait, here's one..."

Denise interrupted, "We decided to go to Mexico."

"What's that?"

"We decided to go to Mexico with friends for Thanksgiving. There's a train that runs through a gorge, and they do a holiday gourmet weekend on the train." Denise's voice was level and low.

Fiona held her breath. This was Denise's first Thanksgiving married. It was also the first time she hadn't spent the holiday with her mother. Denise had to know Fiona expected them for Thanksgiving. Not that there were any firm plans, but they *had* talked about it during the summer.

"Oh." Fiona's voice sounded stunned. "What friends? From Tom's work?" Her words barely filled the airspace on the phone.

"Oh, no. Stephanie and her boyfriend are coming down from Atlanta for this. She read about it on the net, and she suggested it."

"Stephanie. From here?"

"Yeah, she's in Atlanta now, with Coke."

Fiona paused, stung, "I wish you'd said something earlier..." The silence hung heavy.

"Mom?"

71

Fiona sucked in her breath. "Well, I guess that's that then. It is *your* plan. I'll talk to you later, dear."

"Mom!" But the phone clicked dead in Denise's hand.

Chapter Sixteen

Denise sat holding the phone in her hand. "Fuck," she muttered under her breath. She knew she hadn't handled it well, but still, she was angry at her mother.

"What's that about?" Tom came in, rubbing a towel into his wet hair.

"Nothing. Just my mom. She's not happy about our plans for Thanksgiving. I think she just hung up on me." Rhythmically she drummed the handset into her palm.

"You think? Well, did she or didn't she?" He lifted the towel to look at her.

Denise shrugged.

"You said she's been acting weird lately. You should've said something earlier but maybe it's just as well." He plopped next to her on the bed, and continued drying his hair.

"What do you mean by *that*?"

"You know, you and your mom are pretty clingy. It's about time you changed your priorities." He set the towel down in his lap. "So, we packed yet?"

Denise gestured at the open suitcase on the end of the bed.

Tom stood, and surveyed the contents. "Did you get my green shirt? I wanted it for Thanksgiving."

"It's in the dryer. I'll pack it when it's ironed." He nodded and headed back into the bathroom, leaving the damp towel on the bed.

Denise quickly redialed her mother's number but the machine kicked in immediately. She hung up without leaving a message. Suddenly, she wished she was talking to her mother about her crazy schemes with that dead painter.

Chapter Seventeen

"So, you hung up on her?"

"Not exactly, but I ended the call abruptly. I mean I did say something indicating we were done." Fiona sighed.

Amanda paused, "Then what?"

"Nothing. I was really upset. I hung up. I saw my car keys on the desk, picked them up and left. I didn't know where I would go or anything, I just had to get out. As I left, the phone rang, but I just kept going."

"What exactly upset you?"

"Oh, c'mon Amanda. I've had Thanksgiving dinner with Denise every year of her life, and now she ducks out, makes other plans, and doesn't even bother to tell me? We talked about Thanksgiving back in August. She wanted me to know that they were spending Christmas with Tom's folks. Without being specific on arrangements, Thanksgiving here was implied in the conversation."

"I agree that not telling you was wrong, but the rest of this is pretty normal. New husband, lives out of state, supposed to make a life for herself." Amanda was ironing a new batch of linens from an estate sale. "So, where did you go?"

"To Mills. I just went and walked the grounds. It was lovely out, and I hung out in that commons area in Emma's painting. There's a bench there, some of the trees are even the same, only bigger."

"Have you talked to her since?"

"No, I'm not calling. Don't know what I'd say. There've been some hang-ups on the machine, so I think she's called but isn't leaving messages."

Amanda held her iron up to the light, and shook her head. She put it back down on the ironing board and left the room. Fiona craned her neck to see what was going on. She was intrigued by all the little details of Amanda's reclamation efforts. Amanda returned with a plastic jug of distilled water, and carefully poured it in a thin stream into the top hole in the iron. Fiona loved the smell of the damp iron on the fresh linen.

"With all the care you take, you really might want to consider learning to clean and restore paintings. I think the dollar value is much higher than it is for table linens."

"But I really like table linens. What did Mills say about you cleaning the paintings?"

"They want to take it to the trustees, but it looks like we have the green light. I should know by week's end."

"So, you're recruiting?"

"Nah, but it might be fun. You're forgetting, I have a built-in elf on this, Jennifer will be involved, and she's really excited about it."

"She's getting quite an education and adventure out of her special studies units, isn't she? Think of it, she gets to be in on this whole gossipy little treasure hunt."

"Neither of us is complaining about the match."

Amanda resumed ironing. The napkins were worked in ivory linen with autumn leaves embroidered in the corners in amber, chestnut and deep moss greens. Fiona wondered at the delicacy of such needlework for linens geared strictly for the Thanksgiving feast. The thought of the holiday caught in her throat.

"You need a survival strategy." Amanda had been watching Fiona's face. "I can be free for Thanksgiving. It'd get me out of my sister's dreary annual event. Oooh," Amanda paused, "I could even use your empty-nest deal as my excuse. My sister would just eat that up."

"Oh, that's not necessary." Fiona just couldn't picture Thanksgiving. It was true though, that Amanda dreaded her sister's affair every year.

Amanda set down the iron again. "Really, Fiona, we should make this an Emma Caites event. Let's ask Norm if we can cook up a Thanksgiving meal at his house, and pump him for stories about the good-old-days."

Fiona cocked her head to one side, "Maybe. I guess I could ask him."

"Of course he'll say yes, it's not like he has the world knocking at his door on Thanksgiving. It'll be great. See if Jenn can come, too."

The idea wasn't half bad. Fiona could just picture them packed into Norm's adorable little kitchen, spoons aloft to potato mashing and gravy making.

"Okay, I'll ask. But I won't pressure him."

"I don't think you'll have to pull teeth. Anyway, we'll do something no matter the answer. *Deal*?"

Fiona felt like she'd been played. But it was done spontaneously

75

and lovingly. Over the years she and Amanda had taken turns, easing the pains of living for each other. This was no different. Fiona felt blessed that she had such a friend. She couldn't suppress a spark of fun in the idea. "Deal." She reached over to finger one of the finished napkins. "Can we use these for Thanksgiving?"

Amanda looked down at the napkins, and for the first time recognized their holiday theme. "Sure, they're perfect. I'd never get them listed, sold and delivered in time for the holiday, anyway." Amanda was on a roll, "*And*, you need to work on a plan for Christmas."

"Whoa, that's jumping ahead. Let's just get Thanksgiving under way."

"Nope, Fiona, you already know that Denise is spending Christmas with Tom's family. You need to plan something special for you that fills that gap, and then some."

"What's this, the *sour grapes holiday plan?*"

"Not at all, I've been alone my whole life. If you don't give yourself the room to enjoy a holiday, all you feel is the absences. The absence of a lover, the absence of children, the absence of a family, the absence of friends with better plans. As an empty-nester you need to make sure that the holidays have enough in them for your presence. Leave no hole to be filled."

"So, did you have a plan for that?"

"No, because it needs to be your plan. I can't figure out what fills your gap. For me it's the spa thing. I pamper myself. I like nothing better on a holiday than a swim in spa waters, a massage and a good book. Maybe a movie in the evening. I don't know what you like."

"Me neither."

"Well start thinking about it. Come Christmas, we want you booked." Amanda gently folded the last napkin and set it aside with the others.

Chapter Eighteen

Fiona stepped outside to pick up the mail from her box. The air was crisp, making November finally feel like the beginning of winter. A California native, Fiona never missed winter, or even understood the lure of seasons. But she did enjoy the little bit of color that Oakland enjoyed, and she loved the smell of wood smoke when fireplaces were stoked for that holiday atmosphere.

The mail was light, some junk mail, a few business letters and something from the county Bureau of Records. That wasn't so unusual. In her business Fiona often needed official records to date events in the estates she handled. She just couldn't remember having ordered any records for her current cases. She stepped back inside, tearing open the envelope as she did. She sat down in her favorite chair, pulling the thin paper from the torn envelope. She reached for her reading glasses on the end table, unfolding the sheet, and spreading it flat in her lap.

There it was, and only then did she remember having requested Emma Caites' death certificate, all those months ago. It took her breath away. It was as though a friend had died, and here Emma Caites had died almost fifty years earlier. She had to laugh at that. Fiona scanned the vitals: born San Francisco, no spouse, before settling on the section at the bottom listing the cause of death. As usual there were three sections. The first indicated heart failure, a little surprising for a woman of slight build at only fifty-eight. Fiona reflected that Emma had died only a few years older than she was now. She didn't think of herself as an old woman, yet in 1958, Emma would clearly have been considered so. Maybe Emma didn't think she was old either.

The second listed cause was "Sequelae of Calve Legg Perthe Syndrome." Though she'd researched Emma's condition thoroughly, she couldn't imagine how those problems would've contributed as a cause of death. Then her eyes found the third cause listed: "Possible heroin overdose." Fiona gasped. Kicked squarely in the solar plexus, she struggled to recover her breath. *An addict?* Good God, maybe Emma did follow the sordid path of the tortured artist. Fiona felt like she'd happened on a lover's secret infidelity. She reflected on how little she really knew about Emma. How much can you glean from an artist's canvases? She knew for sure that she could never grasp, much less write about Emma, unless she came to an understanding of this new wrinkle. Now there was another layer to Thomas' reluctance. It became even more imperative that she find a bridge to Thomas.

She reached for the telephone, and paused. Usually, her first impulse would be to call Denise. She hadn't spoken to Denise since the Thanksgiving cancellation, and now, with the holiday the next day, she didn't want to reopen that wound. Besides, Denise was probably somewhere in Mexico. It took all her reserve not to dial Denise's cell number.

So, who would she call with this new bomb? Amanda was teaching, not that much would happen in the classroom the day before Thanksgiving. She thought about Norm, and dismissed the idea. Without more information and context, this would rock his world. Fiona had become increasingly aware that Norm was emotionally fragile. When she suggested Thanksgiving at his house he had wept openly before accepting. When Norm's wife died, he had just closed the door on being connected to anyone. Now, with new friends, the door was swinging open in ways that were unpredictable. Somehow, the image of a fading, crippled beauty on junk wasn't what Fiona wanted Norm to contemplate for the holiday. Fiona dialed Marvin's number at the gallery. His distinctive voice took the call.

"Marvin, it's Fiona. Got a minute?"

"If this is about tomorrow, I really don't think I'll be coming. I make it a practice not to be the stray dog at a Thanksgiving gathering."

"Marvin, get off it. I wasn't calling about that, but now that you mention it, we're all stray dogs at this event. Even strays gather for good food and company."

"Just who's going to be there?"

"Me, Norm, Amanda and Jennifer—all single and with nothing better to do on Thanksgiving. Amanda and I are damn good cooks. If you came, it would complete the circle of Emma Caites accomplices. But, Marv, that's not why I called."

"Right."

"Really, I have juicy Emma news. It's really rocked *my* world."

"So, girl, give it up."

"Months ago I ordered her death certificate, and I completely forgot about it, but it arrived today. One of the listed causes of death is possible heroin overdose."

"Jesus."

"I know. It really upset me."

"Not me. I don't need to like this woman. From a collector's point of view, addiction can be an asset."

"Marvin!"

"Fiona, look at Van Gogh. Look at the Impressionists. Nothing fuels value like the story of the suffering, tortured artist."

"It should be the paintings that sell the artist."

Marvin laughed, "Welcome to America, everything is the pursuit of gossip, the cult of personality. Look at the Olympics. It's not so much the athletes' performance that catches attention, it's their overcoming obstacles, and it's the same with rock stars and actors."

"Well, I can assure you that won't sell to Thomas, and I'll need him to fill in the gaps."

"Yeah, well, you'll have to really think that one through before you approach him again. He's protecting her, and it's beginning to look like there's a lot to hide."

Fiona saw an opportunity. "Yeah, so what do you have to hide? What makes you a stray dog at Thanksgiving?"

"That's easy, I'm gay and not currently hooked up. My family rejected me. To them I might be acceptable in the closet, but open? And with *this* hair? Not a chance. I used to celebrate with my partner, but there are issues there too." He paused, "So, what's your story?"

"Empty nest."

"Really? Just that simple?"

"Essentially, yes. There are variations on the theme, she married this summer, moved away, and has never been so distant. They were supposed to come here for Thanksgiving, but I was usurped for a better, more hip opportunity. I'm not sure just now if we're even speaking."

"And Amanda?"

"Refugee from a dysfunctional family, never married, never wanted to be."

"Norm?"

"Widowed."

"Jennifer?"

Fiona laughed, "She's a student who can't afford to fly home.

79

Our sorry lot actually sounds exciting to her. Really, she's a breath of fresh air. Sometimes I look at her and wonder where I failed Denise."

"You didn't fail Denise. She probably just needs space to define herself in her new life."

"Oooh, Mr. Psychotherapy. You *should* come tomorrow, you'd fit right in."

"What makes you say that?"

"Amanda has spent her entire adult life in therapy. It's a spectator sport for her. Whenever I did something questionable with Denise, she'd just say, 'Put a nickel in the therapy jar.' Sometimes I think the two of them talk more easily than Denise does with me."

Marvin laughed. "Okay, I'm intrigued. If I don't come, you'll all spend the day discussing Emma Caites, and I'll be way behind."

"Good. And the theme of the day could be devising the best strategy for reaching out to Thomas. With you and Amanda, we'll analyze the options."

"I thought the theme of the day was great food?"

"Nah, great food is just the starting point, just fuel for the fire."

Chapter Nineteen

Norm groaned, his hands on his taut belly. He emptied the last of his wine, and nodded at Marvin, who'd brought the wines, and had walked them through the choices. They perfectly complemented the tastes and textures of the sumptuous meal. The others spoke animatedly and picked at the food on the table. Norm reached out, and fingered the delicate embroidered leaves on the napkins, such a lovely little touch. Lily would've loved it, a gentle reminder of the season. It almost brought tears to his eyes again.

He had misjudged Amanda. Anyone who saw and collected such details of domestic devotion had to have a soft side. After watching her all day, he could see that the brash exterior was a bluff. When he heard that she was a special education teacher, he knew she was all heart. It reminded him of how Lily had hardened, bit by bit, when the years passed and had not filled their home with children. Hardened like calluses on work-worn hands. Norm wondered what trials had built that wall around Amanda, and immediately he loved her for it.

The day had been very emotional for him anyway. Norm was so thankful to have been included in this gathering. He wondered at his luck, that a soft-hearted moment selling a painting would lead to this, this incredible inclusion. When Fiona had insisted that he carve the turkey he'd put his arms around her and his eyes filled with tears. He was so embarrassed; he didn't want to cry in front of his new friends. For the first time in years Norm felt that he occupied his home, that there was a warmth there that included and filled him. Fiona just embraced him and told him quietly that they all had him to thank for this day, that he had brought them all together. He could almost feel Lily there at his side.

The Thanksgiving meal was really over now, but nobody was yet willing to stop picking, a bit here and there, lingering with the conversation. Norm was exhausted from it all, and when he was this tired these days, his hearing seemed to fade out. There were still desserts to be served, so he was holding firm at two helpings. He'd not felt this full, or this content, since before Lily died.

Early that morning Amanda and Fiona had swooped into his kitchen, and created that dance of festivity that Lily and her sisters always had. It was the mystery of women, working together in that small galley. They laughed and teased, rolled pie dough, and mixed and stirred. Norm sat in the breakfast nook, watching and answering questions. Where was this? Where was that? Did he have any cloves? He gratefully answered the questions, and rifled through the cupboards to find every last necessity. There was an ease and a grace to it that he'd forgotten, soft hands practiced in the rituals of chopping, peeling and timing. He'd napped right there at the table, lulled by the voices and smells. Fiona nudged him to suggest he lie down a bit, but he didn't want to leave the center of it, even if he dozed. Like Lily, the women tidied as they went. Whenever he opened his eyes there was some new facet being prepared, but aside from the growing line of serving bowls, laden with the colorful dishes of the day, the kitchen remained spotless.

And the meal. He hated to admit it, but it outstripped anything Lily had ever prepared. Lily'd always stuck to the basics, didn't go for those fancy ingredients. Norm saw that those extras; the copious garlic, chestnuts, Italian sausage, dried cherries, maple syrup and fresh herbs; all combined into an incomparable feast. Just the aroma of it made him feel blessed. After Lily passed, company had only made him feel lonelier, so he avoided people. He'd even avoided her sisters, whom he loved dearly. But they were painful reminders, their similarities, mannerisms and shared stories. It only made Norm miss Lily more. He'd come to where his solitude was his armor. It suited him, but the bustle and chatter of this day brought back his sense of home. By dint of luck he was part of a project that enveloped him, and carried him along in the flow of the living.

That youngster, Jennifer, was okay too. She'd arrived later, and though she tried to help, the rhythms of the older women were so interwoven, it wasn't easy to step into the fray. Instead Jennifer had sat with him quietly, quizzing him on the details of Emma Caites and about his connections with Thomas. In turn, she told him about the dark and filthy basement at Mills and the treasures they'd retrieved. There again, gentle memories of his first crush on Emma slid the sweetness of the day by so swiftly that he wanted to grasp and savor every moment. Maybe it was the wine, but the whole day had a warm glow to it.

He recounted to Jennifer how, after the war, Thomas, as the young man of the family, had researched a new car purchase for Emma. Until then she'd driven her grandfather's 1920 Oldsmobile-

37A. Thomas was mortified at the old car, and determined that, buoyed by post-war successes, his mother would upgrade her transportation. Thomas had asked everyone for advice on which car would be best for his mother. There he was, all of twelve, stepping into the male automotive world to find her the best car. Norm knew that Thomas longed for fancier, more stylish wheels, but that his mother's tastes, needs and limitations were paramount. Together, he and Thomas had settled on the Studebaker. He'd never seen Thomas so proud as the day he and Emma had come by the frame shop to show off the new car. Emma, in turn, beamed at Thomas, to see how confident and happy her son was to have helped his mother. Coming just before his departure from the frame shop, it was one of his last memories of the Caites, and a sweet one to carry in his heart.

Jennifer pushed him for the names of families who would have purchased Emma's work or frames for it at the shop. She asked him for the details of his favorite pieces, and he took her to see his two paintings. She compared the styles to what she'd seen at Mills, and Norm could see that she was looking at the paintings with a critical and appreciative eye. Jennifer confided in him that she'd fallen into this assignment, and that it was the most exciting thing she was doing at school. She told him how Fiona was teaching her to clean the paintings, and how satisfying it was to watch the colors bloom from years of neglect, and to find the artist's true intent buried under the grime. Norm took her into his shop and showed her some of his favorite brushes and techniques for restoring delicate works. Jennifer's face flushed with the new knowledge. He brought her into his study and showed her his collection of reference books on art. Jennifer's eyes widened when she saw that resource. She thanked Norm for the education, and asked if she could use his library on the Emma Caites project. He was flattered. All the while, Jennifer pressed for particulars of Emma's paintings and of her patrons. As is often the case, one story led to another, and Norm was surprised at the names and specifics of his recollections. From time to time, Jennifer would reach into her pocket for a notebook and jot down details from his stories.

Norm was prepared to dislike Marvin. He'd never been comfortable with the queer lifestyle, even less so when it was obvious. Marvin, with his hair dyed straw-blond with visible black roots and his affected voice and manner, was nothing if not obvious. And Marvin was one of that newer breed, the art dealer. Norm

83

essentially had always run a collectables and second-hand shop. When used became vintage, and vintage became antique, Norm had felt the pinch. He'd always prided himself with having a good eye, but he couldn't compete at the estate sales against these new dealers. With the dealers skimming the cream of the estate sale crop, shops like his had to be satisfied with lesser wares. After a while they catered to students and to the working poor. Norm still made an honest living, but the changing market took the prestige and pride out of his offerings.

But Marvin was charming and engaging. He gave a quick introduction on the wines, and then opened three bottles for tastings and comparison. He brought crackers and cheeses to go with the wines. He raised his glass to honor Norm and Emma Caites, and everyone joined to toast the events that had brought them all together. Marvin spoke highly of the cleaning and restoration work that Fiona was doing, crediting Norm with those successes. He regaled them with horror stories of amateurs ruining paintings with brutal cleaning techniques. Marvin confided that there was even a woman on the internet who advocated rubbing old paintings with *bread* as a cleaner. While it wasn't the most damaging home remedy, Marvin commended that it didn't compare with the professional approach that the old-timers had used, and which Norm had taught Fiona. Marvin was warm and funny. He spoke eloquently of the styles of the early Arts and Crafts movement in the Bay Area, and how you could look at Emma's paintings and see all that, and her French salon education at the same time. Using Norm's little landscape as an example, he showed how Emma made deft use of color and light to establish form. He compared her favorably to local famous artists like Selden Gile and Louis Siegriest. Norm remembered the excitement of the early East Bay art world, and the contributions of Gile and Siegriest in Oakland's Society of Six.

Marvin went on to say that Emma's grandparents, so significant in Emma's development, had been neighbors of Selden Gile, and that they'd known California's pioneer of painting, William Keith, decades earlier when he'd lived in Berkeley. When the San Francisco earthquake had driven the artists out of the city, Emma's grandparents had assisted many of the refugees landing on the shores of the East Bay.

Marvin was a font of information on the artists of Emma's time. He spoke of the increasing difficulty of finding Emma's paintings, and of his wish that this under-appreciated artist would finally be exhibited in a retrospective, posthumous show. He turned to Norm, "If we could get Mills to participate, would you allow us to show your paintings?" Norm was flattered. He was immediately on board. After all, he'd like nothing more than to see his Emma Caites finally get her due in the art world. By the time dinner was served, Norm was totally charmed, and had set aside any reservations he had about any of his companions.

After dinner, the guests all cleared and washed the dishes. Marvin poured Dolce, a lovely late-harvest dessert wine from Napa Valley, and explained that its sweet smoothness was from the sun dried grapes and a bacteria that formed when the grapes were left on the vine long into the autumn. Just then the women came in with the desserts. Norm feigned a groan as apple pie, pumpkin pie and lemon tarts made their way around the table, with generous dollops of whipping cream for each. Norm sampled all the desserts, and pronounced the holiday a complete culinary success.

As the group lapsed into silence savoring the wine and dessert, Marvin produced a wrapped package that he handed to Fiona.

"What's this?" she said, with the box in her lap.

"This is a little something for you, to acknowledge that it was your enthusiasm and tenacity that pushed our project to this point. It appears that we are at the threshold of success, and that is entirely because you pressed so hard." Fiona tore through the wrapping paper to the box below. She carefully opened it and found a tiny painting of a seashore, no bigger than six by eight inches in a gilded frame. The painting was rendered in smooth, fine, tonalist strokes, revealing a restless gray sky over a quiet beach in taupes and beiges. The high water mark was peppered with large rocks, giving way to an otherwise sandy shoreline. On the right, at the crest of the sand rose a tree covered bluff, with beach and bluff receding away to a point in the background. The lapping ripples were suggested by the merest ribbon of white foam, wrapping seductively around partially submerged rocks. At the bottom, in tiny sienna squared letters, was Emma's signature, dated 1932. The painting was serene and exquisite. It brought tears to Fiona's eyes.

"Thank you, it's stunning." She hugged it to her chest, and then, thinking twice, turned it to show the group. "I'd be proud to exhibit this lovely little gem."

Norm excused himself, and retreated to his study. He returned with a large book on cowboy art. The others looked at each other, perplexed. Norm opened the book to where there was a poster, stuck between its pages to keep it flat. He gingerly lifted the poster and laid it flat on the table for the others to see. It was a poster for Emma's painting class, perfectly preserved, though a little yellow with age. The corners had bent and had small holes where tacks had been removed. There was a heavy border around the edge framing the images and text, which lapped over itself in the corners, forming an uninterrupted line with squares in the corners. Across the top within the border was a stylized woodblock type image of the Oakland hills, with a line of eucalyptus in one swale, and the rounded forms of live oaks running just below the horizon line in another cusp between the slopes. An echoing, simpler border surrounded the image. Below that, in all capital letters, it said, "LEARN TO PAINT THE EMMA CAITES WAY." The lower case language of the ad underneath said, "Though Paris trained, the artist is a California native and American through and through. Her belief in the American can-do attitude extends to painting, and the California landscape. You can do it too! Small classes, reasonable rates," followed by a post office box contact. The poster was a piece of art in and of itself, delicately balanced, yet bold in its layout and design. The group was spellbound.

"This border," Fiona said, pointing to the outer border, "It's the edging trim on the hardwood floor in my apartment."

Norm nodded. "I stole that poster. I always felt guilty about it, till now. I used to wonder if Ms. Caites lost students because I took it out of the Laundromat. She used to complain that her posters didn't stay up more than a week or so before they disappeared."

"I can see why," answered Marvin, fingering the edge of the heavy paper stock. "It's lovely. This kind of ephemera doesn't usually survive."

"Well," Norm said, "It's time we all worked on getting together a show."

Chapter Twenty

Fiona came up from the basement, where she'd been giving Jennifer more tips on the cleaning process. Actually Jenn was almost as good as Fiona, now. She'd made leaps and bounds after her Thanksgiving discussions with Norm. Fiona was relieved to have passed the baton, having not quite recovered from her restoration efforts on the self portrait. Most of the cleaning activities had been moved to Norm's shop. It was better equipped and had the ventilation for the task that Fiona's garage couldn't offer, at least not without freezing to death.

Early December had blown in some uncharacteristically cold weather. Oakland wasn't prepared for these dips into the twenties and low thirties. It had homeowners outside wrapping their pipes, and Fiona was relieved to keep the basement closed. It'd keep her heating bill lower.

Five of the seven Mills' paintings were complete. The results were amazing. The dingy little canvases glowed with new life. Now they were working on the Mills' Commons painting, which was turning into Fiona's favorite. In spite of her one traumatic failure, Fiona was in love with the transformation process. She'd saved this last large canvas for when Jennifer's skills were ready. Fiona viewed this painting as the closer for the Mills Board. Actually, whichever painting they were working on at the moment was her favorite, but the Commons painting so manifested the feeling of the Mills campus that she was sure this piece would sway the Board when it came to the point of seeking an exhibition of Emma's work. She'd shown Arthur Bradley two of the cleaned canvases, and he was smitten. Fiona had dropped some hints on the idea of a show, and Arthur eagerly nodded approval. He wanted an update on the research side, but Fiona wasn't ready to reveal what they knew yet, not until she'd tried again with Thomas. She hadn't actively pursued discussions on a Thomas strategy at Thanksgiving because she didn't want to involve Norm in discussions of heroin addiction and illegitimacy. Not on a holiday. Norm had seemed so happy that day that Fiona couldn't bear to tarnish Emma's reputation. It was clear that Norm had carried a torch for her, all these years.

While they'd made great progress on the Mills paintings since the holiday, everyone had been too busy to get together to strategize. Questions of Thomas receded in the hum.

Fiona's eye caught the blinking light on her answering machine. The only message was Marvin, who sounded urgent, and requested that she come to his house tonight. Fiona dialed the gallery, and Marvin answered.

"Hey, what's up?"

"Oh, hello, what a pleasant surprise, how was your holiday?"

"Marvin, it's me, Fiona, returning your call."

"I know dear, but it's not back from the framer's. Give me your number, and I'll get back to you. What's a good time?"

"I gather you can't talk."

"You got that dear. Six-thirty work for you?"

"Six-thirty. *Your* house?"

"I'll have answers for you by then. We went with the gilded liner on that, didn't we?"

"Okay, but you'll have to explain this, see ya later."

"Bye now."

Fiona set the receiver in the cradle and wondered what was up. Marvin had alluded several times to trouble with the partners, but this was weird. It was already getting dark, almost five, so Fiona called it a day. She'd set out some fresh salmon earlier, so she made a quick dinner, and then headed over to Marvin's for the mystery meeting.

"Okay, James Bond. What's up with the secrecy?"

Marvin swung the door wider. "Get in here, girl, I'm losing heat." Fiona waltzed by him and slipped out of her jacket. The room was warm, warmer than she'd allow for herself. Marvin took her coat and hung it in the hall closet.

"You didn't put the heat up for me, did you?"

"No, but I would have. Things are tight at the gallery, so they've turned down the heat. Until holiday traffic picks up they can't justify the expense, at least on the days *I* work. By the time I get home, I'm like ice."

"Things sound pretty grim there. What's the rub?"

"Part of it is the usual pre-Christmas jitters. We do the bulk of our sales in December, so every year it's the same early Christmas anxiety. This year there are extra pressures. It's personality stuff, but I'm coming out on the short end. It's a problem with three partners, someone's always on the outs. It's my turn this year."

"Sounds miserable."

"Well, November helped. Antiques led sales *massively* last month, and if that continues, it'll be okay, regardless of personalities. Money talks."

"This explains the secrecy on the phone."

"I have to be very careful with the Emma Caites work. I don't want to even discuss her within earshot of the partners. I spend a good deal of time shopping the estates and antiques circuit. It's time that they don't see or credit, always a beef. I don't want them thinking I'm enhancing my personal collection on gallery time." Marvin stepped into the kitchen.

Fiona raised her voice, "Even if they aren't giving you credit for the time, anyway?"

"Let's not pretend any of this is rational." Marvin came back into the living room with two generous glasses of red wine. He handed one to Fiona.

She took a sip, "Wow, this is great. What is it?"

"It's a nice little cabernet, my house wine. I'm ashamed to say I get it at Trader Joe's."

"No shame in this, it's lovely. What's the occasion?'

"We're celebrating." Marvin raised his glass. "Today we bought seven paintings."

"Jeez, I'm thrilled, but it makes me wonder if I'll make rent come January."

"We did fine. I give the credit to Jennifer."

"How so?"

"I haven't been making much headway finding Caites work. Since I poked around asking questions at Clar's, they know about my interest. I was there the other day on another matter, and one of the employees took me aside and told me there's a Caites fan with a standing bid on all her work. And the bid's pretty high. Whoever it is, never loses."

"So, we have competition." Fiona bit her bottom lip.

"I guess. We certainly won't have any success at local auctions. At Thanksgiving, Jennifer was pumping Norm for stories. He gave her the names of people who'd bought Caites paintings back in his day. Some of those names are from old Oakland families. So I thought I'd do a little outreach of my own."

"*What?* You cold-called and asked about their art collection?"

"Not quite, but close. I called and explained that we were doing research on an unlisted Oakland artist. I said she was a former Mills student, and this was an academic research project linked with Mills. I told them that our information indicated that someone in their family had purchased an Emma Caites painting pre-1946. If the family still had it, we'd like the opportunity to see it, maybe photograph it. I suggested that they'd get photo credit. I didn't even suggest we were interested in purchase. And, *bingo*. These people love to think of their families as dynastic. You'd be surprised what still lurks in grandma's basement. Our seven paintings came from two families. All were in basements or attics." Marvin fetched the bottle of cabernet, and refreshed their glasses.

"I don't get it, you make a couple of calls, and suddenly the blue bloods of Oakland are crawling through their attics?" Fiona shook her head in disbelief.

"Fiona, these people are my clientele. I get what makes them tick. They are from wealthy, well-educated families. To them, this is a cultural and educational pursuit. They might not give a dime to The Salvation Army, but they'd crawl through cobwebs to participate in arts research."

"Well, maybe that explains cooperation, but not sale. If someone thinks they're worth the time to do research, why would they sell the paintings?"

"She's not listed. That's a big deal, and they know it. Once I said she wasn't listed, they knew. Emma Caites is not in the top tier of her time. She barely ticks on the radar, and not at all outside of Oakland or Berkeley. Unless they actually liked the pieces, from their point of view I'd just identified them as artistic curiosities. None of these works was currently displayed. They all came from storage. You'll see. They're filthy."

"So, how did you get to discussing sale?"

"I described how you first became interested in her. You bought a painting, and wanted to know more about the artist. I was helping you. Suddenly they wanted us to have them. It felt like a treasure hunt. Fiona, I didn't spend more than $200 on a painting, and most were half that."

"You got great deals by being completely honest?" Fiona shook her head, "Go figure. So, do I get to see them?"

"C'mon, they're downstairs."

Marvin had arranged the paintings, each with strong direct lighting, around the walls. They were badly soiled, and that couldn't have pleased Fiona more. There was a broader range of styles than they'd previously seen, two plein air landscapes, two abstracts which didn't appeal much to Fiona, one self portrait, one interior with three women, and one with Thomas, as a youngster, playing in their old car. Even under the grunge, Emma could tell these were lovely paintings.

She turned back to him "Marvin, this is a goldmine. They're gorgeous."

"Which ones do you like?"

"I hate to admit it, but I'm not crazy about the abstracts." Fiona felt she was revealing something she'd rather not. One of the abstracts was a female nude. It was done completely in pastels, and looked cubist. Although clearly a nude, it was tough to identify specific body parts. It was attractive in a modern sort of way, but it didn't hold any appeal for Fiona. The second abstract was an interior in the same style. Emma could tell it was the interior of her apartment. Still, she found the fractured forms alienating. Both bore signatures and dates from the early '50s. "I thought you indicated they'd bought paintings pre-1946?"

"Yes, but this family liked Emma's work, and continued to seek her out. They had both abstracts, I'm sorry you don't like them."

"I can see they're good, I know that time marches on, and of course Emma would branch out, but they don't have the charm of our earlier stuff."

"Well, I love them. They are textbook examples of what was happening in the late forties and early fifties. Emma grew and experimented. It's so important to show her as evolving. I guess you won't mind if I take both abstracts?"

"Not at all."

"So, what do you like?"

"I love Thomas in the car and the self-portrait." Fiona noted that the painting of Thomas showed him as a youngster, just a little older than he was in her existing painting, but it was dated 1951. Thomas was standing on the driver's seat, with his hands on the steering wheel, his head turned and smiling as viewed through the side window. The painting had a warm, sepia glow. "It looks like she worked from a photo. She even captured that old snapshot look."

"Don't be too surprised if it's a little more colorful when clean, but you're right, it's all about capturing that photo-feel."

The self-portrait showed a much older Emma than they'd seen

before. It was an outdoor painting, with Emma seated on the running board of the same car in the Thomas painting. Emma's face was in the sun, and she was squinting just a bit in the glare. The face, while still lovely, revealed crow's feet and some laugh lines. Fiona was pleased at that! Emma looked happy. The side mirror was just above and to the left of her head, with the driver's window forming a kind of halo above her. The feeling of the painting was sun washed and warm. The signature bore the date, 1946.

"Look, this is the last year they had that car. That's the year Thomas helped get the new Studebaker, yet this is still that ancient car."

"It's a great self-portrait. This picking is turning out easier than I thought." Marvin smiled.

"What about you, what do you like next?"

Marvin pursed his lips. He pointed at a plein air painting of the Cameron Stanford house, the Victorian on the shores of Lake Merritt. It was surrounded by eucalyptus trees, though substantially smaller than they were now.

"You want a house portrait?" Fiona was surprised.

"Well, not just *any* house portrait. This was the building that was originally The Oakland Art Museum. I find it very interesting that she painted it, a building that her work never saw. I like the irony."

"Well I'll take the other landscape, the one of the hills." The canvas showed the Oakland hills clad in their late summer, golden grasses. The sky was clear and intense, with both eucalyptus and oak groves.

"Isn't that essentially the same scene as the poster?" Marvin pointed out the familiar lines. Fiona looked closer. Sure enough this was a more detailed view of the same slope and trees.

"Good call, Marvin. I wouldn't have put it together."

"Well, we certainly will in the show. It's a lovely contrast."

"What about this last one? Who gets that?" The final painting was an interior done in a semi abstract style, very similar to the coffee cup from the last batch. It was evening, and three women were seated at a table. There was a lamp on the table, but its light was subdued. The painting, done in deep rusts, roses, browns and greens, had a pensive quality. The women's coats were draped over their chair backs, leaving the feeling quietly casual. They were roughly painted with no clear features, appearing, as did the room, quickly rendered, much like a landscape. It was dated, 1929.

Fiona ventured, "I like it, but I don't love it. You?"

"Same."

"Why don't we leave it then? We'll look again after it's cleaned."

"Okay." And that was it; in less than twenty minutes they'd viewed, assessed and divided the latest haul. Fiona wondered that this had become de rigueur so quickly.

"Hey, it's freezing down here Come on back upstairs." Heading back up, he paused, "We're fifty-fifty in this deal, right?"

"Of course. Why?"

"One of us has been kicking in a little extra on restoration. What's up with that?"

Fiona's jaw dropped. Of course he'd noticed. You couldn't sneak a re-lined canvas past an antique art dealer. She slumped down onto the sofa.

"Well, Fiona?" Marvin sat down across from her.

She sighed. "I screwed it up, so I fixed it. That's all."

"Why didn't you say anything? Did you think I wouldn't notice that a painting was suddenly larger *and* professionally re-lined?"

Fiona hung her head, "You were away. I made a mistake and ruined the painting. I was sick about it. I found a guy and he fixed it. More than fixed it."

"In some ways it's better but the value still suffers for the re-lining. "You must have paid a fortune. You should have said something."

Fiona shrugged, and spread her hands.

"No, really. Partners means communication. Okay?"

She pursed her lips and nodded.

"So, what did it run you?"

Fiona stuck to her plan. "No, I'll pick that up. It's my stupid-tax."

Marvin shook his head, "Fiona, what did I just say about communication?"

She swallowed. "Six hundred. It covered the repair, the re-lining and the finish varnish." Fiona added, "It was pretty damaged, I thought it was a deal." She sighed, and then told him the whole story.

"You got a great deal, and quality work, too. Looks like we found our in-house restoration guy for the tougher jobs. Good work, under the circumstances," he grinned.

"We okay?"

Marvin nodded.

Chilled, Fiona wrapped a throw over her shoulders. In the spirit of this new communication, she broached the other issue that had been bothering her. "I'm a little uncomfortable that the others haven't been included in buying paintings."

"That's simple. Ask them. If they're interested, we'll include them in the pool."

"Really?" Fiona was a little stunned that this was so easy.

"Sure, this has become an ensemble group. Jennifer probably can't afford it, but we can select one of the non-designated canvases, and give it to her. And I'll tell her that her detective work, collecting Norm's stories, led to a new approach in acquisition."

He emptied his glass, "I really loved Thanksgiving, Fiona. It was the best holiday I've had in years. I want to include everyone in this."

Fiona broke into a huge smile. "Yeah, I enjoyed it too."

"The food was stellar. You two really did a great job." He flashed a sly grin. "It competes neck and neck to any *gay* Thanksgiving feast."

"Wow, that's a compliment."

"We still need to discuss how to approach Thomas."

"Yeah, but it's late, and I'd like Amanda in on that. You free Friday or Saturday night?"

"Yes ma'am."

"Then we're on, dinner. I'll check with Amanda, and let you know what night." She hesitated, "And Marv?"

"Yes?"

"Thanks, for making this so easy. For *everything*."

Chapter Twenty-One

Norm had reached for the telephone half a dozen times since Thanksgiving. He knew it might be interfering, and yet he also thought he might be the only one in a position to reach out to Thomas. After all, *he* actually knew him, or at least, had known him. And Norm had always loved Thomas. He had been an exquisite little boy, with all the delicate features of his mother but with more of an infectious laugh. More than most children, Thomas had always seemed complete. Whatever he did, he seemed happy doing it. He had a sort of protective possessiveness of his mother that Norm found especially endearing. His conversation with Jennifer had reminded him of so many little moments he'd shared with the Caites.

Of course it was years before he figured out that Thomas was a bastard. There seemed to be no question of it at the time, the Caites just were who they were, like a salt and pepper set. Nothing seemed missing. There was none of the whisperings or mean-spiritedness that he'd experienced in other situations, especially during the war. There'd been a lot of that, during the war. And of course, the situation in *his* family had punctuated the issues of infidelity for him. Ever since his dad had died young on the job, his uncle had always looked after his mom and him. In late 1946, that got out of hand, and when his aunt figured it out, that was it. He and his mother were cut off from the paternal side of the family. It cost him his relationship with his uncle, his cousins, with the frame shop, and ultimately, with the Caites.

That experience was part of why, later, he so admired Emma. She'd got caught in an indiscretion, in the worst way for a woman, and she was crippled too. But Emma held her head high, not proud or haughty, just herself. His own mother had been unraveled by shame. She became stoop-shouldered and prematurely old under the weight of it. They'd lived like refugees, moving out to Berkeley to get away from the rumors. His aunt had gone very public with the whole affair, exacting every revenge. Living the experience shaped who Norm was, having been through that pain, and watching his mother suffer. Sadder still, he could tell his mother had loved his uncle. Years later she said he'd reminded her of everything that was wonderful that she'd lost in his dad. It was like she'd lost the same love, twice.

None of the group had even mentioned Thomas' birth status. It was obvious enough, especially with all the research they'd done. Norm couldn't tell if it wasn't mentioned because it was so delicate a topic, or if it was because, with their modern perspective, illegitimacy didn't even rate for them. Norm reflected on the group, divorced single mother, never-married single woman, gay man and childless widower. Maybe not so surprising after all, he thought. Marriage wasn't even the norm anymore. Movie stars had babies alone. Very public couples dispensed with legal ties. There were children without marriages, and marriages without children, always a tender spot for Norm. Yet, the group openly wondered why Emma, who was talented and prolific, wasn't more famous. Over the years Norm had also wondered the same thing, and had always feared that Emma chose obscurity intentionally, to protect her privacy and her son. Maybe Emma felt the same wounds as his mother, but didn't air her losses.

Norm still had the old rotary style phone. He reached over, picked up the handset, and dialed the number listed for Thomas Caites, architect, his large fingers stuffed into the little holes in the dial, his wrist and arm arching over with the motion of each number. He had no idea what he'd say, and then a man's voice answered.

"This is Thomas Caites. Can I help you?"

"I don't know if you'd remember me, Norm... Norm Gilbert?"

There was a pause, "Of course I remember you. You babysat me when I was little. You were my best buddy." He hesitated, "Geez, I remember you helping me pick out my mom's car." Naturally, the voice was different, but Thomas still had the direct openness and warmth that Norm remembered.

"Yeah, that's me. We really checked out that car, didn't we? Don't suppose you still have it." Norm joked.

After a long pause, "Well, as a matter of fact, I do."

"Really? I was joking, I didn't mean..."

"No offense taken, Norm, I've always been a sentimental sort. When mom died, I just stuck it in storage. I couldn't bear to sell it; it wasn't worth much then anyway. Back in the eighties I fixed it up, and now it's a classic."

"I'd love to see it some time. It'd bring back good memories."

"Whatever happened to you, Norm? Suddenly you were gone. We still worked with the frame shop, but no Norm. I really missed you."

"Yeah, well, one of those family skirmishes. My mom moved us to Berkeley, which was far away back then. I missed you, too."

"Kids have so little input into the movement of the spheres."

"Yeah, and we spend the rest of our lives figuring that stuff out, if we're lucky. We're like that old Studebaker. We get more valuable as we get older."

There was a lull in the conversation.

"What made you think to call, Norm?"

"Been reflecting on the old times a lot lately, happens when you hit eighty. I remembered about you and that car. It was a real triumph, that. The last for me, and for a while after that. But you can't take away how great we all felt that day."

"I know... Norm, I'd love for you to come by and see the car, maybe have a cup of tea."

"I'd love that. Thomas, there's another reason for the call. Some people I know have taken an interest in your mom's work. I might even be responsible, since I sold the woman one of your mom's paintings."

"Is this the woman with the apartment painting?"

"Yeah, that's her. You'd really like her."

"I talked to her on the phone, seemed nice enough but I'm not really interested in rehashing my mom's life with strangers."

"Fiona doesn't stay a stranger for very long. One minute she's buying a painting, and the next, she's like family."

"I already have a family."

"Of course you do. But someday, somebody is going to follow up on your mom's work. I sure hope so, anyway. She was a wonderful and talented woman. In a funny way, she was family to me. She deserves more recognition than the art world gave her then." Norm inhaled over the phone, "I think you'd want Fiona to be that person. She's warm and sensitive and loves your mom, warts and all."

"I don't know how she could know my mother's warts, Norm."

"All I'm saying is that you can pick how the story is told, and this wouldn't be a bad pick. Your mom could be in a catalogue of unknown artists, or she could shine. You should give Fiona a call. Talk to her."

97

"I've got her number. I'll think about it." Thomas's voice was cooler.

"I won't bug you anymore, but in a couple a weeks, I may just decide to come see that Studebaker."

Thomas hesitated. "Okay, I'd like that, but no pressure."

"Nah. Just for old times' sake. But Thomas, if you do call her, don't tell her I called you, okay? I'm butting in here a bit where I don't belong."

"In all directions, it seems. Give me a call when you're ready to see the car."

"Okey-dokey, Thanks."

Thomas answered softly, "Wow, okey-dokey."

"What's that?" Norm thought he'd signed off already.

"Okey-dokey, it's just you always said that when I was a kid."

"I did?"

"Yeah."

"Well, I guess some habits just stick."

"Yeah. Call me, okay?"

"Sure will. Bye."

Chapter Twenty-Two

"Amanda?"

"Hello?"

"Amanda, it's me, Denise."

"Oh, hi hon, what's up?"

"What's up *there*? My mom hasn't called me in weeks."

"Well, why don't you give her a call and ask?"

"Amanda, she hung up on me. I can't call her."

"As I heard it, that's not quite how it played out. She did indicate she was ending the call. I think you know she was upset, but she didn't just slam the phone down or anything."

"But she hasn't called. She didn't even call on Thanksgiving!"

"She was pretty busy on Thanksgiving. And weren't you in Mexico?"

"Yeah, but I had my cell. She knows the number."

"So why is it her job to call you? And why would she call you when she knows you're traveling with friends?"

"Come on, Amanda, you know what I mean. I haven't spoken to her in weeks. That's never happened, ever."

"Well, your mom has a lot going just now. I'm sure she's aware of the passage of time. But I still don't get why you think she's supposed to call *you*."

"She always does."

"And you're always home for Thanksgiving."

"So, you're on *her* side."

"What, we have sides now? I'm just pointing out that things are different. You're an adult, and it's time you started acting like one. If you have a problem with your mother, call. Or email."

"So she's not going to call me?"

"*I* don't know."

"But she talks to you all the time."

"Oddly enough, sweetie, we actually converse on topics other than you."

"What about Christmas?" Denise fished.

"I understood you were going to Tom's parents for Christmas. You announced that in August."

"That could still change."

"Well if you want a change, you'd better get talking to her. I think she's making plans."

"Is she seeing somebody?"

"*What?*" Amanda couldn't fathom where that came from.

"Is she seeing somebody? Tom says that'd explain it. I mean, why else would she just ignore me like this?"

"She's not seeing anyone. She's not ignoring you. She's just got a life is all. Respect that. Be happy for her."

Amanda could hear muffled crying, a moment passed, and Denise sniffed aloud, "You don't know what it's like."

"Denise, what's really going on?"

"What do you mean?" she snuffled.

"You know, Mexico with no notice, no calls, calling me to pump me for info. What's up? Why don't you just talk to your mother?"

"She's never there."

"So, leave a message. What's got into you?"

"Tom says we're too dependent. He thinks it's good there's some distance."

"What do you think?"

Denise fell apart, sobbing. "I don't know anybody here. I can't find a job. Tom works all day, and then either watches TV or just talks office politics. I don't want to spend any money cause I'm not working. Tom used to complain about the phone bill, so he's relieved that we're not talking."

"Is money that tight?"

"No, no, he's making good money. It's just… it's not really *mine*, you know."

"I think you're homesick. Why don't you come home for a bit before Christmas? Then go on to Tom's folks after. You can pick up a cheapie standby ticket on the net."

"You're not listening. I'd get nothing but flack if I did that."

"Denise, you've got to do something. If you can't find a job, volunteer, get involved in politics or start a business. Get some exercise. Do *something*. If not, come home for a visit. Lots of newlyweds have this problem. Happily-ever-after doesn't mean your spouse is the only one you speak to."

Now Denise was openly crying.

"Do you want me to send you a ticket? A weekend home, for shopping with mom?"

"No. I'm just low. I really can't go anywhere when I have all

100

these job applications out."

"Denise, you're making excuses. At least call your mom, and leave a message if she's not there!" Amanda heard a door slam in the background, and Tom called out.

"I gotta go, Amanda, please don't tell my mom about this. I'll work it out."

"Call her."

"Okay."

"And call me in a day or two. Let me know how it's going."

"I will. I gotta run. Bye."

The phone went dead in Amanda's hand. Once again she was relieved that she'd never married. Now she had to decide whether to say anything to Fiona. She didn't like the sound of this at all, but she knew the first months of marriage were often rocky. Geez, she hated being in the middle. And she didn't even get to find anything out about Mexico.

Chapter Twenty-Three

Amanda was just setting out a tray of cheeses and baguette slices when Fiona pounded on the door to her apartment. The air was filled with the aroma of her famous lasagna.

"I'll get it," Marvin set down his glass of Vouvray and turned to welcome Fiona. Amanda flashed for a second about their usual antics on entry, but decided to let it go. If Fiona was out there on her knees, she'd let *her* explain it. Fiona burst in, breathless, her cheeks flushed.

"You won't believe where I've been."

"Looks like to a bar," quipped Amanda.

"Really?" Fiona checked her reflection at the entry mirror, noting her cherry cheeks. "Geez, I guess I have had a few."

"Well, don't stop now," Marvin passed her an ample glass of the Vouvray.

Amanda rolled her eyes, "At least have a bite to eat with that." She took Fiona's coat. "Get in here so we can close the door."

Fiona settled on the couch, leaned forward and loaded an appetizer plate with cheeses and bread. "So if the theme of the evening was how to reach out to Thomas, we've hit the jackpot. He called me today."

"He called *you*?" Marvin turned back from the kitchen, where he'd been headed with the empty wine bottle.

"Yeah, took me by complete surprise."

"What'd he say?"

"He said he'd been thinking about what I'd said, and that he'd like to meet with me and see if we could connect for this project."

"Good thing we're meeting tonight. When does he want to see you?"

"That's just it. That's where I've been."

"You've already been?"

"He wanted to meet right away, suggested we wind up the week early with a drink at Bateau Ivre."

Amanda smirked, "By the looks of it, that place is aptly named. How'd it go?"

"I think we were both really nervous. At least I was, and *he* sure looked it. You should see him. You'd recognize him in a heartbeat.

Those fine features and arched eyebrows. He has a cute way of looking perpetually surprised. All gray now, but he's exactly what you'd expect. I recognized him immediately from the paintings of him as a kid."

"Was he waiting out front?"

"No. You know that place. It's like a labyrinth in all those little rooms. He was in the back by the fireplace, and I just knew it was him. He was surprised at that, and I explained that he looked just like in the paintings."

"Well, *that* revealed a lot." Marvin winced at the impromptu meeting. "What did he say?"

"'What paintings?' I explained that I'd seen a couple of paintings of him as a child, and that he was a dead ringer for that kid."

"Good girl. I'm glad you didn't tell him we had those paintings. I'm sure our phantom bidder is Thomas."

"*What?*" Amanda looked perplexed.

Fiona interrupted, "Marv and I have been trying to buy up Caites paintings. We've lucked out, and got a bunch recently. You interested in being in on that?

"Maybe. What's the objective?"

"Mixed." Marvin explained. "Fiona mostly likes them. I collected a couple before this. *My* objectives are a little more mercenary. If we get this show together, they'll increase in value dramatically. If not, we just get paintings we like."

Amanda paused. "I hate to admit it, but I'm not really as attracted to that style as you guys. I'm really only into this for the story part."

"She did abstracts in the forties and fifties. Interested now?" Marvin pressed.

"Well, count me in, to look. I might be into something retro. But I'm not so interested in speculation. I already do pretty well with my own pursuits. I'm best with things I know."

"Okay."

But her curiosity peeked out, "What's with the *phantom bidder* thing?"

Fiona stepped in, "Apparently, there's an anonymous bidder at Clars' with a standing bid on any Caites works that come in. And always wins. So we're stuck with estate sales and poaching."

"Poaching?"

"Yeah, Marvin's had some luck cold calling the families that

Norm remembered bought paintings."

"Whoa, was that ever a long shot."

"Hey, can we get back to Thomas? I'm dying of curiosity." Marvin reached for more cheese.

"Oh, yeah. So he got there before me. When I sat down there were appetizers and wine. Right away, he asked me about the original find, the apartment painting, and why I pursued it."

Fiona paused for breath and launched back in. "All I could say was that I really loved the painting. First of all, it was a painting that was clearly done from the window of my apartment, so that intrigued me. It obviously wasn't painted by an amateur. It was as though the painting was a portrait of a loved one. I told him I raised my daughter in that apartment, and it meant home to me. It just warmed my heart to see that it had meant that to someone else, too, and that that person had had the ability to communicate the feeling in a painting. It made me want to know more. He just kept nodding. He asked me about the paintings with him in them, so I described them, you know, the little guy with the paint brush and the kid in the car. He remembered them! He said it always made him feel funny when his mom sold a painting with him in it. Like the Native Americans who feel photographers are stealing their soul."

"Was he weird about those paintings being out there?"

"I don't know, but I decided to just go with my heart. Or maybe my liver. I hadn't eaten, and I was feeling the wine pretty quickly. I told him that his soul looked intact and that I was glad to have seen and enjoyed those paintings because they were done with love, and because there was something universal about them. I'd had similar feelings from snapshots of my daughter, painting or playing. Kids are so direct about what they're doing, no layers, no hidden meanings. It's a pleasure to see the delight they take in the day-to-day, and the paintings conveyed that."

"You did okay, girl, just being you." Amanda was always her biggest booster.

"I hope so. We talked for well over an hour, and then I had to break it off to come here. I told him about the paintings and drawings at Mills, the dark cobwebby basement. I told him Mills had assigned me a student assistant, and that we had restored their paintings. I said Mills was impressed too at the talent, and that they knew so little about her. I asked him if he knew she'd left money to the school. Of course he did. I told him about the photos and records. I tell you I was babbling, carrying on about all the good things that had come out of that one little painting purchase. You know, about Jennifer, the Mills people, and of course Norm. I kept you out of it for now, Marv, because you're a dealer."

"A good call, from an only slightly inebriated interviewee."

"Hey, I just wanted to connect. I wanted him to see that the people who'd taken an interest had done so because of the work, and because they'd come to care about this woman's work and story. He asked me about Norm. I said we'd adopted him because he's so gentle and sweet. He wanted to know about Norm's personal life. I said he was widowed and had no children. He seemed very interested in him."

"So how did it end?" Marvin was keeping the story on track.

"When I said I had to go, he looked me squarely in the eye, and asked me what my objectives are. I felt like a teenage guy, asking a girl's dad if I could date her. *Do I have honorable intentions?*"

"Well, do you?" Now Amanda was smiling.

"*I* think so. I said that at first it was just curiosity, and then I couldn't believe that she wasn't more renowned. I wanted to know her story. Now, I'd like to see Mills provide a forum for a retrospective and maybe, just maybe, if I can get a handle on the information, I'd like to write a biography. I told him that in many ways she was a truly modern woman. I told him what Norm had said, about how she lived her life with her head held high, even though life hadn't necessarily treated her kindly."

"What did he say?"

"He thanked me and said he'd think about it for a few days. If he decides to help us, he has some paintings to share, and he'd be happy to show them at Mills. He also has correspondence and the names of other people who are still alive, who knew her. He shook my hand, and then, as though he'd given it more thought, he gave me a quick hug." Fiona sat back on the couch, exhausted.

"You did good, girl." Marvin was nodding enthusiastically. "That nails it."

Amanda piped in, "Well, there's more. Jennifer called me, she was all excited. Arthur Bradley was very impressed with the before and after photos. He's really excited about curating a show. He wants to know how many other paintings there might be, and if we can get the owners to cooperate in showing them. Fiona, he wants a meeting with you *and* the Board, where you would show the restored paintings." Amanda smiled slyly, "And can you do it Thursday? So, please call Jennifer, that girl is walking on clouds. Bradley was really impressed by her work on the restorations. He's trying to get her to change her major to Art History, and he's suggesting there may even be a scholarship attached to that."

"Alright!" Fiona couldn't imagine anything sweeter for Jenn. It was true that she'd really found direction in this project, and Fiona knew that, as much as Jenn loved it there, Mills was a stretch for her and her family. Her other claim to fame, the rowing team, wasn't the sort of passion that would transcend college.

"So, all great news, should we celebrate with some lasagna?" Amanda was already moving towards the kitchen.

Chapter Twenty-Four

Fiona checked the North Berkeley address three times driving over. She was more nervous now than the first time she'd met Thomas. For once, traffic was light. Berkeley traffic always flummoxed Fiona, between bad parking, university traffic and insane street layouts and barriers, Berkeley had made itself over as The Unnavigable City. At a stop sign, she reflected. Fiona was comfortable with Oakland because it was home. She knew the layout of its districts and its regular blocks of cozy working class homes. To her, Berkeley was foreign and encumbered by "isms," but the issue was hers and not the place. She'd allowed plenty of time, but now found herself unfashionably early. She pulled just up the street from Thomas's home, and turned on the radio to wait a bit before knocking on the door.

Thomas lived in an older stucco home, a particular style that differed from the standard bungalow, but wasn't the more upscale manor style you'd expect in this neighborhood. Fiona's polling place, on China Hill, was located in a house with this style layout. Thomas was on a corner lot, with the entrance at the peak of the corner, set back just enough to give the entry some sense of space and presence. The wide front porch was flanked by two gingko trees, set in small plots with some rosemary and gray santolina. The last few golden leaves still clung to the gingkoes, and the sidewalk was strewn with their gold and yellow fan shapes. The little flanking gardens were the only green space on the street-side of the house. From there, the house ran along the lot lines at the sidewalk, in both directions back from the corner. Fiona knew from having been at her polling place that this layout created a house with two wings meeting at the center, and if no one had added on, there would be a back courtyard which served as a very private garden area. A double garage cut underneath the house on one side, and at some point, a second floor had been added the full length of the house, creating even more of the European perimeter courtyard look. Fiona was pleased to see the addition had been elegantly incorporated into the design of the original home. The second floor windows all sported grilled ironwork window boxes, filled with well-tended geraniums. Fiona wondered how they'd look in season, when the flowers bloomed. She checked her watch and decided that fifteen minutes early wasn't too bad. Besides, her car was getting chilly.

Fiona had hardly rung the bell when the door swung open. Thomas had been waiting. In the full sun, he looked older than he had the other day. Thomas had a slight build, which made him appear a little taller than he really was. Fiona guessed him at about five-ten. He was casually but elegantly dressed in wool tweed trousers and a silk shirt with a knit pullover vest, all in tones of slate-blue and gray. He had a full head of thick, wavy silver hair, worn a little longer than was professional, but which suited Berkeley. That mane of hair framed an oval face with olive skin. His forehead was lined, and he was a bit jowly. He wore frameless eyeglasses that disappeared, once you connected with his crystalline blue eyes. Thomas ushered her in a little formally, with a wave of a hand.

"I hope you don't mind if we meet in my office."

"Not at all. Whatever works for you is fine with me."

From the corner entry, Thomas led her to the left, through a set of French doors, into a little room that was clearly used as a waiting area. The furniture was original Arts and Crafts, oak-framed with rich tapestry upholstery. Beyond that, Thomas showed the way to his office. It was a long narrow room with a desk at the far end, and a comfortable seating area near the entry. There was an oversized coffee table, which Fiona figured was used for spreading plans. The rest of the furnishings were the matching originals to the Arts and Crafts pieces in the entry. More stunningly, the walls were covered with paintings. Shoulder to shoulder, frame to frame, from chest height to about nine feet, like wallpaper with paintings. Almost all bore the now familiar signature. Fiona was overwhelmed. Thomas motioned for her to sit in a Morris style chair in the seating area.

"Oh, look," she said aloud, then, surprised that she'd verbalized.

"Yes?"

"I'm sorry. It's just that I think I've seen that chair in one of your mother's self-portraits."

Thomas nodded, "Likely; all of this furniture belonged originally to my great-grandparents. They left it to my mother. It was our furniture when I grew up. If you look, you'll see it in a number of these paintings." He gestured to the walls.

Again, Fiona's eyes grazed the walls. There was too much, she couldn't focus on any one piece. They were lovely paintings, far and away better than most of what she'd seen. Only a few of their finds were of this caliber. Here and there she saw an interior, many of which contained the familiar furniture.

"Your mother left you some incredible paintings."

"Not at all," Thomas paused. "My mother was a working artist. She rarely kept a painting; they were all sold. It was her living, her passion too, but the passion was to paint, not to have the paintings."

Fiona looked around, puzzled, and it must have shown on her face.

Thomas explained, "I've collected these since my mother's death. Perhaps I am overly sentimental, but I always thought my mother was a great talent. I've been collecting her work for years. I know it doesn't show well crammed together like this, but I keep most of it in my office wing because it's a taste my wife doesn't share. "

Fiona stood and walked slowly around the room, trying to take in the details of the paintings. "Some of these are signed Caites, but after 1958."

"Very good. As you know, from the painting you described the other day, I have been painting all my life. Most of these are my mother's but the rest are mine. I mixed them where the styles complimented. My more abstract pieces are in my residence. Thankfully, my wife enjoys my other work."

Fiona turned and saw a playful smile cross his face. "Do you show or sell your work?"

"A few years back I did, but," he held up his hands, the slender fingers were knotted at the knuckles. "It's not that I can't paint anymore, but I still work in architecture, and the drafting table takes most of what my hands can do these days."

"Do you have an area of specialty?"

"I used to do public buildings, but I am semi-retired now. I only do what I like. My current interest is making today's functions fit and blend with the styles of the past."

"Like the addition on this house?"

"Well, that's not recent, but that's the gist of it. We have so much history and beauty, but our attention spans today would run over all design if we let it. I've seen a great many Bay Area remodels that butchered the blend of old and new."

"I was noting your home before I came in. Usually this style is one story, but you've merged the second story beautifully, bringing

109

something… southern France into the mix."

"Thank you. Ms. Hedge." He tipped his head acknowledging the compliment. "I have some questions for you. I've checked up a bit, and it seems you've been an accountant for almost thirty years. From my experience, this is not a profession known for its artistic sensitivity. And yet, you obviously have a good eye. What brings you to this endeavor?"

"Empty nest."

"No, really. That may be your current circumstance, but there's a frustrated artist in there somewhere, and some training."

"Not really." Fiona paused, "I fancied myself talented in my youth, started college in art school but I suffered from a failure of confidence. I wasn't driven to paint, and my work was never lit from within, if you know what I mean. By second year I was looking for a safe route."

"A little of that put me in architecture…"

"That surprises me."

"Oh, and a little pressure from my mother. She could be very conservative. She believed in having something to fall back on."

"Well, as a parent, I can relate to that."

"Me too. I have two daughters. They're adults, with near adult children of their own, but I still worry. Their mother says it's because I was an only child."

"I wasn't an only, but I have an only, so maybe that explains my worrying ways." Fiona paused and looked around, "Maybe it's more complicated. I was a single mother, as was your mother. I think that leaves you with more of a concern for your child because there's less of a safety net. Your daughters have you, their mom and each other. My daughter has only me. Her father disappeared from our lives decades ago. It makes it harder for me to give her the space to make mistakes. We're struggling with that now."

"Ms. Hedge…"

"Fiona, please."

"All right then, Fiona, I like you. I want to entrust my mother's story to you. I don't want to put conditions on it, but I am nervous, maybe protective of my mother. I think you understand."

"I think I do, and I *am* flattered. But why now?

"Because you asked, and frankly, didn't give me much choice."

"What about your girls, surely there's some interest there?"

"No, and that's probably my fault. My mother passed well before the girls came along. I've held my mother's memory very close. Now I see that it may even have alienated my wife a little. I think, because of me, she chose distance from everything related to mom. The girls adopted that distance."

"Maybe you didn't share well."

The older man looked up to face Fiona, "Why do you say that?"

"It's just that the only-child, single-parent bond is pretty tight. It's hard to make room for anyone else in it, but you have to, to have full lives. Like I said, my daughter Denise and I are struggling with that right now."

Thomas looked up at the paintings. "Maybe there's something there. I'll think about it. I'm going to send you home with some things, correspondence and papers. Most of it is letters from Henrietta, my mother's best friend."

"From Mills College, Henrietta, you mean Wren?"

Thomas looked up at her, "You *have* been doing your homework. Yes. On the top of the first box I've left an envelope with Wren's daughter's contact info. She knew Mother, and has her mother's papers. Start with that, and then maybe I can help you with more. Later I can show you some photographs."

"I brought something for you, too."

"For me? What is it?"

"A few photocopies," Fiona reached down to her folder. She pulled out the first photo that she'd found at Mills, the one where Emma confronted the camera so directly. She handed it to Thomas.

"Oh God, she's so young. You don't think of your mother ever being *that* young. She was beautiful. My youngest has this same look, the same presence about her." Thomas looked up. There were tears in his eyes. Fiona handed him a photocopy of the poster.

"I remember these." Thomas broke into a broad grin. "We used to walk all over town putting these up. That woman worked so hard. Always painting, always teaching. I didn't know there was an option." Again, he looked up at her, "You know, I was shocked when she died. I had no idea there was money. She always worked to support us, and she could have lived so much easier. I think it was pride."

"I think we'll find it just was who she was. Like most of us, a jumble of things, insecurity, pride, thrift, self-reliance. It's part of why I want to find her."

"Thank you for these." He held up the two papers. "I'll share them with my family"

Thomas stood up, and Fiona knew the deal was sealed. Thomas trusted her. "I have a couple of boxes. Where are you parked?"

"Just up the street a bit."

They proceeded out to the waiting room where two boxes were stacked behind the door. Thomas handed her one and picked up the other. "Show the way." At the car they loaded the boxes into the back seat. Thomas hugged her and thanked her for everything. "Next time, you can meet my wife. But first, I have a little backtracking to do with her to get her on board."

"I'd like you to meet the others as well."

"The others?"

"My best friend, the Mills assistant, Norm Gilbert—who you know, and my friend Marvin. He's an art dealer. Oh yes, and the administrative folks at Mills. We've all been piecing the bits together."

"Well," he motioned at the boxes, "There's your homework. Let me know how it goes." He hugged her again, "We'll be in touch, soon."

Back in the car, Fiona could hardly believe it. She was so excited her hands were shaking. Once out of the neighborhood, she pulled over to think. There was no way she'd remember all this to tell the others. The whole time she was unable to focus on even one painting well enough to describe it. There was easily a complex and rich retrospective exhibit, just in what she'd seen today. And then there were the boxes. She stepped out of the car, opened the back door, slid across the seat, and lifted the lid of the first box. Inside were dozens of packets, letters, still in their original envelopes, in ribbon-tied bundles. She wanted to rifle through them, but she knew that she needed to back up and bring order to the chaos. First thing tomorrow, she and Jennifer would begin the task. The bundles would be opened, each letter and its envelope photocopied twice, then they'd reassemble and tie the originals. They'd organize by date, then categorize the letters by topic, and create a time line. Oh, it was all so studious and anal but Fiona could hardly wait. Inside those letters lay the true Emma Caites.

Chapter Twenty-Five

Norm was in his workshop setting out various tools, solvents, soft cotton cloths, brushes and cotton swabs. He was getting to be an expert at teaching how to clean oil paintings. Amanda had called him, and asked if he could give her some tips. Apparently Fiona had been after her to try it, and Amanda had decided that she should at least know the basics. Norm made a trip to his store and picked up a couple of really grubby, little landscapes from the back. Nothing fancy, but cleaned up they'd look nice enough for most folks to hang. He had little energy these days for restoration, so having a workshop full of learning elves had been handy. They'd run out of Caites paintings to work on, but Amanda could learn on anything.

Norm was flattered that they'd invited him to participate in buying Emma's paintings, but at his age he was no longer interested in acquisition for its own sake, or speculation. He loved his two Caites paintings—they came bundled with history and memories. It was enough for him. It did, however, pique his interest, and he'd been racking his brains ever since Thanksgiving for memories of who'd bought from the frame shop, so long ago. He was keeping a little notebook in his top pocket, and jotting down bits of stories when they came to him, following Jennifer's lead. Norm was really pleased that his conversations with Jennifer on Thanksgiving had yielded seven paintings so far, and really nice ones at that. It made him feel like an integral part of the operation and not just a spectator. He was especially impressed with Fiona's little landscape, the one that echoed the poster he'd kept. He belonged with the group. For his part, that, and seeing the others appreciate Emma, was enough for him.

Norm turned on the shop heater, and checked his watch. The workshop would be comfortable by the time Amanda arrived. He'd come to appreciate her edgy humor and offhanded geniality almost as much as Fiona's embracing warmth. Amanda was determined to help him market some of his smaller items on eBay. She even threatened to drag him kicking and screaming into the twenty-first century. Everybody gives in the way that they can.

Amanda rang the bell a half dozen times. Norm grinned. She'd noticed he was hard of hearing, and made the extra effort to see to it that he wasn't left out. She just called it, *stepping up the volume*. He could see why she'd be a good special education teacher. She noticed how and whether you picked up information, and then presented it in the best way for you. Lily had volunteered as an aide in the schools, and always liked the special-ed classes best. She was patient and could appreciate the greater significance of small achievements. Even with her brash exterior, Norm could see some of that in Amanda, too. He greeted her at the door, and noted suspiciously that she had amassed several boxes on the front porch. Electrical cords stuck out of the boxes.

"What's this?"

"It's your temporary foothold in the modern world."

"Amanda!"

"You don't have to keep it, but you have to try it."

Norm knew it was hopeless to resist. He sighed and helped Amanda carry the boxes of computer gear into his study.

She was on a roll and added, "I noticed the other day that there is this little corner over here where I could set you up without disturbing your regular routines."

"I thought you were coming to learn restoration."

"We'll do that, and then I'll set you up on this." She set down the last of the boxes and turned, "Show me the way."

Norm escorted her out to the workshop. He explained the solvents, the neutralizers, and the necessity to keep the canvas from getting saturated. He showed her how to use the brushes, and for delicate work, how just the tiniest of motions with a Q-tip might be all a painting could handle. Amanda was a quick study. She was gently daubing like a professional within the hour. Norm reminded himself that she'd been doing textile restoration for years. Maybe that explained it. He could hardly wait to tease Fiona and Jenn with Amanda's successes. He sat next to her and watched her deftly work the painting. Amanda seemed a little subdued.

"You're mighty quiet today."

"I guess so. I have a lot on my mind." Amanda pursed her lips but kept to the task.

"Want to unload?"

"I can't even quite put my finger on it myself." She shook her head.

"I don't want to pry, but if you want to kick it around..." Norm hated to see her out of her usual groove.

114

"I got a call from Denise, Fiona's daughter. They're going through a rough patch, not even speaking. Denise has been like a niece to me all these years, so when there's friction between her and her mom, it weighs on me."

"I understand. I hate being in the middle, too." Norm couldn't help but think of his own impulsive call to Thomas. "Can't you just tell Denise to work it out with her mom?"

"Ultimately, that's what I did, but it's still bothering me." Amanda turned the painting ninety degrees and leaned over, examining an oily spot on the canvas. She looked up.

"Don't worry. The solvent will take that right off."

Amanda nodded. "You know, without Emma Caites and all, Fiona would be a mess. Denise married and moved to Texas this summer. Fiona was so hangdog, I could barely stand it. She'd spent the whole year before focused on the damn wedding. It's not my business, but Fiona spoiled that girl. When Denise moved on, Fiona was at loose ends."

"So if your friend is okay now, why so glum?"

"I'm worried about Denise, and I wonder if I should tell Fiona that the kid is in rough shape."

"Did Denise say to tell Fiona?"

"No," Amanda admitted, "Just the opposite."

"Then just keep an eye on the situation, and hang tight."

"That's what I figure. Still…it's hard to tell if there's really a problem or if it's just new-marriage adjustments. I'm not exactly an expert in the area." Amanda rolled her eyes in self-mockery. "Part of my problem is I'm a little selfish, or selfish for someone else, if that makes any sense."

"Not really." Norm looked up quizzically.

"Fiona was always there for Denise, for everything. This is the first time in years that Fiona is following her own curiosity, doing things for her. I don't want to interrupt it."

"Then don't. You can't live for young people. They have to get out of their own way. Unless it's damaging, just leave it be."

Amanda nodded, but she didn't look convinced.

Norm continued, "I should take my own advice. Funny how you don't realize something applies to you, 'til you tell somebody else. Young people aren't the only ones learning," Norm shook his head.

"Well, as a teacher, I'm fond of saying, *stop learning, start dying.*"

"Ooh, that's harsh, especially for someone my age."

"You forgot," she laughed, "I'm about to introduce you to a computer. Remember we learn best from our mistakes. What's *your* issue?"

"I think I stuck my nose in where it doesn't belong. I hope I haven't caused trouble."

"How so?"

"After Thanksgiving I was so excited about the project, I called Thomas. I told him to call Fiona and I've been kicking myself ever since."

Amanda laughed. "Well, stop kicking. That one may have worked out just fine."

"What, heard something?"

"Big time. Fiona's met with Thomas, *twice*. Get this, he up and called her out of the blue." She giggled. "You haven't heard because she's swamped with all the documents and letters he gave her." Amanda turned the painting again, and surveyed her handiwork.

"Thank God, I've been just sick about it since I called."

"So, it all worked out. You can stop worrying. Shall we tell?"

Norm shook his head. "Not unless it comes up."

"I'll leave it up to you. I'm just happy with a happy ending." She stood. "I think I have this cleaning thing down. Let's go set up that computer." Norm nodded in agreement. He was so relieved about the call that now; even the computer didn't intimidate him.

Norm sat in his office chair, amazed. Amanda was crawling around on the floor, connecting a series of gray boxes, cords and wires. She even converted his phone cord for a jack and splitter. From the bottom of the box she retrieved a new push-button phone.

"You're not still renting your old phone, are you?"

Norm didn't understand the question.

"From the phone company, are you renting this old phone?"

"Well, sure I am."

Amanda rolled her eyes. "Call them in the morning and change that. You've probably paid for the phone a thousand times over." She clicked his new phone into the jack and attached the computer to the other side of the splitter. "They should be shot for that. Those old phones should have been scrapped years ago. Nobody rents anymore."

Amanda stood up and brushed the dust from her knees. She was covered with dust bunnies from rooting around under the desk. She

116

grinned, "I guess next time I should give notice so you can vacuum." Norm blushed. Amanda giggled. On Lily's corner desk the computer was taking shape. Amanda had explained that she'd set him up his own mailbox, under her account, so he could get email and go online. Norm still balanced his checkbook manually. So this was more than he could grasp.

Amanda stood up and brushed herself off.

"That's what I love, a man who blushes over his housekeeping. I'd die of embarrassment if someone looked under my furniture. Hell, Fiona'd have an asthma attack just thinking about it." She rolled him in his chair in front of the keyboard.

"I've set this up with a number of shortcuts. You won't believe how easy it'll be. We're going to run through this once tonight, and I'll be back Tuesday for real training." Amanda pointed, "Push that button."

Norm did as he was told, and the computer whirred while the screen sprung to life.

"Now, move your cursor to the bottom of the page." Norm just looked at her.

"Oh, I'm sorry. Let's start with some basics."

She ran through an introduction to the mouse, modem, keyboard and the icons on the screen. She had him do everything, patiently pointing, but keeping Norm's hands on the keyboard the whole time. Finally she guided him through opening-up his AOL account and collecting email. Norm was shocked that there was already an email there, waiting for him—a welcome to the computer from Amanda.

He was overwhelmed, "Stop, I can't do anymore."

"Okay, let's just walk you through shutting-down." Again, Amanda patiently walked Norm through the steps, but left his hands on the controls. The screen went blank, and Norm sighed with relief.

Amanda reassured him, "I want you to understand, you won't remember any of this tomorrow. This was just an introduction. Don't worry, we'll do this all again, you can take notes if you like, and we'll keep doing it till you get it."

"Oh Amanda, it's too much, and I'm too old."

"*Stop learning, start dying.*"

Norm laughed out loud.

"Hey, don't worry, I can handle this," she pointed her thumbs at her chest, "Special-ed, Norm, I'm ready."

He laughed again.

"Okay, now for your homework."

Norm blanched. He looked down at the keyboard, terrified.

"Not there, your homework is at your store. I want you to go to your store and find ten small items that you think are good quality but have not moved in six months."

"That's my homework?"

"Yup, that's it. I'll see you Tuesday." Amanda leaned over and kissed him on the forehead.

Chapter Twenty-Six

Fiona and Jennifer had been sorting and copying all day. Their tiny library office was steaming from the copier and their efforts. Fiona had taken the day off work, and Jenn was skipping classes. The next day was their presentation to the Mills Board. Each of them had read bits and pieces of the Caites correspondence, but it needed to be catalogued before it could begin to make sense. It was Fiona's idea to have a set of the documents at the meeting. It lent the air of scholarship to the venture, rather than just a fortuitous trip to the basement for paintings. Jennifer had jumped at the suggestion, and sorted the copied letters by date and life events into five huge, separate binders. They made a duplicate set to keep in the Mills library office.

At Fiona's insistence, the original letters were placed back in their envelopes and retied with the ribbons. There was something elegant and nostalgic about the way Emma kept Wren's letters. She wanted to preserve that integrity, and even felt the bundles might make a nice part of the exhibit itself. Fiona had never appreciated the Mills administrative assistance so much as she had today. Looking at the stacks, she realized there was a small fortune in copying alone. In all honesty, though, Fiona had appreciated Jennifer from the very start. Jenn had an innate sense of organization that mirrored her own. She also had that kid-from-a-large-family ability to roll with the punches. It reminded her of Amanda, without the head trips. Indeed, over the years, she had come through thick and thin with Amanda, had been her steady shoulder when Amanda's family pulled its routine dramas. Jenn was a similar package, without the damage. Fiona had never known anyone so calm and levelheaded.

"So, what have we got?"

Jenn looked up from her clipboard, "We have a small binder, correspondence from Emma to her grandparents. Then the monster—Henrietta's letters to Emma. We've divided those into four sections, France and early Oakland, Thomas, Post-War and the Fifties. For the presentation we have the seven restored Mills' paintings, with 'before' slides, slides of additional paintings from you, Marvin and Norm, and we have copies of the poster. We don't have an inventory or slides of Thomas' paintings."

"I don't want yet to promise Thomas' collection. I'm sure we'll get some cooperation but I can't promise what's not ours."

"So, at a minimum we have twenty-four canvases, the print, and the classroom drawings and studies."

Fiona nodded, "A small show, but still doable. With any number of Thomas' canvases it becomes a blockbuster event."

"Any news from Henrietta's daughter, what's-her-name?"

"Jordan. Not yet. I really have my fingers crossed on that. Have you read any of Henrietta's letters?"

"A smattering."

"Did you notice that it's difficult to decipher from Henrietta's letters what's going on in Emma's life?"

"I'll agree that Henrietta is… discreet."

Fiona snorted, "I'd say oblique." Shifting gears, she added, "If Emma's letters to Henrietta are anything like her letters to her grandparents, it'll change the complexion of the entire search. Emma is direct, to the point of wincing sometimes. Getting Emma's story from Henrietta's stuff is like trying to paint a portrait from a shadow."

Jenn laughed, "Nice painting analogy. Is this what we have to look forward to over the coming months?"

Fiona suddenly missed Denise so much she could barely speak. She missed the banter. She missed her baby. She adored Jennifer, admired her presence, and at the same time, Fiona was tormented that her own daughter didn't have an ounce of the common sense and sensibility as Jenn. Christmas was coming, and Fiona was still in the envelope of silence from her daughter. Fiona swallowed, hard. In spite of it, she grinned and returned the quip.

"I'm working up to art puns." At that, Jenn covered her eyes and groaned.

"Well, I think we are as ready as we can be at this point. Tomorrow's the big day. Hey kiddo, thanks so much, I couldn't have pulled this all together without your help."

Chapter Twenty-Seven

"What have you done to him?" Fiona laughed.

"What ever do you mean?" Amanda didn't do coy that well, and at this, even Jennifer joined in the laughter. Though she was loosening up some, Jennifer was loathe to make direct fun of her elders.

"Come on Amanda, I got an email today from *Norm*... We're talking Norm here. What kind of drug did you give him?"

It was another Saturday night pizza extravaganza at Amanda's. Amanda, Fiona and Jennifer were celebrating the success with Mills. Fiona was serving a Blackstone cabernet—Marv's house-wine secret from Trader Joe's. The Mills meeting went fabulously and they were definitely on board for an exclusive Emma Caites retrospective for June. They had yet to finalize the size of the show, but the Board had been impressed with the before-and-after on the paintings. Arthur Bradley was so solidly in their corner that he had introduced them at the meeting, and then summed it up with his recommendation. The taciturn instructor had then suggested, right in front of Jennifer, that her efforts and anticipated efforts should be rewarded with a full scholarship, now that she'd officially declared Art History as her major. Repeatedly they toasted their successes. They'd know Monday or Tuesday on the scholarship vote, but Fiona was certain of the outcome. Jennifer was near weeping.

"Really, though, Amanda, what's up with Norm? He sent me an eBay listing."

"It a project we're working on together—dragging Norm into the Twenty-First Century. He's got some great things in his shop, but no chance of selling it to his sad, little walk-in crowd. He's stuck with predators like me, scarfing up the good items for pennies."

"Don't you have a conflict of interest there?"

Amanda shot Fiona a feigned hurt look.

"Really, how did you get Norm on a computer?"

"I didn't give him an option. I had just upgraded, so I brought my old computer and set it up in his study. First I showed him the basics. Then I showed him how to use eBay for research, you know, pricing and all. He went crazy. As soon as it was relevant to his business, he was on it. In three days we were listing his stuff for sale. He's really into it and now he's exploring email. The toughest part has been taking the photos, because his fingers are too big for my camera!"

"I wouldn't have expected it. He seems like such a sweet old guy, but not exactly savvy." Fiona struggled with this new view of Norm.

Jennifer piped in, "Don't count on that, he really knows his stuff. He has an incredible reference library for art, antiques and collectibles. I've been using it for Emma Caites, on background."

"Ooh, you're ruining my image of our dear Norm!" Fiona cringed.

Amanda was clear on this angle, "Well, if his image has to include unsuccessful in business, it's one he can afford to lose."

Jenn laughed again, "I'm not sure if that doddering shopkeeper image isn't something he hasn't carefully cultivated."

"It makes me wonder," Fiona said, pouring another round, "Why did he sell me that little painting so cheap in the first place?"

"You lived in her house." Amanda drained her glass.

"What?"

"I asked him," Amanda added, "Never underestimate the power of sentimentality. You lived in Emma's house so he wanted you to have the painting."

"He said that, but I didn't think it could be as simple as that." Fiona shook her head. "Amazing. All this from a little painting." She started gathering the dishes. "We've got dessert too, but let's wait a bit."

"What's random to you is random squared to me." Jennifer added.

"What's that?" Fiona queried.

"You buy a painting and it adds a new dimension to your life. Interesting to ponder, but direct. From my perspective, you, a complete stranger, buy a painting, and suddenly I'm a scholarship contender in Art History. Interesting ripples in the pond."

"Mine, too," Amanda joined, "I drag you to a thrift shop, and I'll kill you if you tell Norm I called it that, and by the next holiday I have new family. It's how little events become the fulcrum."

"It's true of Emma, too. She gets an illness as a kid, and aside from the long range disability, it triggers a course of action that changes her life, and ultimately who she is." Fiona marveled at the complexity.

"Well, do we know that? We suppose it, but what do we know?" Amanda pressed.

"Oh, we know it. Not just her Mills entrance essay, but earlier letters to her grandmother."

"Oh yeah," Amanda reflected, "You're reading all this. So where are we in the Emma story?"

"So far the most interesting things are Emma's letters to her grandparents. I guess she has them from their estate." Fiona took a deep breath, "She was stricken ill at ten, and she spent the next fifteen months in a full body cast. Early in that period, she was shuttled off to her grandparents. Her mother was repulsed by her infirmity, and feared her siblings would catch it. Overwhelmed by Emma's care, her mother was all too willing to send her off to Oakland for its beneficial climate. Essentially, Emma was dumped by her immediate family."

"Wait a sec," Amanda went into the kitchen carrying the empty pizza box, and came back out with a battered hatbox and an assortment of bowls. "Okay, I didn't want to miss anything." Amanda spread the bowls across the table, and then, from the hatbox, poured a stream of beads and buttons into one of the larger bowls.

"What have we got here?" Jenn leaned forward, and fingered the brightly colored bits.

Fiona eyes widened, "Yeah, what is all this?"

Amanda looked up, surprised at their surprise. "It's just some buttons and beads'n stuff. I use'm for repairs to the vintage clothes, or to make matching beads for an outfit."

"You mean you've always had these?" Now Fiona's fingers were rifling through the bowl, too. "They're so cool."

"Yeah, I've had some of them for years. A few months back I bought out a collector's supply, new-old stock, everything. Now I need to get serious about organizing because I have too much to be able to keep track."

"So what are we doing?" Jenn was eager to get her hands on the colorful bits of glass and vintage plastic.

Amanda smiled, "We?"

Jenn poured a handful of beads from one hand into the other, "Yup, we. You don't think we were going to do story time while only you got to play with the gems, didja?"

Amanda's smile broadened, "Okay, so the first sort is simple, buttons or beads, then color and size. We won't finish but we can get a start."

Jenn dove her hands into the bowl, and scooped out a luscious measure of bright baubles, which she placed in front of her on the table. In no time her fingers were flying, picking and sorting, then dumping her little piles into the bowls between them. Amanda nodded and followed suit.

She looked up at Fiona, "Well?"

Fiona pulled her chair up closer to the table, and reached for her own bowl.

"No silly," Amanda giggled, "You're supposed to tell the story."

"Oh, okay. Where was I?" Watching the mesmerizing colorful beads and buttons as they clinked into tidiness, Fiona continued, "After her rehabilitation in Oakland, she went back to San Francisco to live with her family. Emma's grandparents grieved for her physical pain and the emotional rejection. They were determined to make up for it, for the difference in her East Bay life, for her subsequent exile to her parents' home in San Francisco. They spared no effort to enrich her environment, her education. Think of it, at fifteen, when she returned to San Francisco, she had completed all of her high school requirements, she spoke, read and wrote French fluently, could read Latin and had a smattering of German. She was well versed in political and philosophical discussion. These were interesting times; there was a war on and a fierce debate in the country about involvement or isolationism. Emma had already become an accomplished painter. She knew needlepoint, knitting and the domestic arts."

Fiona reached out and caught a large rolling amber bead that had escaped Jenn's flying fingers. She deposited it in a cup of similar amber beads. Jenn nodded.

"Her grandparents were California old money, if there could be such a thing. They were patrons to the arts, and knew many of the Californian legends. It would not be unusual for Emma to experience a dinner event with such notables as Jack London, Ambrose Bierce, Xavier Martinez or any of Oakland's later, Society of Six, artists. They lived a stone's throw from Seigrist's famed Rockridge cottage on Chabot."

Amanda paused in her pickings, "Chabot? You mean just up here off College?"

"Yeah, just up the hill from there. We can't prove that any one of these meetings ever occurred, but with her grandparents, it's clear that she lived a life peppered with the best minds and talents as the area had to offer. She matured in an intellectual and artistic atmosphere. Because of her illness, to Emma, home was Oakland and her grandparents. Young Emma had almost no emotional connection to her family in San Francisco. Her twin siblings, six when she left, were now eleven. They barely knew her. Her mother, always a social butterfly and a bit of an airhead, could not relate to this metamorphosed young woman." Fiona paused, and noted the quiet punctuation of the buttons and beads, plinking into their respective containers. A cup of cobalt colored beads caught her eye. Jenn was relentlessly pursuing a collection of orange glass buttons, and Fiona's eye followed, scanning the big bowl for those flashes of orange. She looked up to find both Amanda and Jenn looking directly at her, grinning.

"Oh!" Fiona caught herself and returned to her story, "You see, at fifteen, Emma had recovered as much as she ever would. One leg was two inches shorter than the other, and her hip was fragile. She wore *special* shoes to even out her leg length. She walked with a cane, and was careful for the rest of her life to bear her weight on the cane to ease deterioration of the hip. Doctors had warned that she should avoid ever carrying excess weight, and the rigors of pregnancy or childbirth. In short, given the social expectations of the day, her prospects were limited. Her parents insisted that she return to San Francisco for its enhanced 'social opportunities.' Frankly, at fifteen, they wanted to marry her off, and quickly."

Fiona caught her breath. Lulled by the story and transfixed by the beads, Amanda and Jennifer were spellbound.

"Let's get dessert, and then I'll continue."

Amanda nodded, and with the back of her hand, swept the loose beads in front of her off the edge of the table and back into their original sorting bowl. The three filed into the kitchen where Amanda had elegant Pot de Crèmes filled with lemon curd. She pulled out a fresh baked gingerbread, and cut generous wedges, which she heated briefly, serving each one, with its own lemon curd cup and a shot of fresh whipped cream. Amanda made up a pot of spearmint tea and loaded it on a tray, and stopping briefly to consider the beady mess on the dining table, brought everything out to the living room coffee table.

After a few bites, Jennifer cleared her throat, and her

companions looked up. "This is amazing. I've never tasted such a combination. It only brings up one question."

"What's that?" Fiona thought this was serious.

"If the two of you can put out a spread like this, and I remember Thanksgiving, why do we always eat pizza?"

They laughed so hard Amanda almost snorted her tea, and Fiona choked on her gingerbread. Point taken. For twenty minutes they discussed food and savored their desserts. Finally, when only slow Fiona had yet to finish up, they retired back to the dining table and their sorting. Fiona returned to the story.

"I warn you, Emma's letters from the San Francisco 'home' to her grandparents in the East Bay are heartbreaking. They start out normal enough. She tells them how much she misses them and the comfortable rhythms of the home she had come to see as her own. She yearns for the food, the evening conversations. She pines for the garden strolls, gathering flowers and herbs with her grandmother. While more eloquent than the average fifteen-year-old, they are letters about being homesick. The focus is on what's missing. Through them we can see a lonely teenager longing for her family."

Fiona gathered her companions' dessert dishes and took them to the kitchen. Returning, she took up where she'd left off, "The pain, though, is in the details she recounts of her day to day life in the Caites home. Her parents, arguably to minimize her time on the stairs, have fixed up the tiny servant's room off the kitchen. Her old room upstairs is occupied by her little sister. There is a guest suite downstairs, but there is never any suggestion that Emma should take the guest quarters or share the room with her sister. She is physically excluded from the rest of the family. Her siblings treat her as a curiosity. Their friends are whisked away, and Emma's presence in the house is always discussed in hushed tones.

Emma actually likes her diminutive refuge, but there is no room there for her art materials. Instead of making room for them elsewhere, her mother takes her art supplies and books, boxes them and stores them in the attic of the garage. This is accessible only by a rough ladder, which of course, Emma cannot safely negotiate." Fiona paused, "If you can wait a bit, some of this is so sweetly written in her letters…" Fiona walked over to her purse, which was perched on a stack of papers. She carried them back to the table, and began leafing through them while the others continued sorting the beads and buttons.

Fiona peeled through the pages, and then finding what she'd wanted, resumed, "Ah, here, like this," and then quoting, "*I've taken to sketching on small tablets in pencil, though Mother finds it distasteful. I am unable to discern what it is in my artistic pursuits that she can support. Landscapes are forbidden entirely, though Mother permits me to draw "likenesses," which she sees as an acceptable parlor activity. Art then, is reduced to some light entertainment value befitting a young woman in courting.*" Fiona was shaking her head.

"Emma repeatedly requests that she be permitted to take painting classes. A noted artist-couple of the time, Arthur and Lucia Matthews, remained in San Francisco after the quake, and Emma wanted to approach them about private instruction or an apprenticeship. Her parents will hear nothing of it."

Turning back to the copies in front of her, Fiona continued, "Emma tells her grandmother, '*As my mother understands it, Lucia works in the craft shop, supervising employees, most of whom are men, whilst Arthur Matthews is out painting nudes! My mother finds this conduct, these shared competencies, entirely unseemly for a woman. The Matthews, in her estimation, are coarse people who do not fit well in society. Other than simple caricatures, all my artistic endeavors are either forbidden or made impossible.*'"

Fiona looked up from her papers, "Similarly, her parents saw no place or use for further education. Emma had already finished high school, so, in their minds, her education was complete. Seeing her as a little rough cut, they do offer her classes at a finishing school, which Emma explores but rejects when she discovers the curriculum covers basic domestic arts, fashion and dance."

Leafing again through to Emma's letters, Fiona selected one and quoted, "*Dance! Can you imagine? Grandma, does she even see me? She is so mortified by my cane that she refuses to recognize that the freedom it gives is more valuable than whatever grace is lost in its employ. When Mother discovered that I can maneuver some without it, she immediately insisted that I dispense with 'that ugly bit of crippledom'. When I resist, she stoops to stealing my cane away at those social occasions where she hopes to market me to prospective suitors. Dearest Grandmother, what can I do? Am I to participate in the crutch of fraud on which my Mother leans to sell me?*"

Fiona let the papers settle in her lap, "Our Emma is captive. She has no outlet for education or intellectual stimulation, and she longs for the earnest and intense dinner conversations she remembers from Oakland. When she tries to engage her parents, or even her siblings in discussions of current events or art, her mother chides her, and suggests that she is not in the East Bay's Bohemian culture anymore, and that it is high time she learned to engage in polite discussion. In keeping with the mores of the day, Emma is not permitted to leave the house unaccompanied, and takes to assisting the servants in their activities in the kitchen. Again, when her mother learns of her scullery endeavors, Emma is punished and sent to her room." Fiona sighed and took her last bite of gingerbread. Her companions paused from their sorting while Fiona chewed thoughtfully.

"The absolute worst for Emma is her mother's constant efforts to invite suitors to the home. These are formal parlor events, with limited discussion, and certainly no substantive content. The young men are dolts from 'good families,' the problem sons who might be well suited to a match with a beautiful cripple from money."

Fiona flipped through the pages, and continued, "Emma notes to her grandmother that, '*At least two of these prospects were obviously homosexual, but they were proffered without any acknowledgment that that might be an impediment to a match...at least from my parents perspective.*' One after another Emma rejects these suitors, to her mother's dismay."

Fiona paused, watching the growing accumulation of gem-like bits in the bowls and ramekins spread across the table. She sighed, "Ultimately her mother alerts her, in no uncertain terms, to her limited options, emphasizing what an unattractive package Emma is in the market. She reminds Emma that there is a war on, and that the already short supply of quality husbands is unlikely to provide opportunities to uppity cripples such as herself. Her mother informs her that a spinster, even a crippled spinster, cannot expect to live off of the resources of her family forever.

"Emma's years in San Francisco are wasted. She is unable to enhance her skills or broaden her intellectual horizons. Her only salvation is the public library, but even then, her mother seeks to censor her selections. Emma takes up reading French literature, in French, to thwart her mother's restrictions. All the while, Emma repeatedly writes and begs her grandparents to bring her home. While they are horrified at their daughter's narrow bourgeois

128

attitudes, they reply to Emma that their hands are tied.

"Privately, in separate correspondence, her grandparents are overwrought at the damage being done to their delicate and delightful granddaughter. They abhor their only daughter's shallow values, and scheme to find an acceptable salvation for Emma. They visit regularly, and take Emma—and her siblings if they're interested—to cultural events in the city. These visits are heartbreaking as they see all their efforts to let Emma bloom undermined by the most mean spirited and limited view of her potential.

"The deepest tragedy is that ultimately, Emma's salvation is brought about by her grandmother's death in 1918 from influenza. Emma was overwrought by the loss; in her mother's opinion, another symptom of her defective and unbalanced nature. Emma's parents blame the grandparents for having spoiled the girl, and for having trained her in unsuitable ways. When her grieving grandfather requests that Emma come to live with him, to run his household, Emma's parents leap at the opportunity to be rid of the albatross.

"Emma, at last, is free to return to Oakland, but it is an Oakland less sparkling and far lonelier than she left it. She and her grandfather are refugees, from loss and pain."

Fiona looked up at her companions. Their hands sat idle.

"This is all in the letters?" Amanda had tears running down her cheeks.

"Yes, every detail."

"Our Emma was made of stronger stuff than we knew."

Chapter Twenty-Eight

Christmas shopping. Normally, Fiona loved the holidays. This year, she was dreading it. If Amanda hadn't insisted, she'd have just let the whole thing drop. Amanda was right of course. Marvin was inviting the group, including Thomas, to a pre-Christmas dinner, and she wanted to have something small, but special, for each of them. Without the efforts of each and every one of them, the Emma Caites project would never have been launched. Fiona marveled that it really was an ensemble endeavor. She realized how much she looked forward to the Emma events with the group. Like Amanda said, it had become a second family. So shopping should not be such a chore. Besides, Amanda could help her pick something for Denise that wouldn't push any buttons. Fiona always agonized over the details. Denise—or should it be Denise *and* Tom? Separate gifts for each of them? Household or personal? At least, since they'd just done the whole wedding thing, Fiona had a pretty good idea of what they already had. She wondered what Amanda had in store for her today, since there was always a hidden agenda with Amanda.

Fiona heard the honk downstairs, grabbed her coat and scarf, and headed out through the garage below. She hadn't looked at her garage the same way since she learned that Emma had given painting lessons in there. Now always in her mind she could see a semicircle of easels and hopeful beginners. Thomas said that he had always participated in the classes; he was her shill. If that kid could paint, hey, anybody could. They'd do basic exercises here, in tempera on paper, before going out to the hills to paint the landscapes. Amanda honked again. Fiona rolled down the garage door and climbed into the passenger seat.

"So, what's on the agenda for the day?"

Amanda grinned, "Mostly that we have a good time. The shopping is extra. Do you know what you'd like to get?"

"I have some ideas. I'd like a quality French beret for Norm, legwarmers in outrageous colors for Jennifer and some kind of organizer bag for Marvin."

"What, Marvin's not organized enough?" Amanda's face showed her skepticism.

"When he came to assess the Mills' paintings, all his things were loose. He made several trips to the trunk of his car to get it all. You?"

Amanda was ready, too. "Okay, for Jenn I want to get these fun hairclips I saw at a shop on College Avenue, for Norm, I already got him a book on eBay marketing, which, of course, I got on eBay. For Marvin, I want to get him one of those Wayne Thiebaud t-shirts with the pies and cakes on it."

"So let's start on College, and then we'll end up at the Oakland Museum for the t-shirt."

"Cool beans."

This was why Fiona loved to shop with Amanda. Some women liked to amble through shops looking for ideas. With Amanda it was a targeted mission. If something fun came up along the way, fine, but with Amanda, you got the job done.

"What about Denise?" Amanda was leaving no stone unturned.

Fiona hesitated. "We can talk about her along the way. I'm really stumped on her, and it's not because I don't know her tastes."

"So, you heard anything?" Amanda was hoping Denise would have called.

"Not a word," Fiona's jaw tightened.

"So what weird message does it send, giving a gift to someone you're not speaking to?" Amanda queried.

"A *different* weird message than the one where a mother doesn't remember Christmas for her only kid."

"*Ooooh.*" Amanda changed the subject. "Given any thought to your plans for Christmas?"

"Nope. Amanda, I've been so busy, I haven't really had time."

"I know. But that way it sneaks up on you. You're always welcome to join me in Calistoga for a holiday of decadent pampering."

"Not really my style, but I'll keep it in mind." Fiona was tense about the impending holiday.

Other than the parking, their search on College worked out very well. Amanda's hairclips were just the ticket and the same shop had legwarmers which Fiona picked to match the clips. A men's shop up the street had lovely berets. Fiona and Amanda debated the color, and settled on a dark burgundy. The organizer bag was a bit of a problem, until they passed an upscale hardware up by Ashby. There, in the window, was an old-fashioned canvas tool bag with leather trim and handles. It was perfect. They hopped in the car, and headed

131

to Lake Merritt and the Museum Store. The place was full of kids and the line for the cashier was serpentine. Amanda found Marvin's t-shirt, then dutifully searched out the end of the line. Fiona shopped the book section, and noted with particular interest a number of beautiful books on California paintings during Emma's time. There was a beautiful book on Arthur and Lucia Matthews. Fiona remembered the names from Emma's letters, and snapped it up. Digging further, she found a reference book with exquisite photos of Northern California plein air painters. Before she could do any more damage, she joined Amanda in line.

"What's that?" Amanda inquired nosily.

"For reference and maybe a gift for Denise."

"Interesting choices. Which is which?"

"The Matthews book might be the gift."

Waiting in line, Amanda browsed through the two tomes. "It might just be a brilliant selection. It shares what you're doing, but makes no comment on the other issues. Plus you can glean info from it before you ship. Nice."

"I think that means once we're through this line, we're done." Fiona was relieved.

"Now we can eat. I'm starved."

Fiona checked her watch. "Let's go back to my house for that. I've got great leftovers and I've about had it with the crowds."

They recovered over steaming bowls of potato leek soup and sour dough rolls. Amanda asked about Henrietta's letters.

"They're a great source of information about Henrietta and her family, but she doesn't comment much on the details of Emma's life. She discusses art a lot. Henrietta married a career diplomat; she traveled all over the world. Everywhere she went, she connected with the local culture and art. Obviously she and Emma always shared an appreciation, not just of art, but of its place in life, in society. Her letters comment on current events, through the eyes of whatever culture where they were stationed. They are great letters, but not good gossip. They'd be worth investigating for some other book even, just not very illuminating of Emma. Sure there are occasional platitudes, but I gather she was a little more straight-laced than our Emma. I've made a copy for Jordan, if we ever connect."

"So you didn't get anything?" Amanda couldn't believe all those letters yielded nothing.

"No, I got a lot. From the envelopes alone I got every address where Emma ever lived after Mills. I know her lodgings in Paris, the school she attended, the museums she went to, or that were recommended by Wren. I got the gist of things. In person they must have been really close confidants, you can tell because they write in a sort of code. In Paris, Emma seems to have had a disastrous affair with a man named Peter, but the references make no sense. They talk about tulips? Wren knew that Emma had inherited money from her grandparents, and that it tore her family apart. Wren calls it, *the heavy burden of freedom.*"

"Well, you could see *that* coming from Emma's relationships with her family. Putting that in code could only be a favor."

Fiona glanced up and saw that Amanda's face had clouded over. She was never far from her family's brutal past. Fiona pondered whether any of us ever escape the injuries of childhood, and whether all our talents *and* flaws weren't just outgrowths of early coping. Fiona's own mother had hardened herself to the emotional neglect of a workaholic husband. Fiona wondered whether growing up in that house had taught her not to connect in a way that had doomed her marriage. She shuddered to think what ripples on that theme Denise was acting out now. She borrowed Amanda's phrase, "Put a nickel in the therapy jar."

Amanda looked up, their eyes met and both laughed.

"So, why don't you go to Paris for Christmas?"

"What?"

"Have you ever been?

"No."

"Well, why don't you do one of your magic internet deal searches and get a quickie getaway to Paris for the holiday." Amanda was serious.

Fiona was stunned. "What would I do there?"

"I dunno, check out Museums, visit the addresses where Emma lived, get the feel of neighborhoods. In France they have restrictions on changing the facades of historic buildings. It's likely that a lot of what she saw is still intact. The Paris of the twenties was a wild place. You know, Hemingway, James Joyce, the Murphys, Gertrude Stein. Go to France, drink absinthe."

"That's a crazy idea."

"You got another plan?" Amanda was really pushing for a Christmas plan.

Fiona was silent on that.

"You could just call her." That Amanda always had the logical alternative.

"I need to give Denise her space. I need some, too." Fiona wasn't sure if she was taking the high road or sticking her head in the sand.

"Then go to France. What the hell. Why not?"

Chapter Twenty-Nine

"Excuse me. May I please speak with Fiona Hedge?"

"Speaking."

"Oh good. This is Jordan McCann. Henrietta was my mother." Her voice was steady, but a little reedy. Fiona suddenly realized that Jordan was elderly. Somehow she had envisioned her as a contemporary. She must be at least as old as Thomas, and probably older. Fiona was struck by the feeling that she was catching this opportunity just in time.

"Jordan, I've so looked forward to speaking with you. Did you understand my letter, what I'm looking for?"

"Actually, I understood perfectly. In a way, I've been waiting years for that letter."

"Really, what made you think such an inquiry would come?"

"My mother was pretty astute. She always recognized Emma's talent, and knew, for a variety of reasons, she had gone unrecognized. She told me that someday, someone would pursue it. We always thought that it would be one of Thomas' daughters, but they've never caught the interest. My mother made me keep all of Emma's papers and things for exactly this occasion. I'm pleased that it came in my lifetime. If I might ask, what brought you to this endeavor?"

"It was a fluke really. I found a painting that I loved. You see, it turns out that I live in Emma's old apartment. The painting is of the complex as seen out my window. When I saw it I knew it could only be my place. I bought it and restored it. It made me want to know more about the artist. And those inquiries have led me to you."

"Thomas contacted me. He seems to trust you and suggested I should talk with you. That says a lot."

"Yes, I think we've established a rapport but he's still somewhat tight lipped. Parts of this are awkward, maybe even painful."

"That's a thoughtful way of approaching it. Ultimately, what will you do with all the information?"

There it was. Fiona sensed *the test.* At every juncture she had to establish herself, with Norm, with Thomas. Emma Caites seemed to generate great loyalty among those who knew her. She answered sincerely, "Well, we've already arranged for a retrospective show through Mills College. That will be in June. The exhibit will bring some recognition to Emma. At this point we have enough information for a bare bones exhibit."

She continued self consciously, "I understand the position some would take that the work should speak for itself. I suppose I could stop now, but I'm not finished. I need to understand more. My personal goal is to write her biography. She was an amazing woman and an incredible talent. I have come to relate to her and her integrity. I raised a daughter alone in that same apartment, without any of the social and physical limitations that challenged Emma. I think the times have changed and that the personal reasons that may have kept her out of center stage are no longer areas of judgment. I think she can shine without anyone suffering for it."

There was a long pause on the other end. "Ms. Hedge, I believe we have found the right person for the task. And when you get to the tough parts, have you thought how you'll approach Thomas with that view?"

"Write it up first. Write it honest and clean. Write it without judgment, but acknowledging how the judgment of the day had an impact. The remarkable thing about Emma was that she painted. She didn't really have to, not financially anyway. Obviously she didn't do it for the recognition. But she got up every morning and was an artist. From her work, you can see that she continued to explore the medium, to stretch herself for her whole life. She never gave it up. If Thomas can see that, and I'm sure he can, he'll be on board for the story. It is who she was."

"I'd love to meet you Ms. Hedge."

"Please, call me Fiona. We really should meet. It will have to wait until after the holiday, though. I'm going to Paris over the holiday. Early January, perhaps?"

"Are you going for this project?"

"In part, yes. I don't have much to go on but I have her addresses and the school. I'd just like to see it, you know, to place it in my mind."

"I have Emma's correspondence to my mother. I think you should have it before you travel."

"How much of it is there? Perhaps I could come down to L.A. and pick it up."

"No, I'll have it sent by courier. That way, you could have it by the end of the week."

136

"I really appreciate it. This will really make the trip more focused. I may even get to read her Paris letters in Paris."

"I hadn't intended to send them in advance, but if your mission has you traveling halfway across the world to catch the flavor of the place, you really should have the letters. But of course, I'd still like to meet you."

"And I want to meet you, as well. It's been difficult to get a feeling for Emma, there are so few people left to interview. Did you know her well?"

"Yes, in two ways. She was such a big fixture in my mother's life that she was often part of our conversations over many decades. Mom would read her letters aloud, with some censorship, I assure you. Then, when I was old enough for college my mother sent me back to Mills. Emma, or Aunt Emma, as I called her, kept an eye on me. I used to spend time at the apartment... well, now *your* apartment, with her and Thomas. She was the best aunt you could hope for. When my brother was missing in action, she was a huge comfort to me and to my mom. We came and stayed with her often. We were there when we got the news."

"You lost your brother in the war?"

"Yes, in the Pacific. It was strange, because a year later, Emma's brother was also killed. I always felt that we had a lot in common."

"Have you ever had the opportunity to read your mother's letters to Emma?"

"No, do you have them?"

"Yes, I got them from Thomas. They are wonderful letters, though not what I'd hoped. But I imagine they'd be much richer for you."

"What was missing?"

"I was looking for something more gossipy, something that told me more about Emma. These are newsy and philosophical, but not personal."

"Well, my mother *was* a diplomat's wife. She was nothing, if not proper. I think it's why she and Emma got on so well. Emma was a free thinker and spoke her mind. My mother always loved that about her. In Emma's letters to mom, you'll get what you're looking for."

"I've made a full set of copies of your mother's letters. Would you like me to send them to you?"

"Yes, please do. I'd love to read them, and share them with my daughter." Jordan paused, "This does raise an issue that is a bit sticky."

"What's that?"

"Well, I don't *think* it's a problem. Understand, my mother never wanted me to give the letters to Thomas. You see, Emma didn't want Thomas to know who his father was. I've read all Emma's letters at least twice. I don't know if a reading of these letters would reveal that, especially given your other research. But if it does, I have to ask you to honor my mother's and Emma's wishes."

"She never told him who his father was?" Fiona was flummoxed.

"Not that I know. And, like I said, I've read the letters. She never directly reveals it in there either. I know my mother knew, but she never told me, even after Emma died."

"Did you know her towards the end, you know, later in the 1950s?"

"I last saw her after her fall, in '55. I could barely stand it."

"I don't know anything about this."

"Oh, her hip had been deteriorating for years. Nothing they could do for it back then. They wanted her to move to a nursing home, but she would have nothing of it. One day her hip just failed. She fell in the kitchen and was there, on the floor, for a day or so. Emma had a hospital bed put into the living room and just continued on. She had to use crutches or a wheelchair, which she hated, but she *wasn't* leaving her home. She couldn't bear any weight on that leg, the hip was completely destroyed. I know Thomas struggled with it, but in the end it was Emma's choice. I think life became almost unbearable during this period. I don't know how she dealt with it. I came to visit once, and she tried to be hospitable, but you could see the pain etched in her face. She must have aged about forty years in those six months. I was moving to Europe for a few years. When I saw her, I knew it would be the last time."

"I didn't know," Fiona said softly. She was taking the news badly. She couldn't bear the suffering, *or* Emma's stoicism.

"She continued to paint. Lord knows how, but there are canvases dating through 1957. She died in January of '58." Jordan's voice was low.

"Are you sure about the paintings?"

"You'll see it in the letters. And Emma was still selling into 1957. Talk to Thomas. I think he has some of those later works."

"What was your relationship with Thomas like?"

"Sort of like cousins. We were close for a while when we were

138

younger. Later, we drifted, after my mom died. He was really close to her. After that we got caught up in our own lives, you know, mostly Christmas cards, occasional emails. I hope there's no friction, I don't know."

"Why would there be friction?" Fiona didn't understand.

"Well, I wouldn't give him the letters. So I told him I might work on a book on my mom, needed them for reference and all."

"But you were honoring your mom's and Emma's wishes"

"Yes."

"This is a lot for me to digest." Fiona added, "I didn't have much on the later years. I am so sorry to hear about all the suffering."

"What you're doing may make up for some of it."

"Thank you, I hope so." Fiona was humbled.

"When you visit, I have some paintings I'd like you to see. Maybe you'll want them in the show."

"Do you think you could come?"

"Pardon me?"

"To the Mills exhibit, I'd love for you to be there."

"In June? I'll think about it, it is a lovely time. In the meantime, watch for the letters. And I can hardly wait to hear about your Paris trip."

"Thank you, you've already been more help than you know."

Chapter Thirty

Amanda fidgeted all day over it. Finally when she got home, after a glass of Pinot Grigio, she tried to weigh the pros and cons. It was, after all, none of her business. Added to that she was irritated—never the best frame of mind for her to reach out and try to talk sense to anyone, much less someone she loved. Another glass though, had the pros talking. Then again, she really was the only one in any position to reach out between the two of them. What they both had in common was that they were stubborn. *Really* stubborn. Part way into her third glass, Amanda picked up the phone and dialed Texas. Perhaps the wine is why she forgot the time difference.

A man's voice groaned, "Hello?"

Amanda wasn't expecting that. In fact, she'd completely forgotten about Tom's existence. Sometimes that happens on a crusade, especially after the third glass. "Excuse me, who is this?"

A pissed and sleepy voice answered, "Tom. I live here. And who the fuck are you?"

Oh yeah, *Tom*. "Well, I'd like to speak to the lady of the house, *if* you don't mind."

There was a pause. She could almost see him rolling over and looking at the clock, "At one-ten a.m., I *do* mind. You selling something, lady?"

"No, I just want to talk to Denise. And who are *you*, the fucking gatekeeper?"

"Might be. Who the hell are you?"

"I'm her aunt."

"For your sake, there better have been a death in the family." Another long pause, rustling and then a muffled, "Denise, hon, some woman's on the phone, says she's a relative."

It felt like forever. Amanda thought about hanging up. But these were young people—strong chance of caller I.D.

Then a couple of clicks and Denise's voice kicked in, "Honey, I've got it, you can hang up." Another click. Amanda waited. Maybe she was in the clear. "Hello?" It was Denise's sleepy voice.

"I thought you said you were going to call your mother."

"Amanda?" Denise was whispering, almost hissing, "What are

you, nuts. It's after midnight."

"I've been busy. So, why didn't you call your mom?"

"It's not that simple."

"She's your mother. Of course it's that simple."

"You don't understand. It's not just *me* now."

"What, now someone *else* is involved in your relationship with your mother?" Amanda wasn't going to let that sit. Not tonight.

"No... Well, yes, I'm married now. It's not just me."

"Denise, when married means you can't talk to your mother, there's some serious shit going down. What is it?"

"You won't understand."

"Oh honey, I've been in some pretty twisted relationships, I am the Queen of Dysfunctional, believe me, I *do* understand. But you've got to actually talk to be understood." Amanda pressed.

"Well, that's a competition I don't want to win."

"Touché."

"Are you drunk?" Denise really knew her aunt.

"That's a matter of degree. What I *am* is concerned that you haven't spoken to your mom in over a month. It's the holidays, what is the matter with you?"

"Are you asking *her* the same thing?"

"She didn't unilaterally cancel Thanksgiving without notice."

"What, so *I* started it?" Denise was being petulant.

"Cut it out. You know this is yours to fix." Amanda didn't give her any room to wiggle.

"There's nothing I can do now. Christmas is set."

"You don't have to rearrange the schedule. Just call."

"It's not that easy."

"It's *always* just that easy." Amanda drained her glass.

"Easy for you maybe, but then you've chosen to live alone."

Amanda sighed, "You did this when you were a little kid."

"Did what?"

"You'd cover your eyes and then say, *'You can't see me.'*"

"What the hell are you talking about?"

"Think about it, okay? And call you mother. We *can* see you. Nothing's changed."

That was it. Denise whispered, "It's late. I gotta go."

And then she hung up. Amanda put her head in her hands. *Fuck!* That certainly went well. What were godparents for anyway? She emptied the bottle.

141

Chapter Thirty-One

The doorbell rang. Fiona jumped. She wasn't expecting anyone. It wasn't like she had the kind of business with a walk-in component. She went to the window and looked down onto the front porch. There was no mistaking the top of *that* head. Bleached blonde, dark roots. Marvin was stepping from one foot to the other, rubbing his gloved hands together in the cold. Fiona darted down the stairs and threw open the door.

"Get in here, it's freezing out."

"Girl, you don't know freezing. But my blood's thin from twenty years in sunny California."

"So, what's up?"

"My car's downstairs. Come give me a hand." He looked like a kid on Christmas morning.

He led the way through the kitchen, and down the back stairs. Fiona grabbed a jacket and padded along behind him. His station wagon blocked her garage entrance. The seats were folded down and the back was stacked with canvases, their stretcher bars crisscrossed over each other. Fiona swallowed hard. Mostly she'd recovered, but sometimes the idea of paintings brought back that sick feeling in the pit of her stomach and the image of peeling paint. She breathed deeply.

"You've been having *way* too much fun."

"I just couldn't resist dropping by. I can't take them to the gallery, and I work late tonight. I'm bursting to show you these. They're the best yet."

Fiona took the first one from him, "Where to?"

"Upstairs, where it's warm."

They each made three trips ferrying the canvases upstairs. In the spirit of being a good sport, Fiona tried not to look. But he was right, they were lovely. She followed him up the stairs with the last load. "Where did you get these?"

"Fiona, you won't believe it. *She* called me."

"Who?"

"One of the Knowlands' grandkids. She heard from my last seller that I was interested in Caites. She inherited these from her grandmother, but never liked them."

"I can see that by the way they've been treated."

"Yeah, filthy *and* damaged. You'll get to learn how to repair a ripped canvas in this batch."

Fiona did a quick calculation and hoped he did well on the price. She'd just put a trip to Paris on her credit card and didn't want to ask Marvin to wait to be reimbursed. "So, what's the damage?"

"You won't believe it."

"Please, don't make me guess. You're killing me here."

"Fiona, the whole lot was just $520."

"Jesus. Has she got any more?" Fiona started moving paintings into the light, "What did you do to her?"

"Really Fiona, she set the price. I mean, obviously she knew about the earlier sale. I did point out that the condition here didn't approach her friend's paintings. Obviously these were not well stored or cared for. So she does a little mental calculation and blurts out the price."

Fiona looked up, "*That* price, the $520?"

Marvin nodded. "So I paused for a minute, not too long, because I knew I would accept her offer, but I didn't want to look too eager."

"If you're taking them at her price, what do you care if you're eager?"

"*Reputation*, my dear and I may deal with this family again. In seven months these may be valuable paintings and I don't want the Oakland art world pissed because they think I poached some family's heirlooms."

"Okay, let's have a look at them."

There were two interiors and four landscapes. Both of the interiors, dated 1948, were from the inside of an old soda fountain. The first was a panorama. Under the grime, were gleaming oak floors and a long counter, its surface space broken up at regular intervals by napkin dispensers and salt and pepper shakers, and the same rhythm echoed below by built in stools. On the right hand side were oak booths, foreshortened towards the back, with red vinyl benches peeking out of each booth, repeating smaller and smaller. The table tops and counter were a polished black surface. The first booth, the only one you could actually see into, had dirty dishes and coffee cups on the table. The image was serene and welcoming.

The second painting was a close-up of one of the booths. The black tabletop gleamed under a coffee cup with a spoon in the saucer. The spoon, though impressionistically painted, had all the right reflections and highlights on its restaurant stainless steel surface. Just above and to the left of the coffee cup was a juke box selector. On the far left side of the juke selector were the ubiquitous salt and pepper shakers and one of those tall, fluted glass sugar dispensers.

Fiona sucked in her breath. "Choosing isn't going to be easy this time."

"I know, honestly, I want them *all*."

Fiona laughed, "A deal's a deal."

"Fiona, this isn't even about speculation. These are simply incredible."

She turned her attention to the first landscape. It was a sweet little forest scene. A stream in the foreground broke up the space, creating an open area from which to see the trees. Reflections in the stream showed the varied greens of early spring. In the foreground were moss covered tree trunks, their branches just forking at the top of the painting, with little foliage visible. Behind them, the forest foliage led the eye along a small path. The colors were the powdery greens of young eucalyptus, bright light greens for new deciduous 'mouse-ear' sized baby leaves, shining in the sun and the deep grays, silvers and rusts of the peeling eucalyptus trunks. The effect was peaceful, with golden sunlight streaming in wherever there was a break in the canopy.

The next painting was a little smaller, and it totally spoke of summer. It was a view of the boathouse on Lake Merritt. Behind it you could see the lake, peppered with little sailboats. Fiona laughed. Learning to sail on Lake Merritt was almost an Oakland right of passage. The part of the painting that totally completed it—that made it speak—was the jumble of bicycles, abandoned on the lawn in front of the boathouse. This was where the kids were. Bikes in all colors, their chrome fenders glinting in the sun, lying on the ground, leaning against a wall or a tree. This canvas had a long tear in it, but clean edged, with little damage to the painted surface. Fiona had seen worse.

She flipped the next piece. It was a large canvas, not like anything she'd seen from Emma before. It revealed a hilltop cut diagonally by fence posts, with a body of water and other hills roughly painted in the far distance. The hilltop itself was occupied by sheep, standing sheep, grazing sheep, sheep at attention; fat woolly critters rendered in bold brushstrokes, their big ears flopped sideways. The painting was funny, but on second viewing, impressionistically accurate. Fiona couldn't put her finger on why, but this was a humorous view of the countryside, or at least lighthearted. It was dated 1951.

The final painting was a windblown, early winter painting of a delta area. There were wisps of snow, caught in the marsh grasses and skittering across fresh thin ice. The painting centered on a clump of grasses still standing, where most had already been flattened by the end of the season. Snow was caught in the clump, the white in contrast to the gold and beige of the dry grasses, and the deep browns of the water through the ice. The sky was gray and the background faded to a leafless woodlot, in taupe and grays. The grasses in the central clump were delicately rendered, the only part of the painting whose details had not been obscured or dulled by winter.

Every canvas was superb. Fiona could hardly wait to see them cleaned. In spite of her anxiety about cleaning, her enthusiasm returned. She turned to Marvin, "I can't decide. One of the interiors and two landscapes. I'd love whatever I got."

"Hey, you're not getting off that easy. I'm not making this decision alone."

"Well, if I *had* a preference, I'd pick. But I love them all."

So Marvin started the process. "Okay, I'll take the panorama of the soda shop, because, in its own way, it's so Hopperesque."

"Fine with me, I love the intimate little cup and juke box."

"Now this one is tough. I'll be honest, I'm not crazy about the humor in those sheep, yet it's well painted." Marvin squinted at the landscape.

"I'll take them. They make me laugh, those sheep."

"I'd like the bicycles. It's just so fifties, that one's fun, to me."

"Okay," Fiona had liked the bikes too, because they *were* fun, but so were the sheep. For her next pick she selected the quiet forest and stream.

Marvin nodded, "Good choice. And that works because I like the grasses. I like the late-life winter symbolism."

Fiona looked at him to make sure. "So, we're happy?"

Marvin laughed, "No, really I want all of them, but I'm happy with my picks."

Fiona looked at all of them, strewn across the room. "These are really good Marvin. These, with the others, are enough for an exhibit, even without Thomas."

"Yeah, I know. We're on our way."

Fiona fetched her checkbook and wrote Marvin a check for half the $520. "Best money I ever spent."

"Me, too."

Chapter Thirty-Two

Fiona stood in the open doorway, signing for the boxes, and fretting over the heat loss. The UPS driver helped bring them in, and stacked them, all five, in the living room. Somehow, Fiona had been hoping for something less voluminous, something more travel-kit sized. She only had a few days before she left and still had some shopping to do before Marvin's dinner. She sighed and opened the first box. Inside, Emma's letters were loose. *Rumpelstiltskin.* Emma closed the box and called Jennifer.

"Jenn, have you taken your finals yet?"

"Last one's tomorrow. I can hardly wait till it's over. Why?"

"Afterwards, do you think you can give me a hand with another organizational project?

"Sure. Does that mean you got Emma's letters?"

"Yup, five boxes of documents. I want to get them ready so I can take at least some of it with me."

"May I suggest something?" Jenn was sounding professorial.

"Sure."

"Are you planning on bringing your laptop?"

"I really hadn't thought about it. Why?"

"We could scan the documents, and then enter them into a database, by date. Then you could bring the lot of them with you, carrying only your laptop."

"Wouldn't it take forever?" Fiona stood looking at the five boxes.

"A little longer at the outset, but then they'd be in there, retrievable by date, sortable by any parameter you entered." That Jenn was a godsend.

"I don't know where you get all this but, okay, where do we start?"

"I'll be over tomorrow after my exam. We'll go pick up the equipment and software, and then we can get it done before the party." Jenn sounded so confident.

"Are you *sure* you know what you're doing?" Fiona couldn't imagine taming this pile of loose paper.

"Yeah, I just helped someone do this at the library. Art Bradley volunteered me because he thought it would be good for me. He has

147

some image of me as a future data-wonk."

"You're a lifesaver, and maybe by extension, so is he."

"Let's not get carried away. Though I have to admit, I was impressed that he was even aware of the database software. Lots of the older professors are real fossils."

"I'll remember you said that." Now Fiona was feeling fossilized. Jennifer just laughed.

It took the two of them several hours, hooking up the scanner and loading the software. Fiona was really impressed with the software flexibility. Once she was used to it, she might enter Wren's letters too. Finally they started feeding in the documents. Fiona sat at the computer, viewing the scans as they were entered, to make sure that they were clear. For each, she'd enter the date on the letter, or the postmark. Later, when she read them, she'd sort by date, and then enter the topics covered. This was really a historian's dream, though she *would* miss the feel of the paper and the visual quality of the handwriting. It was never quite the same, reduced to black and white on a screen. They worked at it all that evening and through most of the next day. Finally, it was all entered, almost four decades of regular correspondence. They took turns at the laptop, searching for time frames, and looking at Emma's neat squared handwriting, flowing in even lines across the screen.

"Well, it sure beats lugging five boxes of documents. Jennifer, this was a great idea."

"Plus you can email us and let us know what's up."

"How would I do that?" Fiona was serious.

"Oh, your hotel will have WiFi, or an internet café will."

"Yet, another thing to check."

Jennifer rolled her eyes. "I don't get *this* level of technical resistance when I help Norm."

"Oh my God, you too? Now he's sending *me* email jokes!"

"It's really impressive how he's taken to it. I think it's a generational *and* gender difference."

Now Fiona shook her head, "This I have to hear."

"Well, the generational difference is pretty well accepted. We've all heard the jokes where if you need technical help, ask an eleven year old. Kids approach computers without fear because they're used to them."

"So where's your gender difference?"

"In older groups, where the individuals have some level of

computer anxiety to start, I think men fare better once they see the computer as a tool for accomplishing some other task. I think they relate to tools more than older women do."

"Interesting hypothesis. I don't know how you'd test it. Besides, there are plenty of middle-aged women who are computer proficient. Look at Amanda."

"Amanda's proficiency isn't innate. She struggles, but takes mastery as a point of pride. Plus, she feels compelled to succeed at it in front of her students."

"You've discussed this with her?"

"Sure, because of Norm. He's her star pupil."

"So if I have trouble with this, I should ask Norm for help?" Fiona joked.

"Soon."

"Does he have database software?"

Jenn gave her a funny look. "No. Inventory tracking software. Like I said, he's really into this."

"Okay, I'm appropriately shamed. I'll send everyone Paris emails." She closed the laptop with a click. "On another, more mundane topic, are you ready for Christmas?"

"Ready as I need to be. My folks will just be glad to see me. My big present to them this year is the scholarship."

"I would guess so."

"It's a relief to me, too, because I could see them sacrificing for this. Then this project comes along, and for the first time one of my interests pans out. I think they're relieved on a number of levels." Jenn smiled, "They don't think I have a long-term future in rowing."

Fiona snorted. "Yeah, I was meaning to talk to you about that."

Jennifer changed gears, "I may have cheated a little on Christmas gifts."

"How so?"

"I took some of the photo images of Emma's paintings and turned them into note cards. Mostly for my sisters but you might want to look at them. I think they're a marketable item."

"Bring them to the dinner, and the group can discuss them. I don't think we'd want them in wide circulation until the exhibit, but maybe after that. Shall I pick you up?"

Jennifer flashed a wide grin, "Sure, but you know you're spoiling me."

Fiona winced, just a little inside. "It's my pleasure."

Chapter Thirty-Three

The day of Marvin's dinner opened with a miserable, cold and windy rain. Amanda called it Bay Area Christmas shopping weather. It was perfect for the solstice, dark on dark. Fiona loved this full-on winter. If you could stay in, the contrast made it perfect to curl up with a good book, or in front of a fire. But tonight they all had to schlep to Marvin's. Fiona was glad she'd offered to pick Jenn up, this was no weather for public transit. Since parking was tight near Marv's, Fiona followed up with an offer to shuttle most of the group. She'd start with Jenn, then swing around to Norm's then Amanda's. Everyone was relieved to simplify the evening.

Fiona spent most of the day packing, or finishing up end-of-year work projects so she could head to Paris the following day with a light heart. Mostly she was ready, but Fiona would check and recheck every detail until she was confident she'd anticipated everything. It *did* keep her from obsessing about Denise.

While Fiona thought of her daughter constantly, she was so busy she never did that sit-in-front-of-the-phone-suffering thing. She'd mailed her gift with plenty of time, even to accommodate their travel plans, and having done so, closed the door on its being Christmas. Yet, she hadn't spoken to Denise since well before Thanksgiving. Underneath it all, Fiona still felt wounded at how Denise had handled Thanksgiving. There was, in its wake, a sort of stunned silence. Fiona wasn't ready to break out of that quiet, but it felt odd to be headed off to Europe, without even having told Denise that she was going. Fiona knew that the larger issue was about Denise making adjustments to married life. Many women make the mistake of shortchanging their other relationships. That was something you had to learn first hand and Fiona knew it was unlikely that she could help in the process. She just hoped Denise was making healthy choices.

The phone rang, interrupting her dilemma. Jennifer wanted Fiona to pick her up early. A tree was down on campus and the power was out. Jenn didn't want to sit around in the dark, with no working clock, waiting for the appointed hour. Fiona was relieved to get underway. She'd loaded the car hours before and had just been sitting around, waiting.

The campus was pitch black. The windshield wipers kept up a steady beat, adding rhythm to the storm. Jennifer found Fiona by her headlights, and climbed into the car, chattering like a magpie. "Really, it's like they'd never had the power go out before! What's with these Californians? A couple of hours without the internet won't kill them." Apparently the dorm scene was bedlam, so Jennifer was thankful to be making her escape to spend the evening with adults. She sat in the front seat, hugging a plastic shopping bag to her chest, babbling about exams, going home, getting to meet Thomas and anything else that flew into her head. Fiona laughed at her jitters. The blackout had her attention, too.

Norm was a little more level-headed. Fiona pulled up as close as possible and Norm dashed out to the car, slipping into the backseat behind her with the agility of a gazelle. Sometimes that man really surprised her. Since they'd met he'd been getting younger. She remembered his frail, small figure in the hospital. He seemed transformed.

"Ladies, it's a wild and woolly storm we're expecting tonight!"

"I haven't been listening to the radio, just Jennifer's tree-down report."

"Severe winter storm warnings, high winds. Jenn, you had a tree down at Mills?"

"Yeah, so there was no power."

"That could happen a lot tonight. Anyone know if Marvin has an electric stove?"

"Gas," Jenn answered, "I helped yesterday with some of the preparations."

Fiona giggled, "I see you have your priorities in order—check the food first."

"Yup, I know what's important. I brought candles too, just in case."

Traffic was terrible getting to Amanda's. The signal lights were swinging wildly in the wind. Holiday banners, hanging from the street light standards, whipped mercilessly in the bluster. To Fiona, it all just added to the excitement of the evening. She hadn't realized how much she was looking forward to this dinner. Amanda was waiting in her apartment foyer. Fiona could see packages in her hands, so she popped the trunk as she pulled to a stop. Amanda saw it and dove between the raindrops to deposit her goods into the back, and then zipped into the back seat behind Jenn.

"Whew, it's nuts out there," she announced, wiping the rain from her face.

"Duh," Fiona snickered. It was true what they say, that at their very core, communications were always about the weather. They pulled up to Marvin's, actually you couldn't miss it. His house had about a million lights on it. *Christmas Central*. This must be where the little kid in Marvin expressed itself. Tasteful, refined Marvin had every holiday gimmick strung-up on the exterior—blinking lights, colored lights, snowflakes, you name it. It looked like a fireworks shop on a street of mortuaries.

Everyone in the car howled at the same time.

"I dunno, do you think Marv likes Christmas?" laughed Amanda.

"Well look at that," noted Norm, "Who'd've thunk it?"

"No power outage here, at least not yet", chimed in Jennifer, "Just wait till he plugs in the blender."

"Yeah, he may take down the whole city." Fiona chuckled. The evening was off to a festive start, and they weren't even in the door.

There was nowhere to park so Fiona pulled up and let the others out. They unloaded the trunk and motioned Fiona off to look for parking. She found a spot down the street, and grabbed her umbrella, which lasted about ten seconds before eviscerating itself in the wind. Fiona just grinned and sprinted up the street in the rain.

Inside was warm and the aroma intoxicating. Strains of Bing Crosby singing *White Christmas* played softly just under the hum of conversation. The others had shed their coats and were talking and laughing. Marvin met her at the door with a glass of white wine and a hand towel to dry herself off.

"Thanks, I needed both of these. What are we drinking?"

"A Vouvray, for starters."

If the outside of Marv's house was a holiday riot, the inside was the opposite. The only Christmas décor was the tree. It was a small noble fir, no more than five feet tall, raised up on a round table. It was decorated simply and elegantly in whites and silver, with a touch of gold in the star at the top. The table was draped generously with a luxuriant fabric. A heavy white and silver damask with subtle arcs of silver woven into its elegant fluid tone-on-tone pattern. The effect was of snowdrifts. Fiona stepped closer to examine the ornaments on the tree. They were flat, hammered, silver squares and rectangles with images worked onto their surfaces. They were primitive, yet simple and beautiful. There must have been fifty of them on the small tree, the only decoration except for strings of tiny white lights, and silver and white satin ropes. The lights reflected off the hammered facets on the ornaments.

"Excuse me, Marv?"

Marvin stepped over from where he was refreshing wine glasses.

"What are these?"

"Ah, aren't they lovely? They're Milagros, miracles. They're religious artifacts from Mexico, Central and South America. Each one represents a wish or prayer, blessed and fulfilled. Some are generic—the sacred heart with flames, and some are specific." He reached out and pointed to one with a leg on it, "Here the parishioner sought help from being lame. So they tell little stories."

"Wherever did you find them?"

"Remember me, antique religious art? I have a couple of connections, one in Peru and one in Mexico."

"So these are all old?"

"Mine are, and all silver. They still make them, but now they're usually silver and tin. These have a history going back to the days of Spanish colonization."

"You sell these in the gallery?"

"A little. I'd like to push them harder, but the partners resist them as tchotchkes. This guy in Peru is collecting and selling them to raise money to restore old churches. I'd like to give him the business."

"I'd like to buy some. We'll talk when I get back. The tree is incredible, and with the explanation, it's even better. A tree like this in *your* gallery could sell these by the hundreds."

Marvin took an exaggerated bow, "We aims to please, ma'am."

They turned and joined the rest of the group. The music shifted. Fiona cocked her head to listen and suddenly recognized the Beach Boys singing Christmas tunes. She giggled convulsively. Marvin caught her eye, noticed her recognition and smiled.

The coffee table was laid with hors d'oeuvres, savory goodies delicately wrapped in prosciutto. These lovely morsels were set up either fan-folded on crackers or rolled, plain, with alternate fillings of caviar, deviled egg or dill pickle. She guessed that Jennifer and Marv had prepped this the day before. The deviled egg had fluted edges and florettes, piped onto the crackers. The caviar spilled out artfully across the tray and Japanese pickled ginger framed the edge. A cheese tray with grapes and sliced fruit graced the sofa table. It dawned on Fiona that she hadn't eaten all day. She took a plate and sampled. The appetizers were as delicious as they were elegantly presented. The deviled egg in particular was intriguing, Fiona could taste the Dijon, but there was another flavor.

"Jennifer, what's in the deviled egg?"

Jenn looked up, smiled and said, "You'll have to talk to Marvin. I don't know if I'm authorized to divulge the secrets of Marv's kitchen."

Amanda guffawed, "Such loyalty! Just *whose* assistant are you?"

Marvin yelled out, "Horseradish," from the kitchen. "There are no secrets among friends."

Norm jumped in on this, "Besides, Jennifer isn't *anyone's* assistant, she's a member of the team."

Fiona looked around, and thanked Emma Caites under her breath. These five friends had come together because of her and had forged new bonds in all directions. She noted the missing invitees. "What about Thomas and his wife, are they coming?"

Marv answered, "Looks like we've got Thomas. He called, but he's coming alone."

Fiona stuck her head in the kitchen, "That's a recurring theme. I wonder if there's an issue." Amanda sidled up next to her.

"What do you mean?" said Marvin, without looking up from what he was doing.

Fiona explained, "I mean there seems to be some antipathy between Thomas's wife and his deceased mother."

"How can that be, doesn't Emma's death pre-date his relationship?"

"Yes, but his office is a shrine to Emma. Paintings, furnishings, I think Thomas segregated his life. He excluded his past from his present and that alienated the women in his life."

"That could work to our advantage, so don't mess with it." Marvin's eyes met hers as he put the last of the garnish on the tray.

"Ooh, that's cold."

"I don't mean financially but sometimes wives get involved and before you know it, they want to hang the show. Almost every straight middle-aged woman I ever knew is a frustrated decorator." Amanda winced at his assessment. He continued, "If you want to make nice, do it at the opening."

"It may not be up to us anyway," Fiona deflected.

"Rarely is," he smiled, handing her the elegantly finished platter.

154

"Marvin?" Now, Norm had a question, "What's this piece over here?" Norm was standing in the living room looking at a low relief bronze hanging on the wall. Fiona joined him.

"It's one of the Stations of the Cross," she replied. "Hey, I didn't do Catholic school for nothing." At that, Amanda came over to look.

"It's the Second Station, Christ Receives the Cross. This is beautifully done." Amanda grinned sheepishly, "I spent a lot of time in high school, doing penance. I really got to know my Way of the Cross."

The piece was in the traditional arch top format, but instead of a literal picture, the space was broken up on the diagonal by the cross image. On second look, you could see Jesus' sinuous shoulder and torso powerfully rendered in the lowest angled notch formed by the crucifix. His face was barely visible in the next notch up, counterclockwise, with the crown of the head completing the image at the top. The piece was simultaneously dynamically abstract but still representational.

Fiona called out, "Marvin, this is a lovely interpretation, is it an antique?"

Marvin came out and stood by the door, wiping his hands with a dishtowel. "This one's not an antique. It's by a Canadian artist, Guylaine Claire. She did a lot of things but earned her bread and butter on Catholica. I liked this piece because it's graphically dynamic and still has the traditional human imagery. The cross really cuts up the space. It's a different view than the tradition, but the sculptural representation of Christ's body, almost hidden behind that bulk of the crucifix is phenomenal." He paused, "So much of the Catholic abstract and modern work has all the charm of a Hallmark card, but this piece has it all." He looked directly at Fiona, "There's a story there, too. Maybe someday we'll get a chance to explore it."

Fiona was puzzled by his comment, but let it go and continued with the discussion of the bronze. "Interesting, as a solo piece, it has that whole, 'one's cross to bear' symbolism yet in the set it reverts to Amanda's Way of the Cross. How did you get just the one?"

"Oddly enough, new items you can buy individually. You just have to know where to shop." Marvin winked, "I know all the best sources."

The doorbell rang. Fiona glanced at Marvin, "I'll get it. Thomas knows me." Marvin nodded, reached across the table, poured a new glass of wine and handed it to Fiona.

Fiona opened the door and greeted Thomas, handing him the glass as soon as he had set down his packages and freed himself of his dripping jacket. "Come on in and meet the crew. Once you shake off the cold, you'll find some savory goodies to start the evening." Wine in hand, Thomas followed her into the living room. Fiona studied the faces of her friends as she made the introductions. Each knew Thomas as a story, a face in a painting, as an extension of Emma Caites. Marvin and Amanda responded about the same, both respectful and direct.

Marvin shook his hand, saying, "I've been an admirer of your mother's work for many years. I understand that you paint as well. It's a pleasure to meet you."

Similarly, Amanda was formal, "Mr. Caites, a pleasure. I can see the resemblance."

But Norm surprised Fiona. Without a word, he stepped up to Thomas and embraced him like a long lost brother. There were tears in both their eyes.

The best response was from Jennifer. She marched forward enthusiastically to take his hand and exclaimed, "You're the boy in the painting. I'd recognize you anywhere. *I* restored you." Then she blushed deeply, "The painting I mean, of course." But having said it, perhaps it was true.

Thomas beamed. "I'd love to see that painting."

"Oh," she said, recovering, "I'd love to show you. We all have so much to share."

Thomas looked around the room warmly and then directly at Fiona. "Thank you so much, thank you all. If I ever had any doubts about this project, they've all just disappeared." Then turning to Marvin, he said, "I understand you have a few of my mother's pieces here. Would you mind giving me a minute to visit them?"

"I'd love to. This way." He ushered Thomas down the hall. On the way, he turned to Jennifer and said quietly, "Hon, drop the oven down to 275, we're going to slow this down just a bit." Jenn nodded and headed into the kitchen. Fiona took the opportunity to grab a towel and wipe up the pools of rainwater she'd noticed draining from the coats and umbrellas in the entry.

Amanda followed her. "He's gorgeous, what a gem, and the spitting image of his mother." She helped Fiona with the cleanup, then they headed to the kitchen to see if they could help out there. Jennifer chased them out, shooing them with her hands, laughing, "It's a surprise, *out, out, out!*"

They retreated to the living room and munched with Norm on the last of the hors d'oeuvres. Amanda stacked the dishes and brought them in to Jennifer, who accepted them and wordlessly handed Amanda another bottle of wine. Amanda circulated, topping-off glasses. Fiona was telling Norm and Amanda about the Milagros when Thomas and Marvin returned. Thomas joined right in.

"Yes," he added, "It's a stunning and sensitive way to display them. I can hardly wait to tell my wife, she'll be so impressed. She's partial to religious antiques, especially primitives."

Without a word, Marvin reached over to the tree and selected one of the Milagros. He extended it to Thomas. "Please give this to her, it's one of my favorites. It symbolizes healing in all of its miraculous ways. When we meet again she must know that she is welcomed by everyone." Wordlessly, Thomas nodded his acceptance, taking the Milagros and thoughtfully fingering its hammered surface.

Marvin bowed, "My friends, if you'll excuse me, I need a moment to set-up for dinner. This is an American solstice dinner, our celebration of friendship and the annual promise of the return of light." Marvin disappeared into the kitchen, with Jennifer in tow.

Amanda giggled. "What has he done to that girl, she's become quite the little sous-chef."

Fiona countered, "Come on, we're just jealous we didn't think of it first. At Thanksgiving we almost ran her out of the kitchen."

Amanda turned to Thomas. "This is a crew of conscripted talent. Fiona has all of us learning art restoration and history. It's been a wonderful adventure."

"I'm sorry I missed the beginning of it. I resisted at first but I assure you, I'm in now. I am so excited about this. Something Fiona said at our last meeting really stuck with me."

Fiona was stumped, "Thomas, what did I say?"

"You suggested that to fully appreciate my mother, I might consider sharing her." Marvin and Jennifer joined them, but did not interrupt. Thomas continued, "I've been talking to my wife more, about my childhood, my mom. I've never done that before. We've been married over fifty years and I've just started sharing all this.

It's been incredibly sweet. I wanted her to come tonight, but she wanted me to be sure first. She's very reserved. Now I'm sorry I didn't insist."

Marvin stepped in, "Next time, you must be sure to bring her." He signaled to Jenn and then announced, "Dinner is ready."

Everyone filed into the dining room. The table was simple and elegant. The only décor was an arc of fresh cut holly, meandering through the center of the table. The guests were seated while Marvin and Jenn delivered two lidded terrines, which they set into open areas in the holly. Jenn lit the candles and dimmed the lights. Marvin reappeared with another terrine of cream of spinach soup. He ladled a serving into each of the bowls stacked at his place, into each of which Jennifer sprinkled grated pecorino cheese before serving. When they finished, Marvin and Jennifer sat down with the others. "Please, everyone, enjoy."

Fiona sipped her soup. It was smooth and rich, an edge of garlic in a full bodied chicken-spinach base. The cheese garnish gave it a perfect salty, ripe finish. Fiona turned to Marvin, "This is incredible." And then to Amanda, "Just amazing, this soup is like poetry. Our work is really cut out for us now." The others laughed.

Norm smiled at Thomas and said, "If this is going to be a competition, I am a happy man." When they finished the soup, Marvin and Jenn got up and cleared the soup dishes. Jenn returned with a steaming dish and Marvin carried in the main entrée, a dramatic crown roast of lamb. It was a stunning presentation. Each of the rib ends was decorated with a parchment collar that tapered up to a delicately cut snowflake. It was airy and elegant. Without a word, the two began serving. Onto each plate, Jennifer spooned a thin bed of cranberry coulis. She held each plate as Marvin carved the roast into individual curved, dainty chops, placing two into each pool of coulis, while Jennifer passed the plates. When the last plate was assembled, Marvin invited them to help themselves from the two lidded terrines.

"We have roasted mashed yams with potatoes and garlic sautéed greens. There is fresh ground pepper and butter to finish."

Fiona opened the terrine next to her. In it she found a rich mixture of orange yams and creamy potatoes, swirled together in the French way. She served herself and then her companions to each side. Marvin took over and spooned out portions for the others. Norm opened the greens and sighed as he was hit with the aroma of sesame oil and roasted garlic. There was near-silence as the guests assembled their plates. Completed, each plate was a feast for the eyes as well. The curved chops nestled into the cranberry, the orange set against the green of the collard and kale mixture. It was beautiful. Jennifer stood and retrieved a bottle of red, a Sterling Merlot, and filled the glasses set at each place.

Amanda couldn't contain herself, "Marvin, it's almost too pretty to eat. *Everything* is perfect."

Marvin raised his glass for a toast. He said, "First, I want to celebrate the best of times with good friends, but I also want to thank Jennifer, who approached me about assisting today because she wanted to show her appreciation to everyone for helping to bring about all the changes in her life, and to credit the woman who, many decades ago, made this all possible, Emma Caites." They touched glasses and started in on the sumptuous meal.

Norm was the first to speak. "Marvin, Jennifer, this is the best meal I've ever tasted. Dear God, Lily, forgive me but it's true, it's perfect. I've never tasted lamb like this, so tender, and what is that herb?"

"Rosemary," Amanda volunteered, "I'm taking lessons, Marv."

"What I want to know," Fiona queried between bites, "Is how did you rehearse this? It was seamless." Fiona thought about working with Jenn and realized one of her gifts was that she anticipated your needs, even before *you* knew it.

"Jennifer was a total partner here," Marvin nodded, "We walked it through verbally but she was always a step ahead." Jennifer blushed again.

"I don't even know how I'll describe this to my wife." Thomas gestured with his fork at the spread before them, "She'll never believe it. We've been to some of the finest restaurants in the world and nothing could touch this."

"I don't even know how I'll tell my mom, said Jenn, "And *I* witnessed every step."

"Is there orange in the coulis?" Fiona closed her eyes and tasted it again. "Mmmm, perfect."

They lapsed into silence as each savored the tastes and textures of the meal. Jennifer topped their glasses, emptying the second bottle of Merlot.

Outside, there was a flash of lightning. Seconds later, thunder crashed and rattled the house.

159

"Fiona, are you ready for tomorrow?"

"Packed yes, I'm not so sure about ready. I hope this storm won't cause problems."

Thomas looked her way, "Are you traveling for the holiday?"

"I am going to Paris. I have your mother's addresses from the twenties, a stack of old correspondence and I'm hoping to trace her footsteps."

"Oh my. I'd love to get your impressions when you return."

"You don't have to wait for her return. She's going to send us email updates, right Fiona?" Fiona sensed just a bit of nagging in Jenn's nudge.

"That's a good idea, Fiona," Amanda added, "That way there'll be a record, in case of any kind of data loss."

"Okay, okay. I'll send summaries to all, and a full transcript to my own email address." She speared her last forkful of lamb, swirled it in the coulis, and popped it in her mouth. She closed her eyes and swallowed, "Amazing. I am going to Paris, and I don't think that all of France could compete with this meal."

Marvin pushed his chair back. "Let's retire to the living room. We have some little gifts to hand out. Then we can consider dessert."

"Oh my God, insult to injury, there's dessert. Fiona, we'll never hold our heads high in a kitchen again." Amanda dropped her head to her chest.

"Not a problem ladies. It just raises the bar. This is my answer to Thanksgiving, which was stunning."

"I can hardly wait," Norm grinned widely.

They stood, and the men headed for the living room. With a nod, Fiona, Amanda and Jennifer began clearing the table and stacking the plates. Marvin protested weakly, but there was no changing this. In just minutes, with the dining room clear, and water on for tea, the women joined them in the living room. Everyone reached for their stashes of gifts for the holiday.

Norm stood and announced, "Since Marvin and I worked together on this, and since they're the same for everyone, we'll go first."

Marvin retreated to the dining room closet, and returned with a stack of wrapped boxes. They were all the same, except the top one, which had a bow on it. Marvin handed that one to Thomas, and distributed the rest. They all busied themselves tearing the paper

160

from the boxes. Inside were beautifully framed giclée copies of the original *Emma Caites Way* painting lessons poster. For Thomas, his frame contained the original. The room filled with oohs and aahs as each one realized what was in the frame. Thomas was stunned.

Norm went over, and gave him another squeeze. "Now I'm glad that all those years ago I lifted that poster from the Laundromat."

"I'm looking forward to sharing this with my wife. Thank you." Thomas held the poster appreciatively, taking in its detail.

Fiona turned to Thomas, "I want you to know, we've decided that this should be the title of the exhibit, 'The Emma Caites Way'."

Marvin stood up, "Wait just a second, Norm and I were playing around with that idea when we did these copies." He stepped out of the room again, and brought back a rolled poster. It was mostly a duplicate of the original, except that the wording was cropped to delete the references to the painting lessons. The banner across the top was now, "The Emma Caites Way." It retained the language about her Parisian training and California background, and the American can-do attitude. Across the bottom where the contact information had been, it read, "An American Painter Rediscovered. Emma Caites. Mills College Gallery - June 22 to August 3, 2008."

Thomas began to cry. Fiona took his hand, "Are you okay? Is it too personal, too brash?"

"I can't believe it's really going to happen. It's so wonderful. All those years of collecting—I never trusted that my mother's work would be appreciated. And here you all love her for the work. It's what she'd have wanted."

Amanda looked up at Marvin, "Whaddya think, a little dessert and tea?" Marvin and Amanda headed to the kitchen to collect the goodies. She came out a minute later with a tray of mugs and a steaming pot of tea. "Well, He's done it again guys, you should see the dessert. He may be trying to kill us all. Bread pudding with bourbon sauce." Amanda poured, and handed out mugs of tea.

Marvin came out with a second tray. From it he served each one a small portion of bread pudding, served warm, the New Orleans way, each in a pool of rich bourbon sauce.

Jennifer shyly handed out neatly wrapped packets. They all gently unwrapped them to find a collection of printed note cards taken from Marvin's photos of Emma's paintings.

"Oh my!" Amanda's eyebrows went up, "There's brilliance in *this* concept."

It was Amanda's and Fiona's turn to distribute gifts, and there were hoots all around as each opened and grasped the personal acknowledgments. Norm put on his beret, and Jennifer danced in her leg warmers and hairclip. Marvin laughed at the pies and cakes t-shirt, for which Amanda apologized because they were out of bread pudding. Marvin was puzzled about the tool bag, until Fiona explained. He immediately pulled out his appraisal gear, and loaded the bag. Everyone roared and joked with every gift. Thomas, now at ease, laughed with them. As the evening ended, he said he had a gift for Norm and he went to the front entry for his package. He pulled out a large wrapped box, which he handed to Norm.

Norm tore away at the wrapping, revealing the box below. He opened it, and his mouth fell open. He was speechless. Finally he looked up with tear-filled eyes, and said, "I remember the photo, it was taken when I got my new bicycle." He turned the framed painting for the others to see. There, in sepia tones, was a lovingly painted portrait, of a young Norman, all of ten or twelve. He was beaming, as he stood proudly holding the handlebars of a bicycle, clearly a year or two too big for him. The painting was signed and dated, 1952. It was painted fifteen or sixteen years after the young boy had posed for the photo, long after they'd lost touch.

Norm turned to Thomas, "I don't know how to thank you. This means so much to me."

Now, it was Thomas's turn to embrace Norm. "It was her way of keeping you in the family. It was one of the few paintings that she kept."

In their silence, the thunder rolled again.

Norm turned, breaking the spell, "This has been quite an evening. I could never have imagined this. It's beyond me. I'm too old for this and I'm exhausted, but I don't want it to end."

As they each reflected on the heartfelt connections of this solstice celebration, Jennifer said, "Yeah, we sure packed a lot into the shortest day of the year." They laughed again, and began to pack up for the stormy ride home.

With Hugs at the door, and good wishes for the holiday, Thomas invited Marvin to bring his new tool bag to inventory Emma's paintings at his house. He said to bring Norm so he could see Emma's car. After the warm blur of leave taking, Fiona skipped down the street in the rain to fetch the car. Back at Marvin's, they loaded up and rode home in exhausted, near silence.

Chapter Thirty-Four

Fiona woke up to the alarm, just a little hung-over. Given all the indulgences, she was lucky it wasn't any worse. Yet the prospect of traveling overseas queasy or with a headache wasn't appealing and Fiona was glad she didn't have to fly until early afternoon. After downing a couple of aspirins, she wrapped up in her robe, and padded about the apartment, sipping her first cup of coffee. The storm had passed, and the early morning sun was sneaking in at oblique angles across the yard. It was still chilly and wisps of fog rose intermittently from the wet pavement. Fiona waited by her upstairs window, cupping her hot coffee mug in cold hands, knowing that in just a few moments the sun would rise to the angle in the painting and illuminate the courtyard with the rosy light that Emma Caites had captured so many years ago. It had recently become her favorite way to bring in the day.

Fiona thought about Marvin's dinner and what a tremendous success it had been. She reflected on the changes in her life, and realized that for the first time, in a very long time, she was happy. Not that she'd been actively unhappy, but that her happiness had, in the past several years, been through or for others, mostly Denise. Today she was setting out on an adventure, and it was something she wanted to discover on her own. Perhaps some of her reticence in calling Denise was an effort to keep the Emma Caites pursuit for herself. That didn't entirely make sense; she'd shared and conscripted so many others in the venture, but she knew that her motives were mixed. She was tired of Denise minimizing or criticizing her endeavors. And yet, what Thomas had said last night really hit home. His life was improving with the sharing of what he loved. After that, she knew that she had to call Denise this morning, before she left. First though, she was going to enjoy her sunrise and her coffee. She took another sip, and at that moment, there it was. She stepped back and took in the painting and then the view, and wondered at a woman who'd enjoyed this same moment enough to paint it as a regular theme.

She drained her cup, poured another, and self-consciously sat down at the phone. With the time difference, she'd be right on schedule to reach Denise. She held her breath, and punched the familiar numbers. On the other end, she heard it ringing and then click over to the machine. Fiona didn't know for sure whether she was disappointed or relieved. When she heard the beep she said, "Hey Denise, I'm so sorry I missed you. You can reach me on my cell till mid-day but after that I'm headed out of the country till the New Year. I'll be checking email if you need to connect." She paused for just a second, and added, "Hey Hon, I hope you have a great holiday. Talk to ya soon." Then she replaced the handset in the cradle. And that was that.

Fiona made a light breakfast, and grabbed the paper from the front steps. She slid it out of its plastic sleeve, but the paper was still a little wet, so she spread it on the table in front of her while she ate her breakfast, and finished her coffee. Fiona checked her watch. There was plenty of time to shower, pack the last few items and call the cab for the ride to the airport. She picked up the cordless phone, and brought it into the bathroom with her, just in case Denise called back.

Finally, she was ready. She called the cab, and carried her bags to the front door. As she set the laptop case down in the entry, she noticed something in the outside pocket. She reached in and pulled out a wrapped package, then shook her head, smiling. It had to be Jennifer. She peeled off the wrapping and opened the box. In it she found a laptop charger/converter for European power. There was also a little notebook into which Jenn had written computer travel tips, tech support numbers and the addresses of computer stores in the Fifth and Sixth Arrondissement. Fiona threw her head back, and laughed. That girl was amazing. She tucked the package back into the side pocket, hoping she'd never need it, but looking forward the Jennifer's notes in any event. The cab honked out front, and finally, she was on her way.

164

Fiona was exhausted. Never capable of sleeping on a flight, she had spent most of the time reviewing her notes, and chuckling over the copious Post-its Jenn had attached to them and to her itinerary. That girl was even more anal than Fiona, and Fiona had to admit, that was a stretch. Fiona could almost hear Amanda's singsong, *"Put a nickel in the therapy jar!"* and laughed aloud at it. With the holidays, and their respective work and exam schedules, neither Fiona nor Jennifer had had time to read the correspondence Emma had written to Wren. At best, as they'd scanned it, they'd sorted by date, and the two of them had gleaned where Emma had lived during her Paris years, from the return addresses on her envelopes. The whole objective of the trip had been for Fiona to walk in Emma's shoes through Paris. Outside of the letters, they had little hope of tracking Emma down in Paris, as they had at Mills. Initial inquiries to the Ecole Des Beaux Arts had revealed that no academic records from the school had survived the war. Moreover, Fiona, with only her high school French, was at a huge disadvantage in Paris. She thought that it wouldn't matter too much, with most of Paris closed during the Christmas break. What little official information might exist was unlikely to be available on this trip. Nor did Fiona expect that she'd be able to locate any of Emma's paintings in France. It would have to be enough to read her story and to simply absorb the atmosphere of her chosen city.

For her hotel, Fiona had settled on the Hotel Angleterre at 44 Rue Jacob. Under its former name, Hotel Jacob, this was the very hotel in which Emma had resided for her first school year in Paris. A glance at the map revealed why—on the corner of Rue Bonaparte and Rue Jacob, the hotel was just up the block from the École Des Beaux Arts. In the Sixth Arrondissement, the area was well served by restaurants, hotels and shops, and just a block, the other way, from the Metro station at St. Germain des Pres. It was within easy walking distance across the Seine, of the Tuileries, the Louvre and Notre Dame. With her limitations, Emma had selected her location to minimize walking, and maximize the availability and attractions of Paris and her school.

Jennifer though, was not so sure. She'd read every online review of the Hotel Angleterre, and was not impressed. Reviewers either loved the hotel, or hated it. Americans in particular were less than impressed. Named for its former position as the English embassy back in the 1780s, the ancient hotel apparently banked on its illustrious past instead of maintaining its current amenities. Ernest Hemingway had stayed there late in 1921, and while that certainly had caché today, it meant nothing at the time of Emma's arrival for the fall semester in 1925. Back then, Hemingway wasn't even *Hemingway* yet. Certainly Emma wouldn't have known any difference in her not-yet-famous predecessors in a then-cheap little hotel in the Sixth. Fiona didn't care. She was adamant that she wanted to be in Emma's hotel, if not her very room. Jenn's Post-its were full of warnings and alternate locations, just in case the hotel was not up to Fiona's standards. Fiona decided *she* could stand any hotel that Emma could stand.

Though arriving whipped at mid-day, Fiona was tempted to ignore all the scientific advice and warnings about jet lag. All she wanted was to catch a quick nap, just a little refresher. But she was stuck—her room was not yet ready when she checked in. So she left her luggage, all but the laptop bag, and headed out for a bite to eat. Immediately around the corner she found a bustling café, Pre aux Clercs, where she ordered a hot chocolate and a croissant to tide her over. The waiter was genial, and despite the press of lunch business, made no comment that she was alone, or that she opened her laptop to read some of Emma's early letters. After a bit, and despite the fact that she felt no pressure at all to vacate her table, Fiona's well behaved American guilt got the best of her. She packed up and decided to walk up Rue Bonaparte, past Emma's old school, the famed École Des Beaux Arts, to the Pont des Arts, then over to the courtyards of the Louvre and the Tuileries gardens.

Fiona was so tired that the world shimmered, just a bit. She felt as though she were strolling through history. Except for the glass pyramid at the Louvre, most of what Fiona saw was old enough that it would have been much like it was when Emma was there. Paris is the city of the well preserved. Local custom and regulation force landowners to maintain their building facades, and as a result, little changes over time. The biggest renovations to Paris since Emma's departure had been from the war. Added to that, the French were famous for re-purposing buildings. Fiona knew that the former Gare D'Orsay, a train station in Emma's time, was now the Musee

D'Orsay, an elegant grand train terminal which they'd remodeled inside into a famous art museum. To the credit of this Parisian fastidious obsession with its past, she was able to see Emma's Paris. Fiona was wrapped in her warmest Bay Area coat, which was barely enough for the crisp, Paris, December afternoon. She searched the Parisian women, whose outer garments did not seem to be any more substantial than her own, yet they did not appear to be bothered by the cold. She pulled her scarf tight and wrapped it an extra loop or two around her neck, buttoning her coat up as high as it would go. She vowed to go shopping for a hat and a decent pair of mittens or gloves.

Though the bones were there, December was not a kind month in which to visit the Tuileries gardens. Fiona could see how spring would bring foliage and flowers to the formal gardens, giving them light and elegance. Even now, though, the area was full of walkers and tourists. The light was fading fast, and the early evening brought the chill, the wind whipping along the river catching Fiona's breath. She crossed back over the Seine at Pont du Carousel, shielding her windward side with her laptop, and headed back up to her hotel on Rue Jacob. She was glad for Jennifer's coaching on the general layout of the area. She was especially relieved that her cold fingers didn't have to wrestle a map. On the way back to the hotel, a light snow began to fall. The snowflakes danced under the street lights. The Parisians picked up their pace, but laughed and pointed at the welcome sign of the season. Fiona was entranced; suddenly it didn't feel quite so cold as she walked back to the hotel, hands dug deep in her pockets, her head tilted back, catching snowflakes on her face.

Chapter Thirty-Six

From: fionahedge@yahoo.com
Subject: Paris First Impressions
Date: December 23, 2007 12:09 PM
To: artantikmarv@sbcglobal.net, ohamandakins@aol.com, norminisstormin@aol.com, jennsullymills@gmail.com, thomascaites@mindspring.com

Okay all. I arrived wiped out. I ignored all your advice, stayed awake the whole flight after staying up all night. I did my first day in Paris positively bleary. Some quick notes, they really have winter here. It's too cold for me, as Marv says, thin California blood. This place is enchanting. Norm, everything is vintage, if not antique. This may explain why everyone thinks the Parisians are snobs. They have a lot to be snobby about. The architecture is incredible and the history, if you're aware of it, surrounds you until you feel small and insignificant. I don't know how the French live day to day with the weight of such beauty. But they do; they know, and they take it in stride as a birthright. Whew.

Location, location, location. Jenn, you were right and wrong about the hotel. It is small. The entry and public areas are lovely and I understand there are about four nice rooms—the ones featured on the website. The courtyard looks as though it must be lovely in summer, but freezing now. One of the other guests, a regular, laughs and says the courtyard is stunning, and essential in summer, since the building has no air conditioning. My room is not a featured room. It is small, clean and near to threadbare. Thank God it's clean, coming in tired that would have been the one flaw to turn my head. The furnishings are early Goodwill. They can only get away with this (and the prices) because of where they are. The Louvre, Notre Dame, Musee D'Orsay. All within easy walking distance. I understand that it's true that Hemingway stayed here, but well before he had a name and could afford better. Apparently, in the interests of preserving all that history, they've decided not to upgrade. It's not what I would have picked as a luxury vacation, but it really puts me in mind of our young Emma. Her school is just down the street. Most of the art students have vacated for the holiday, but there are a few stragglers. Nothing has changed since my brief days in art school, intense young men with poor posture, shabby clothes and permanent cigarettes. I think the coffee cups have been glued into their hands. There couldn't have been an easier landing spot for a young woman trying to keep convenience up, costs and mileage down.

I've been reading Emma's early Paris letters to Wren. I feel as though we have arrived at the same time, to explore the same city. Paris, with its ample history and architecture conceal the fact that that exploration is separated by over eighty years! While Emma could have afforded better, I am learning that she is a very frugal girl. She also wanted to blend. In one of her first letters to Wren she recounts a mistake she made initially at Mills. In their painting class, Mills students were required to show framed paintings for class critique. Emma rummaged in the basement of her grandfather's home to find some available frames, which she used for the critique. Unfortunately for her, they were Newcomb Macklin frames, a fact not lost on her classmates. She was teased mercilessly thereafter, and the professor noted, with an edge, that it was good for her that the quality of the work displayed was adequate to the frame. Emma never again made the mistake of an inadvertent display of wealth.

In her letters, Emma points out that in the interest of blending, she is able to hide behind her well honed Parisian French. Her tutor during her body-cast days was Parisian, and had drummed pronunciation into the poor captive student. Now Emma is thankful for what, at the time, seemed like needless torture. She registers and handles her early class assignments without any apparent notice that she is not French, even Parisian. That same tutor had recommended Hotel Jacob when she learned that Emma would be attending Beaux Arts, another blessing, since she can walk to school without too much difficulty. Emma notes that while the

169

students here are from everywhere, she prefers, at least initially, to stick with the French. "The Americans," she writes, "Are brash, loud and separate. They make no effort to speak French and complain constantly about the foreign food!"

Emma is a little older than many of the other students. Unlike most of her classmates, Emma already has a degree in art. She is here to hone her skills, but, as we've seen, she has her own style and is comfortable with her world-view in art. This leads to some frustration in the classes, which not only start with the basics, but do so with an annoying level of "French Salon Snobbery." Emma tells Wren, "It's as though they (her professors) are locked into a historical view of art, mindless of the incredible changes over the past forty years, changes largely originating in France! They treat us like children." In her discussions with Wren you can hear Emma's voice. In one typical rant Emma reminds herself (and Wren), that "this is the school that rejected Cezanne!" But then concedes, "It was also the training ground of Monet, Renoir, Seurat, Sisley and Degas. So," she tells her friend, "I hold my tongue and do the exercises."

Even in that she is careful. "Women in art and in art schools is a recent phenomenon. The École has only admitted women since 1897. This was not too much of a difficulty at Mills, our all-female institution. However, here," she confides to Wren that she, "dares not excel too flamboyantly." Already I see shades of the Emma we know, the one who avoids attention and acclaim. She complains, "There is an institutional paternalism that grates on me; life drawing classes and anatomy classes exclude female students entirely. In an academy tied to classical study and imitation, exclusion from life drawing is the "mark of Cain" to future success." Quietly Emma and some of the other women organize independent study groups for the women, who hire their own models (or pose for each other) and push on regardless of the limitations of the day.

Emma also objected to being measured in an artistic world that strove for the elimination of medium from finished product. "The classical training of antiquities emphasizes the 'licked finish,' the deliberate, careful obliteration of brushstrokes and painterly expression." Emma missed the easy loose and rolling relationship with paint and with the landscape that characterized the plein air approach of her California home. "Parisians" she notes "simply lack the physical space to have perspective on landscape. It's no wonder that this urban environment leans towards a classical approach, as they so rarely have the ability to step back from their world enough to see it." She thinks it's a wonder that the impressionists arose out of France, and comments that most of them had to leave Paris initially to explore those early experiments in light and form.

I am constantly impressed by Emma's artistic presence in her letters. She is not only well informed of the then-current art trends, she demonstrates the depth of that understanding by comparing the cultural differences between the raw and new panoramas presented by an undeveloped California and the refined, developed and controlled environment of urban Paris. And then, in a particularly charming voice, she can jump to detailed descriptions of the totally mundane aspects of Parisian housekeeping and life. In one early letter she laughs that nothing has changed since Degas' views of women and bathing or women and laundry. Her own domestic affairs are almost as difficult, doing laundry in the tiny sink at the hotel. She boasts to Wren, "I've purchased two tinned laundry tubs, which I use both for occasional sponge bathing and washing out my personal effects. The Parisians," she jokes, "Are not above frequenting the floating baths and laundries along the Seine, but I am missing my grandmother's tidy home in the Oakland hills and the regular hot baths, made easy by household staff."

I am searching her letters for hints of where she ate, cafés and landmarks I can visit. Through her words I am seeing her Paris and the contrast to the sophisticated bustling metropolis of today.

I laugh though, to catch a whiff of perfume as I walk down the street, after one of Emma's diatribes about the French and their penchant to perfume over, and in lieu of, basic cleanliness. That's it for my first day in Paris. I'm beat.

Fiona

Chapter Thirty-Seven

Fiona woke early the next morning. In the dark of her hotel room, it took a few minutes to summon up where she was. As she sat in bed she set about to plan the day. She was torn. On the one hand, she needed to put in some time with Emma's letters, time that would guide and inform her sojourn. On the other hand, here she was, in Paris, with the clock ticking. It was Christmas eve-day. And she needed gloves.

She decided that if she could, she would poke around Emma's old school, even if just to catch its flavor. Since she needed to shop for warmer gear, she considered Galleries Lafayette or Au Printemps. Fiona remembered some reference to Galleries Lafayette in one of Wren's letters, so it was a tie to both a past in Emma's day, and hopefully for her, a warmer future. Fiona had no idea if the French engaged in the same pre-Christmas consumer frenzy as the Americans, but resolved that in any event, shopping on this day should be done early. She also wanted to keep track of walking distances, and was eager to check how far it was to Notre Dame.

Fiona got up out of bed, and threw back the curtains. It was bright white outside! There was a coverlet of soft fresh snow, not deep, only an inch or two, but evenly covering the courtyard outside. Fiona took a couple of snapshots of the courtyard, which in cold winter weather had not been so inviting, but with the snow, became picturesque. So she wouldn't forget it, Fiona slipped the camera into the pocket of her coat. She checked her watch, it was very early yet. She showered, dressed and settled in with Emma's letters until the Hotel's continental breakfast arrived. Fiona could easily skip a more substantial breakfast, but *wasn't* going out in the world without coffee.

Emma's letters were full of the details of everyday. She noted the personalities of her instructors, chafed at the banality of the assignments, discussed the details of finding cheap cafes and places to do laundry. Students were expected to produce work in addition to their actual class assignments, but were given no studio space in which to work. Many students rented little walk-up studios, dreary unheated little spaces in which to work and sometimes live. Always, despite how squalid the studio, students would exclaim that *their* studio had the most incredible light. Many windows though, translated directly to cold and drafty.

While her hotel was not fancy, Emma had hot water and a shower. Soon, she found that she was able to exchange bathing privileges for limited studio space. Her letters were full of funny stories of smuggling art students in to bathe, as she was sure the hotel management would not appreciate her entrepreneurial spirit. She joked that in lieu of a reputation as a starving student sharing a shower, she would earn one far less savory for sneaking them in to her room.

In nice weather students would gather in the parks and public spaces to paint *en plein aire*. This was not officially encouraged, since the school preferred they spend their unscheduled time at the Louvre, copying old Masters. Nonetheless, the students were young, and followed the call of sunshine and fresh air. Emma was making friends.

Fiona looked up at the knock. Her breakfast had been delivered. She put the tray on the little table by the window where she was reading the letters on the computer screen. While she ate, she signed on to the net for a map to the department stores on Boulevard Haussmann, and made some notes in her little wire bound notebook. It looked to be just over two miles, perhaps a challenge for Emma, but Fiona decided she could use a stretch after the flight. She closed up the laptop, and put it in its carrying case. The coffee smelled so good, Fiona decided to forego her usual cream, and was not disappointed. She was enjoying the careful attention to detail, the exquisite little thermos carafe that the coffee came in, the side order of freshly cut fruit and the delicate, airy texture of the croissant. Jenn had been right, the room was a disappointment, but the service was not. Finishing, Fiona put her tray outside, then donned her coat and scarf. She decided to bring the laptop, so she could continue her reading when she stopped for a break. She slung its case over her shoulder. She chuckled that it made such a good wind break.

Fiona set out for the shopping district. It was cold, but the air was still, so, at a walk she was comfortable. She took the route from last night, over the Pont du Carrousel and diagonally through the Tuileries. This early in the day, the Parisians were out with their dogs, frolicking in the snow. Fiona stopped to take a picture of a black and white spotted dog in the snow, surrounded by the black and gray footprints of dozens of other dogs. She turned right at the

Place de la Concorde, noting that the gilded peak on the obelisk would make it an easy landmark for finding her way back. Just beyond that was the Madeleine, the Greek style temple dedicated to Mary Magdalene. Fiona stopped to reflect on the imposing structure. It's not that she didn't like it, but it seemed an odd fit, such an imposing and masculine structure, to house the softer and more feminine charms of Mary Magdalene. Fiona knew that Madeleine, as she was known in France, had a better and more spiritual reputation here than in the States, where she was considered a repentant whore. But this building, somehow, did not fit either image. She snapped a quick shot, headed north on Rue Tronchet, and made the right on Boulevard Haussmann towards the Opera Garnier. By now the shops were beginning to open, and the French merchants were out, sweeping the snow off the sidewalks to the curb. They yelled out in greeting to one another, exclaiming and gesticulating about the snow. Fiona's weak French could catch the gist, not the specifics, but it was all in great fun. Clearly the shopkeepers enjoyed the minor inconvenience.

She decided to breeze through the first of the two major stores, Au Printemps, and then zip over to the other, Galleries Lafayette. Au Printemps had an impressive exterior, with twin rounded corner turrets in the grand Belle Époque style. It was early, and she was one of the first customers of the day. Inside, Fiona was a little disappointed. It was a department store, not so different from any upscale store back home. She laughed at her expectations. Did she somehow think that the French were an exotic species that would only have exotic stores where they purchased their scarves and mittens? She found the accessories department, with hats, scarves and gloves. The onset of winter weather and the gifting season had laid low their stock. There was little selection. The saleswoman tried to direct her to the gloves in a glass case, but they were expensive and too stylish for what Fiona had in mind.

She proceeded to the Galleries Lafayette. She wasn't in the store two minutes when she found the exotic she had desired. Looking up, there it was, towering many stories above her, the ceiling was a splendid stained glass and steel dome. Above, near the dome, tiered gilded balconies scalloped towards the light, a ring of intensely colored arch-topped windows. From there the dome was segmented by its structural steel supports, with the color saturated stained glass elements weaving through the open spaces between the ribs. The areas between the lacework were pieced with clear glass, except at the top where the supports came together at the top of the dome. There, the clear squares gave way to softly colored blues, growing more intense, and weaving in rondels with intense colors around the central core of the dome. Fiona was spellbound. She placed her hand on a display case to steady herself, her head thrown way back and her mouth open. Long live the industrial revolution! The French had taken the then-new technologies of steel engineering and built Palaces of Commerce. Fiona regained her composure and stood up straight. The saleswoman behind the counter was smiling. In lightly accented English she asked, "First time?"

"Oh, yes," answered Fiona, "It's so beautiful."

"Oui, Merci."

Fiona looked around to get her bearings. Finally she saw a directory that could guide her.

"Thank you," she said to the saleswoman, as she stepped over to the sign. Out of the corner of her eye she saw the saleswoman, still smiling, reach beneath the counter for a cloth, and deftly polish away Fiona's handprint on the glass, as though this happened all the time.

With some initial trouble in translation, Fiona finally located the accessories department. Like Au Printemps, stock was low, but Fiona spied some matching sets of knitted scarves, hats and gloves. The hats were the traditional cloche style, with a subtle rolled edge at the bottom. She reached out to touch one of the sets, in a soft deep burgundy, and noticed the knit had an unfamiliar heft. Fiona flipped the tag—they were made of Merino laine, wool. The price was higher than she expected, but so was the quality. The saleswoman approached, speaking quickly in French. Fiona, not understanding a word, looked blankly at the clerk. She fingered her own acrylic scarf. *Schmatta.* Most Californians never invested in quality, winter accessories.

"Is very fine, ce, fait du laine... wool, very warm." The saleswoman was doing her best.

"Yes, I see. I'll take it. Je veut l'acheter."

The saleswoman beamed back at Fiona, took her hand, and led her to the register. Right there, on the rack next to the register, was a coat that made Fiona drool. It was knee length, in a loden green, boiled wool. It was very tailored with an attached half cape, which Fiona figured must work as a sort of rain fly. There was a generous

176

collar that could be folded flat and high up on the neck for better coverage. Below the bottom of the cape feature, the coat belted with the same fabric held by a dark bronze buckle, and then the body of the coat flowed down in a full A-line for an easy stride. On the back was a short kick pleat, with a reinforced triangle appliqué at the top. There were matching, working belt trims on the sleeve ends, with matching smaller buckles, so you could cinch the sleeves tight against the elements. The buttons were the same dark bronze, with just the simplest, small reveal at the edge. Everything was finished with topstitched flat fell seams, so the coat looked trim and neat. Only its fullness and the cinched belt at the waist kept it feminine. Fiona wondered if the weight of the boiled wool would make it too bulky on. She felt the fabric. It had an incredible hand, tightly woven against the wind, but pliant. She crushed it in her fist, and let go. Not a wrinkle, the fabric fell away as it had been. The saleswoman watched and nodded her approval at Fiona's selection.

Fiona unbuttoned the coat on the rack. It had a zip-in liner for added warmth, and a separate front zipper, just inside the line of buttons.

Without a word, the saleswoman's fingers ran through the coats on the rack, and selected one, which she slipped from the rack and held it open for Fiona to try on. It slipped on smoothly and fit perfectly. Fiona did up the buttons, buckled the belt and stepped in front of the mirror. It was stunning. The clerk nodded her approval. Fiona reached for the tag inside the sleeve. The coat was "on sale", but even then, the number looked amazingly high. She quickly calculated the currency conversion, over eight hundred dollars, *on sale*, but it didn't matter. Fiona knew she was going to buy it. A little voice in her head said, "That could be four paintings," but she quickly silenced it. The saleswoman then picked up the scarf set, and held the deep burgundy against the loden green. She nodded again. She was right, the complementary contrast was perfect. Fiona nodded back. She unbuttoned and slipped out of the coat. The saleswoman motioned for another clerk to come assist with finalizing the sale.

Fiona turned to her, took her hand, and said, "Merci."

"No, madam, I thank you. A pleasure..." she hesitated, then added haltingly, "And almost without words."

They both laughed. The saleswoman reached out and gave Fiona a quick hug. "You are beautiful in it."

Fiona followed the junior clerk to the register. There, the cashier ran the credit card, and while waiting for the approval, she took the coat and began to fold it, to wrap and bag it.

"I'd like to wear it," Fiona said, then wincing, "Je veut le porter." High school was so long ago.

The cashier just looked at her blankly. To help explain, Fiona tried to hand the clerk her old coat.

"No madame, Il n'ya pas d'exchange."

"No, no, I just want to wear the new coat." The cashier pushed her old coat back to her. Fiona, remembering to take her camera out of the pocket of the old coat, had an idea. She said slowly, "Savez-vous ou je peut donner mon manteau aux pauvres?" She held out the old coat and said, "I'd like to give this for the poor and I want to wear the new coat."

The cashier looked confused and offended. Fiona was mortified, "No, not you. I didn't mean you, for the *poor*." Fiona reached for her new coat but the cashier, determined to bag that coat, would *not* let go. Fiona tugged at the coat, again, but with no luck. She then tried, once more, pushing the old coat across the counter. The cashier still would not let go. The credit authorization now came through, and the machine spat out the receipt for Fiona to sign. The cashier just stared at it, refusing to surrender her grip on the coat. She nodded at the old coat, "Les Galleries Lafayette ne prennent pas des vielles vêtements."

"Not for the *store*, for the *poor*, les pauvres."

"Les pauvres ne sont pas ici."

Right, I get it, thought Fiona, the poor aren't here. "Mais, ou est-ce que je puis donner mon manteau aux pauvres?" Fiona was wishing she'd never mentioned the damn poor but she had just wanted to know where she could go to make such a donation.

"Pas ici," spat the clerk through clenched teeth. Fiona recoiled. The clerk saw Fiona's grip momentarily loosen, and jerked the new coat clear, rolled it quickly in tissue, and stuffed it in a large bag. She *threw* the knitted accessories on top and before Fiona could even react, tore the receipt from the machine, and shoved it in front of her on the counter. Fiona sighed, and signed the slip. Meanwhile, the cashier was *stapling* the bag shut. Fiona began laughing. This was ridiculous. All she wanted was to wear the new coat.

To Fiona's surprise, another customer stepped in and began rattling away in such rapid French that Fiona couldn't understand a word. One thing *was* clear; the cashier was taking it in the ear. Heads turned towards the raised voices. A supervisor arrived and listened to Fiona's rescuer. He thanked her, looked at the signed receipt and shook his head—the day before Christmas; *this* was not good for business.

The helpful customer turned to Fiona. "I am so sorry, there is no excuse. It is only because you are American that she does this. I will gladly take your old one to my church so we can find someone who needs a warm coat." Fiona thankfully gratefully handed over her old coat. "Merci, merci," Fiona was so relieved that someone finally understood her. She leaned over to take the bag with the new coat, while the supervisor was yelling at the petulant clerk. He then gently took the bag from Fiona's hands. Now Fiona was confused. She'd just given the old coat away, and now the supervisor was taking her *new* coat. She gripped the bag, and held. He quickly let go of the shopping bag and ripped up the store copy of the slip, showing Fiona that the sale was cancelled. He turned to the cashier and yelled again.

"But I *want* the coat," said Fiona. Any pretext of trying her French was gone. She whirled around, reassured to see that her rescuer had not left. Fiona was in fear of losing the transaction, and ending up with no coat at all.

The woman was now laughing. "He wants to give you a discount. They want to run the sale again."

Suddenly the scene made sense. Fiona said, "No, no, that's not necessary. I just want my new coat." But the manager persisted, directing the now surly clerk to rerun the transaction. Beet-red with embarrassment, Fiona wanted to flee, but she *wasn't* going to leave without a coat. By then a small crowd was watching the fuss. The supervisor soon presented a new slip for her to sign. Without even looking, she signed and grabbed the bag. "Merci, Bonjour." She shook his hand forcefully, smiling painfully at the assembled crowd. Again, she nodded to the manager, who handed her the receipts. She shoved them into the pocket of her trousers, turned, and fled. Her rescuer followed, barely able to contain her giggles.

In the vestibule, Fiona ripped open the bag and retrieved her new coat. She slipped into it, just at the woman caught up with her.

"It's okay, you didn't do anything wrong." The woman was laughing so hard, that Fiona could barely understand what she was saying.

"I am so embarrassed. I didn't know what was going on there at all. My French is not so good, they talked so fast. Thank you for helping me."

The woman held up the old coat. "Thank you for a gift to one of our parishioners."

Fiona finished buttoning and buckling, pulled her laptop case over her shoulder and looked up at her companion.

"It's a fine coat, you look lovely," said her new friend, "I can see why you fought so hard for it." She threw her head back, and roared. Fiona began to see the humor. They stepped outside.

"It was very nice that you wanted to pass on the old coat, it's a good coat. With this weather," she waved her arms at the snow, "somebody will be very lucky." She paused, "I am the parish secretary for St. Augustin's."

"Thank you. And thank God your English is so good."

"So, are you here for the holiday with your family?"

"No, I'm alone, doing research."

"Alone, on Christmas? Come tonight to midnight mass, it is very beautiful. I will sit with you. We have music and a choir of angels. We're not a famous church but it is a lovely service. Many Americans come, just to see it."

"Midnight mass?" Fiona, the former Catholic, was amazed to even consider it.

"Yes. Come down a little early, so you can see these store lights in the dark, then walk to the church. I will meet you. You will enjoy it and I will enjoy having you as my guest. I can hardly wait to tell everyone about this funny scene today!"

Fiona wrapped her new scarf around her neck. "Okay, I'll come. I'll see you at midnight at, what was it, St. Augustin?"

"Oui, at Boulevard Malesherbes." The parish secretary embraced her, and set off into the day. Fiona shook her head. She was going to midnight mass, and she forgot to get the woman's name! She needed coffee. Fiona set off down the road, determined to stop at the first café.

But then, heading south, she saw the Opera Garnier. If ever a building suited its original intended use, this one did. The Paris Opera was a grand event in itself, a triumph of arches, friezes and columns, of gilded sculptures and a huge patinaed-copper dome. It was a celebration of drama, a testament to overdone. Fiona took out her camera, and tried to capture the force and lyrical nature of the

180

grand building. There wasn't enough room to back up and give the Opera the space it needed in the photo. She crossed the street, and had to take the photo with busy holiday traffic whizzing by. She wondered what Emma Caites would think of the Opera. Emma seemed more direct, with less artifice. Yet, opera was nothing but lovely artifice, so the housing seemed fitting. She walked on by the building, stopping at each new angle to try again to shoehorn that vaulting edifice into a tiny, rectangular photo. Pausing, Fiona realized she was exhausted. She also realized that she needed to find a home-base. Her room was comfortable enough, but it wasn't what she needed. Fiona was a territorial person, and needed some public space that could be her touchstone. She decided to return to the Sixth and find a café, maybe Pres des Clercs, where she could dig in for a bit.

She was grateful, and occasionally exultant, in her new coat. Heading south to her adopted turf in Saint Germain des Pres, she was warm and comfortable. The wind had picked up some, but in her now zipped, buttoned and buckled state, swaddled in Merino accessories, the weather couldn't touch her. Every now and then she'd slip her hand out of one glove to feel the supple fabric of the coat. Fiona took Rue de L'Opera down to the Louvre and cut through the courtyard there, past that greenhouse pyramid to the Pont des Arts and back over to the left bank. Starting down Rue Bonaparte, she thought she'd poke around the École, but realized she'd run out of steam for adventure. On her way back to the hotel, she happened on another café, La Palette, right at the corner of Rue Bonaparte and Rue Jacob. She slipped in, and found a table near the back where it was warm. Now seated, Fiona realized that she was starving. The waiter soon brought a menu and she stared at it uncomprehending. She was too tired, hungry and rattled to understand any French at all.

At the table next to her, a couple was sharing a large warm tart with onions and cheese. That was it. When the waiter returned, Fiona pointed at the tart and nodded enthusiastically. He laughed, recognizing the failure of language. Another tourist pushed beyond the brink.

"A boire?" he said, staying in character, and that was what she needed.

She searched her French vocabulary, "Vin, blanc. Et des fruits, peut-etre une pomme?" He smiled widely. In minutes he delivered a piping-hot cheese and leek tart, with sliced apples, grapes and a glass of white wine. Fiona bowed her head to him in silent gratitude. She pulled out her laptop, and resumed reading Emma's letters while she savored her lunch.

She paused and remembered the morning's drama. She hated that helpless feeling. She hated not knowing what to do, not understanding the territory or the language. And yet, it seemed to work out. She remembered that first day in Norm's shop, and chuckled. Surely in a day or so, she'd be laughing at the coat fiasco, but for now she wouldn't report on it. Just like the last time though, she'd prevailed with the goods. First, the Emma Caites painting and now, the coat. She reached into her trouser pocket, where she'd shoved the receipts while dressing in the vestibule of the Galleries Lafayette. There, on the unsigned copy, was the total. She did the conversion. The manager had cut two hundred dollars off the total purchase price. Fiona was stunned. She hadn't even thanked him properly. She pictured the scene, and then she laughed out loud. Fiona reached for the grape shears to clip the tags from her new coat. Yet another story, *if* she could ever get up the nerve to tell it. She shook her head, and returned to Emma's letters.

Fiona looked up to see that Business had slowed some. The waiter had cleared her dishes and given her a cup of that dark, delicious Parisian coffee. The tables had changed over several times, as Fiona relaxed into the rhythms of the café, and just kept reading. Finally, when the light began to fade, she closed the laptop and finished the last drops of coffee. If she was going to attend midnight mass, she would definitely need a nap. Her sense-of-time was off, and she was yawning at the table. As she stood to pay her bill, she realized how comfortable she was in this café and decided she'd found it, her home-base. She was relieved that the waiter hadn't even blinked, though she'd been at her table for almost three hours. She tipped generously, and headed back to Hotel Angleterre for a rest before Christmas Eve.

182

Chapter Thirty-Eight

Fiona awoke with a start, for the second time that day. This time the telephone was ringing. She picked it up, but there was silence, then a click. It was the hotel, with her post-nap wake-up call. She groaned and rolled over to get up. *Jet lag.* She lay there for a few minutes, ruminating with all she'd learned about Emma today. She was pleased, and relieved, that she really liked the young woman whose words shone through the decades in those letters. Fiona had worried how she'd handle it if she hadn't liked Emma. Now, she could let that fear go. Emma wasn't perfect, but she was uniquely herself. In her mid twenties she had more confidence about her art, and her perspective on art, than Fiona did now, on almost *any* topic. And yet she was delightfully flawed. She was a quality snob and tried to conceal it, so in some ways Paris suited her. But she missed the earthy appreciation of raw talent that characterized so much of the Bay Area art scene. Fiona liked reading Emma's constant debates about classical training, guild training, and their impact on, or erosion of, talent. Through the ages, art students remained melodramatically serious.

Fiona got up and dressed to go out. She wanted to be a little dressier for the evening. As the guest of the parish secretary, she didn't want to go American and wear jeans. She'd brought some heavy lined wool trousers in almost the same burgundy as her new accessories, which, with the new coat, would be dressy and warm. She headed back to Le Palette for a light supper before she left for Mass. The snow had stopped and it was really crisp. Though she was warm in her new winter gear, where her face was exposed, she could feel the nip. Le Pallette was quiet this evening, only half full of holiday stragglers. The waiter recognized her, and set her up at a small table near the furnace grate. As he led her to the table he remarked, in English, "Great coat." Fiona blushed. She ordered onion soup and the house salad. Earlier that afternoon she'd seen that the onion soup was a hearty affair, topped with French bread and melted Gruyere, the perfect combination to fuel a chilly night out. The waiter served the soup along with a glass of red wine, which she hadn't ordered. She tried to correct him, but he explained, in English, that the soup and the wine were very good together, and it *was* Christmas. Fiona nodded her appreciation and sipped the wine. One could really learn to love a country like this.

When Fiona had nearly finished her meal, she asked the waiter to call a taxi, feeling it was too far and too dark to walk all the way again. Partly it was a security concern, but also, she didn't see the point of walking at night when you couldn't actually see Paris. The taxi arrived just as she'd paid her tab. She directed the driver to take her to Galleries Lafayette. Even before they arrived on Boulevard Haussmann, Fiona understood why everyone said you had to see the Christmas lights in Paris.

She paid the driver, and stepped into a world transformed into a beautiful, almost surreal landscape of illumination. Many of the stores had individual light displays, which alone were incredible. Adding to that, most were awash with color—gelled floodlights as intense and saturated as theater lighting. Au Printemps, with its rounded lines and turrets, was illuminated in an intense raspberry glow. Tiny lights followed its contours, emphasizing its timeless architecture. Down from it, Galleries Lafayette was bathed in an amber glow. One immediately conjured images of Degas' ballet and his dramatic theatrical luminescence. Up and down the streets, the entire façade was a spectrum of saturation. Above the entrance to Galleries Lafayette was an iron grill structure, shaped much like the rose widow at Notre Dame, into which small colored lights were woven. The effect was stunning; the entire area above the awning became an illuminated stained glass window, tying it to the dome inside. None of the lights blinked, flashed or danced, no music was piped to the sidewalk. This display was elegantly restrained and beautiful. But then, there were the window displays. All along the inner edge, ramps had been installed so children could see up close into the store windows. The light show and building washes had been graceful, artistic displays, but the store windows were magical mechanical enchanted dioramas. Christmas villages, with working parts, fantasy scenes with benevolent creatures, favorite characters from fairy tales—all were mechanically acting out the scenes of French childhood lore. Stores were now closed but couples and families strolled the sidewalks, working off Christmas Eve dinner and reminiscing. The glass was smudged from the enthusiastic noses of little children, pressing closer to the dream. The total effect was both sophisticated and sweet. That this was how the City of Light celebrated Christmas, and it made perfect sense to Fiona. She ambled aimlessly awhile longer, taking in the light and the people. It was very late but there were still many little ones out with their parents, soaking in the glow. Most were mesmerized—despite the hour, few of the children fussed. Fiona checked her watch, and turned west down Haussmann towards the church. It wasn't far, and with the crunch of the remaining snow under her feet, Fiona found the walk almost romantic. She was not alone on the street. Many were now leaving the illuminated shopping district, and winding their way to the quieter square and finally the church. Fiona made the right at Place Augustin, and the church greeted her across the open square.

St. Augustin's was an almost hectic blend of vaulting steel architecture meeting and blending Roman and Byzantine features, rounded cupola-topped turrets and a tall gothic body, with Roman arches gracing the front. There were niches with sculptures of the apostles. Without its height, the church would have been too busy to carry the gravity of its purpose. Within that soaring, gothic height, the church found its solemnity. Above the door was another rose window, illuminated from within. Fiona couldn't help but notice the similarity to the lighted grill at the department store, and chuckle at the meeting of sacred and profane in those imitations. Fiona followed the illuminated rose window to the front of the church, searching to find her own department store angel. She was there, to the left of the entry, searching the crowd for Fiona.

She stepped up to the door, and her friend called out, "Nice coat!" Fiona laughed. They filed in together, and Fiona followed her to their seats. They were right up front, on the left in front of the altar, and close to one of the big organs. The main altar was positioned below a huge dome. Inside, you felt so small, that there *had* to be a God.

They sat, and her friend turned to her, "I'm sorry, I didn't give you my name. I am Jeanne-Marie Baptiste."

"I'm Fiona Hedge. Please, call me Fiona."

"Fiona, you are famous today. Everyone loves the story of your coat. It is a story that is French and American at the same time. "

"I am only now beginning to appreciate it. I was too stunned at the time."

"Fiona, what kind of research brings you to work through your holidays in Paris?"

"I am researching the life of an American artist who came to study in Paris during the 1920s."

"So, you are a student?"

"No, I am an accountant."

"You are an accountant, researching an artist?"

"Yes, I guess that seems odd. I am doing the research on my own."

"What will you do with it? I don't understand."

"I'm hoping to write a book. So far I know that my research has inspired her American university to exhibit her work. Even just that has been very satisfying.

Excuse me, but the French would never understand this, it is so American. I lived in New York for several years so I understand this a little. Everywhere in America there are waiters who want to be actors, plumbers who paint on the weekends, lawyers who want to be writers. Everyone does everything. This is not the French way. Our waiters are content to be waiters."

"And my experience is that they are very good at it."

"Yes. Thank you. But it is a curious thing, this American *cross-training.*"

"That's interesting, because it is something that my painter noticed, even in the 1920s. About the difference in cultures."

"Really? I would like to know more about your painter."

"Jeanne-Marie, when I'm done, I'll send you the book."

"Oh good, then I can share it with the same people who know about the coat. They will be intrigued by an accountant *and* writer who focuses on art-biography," she laughed, "This is so *very* American." Fiona chuckled at that. The organ started up and the choir filed into their station.

Fiona recognized some of the melodies but didn't know the words to the songs, she didn't have to—it was like enjoying opera, or instrumental music. The organ was incredible. In dramatic moments, the pews shook with its presence. The choir filled in the tiny spaces, truly like angels. Lilting and soaring, as one voice, the organist and the choir were a duet, playing off each other in timing and tone. The eighty feet of open space below the dome made the music echo and added depth to the sound, like shadows in a painting. Fiona was spellbound.

Jeanne-Marie, seeing Fiona's face, reached over and touched her arm. Their eyes met, and Jeanne-Marie nodded. She leaned over and said, "It's wonderful to share this, it makes me see it more." Fiona nodded.

She looked around the church. There were the Stations of the Cross, positioned along the sides of the central nave. A Catholic all her life, she'd never given much thought to them until Marvin's dinner. Amanda's reference to the Way of the Cross reminded her that there was a whole meditation of worship based entirely on the Steps of the Stations. There was a depth to it that resonated here in the old church. St. Augustin's was large enough to have side chapels, and Fiona knew that they often had their own set of Stations. There were candles and flowers everywhere. This church was decked out for Jesus' birthday party. The priest stepped forward, dressed for high mass in embroidered silk and damask robes, and began intoning the Mass. Again, the experience was out of step with Fiona's experience, as it was entirely in French. She stood and sat and knelt in concert with the others, on cue. Yet tonally everything was the same. Several times in the gospel she recognized the words—and the call back, *"L'agneau de Dieu..."* and it resonated in her head from her childhood, *"Lamb of God, take away the sins of the world, grant us peace."* World over, these tones reflected the core of a belief system going back two millennia. Even if she did not share fully in the belief, Fiona was in awe of the achievement. As a High Mass, the ceremony included all of the pomp; the altar boys came down the central nave in formation, bearing banners followed by the waving pendulum-swing of the smoking censers. Art, music, fragrance, physical action, the mass was an assault on all the senses. Fiona was charmed. She even followed Jeanne-Marie up for communion, queuing for the fundamental rite of Christianity, the sacrificial breaking of bread that bound them together in a brotherhood of suffering and peace.

At the end Fiona sat while the others pulled on their coats. She paused, absorbing the energy of the event. She couldn't imagine anything that would encapsulate a Christmas in France like this Mass, and she was in awe of the cascade of events that had brought her here.

Jeanne-Marie turned to her, "It's late, but I am so pleased that you joined me. If you are still here, perhaps you will join me for dinner the day after Christmas?"

"I would love to." Jean-Marie handed her a slip of paper with her address and telephone number. "About six o'clock, on the twenty-sixth then?"

"Yes. Thank you, so much. If you need to reach me, I'm at the Hotel Angleterre."

"In the Sixth?"

"Yes."

"Come then," Jean-Marie said, standing, "We need to find you a taxi." They stood and pulled on their coats. Jean-Marie led her outside to a cab-stand on the opposite side of the square.

"I'll see you then for dinner," Jean-Marie embraced her.

"Thank you for a magical evening. It was wonderful." Fiona climbed into her cab, closed the door and waved as they pulled away.

Back at the hotel she was tempted to just fall into bed. But she knew that if too much time went by, she'd start missing the details of Emma's letters in her report to the others. So she forced herself to sit down at her little table, and spill the day's impressions. Finished, she climbed, exhausted, into bed. In her head echoed the words, *"Lamb of God, take away the sins of the world, grant us peace."*

Chapter Thirty-Nine

From: fionahedge@yahoo.com
Subject: Paris First Impressions
Date: December 25, 2007 1:58 PM
To: artantikmarv@sbcglobal.net, ohamandakins@aol.com,
norminisstormin@aol.com, jennsullymills@gmail.com,
thomascaites@mindspring.com

I'm in love. I'm in love with a city. I'm in love with Emma,
who proves again and again to be an extraordinary woman.
But first, in response to your various questions:

Yes Jenn, don't worry—in addition to these reports, I'm
keeping copious notes both by hand and on the computer.
Thank you, thank you, for creating those time-chart templates.
It makes it so easy to do the notes and then sort, so they all
end up in order. Also, thank you for the feature that sorts by
topic. Often I see something unrelated to Emma specifically,
but in syncopation, and thus a possible influence. I can chart
it (like with the Hemingway hotel connection) and then it just
sorts as background, but I don't lose the reference. You're my
angel.

Marvin, forgive me for being such a technical klutz. I would
love to send you my photos but I appear to have brought the
wrong cable. I cannot download the images, or I'd be sending
them. Oh well, I have several of those little chippy storage
things, so I'll just save them for my return. Thank you for the
Christmas surprise. I spent part of my morning reviewing your
photos of Thomas's collection. Maybe when I get back a slide
show is an excuse for a dinner? Amanda, are you up to it?
After Marvin's Christmas we really need to show our stuff.
Amanda, you won't believe what I did for Christmas Eve!
Midnight mass! It was stupendous and the end result of a
shaggy dog story that can wait.

Norm, the food IS incredible. I'm mostly doing just café
fare—but when you think that the comparable American
cheap-eats option is McDonald's, it's a national

embarrassment. Today I had an onion/leek/cheese tart that was enough to bring you to your knees. With fresh fruit and a glass of wine, it was splendid. For dinner this evening, onion soup—I guess French onion soup, by definition. I didn't order wine but the waiter brought it anyway, because it was right for the soup, and it was Christmas. (Like I said, I'm in love with a city.)

Thomas, it's clear that there's a romance on the horizon for Emma. I guess I'm inhibited but I feel funny reporting to you on your mom's affairs. I've decided to just wince and report. I hope I don't offend in any way.

Our Emma has settled into Paris well. Despite her initial intention to find an apartment quickly, Emma has decided to remain at the hotel for awhile. She can afford it, (I can attest to the fact that the room is not too showy. I think I have the same furnishings as she did then.) The most important reason is that it is so close to the school. Since she arrived just before school, all nearby student-worthy apartments had already been snapped up. Still, she tells Wren that she keeps her eyes open for those "À Louer" signs in the windows in the neighborhood. The hotel has some benefits—free breakfast at least if you're satisfied with light fare and she has her own small bathroom, with a shower. That was a big deal then, as many students found themselves in walk-ups or studios without hot water. The one thing Emma cannot do is that she cannot use her room for painting. The smell of turpentine is an immediate giveaway if she does and the concierge is a nut about it. He thinks the smell will offend other guests and that it's a fire hazard. So, Emma learns early to swap studio space for hot water. Her letters to Wren are full of funny anecdotes of close calls where she and her friends avoid shower detection by the concierge.

Her days are routine. She arises early, has a light meal at the hotel, usually coffee, fruit and bread. She hurries to school, so she can squeeze in as many hours as she can painting. Emma is already a more than competent artist. She bristles that so much of what the Beaux Arts has to offer is

"mindless copying and rote transcription to two dimensions."
However, she is determined to milk all that she can from the
instruction and so, bends to their will. There are some
instructors who do not like her. (One in particular, a M.
Duprès) To Wren she explains, "I'm not sure if I've attracted
his ire by being a woman or by being a woman who is
proficient. In his class, a drawing class, I cope with the tedium
of his boring little routine still lifes by being very fast and
accurate. I have a distinct advantage here, with years more
experience than my classmates. Since the objective of his
formal 'salon' instruction is near photographic perfection,
there is little to no artistic interpretation in his class. I've
learned to render my drawings with speed and precision,
much to his annoyance. Despite his stature, he is a small-
minded little man." It is almost a game to her, to complete his
assignments in as little as half the time allotted, and to do so
with amazing accuracy. In her comments to Wren, she
compares the exercise to timed chess matches. "The more I
do, the faster and more accurate I become. Duprès is beside
himself, sweating and tugging anxiously at his stiff celluloid
collar. When he presses me to use the full time allotted, I take
special pains to illustrate the ugliness of the still life, his poorly
arranged elements, the finger smudges on the plaster
models, all the little things that make his display a sad and
grimy imitation of art. This drives Duprès to distraction and yet
I have performed exactly to his instruction." He is harder on
her than on any other student, a fact not lost on her
compatriots. Under the knife of his cruelty Emma has become
the underdog of the class. Privately, and only to Wren, she
concedes that "he has honed my skills, and though I quietly
detest him and his determined pettiness, I begrudgingly credit
Duprès with eliminating laziness from my style and giving me
the advantage of speed. We are well matched, Duprès and I,
he is a petit martinet and I am stubborn enough to benefit
from his meanness."

These skills she uses for painting in all other phases of her
education. The school has a special relationship with the
Louvre, so that in closed hours students are permitted entry in
order to copy the masters. Each semester a class is assigned

to copy at least one major masterpiece. The program does not have enough Louvre time in class, and so students are forced to spend their spare time finishing up their assignments. With her enhanced speed, Emma completes her copies early. The first semester it's Gericault's Raft of Medusa, one of the most difficult paintings assigned. She is quick about it and spends her free weekend time painting outdoors. If weather does not permit, she goes to the Musee to assist her classmates in their work, or does additional copies of popular paintings for sale on the sidewalks.

The school turns a blind eye to students painting and selling their works. Officially it is discouraged, but nothing is ever done or said about it. Emma is a prolific plein air painter. She loves it and it is, at least in her first year, the only place where she can spread her creative wings. Before the end of her first semester Emma has worked out her outdoor practice. She explains to Wren, "On a nice day I will take up to six small canvases with me. Because of my limitations, I cannot carry supplies and more than six blank canvases, and then, I am strapped down like a mule. I cannot carry more than three wet canvases back to the studio, so, I must sell at least three on the street to keep painting. This practice keeps my ambitions and my prices in check." If, in a week, she sells three paintings, Emma covers her expenses for the week. By November, weather permitting, she regularly sells a minimum of three or four canvases each week. Other students become convinced that her sales are essential to her finances. They marvel at her ability to paint saleable goods repeatedly without the work becoming formulaic. Emma advises, "It will not become a formula piece so long as you paint the light. Once you begin to color in a drawing in your mind, the thing is done in." She is not like the tourist painters who report each day before the Eiffel Tower to render it endlessly, and deadeningly. Secretly, Emma resolves never to paint the Tower, or the Arc de Triomphe or any of the other standard tourist venues. (Though, because it's close and lovely, she will paint Notre Dame.) Emma begins to paint outdoors with some of the students from the advanced classes and falls into a group of friends who paint together.

192

"When asked, I freely give out the secrets to my sales successes. They are: Never paint a subject once you have become bored with it; once you set up, keep painting (my belief is that purchasers connect when they see the artist in the act of painting and that that generates sales. It is not enough to sit, smoking, in front of your work); Pick a theme to explore in a particular scene, changing light, moving people, whatever you fancy, so that the paintings you sell do not all look alike (AND be prepared to explain your theme to the prospective buyer); and if you want to sell to tourists, bring completed dry paintings to sell." Emma explains that tourists may have money to liberate, but they cannot be bothered to transport wet oil paintings. (She also suggests watercolors for the same reason.) Slyly, she advises, "The artist who wants to sell on location should always have a small dab of paint on the face, or perhaps on one's lapel."

Her companions scoff at her theories, but Emma continues to outsell them all. One even suggests that Emma's sales are the result of the sympathy she garners by painting while leaning on a cane. This offends Emma and a challenge is on. The young man making the comment is to set up in a similar location at the same time, and is to paint leaning on a cane. Other students volunteer to observe both artists, to make sure there's nothing unusual about the session. Naturally, and thankfully, his false impediment does nothing for his sales. Emma remarks to Wren, "Thank God, it was a good outcome, or the École des Beaux Arts would've become the academy of cripples, spread out through Paris with canes, eye patches and crutches!" Emma is intensely competitive with herself. She sets goals, meets them and sets them again. She did not arrive in Paris expecting to be self-supporting as a student there, but by mid-year it has become a point of pride for her that she does so, and that she does not need to rely on her inheritance for her daily needs.

Emma has favorite places to paint. "I prefer quiet spots, which are specifically Parisian. I love to capture the shifting light on the arches of Pont Neuf, the open park scenes of

193

Luxembourg Gardens or tiny little urban spots, like the view at Cours Rohan, a tiny green courtyard study of some fashionable apartments. In these places, I encounter locals. I love to sell my work to Parisians. They have more refined tastes and their francs are not loosened merely by the heady mix of travel and novelty. Locals prefer images of 'their Paris' not the one frequented by tourists."

I think that Emma was popular, though it's unlikely she was aware of it. Her letters are full of tales of collegial fun and exchanges of assistance. I am watching for repeated names of friends, waiting for the budding romance we know is in the offing. But Emma is universally available to her friends. She reports their trials and tribulations to Wren, as if they were her own. Perhaps because she has no family, she easily adopts friends and shoulders their burdens with her own. She does not report on romantic intrigue. I suspect she doesn't contemplate it for herself and so may be oblivious, even if there were overtures in her direction.

On the tourist front (my own) I am splitting my time between the letters and the sites. I don't know which is the more compelling of the two. I feel guilty if I just visit the standard Paris fare, without looking for it through Emma's eyes. Inadvertently I happened upon a lovely café, La Palette, which was also a favorite of Emma's. Tomorrow I'll visit Notre Dame, one of Emma's haunts, even though it was popular with tourists and impressionists. Hopefully I can also get to her school, though with the holidays, that may be limited.

It's been really cold here. I had to buy a new coat and some woolens. Shopping was quite an experience! I selected stores that would have been around for Emma, but also had the opportunity to experience a Parisian Christmas for myself. Hope all is well with all of you back home. Merry Christmas!

Fiona

Chapter Forty

"Ho, ho, ho! Who am I?" There was a pause on the other end, "Hello... Amanda?"

"Yeah, who's this?" Amanda didn't recognize the voice.

"It's me, *Denise.*"

"Oh, hi Denise, you'll have to speak up a bit, I'm at a spa, and there's some background noise."

"You're at a spa?"

"Yeah, duh. It's Christmas, what have I done for Christmas for the past hundred years?"

"Oh yeah, Where are you?"

"In Calistoga, this year. So, you're at your in-laws?"

"Is my mom with you?"

"Nope. She's in Paris."

"Paris?! What's she doing in Paris?"

"I dunno. *I'm* here."

"Cute. Did she go with somebody?"

"Nope, just by herself."

"Amanda, what's up? My mom wouldn't go to Paris alone."

"Well, since she did, I guess you're wrong about that."

"She's never been to Paris. She wouldn't go without researching it half to death."

"Well, you're half right. It was a short notice trip, but she made every effort to research it to death, she just ran out of time. I'm sure she'll do just fine now that she's there."

"Short notice, that's not like her either. Amanda, just what's going on with her?"

"Denise, like I told you last time, you have to pick up the phone and ask *her.*"

"I've been trying, but she hasn't answered. She left a message a few days back—said she'd be out of town. She never mentioned Paris."

"Well, I don't think she needed your signature on a permission slip. She left a message?"

"Just a *sorry-I-missed-you, happy holidays* thing."

"Okay, well last I heard she was walking all over Paris in the snow. Sounds like she's having fun."

"She called you?"

"No, an email. Just an update. You could email her."

"Can't, I'm at my in-laws. Never thought to bring the laptop, and they're in the dark ages, in that department."

"Well then, I guess you'll have to wait till you get home. What's your return date?"

"January second."

"Well, she'll likely be home before you. Before New Years, if I remember."

"You don't know?"

"Well, it's on the calendar at home, but I didn't tattoo it on my arm or anything. How's Christmas?"

"Okay, I guess. I just wanted to talk to my mom."

"Well, that's a good sign."

"I'm a little shocked. *Paris?* That's, well, not like the mom *I* know."

"There's still room for your mom to surprise you, kid. She spent a lot of time living and working for you. It's her turn now."

"So I'm learning. How's *your* holiday?"

"Like I like it, quiet, serene and loaded with decadent pampering."

"What'd my mom get you for Christmas?"

"Sterling silver napkin rings. They're gorgeous."

"What'd you give her?"

"Long underwear."

"No. Really?"

"Really! The silk stuff. You know how cold-blooded she is, she *was* headed for Paris in December."

"Oh."

Amanda heard voices in the background.

"Well, I gotta go, would you tell my mom I called?"

"Yeah, but leave a message on her machine, too."

"Already did. Thanks Amanda. Talk at ya later."

"Bye kiddo, have a happy holiday."

The phone clicked. Amanda folded her phone and put it on the pillow beside her. It *was* an improvement, incremental, but an improvement.

Chapter Forty-One

From: fionahedge@yahoo.com
Subject: Paris Impressions
Date: December 25, 2007 11:58 PM
To: artantikmarv@sbcglobal.net, ohamandakins@aol.com,
norminisstormin@aol.com, jennsullymills@gmail.com,
thomascaites@mindspring.com

I'm feeling a little sheepish. I spent the better part of the
day reading, and then re-reading Emma's letters. Thank god
they know me now at La Palette, and I can drink coffee all day
long without interruption or judgment. All this time I've been
waiting for the arrival of the grand romance, the sweeping
entry of the Dutch Lover. I should have known better. Love
doesn't announce itself. It sneaks in the back door. Our Pieter
has been around all along, only since he's in France, he's
known here as Pierre. I've backtracked a good deal here, to
retrieve bits that turn out to be essential to the story. Please
bear with me as I catch us up.

Pierre has been part of Emma's landscape almost since
she arrived at Beaux Arts. Emma has mentioned him
regularly in her letters, as she did all her friends. The earliest
mention was way back in September, when she remarked to
Wren that she hoped she had not offended her classmate in
inquiring about his accent. He spoke perfect French, but not
Parisian, and she was curious. He explained that his father
was French but his mother was not, and that French was his
second language, after Frisian. There they were, the first
clues. The name, translated, the language, I just never put
two and two together. I suppose, if it's any excuse, Emma
never got it either. That's both endearing in her naiveté, and
heartbreaking, since I think the reason may be that her
mother had so drummed it in to her that she was not a
marriageable package, that Emma never considered herself
attractive. So, the clues were building. Since Emma didn't
discern the interest, of course she didn't report on it. For

example, later, during the "cripple challenge," Emma had reported, as humor, Pierre's remark that her consistent sales were clearly the result of talent, but that the challenge wasn't on point because it didn't address the factors of charm and beauty. Emma clearly didn't understand that the remark wasn't humor. She understood and was flattered by the recognition of talent, and that was the basis on which she judged it, and herself. She turned it to a funny story for Wren. In its context though, it was an outright compliment, if not a direct come on. Clearly Pierre had been attracted to her from the outset.

From Emma's perspective, Pierre was one of her friends. Lacking in family, Emma builds family and family connections wherever she goes, maybe to recreate the warmth and community she'd enjoyed in her grandparents' home. She is mother, sister and mentor to all. It's probably why her classmates so supported her when M. Duprès made her the class whipping boy. As you'll see, Pierre becomes Pieter when their relationship changes, when he welcomes her to his other, Dutch (or Friesland) self.

Pierre and Emma had a special bond, both of them being outsiders within their circle of French students. For Pierre, there weren't any other Dutch students. His French was good, but accented. He was a foreigner. Both of them were outsiders on other levels as well, Pierre, with a French father and last name, was never fully Dutch. From Friesland, even among the Dutch he was a minority. Emma was an American in Paris, during a decade of Americans in Paris, but unlike the famous expatriates of the '20s, Emma did not connect with other Americans. As a talented and accomplished female artist in a time when that was rare enough, Emma's strategy had always been to blend. She did not strive to attract attention, almost un-American in itself. I don't know how much her handicap figured into her public persona. We know it affected her expectations in terms of romance. She had none. Aside from tailored footwear to accommodate her differences in leg length, Emma made no effort to conceal her disability. She used her cane constantly. It is so much a part of her self-image that she includes it in every self portrait and photograph we've seen of her. I cannot tell if this is matter of fact, or defiant. In her letters, Emma mentions the then-popular interest in eugenics back in California. She is from the class and culture that most supported the movement, but as a cripple, she is aware that she is viewed as a defective— echoes of her mother's litany. This viewpoint is further driven home in their reactions when others learn that the disability is the result of illness. Far preferable would have been an accident, just as crushing in result, but less of a judgment of her personally. Even her grandparents inadvertently fed this insecurity, when they endeavored to give her "a life of the mind," insofar as it presupposed that a normal life would not be available. The best of it is that it fueled all of Emma's strengths. She was brilliant, charming, witty and talented. Though oblivious, she was beautiful. So too, though, it may have charged her insecurities, driving them deeper.

Emma and Pierre were also similar in how much of themselves was connected to the importance of their formative families. Emma, though now orphaned from her grandparents, still holds them dear in her heart. Their presence in her life informs every decision, every move she makes. She is homesick for a home to which there is no return. There is only bitterness in her estranged relationship with her parents and siblings, so much so that she rarely includes them when she recounts her life to others. Officially she is the orphaned granddaughter. Pieter is the oldest, and only, son in a boisterous loving family. His father had been a promising young artist but upon falling in love with a Dutch beauty, he had given up his direction, converted to her faith and been taken into her family's business as a wine merchant. The living was steady, but not rich. It leaves his artistic nature unsatisfied. When their son, Pieter, shows talent, he nurtures it, against his wife's practical, Dutch inclinations. Pieter is the family tease. He tortures his sisters, to their total delight. Yet, he is always the one to remember a birthday, to bring a flower to a sister with a sad face, to lend a hand in the women's work of the day, especially if he can do so with a joke or a laugh. Art school is his father's indulgence, one made at great expense to his family. The pressure is intense, as success in art school promises a meager future and the loss of the only male heir from the family business. His father yearns for Pieter's artistic success. His mother, tight-lipped, does not share that enthusiasm. Pieter believes that each of them do so out of complete love for him. He desperately misses the chaos of the family household, the press and babble of blonde sisters, the daily chores and rhythms of a hard working family that laughs and loves under the yoke of living.

Pierre shares his family stories with Emma, who recognizes in them the warmth of her old home, and she basks in that warmth from the edge of the circle, happy to have a glimpse of the hearth fire. She writes to Wren about vicarious family and how, in sharing in it, she misses her grandparents and her Mills circle less. At this point Wren is pregnant with her first child and Emma urges her to take a hands-on approach. Wren's own family had been distant and Emma reminds her how she suffered for it. I must say, I remember Jordan's genuine warmth, and wanted to whisper through the decades to Emma, Wren did just fine; she raised wonderful children. My heart aches for Emma that vicarious was enough, ever the outsider.

From very early in their friendship, Emma helps Pierre to shop or advises him on little gifts to send home. For his mother's birthday Emma drags Pierre to the Moulin Rouge for an afternoon of pastel sketches, so he could send his mother a picture of a French windmill, with a wink and a nod to the risqué connection. (In the meantime, she sells three such pastels fresh from the easel, with Pierre shaking his head in amazement.) Sisters are treated to more benign subjects, fancy hair ribbons along with sketches of the Luxembourg Gardens, Notre Dame or picturesque café scenes. Since Pierre's funds are tight (and allegedly so are hers), Emma insists that they make art their recreation. Pierre's work is very good, but not fast. In an afternoon where Emma can complete six small canvases, Pierre is lucky to finish one or two. Emma credits the evil M. Duprès. Pierre blames his

Dutch heritage.

Growing out from this bond, and her friendships with others, Emma is instrumental in creating the weekend painting group. She takes their personal intimacies and builds social networks. Pierre, more reticent than Emma, is thrilled with the inclusion into the larger group, but perhaps had hoped for more cherished connections. So, on any given clear weekend Emma, Pierre, Simone, Jean Luc, Joseph, Emile, Georges, and Isabelle carry lunches and easels all over Paris. Others come from time to time, but the eight remain the group's core. Pierre is solicitous, he assists in carrying Emma's gear, or he argues in favor of sites that will be easy access for her. Emma tells Wren that this is evidence of his thoughtful friendship, but sees nothing beyond it. Indeed, Emma fails to see romance at all. When student friends hook up or break up she is shocked, blind to the pulse of liaisons all around her.

Emma's quest for artistic challenges outstrips those of her friends. She visits galleries and museums all over Paris. She complains to Wren that her friends, as students, are content to be artists on their class schedule. "The Parisians," she writes, "Are complacent because of art overexposure. They literally trip on art and history in the cobblestones of their streets." Emma reads voraciously and argues the cause of modern art, even while attending the most conservative art establishment in all of Europe. She sends Wren all the reviews of the private galleries, along with her own impressions of new works. On weekend painting sorties Emma experiments with Fauvist and Cubist interpretations. Her companions are shocked, yet the work sells. In short, Emma's Paris experience, though rich with friends, is art driven.

In the spring, when art students are obsessed with blossoms and new green, Emma is obsessed with gray days and rain reflective cobbles. She spends long cold wet Saturdays painting Pont Neuf from under an umbrella or from below the arches. These studies, in grays and shades of mauve, sell before they are off the easel. Emma has become Paris, the Paris Parisians live in. Her buyers are shocked when they learn she is not Parisian. When she wants to paint the bridge at night, Pierre insists on accompanying her. Initially, he does not intend to paint. But her enthusiasm and the indigo hues of the night broken by the golden glow of the street lamps bouncing off the dark river and the cobbles win him over. They each undertake to work on larger canvases, long studies, well into the night. These nocturnes are the best work Pierre has done all year. Each night he walks her home and marvels at the subtle beauty of the dark and his progress. He calls her his muse, to which she laughs and asks why his muse carries a bullwhip.

The end of the school year is approaching. Pierre will be returning to Holland, Emile to Normandy and Simone will be going home to Provence. The rest of the group vows to stay in Paris, though it's not much of a vow as they're mostly too poor to travel. Emma plans to stay; she can paint and support herself. Oakland holds mostly painful losses for her just now.

At the end of each semester, students are expected to display their best work for critique. Both Emma and Pierre select some of their larger Pont Neuf nocturne canvases to display, a fact that does not go unnoticed by their classmates. One student, Paul, never one of Emma's favorites, teases her, suggesting there is something untoward about long nights spent painting with Pierre and laughing that Emma chose to advertise their trysts by showing the same paintings. Emma is taken aback, blushing. The work speaks for itself— obviously they were painting! But she responds tongue in cheek that if he (her tormentor) could paint half as well while trysting, he'd be ready to graduate now. The collected students laugh and the joke is turned. Emma, though, is rattled. She leaves the campus and takes refuge in a café au lait and a pain du chocolat at La Palette. There she writes to Wren, for the first time questioning her feelings for Pierre.

Emma needed to return to school to finish her display. Also, the year-end class photo was scheduled at the end of that afternoon. Walking back to school, Emma sees a For Rent sign in an upstairs apartment on Rue Visconti. It is precisely what she'd been waiting for all year. Immediately she knocked on the building manager's door. He showed her the apartment, a small two bedroom (with good light), on the third floor. It's larger than she needed, but the price is reasonable and perhaps the second bedroom with let her dispense with a studio. She secured it immediately, pulling out the loose bills from her purse that she stuffed there each time she sold a painting. The manager counted the crumpled stack of currency looked her up and down twice and then gave her the key. Later when she recounted the events of rest of the day, she reported to Wren that the earlier tasteless exchange had put her in precisely the position to find her new home. It is so Emma to find that silver lining.

Back at school, she was elated. She set to completing the hanging of her display space for critique. She ran into Emile, who reported that Pierre was looking for her. Emma crossed the courtyard to his class, where he, too, was finishing his display. He turned to her, concerned, but she was glowing. Pierre had heard of the exchange between Paul and Emma, and was worried for her. But the Emma he finds is exuberant. He was confused. Their next exchange so rocked Emma's world that she reported it, word for word, to Wren:

"I found him there finishing up his display and told him Emile had sent me. He reached out and touched my shoulder in a sweet gesture of concern.

'I heard about Paul, I was so worried for you.'

I nodded, 'He's a fool. I was embarrassed is all. I'm okay.'

'You responded well, put him in his place. The whole class was abuzz with it.' He shook his head, 'Perhaps I should not have showed the nocturne.'

I chided him, 'Don't be silly, we show our best work.'

'Always the art.'

'Yes, of course. It's why we're here. Whatever else?'

He answered, 'Sometimes,' and he reached up to brush a stray hair from my face, 'Sometimes I wish there were more.'"

She confides to her friend, "Wren, I was so stunned. I never thought…. face to face with feelings I couldn't understand. My lips quivered and tears spilled down my cheeks. I was ashamed. I tried to turn away, but Pierre pulled me close and held me. I didn't know what to say.

And the call rang out, 'Photographer in the east wing!' It was time for the class picture.

We parted. Pierre wiped my face with the back of his hand. We walked side by side, wordlessly to the east wing, where the photographer arranged the members of the class by height and shot the year end photo, twice. I winced, blinded by the flash and by the turn of the day. Pierre found me, he told me he had to finish his display. Could he meet me after at La Palette at six?"

—That's it, my friends. It's as far as I've read. I hate to leave you hanging, but today, to make sense of this I've had to review almost everything. Tomorrow, Luxembourg Gardens, more story and dinner with Parisians!

Fiona

Chapter Forty-Two

From: thomascaites@mindspring.com
Subject: Paris Impressions
Date: December 26, 2007 10.00 AM
To: fionahedge@yahoo.com, artantikmarv@sbcglobal.net, ohamandakins@aol.com, norminisstormin@aol.com, jennsullymills@gmail.com,

Fiona,

I have two class photos from my mother's stay in Paris. Since your email I've been peering at them and I think it's clear which one was taken on the heels of the day you've described. It is difficult to see one's beloved mother through new eyes but I'm understanding her more in the past few weeks than ever before. I am finding new avenues of appreciation and loving her more for this new perspective. You have me looking at every photo, every painting. Don't be shy. Keep telling the story you're discovering. Again and again, thank you.

Thomas

Chapter Forty-Three

The phone rang, but this time Fiona was already up. She reached over, lifted the receiver and hung it up. She had the curtains thrown wide open, the pale winter sun streaming in. She was dressed sitting at the little table overlooking the courtyard. The laptop was open and Fiona was poring over Emma's letters. Her day was planned, with as much crammed into it as possible. Initially she'd hoped to read all of Emma's letters on this trip, and now she was realizing she'd be lucky to get through Paris, while in Paris. Tonight she had her dinner date with Jeanne-Marie Baptiste, so she needed to maximize her daytime hours. These early morning hours she dedicated to reading Emma's letters. Once the day began, her priorities were to check out the little apartment on Visconti and to see the Luxembourg Gardens, another favorite painting spot of Emma's. She also needed to pick up some wine, or an appropriate gift, to bring to dinner. For that, she'd scout for an open shop along the way or, if time permitted, she'd go to Bon Marche. She'd checked her watch ten times by the time the knock on the door signaled the arrival of her breakfast.

She poured the black, rich, Parisian coffee. Fiona had now completely given up on cream. She didn't want to cover over the flavor of the coffee. She made a mental note to get information on the coffee, so she could try to make it at home. This made Peet's taste like instant, and she was already as picky as they come. Fiona munched on her croissant as she immersed herself in Emma's affair with Pieter. Aside from her descriptions of life with her grandparents, Emma had never been so happy. Emma was surprised that this bliss did not result in decreased productivity. Indeed, the more of life that Emma experienced, the more she poured into her canvases. Fiona mourned that these were lost to them, that there was no easy mechanism to track down Emma's paintings from half a world and eighty years away. Though she was enjoying the romance, Fiona was just a little jealous. There was an intensity to the way Emma went about working and loving that Fiona had never known, except maybe in the intensity of loving as a mother. Emma was fiercely and tenderly in love and, through the force of it, colors were more vivid, textures more real, food more delicious and the very air more filling in her lungs. Fiona reflected on her own relationships, her marriage, and none of them had so gripped her as Emma was in her love with Pieter.

Fiona savored the last of her strawberries and peaches. And even though it would have slowed her down, she wished there was just one more cup of that dark, rich coffee. She flipped the laptop closed, put the tray outside in the hall, and wrapped herself up in her winter duds for the day's trek. Fiona packed up the laptop, slinging it over her shoulder, thinking that she'd find time at lunch to read some letters. She was having second thoughts about dragging it all over Paris, but couldn't let go of the possibility of sneaking in a few more letters during the day. The romance was addictive.

The day was crisp, but not cold, as Fiona set out down Rue Bonaparte to Emma's old apartment on the corner of Bonaparte and Rue Visconti. The location was perfect, almost immediately across from the school. Fiona found it immediately, and based on Emma's description, was able to pick out the proper apartment on the third floor. She photographed the building from all angles. Before she moved on, she wanted a picture of the mailbox at the entry, the place where Emma had sent and received letters from Wren and Pieter. She mounted the steps of the old building, and peering through the sidelight windows, was taking a shot of the brass mailbox just inside the entry, when a tenant stepped out and held the door open for her. Fiona shocked herself by coolly nodding her thanks, and stepping into the foyer. Now focused, she got some incredible shots of the mailbox and the stairs heading up from the entry. She felt like a cat burglar, but Fiona followed those steps up to the third floor. Once past the public entry, which was burnished like an heirloom, the corridor and stairs took on a much more pedestrian feel. The walls hadn't been painted in decades, if that, and the building had the strange aroma of cooking oil and old library books. Uncertain just what she'd do when she got there, Fiona headed up to the door of Emma's old apartment. She looked out the window at the stairwell and felt sure she was in the correct location, given Emma's description of where the "À Louer" sign had been in the window. At the third floor, she stopped at the first door on the right. It was an unpresuming door, three panels with a brass knob. There were several locks, ascending above the knob, the paint peeling where the indented panels met the trim edge.

Fiona stepped back to get a photo of the door. Just as she did so, a young woman opened the door and peered out at her. Unprepared for this, Fiona snapped the shot, the brilliant flash blinding the tenant.

"I'm so sorry. Excuse me!"

The woman stood, half in, half out, blinking her eyes. She didn't move. Her short dark hair lay in odd directions, sleepy crop circles that said she'd only just woken up. Fiona realized it was pretty early, for the day after Christmas.

"You are English?"

"American."

"Oh, I see. And why do you photograph my door?"

Fiona stammered, "Many years ago an American art student lived here, I am writing about her life."

The woman paused to reflect on the explanation. She was wearing a colorful set of cotton knit pajamas with boomerang shapes printed all over them. Fiona blinked. The pattern reminded her of the Formica countertop in her childhood kitchen. She reflected in the moment that she really liked those pajamas, but thought better of mentioning it.

"How many years ago?"

"1925." Fiona saw the woman knit her eyebrows as she struggled with the numeric translation, so she added, "Dix neuf cent vingt-cinq."

"Ah. Famous?"

"No. Not yet."

The woman laughed. "And *you* will make her famous?"

Fiona noted the incongruity, and smiled back. "Probably not."

"A L'École des Beaux Arts?"

"Yes."

"I am a student à L'École des Beaux Arts. How can I help you?"

"Could I… see the apartment?" Fiona could hardly believe she was asking. The woman looked almost as surprised.

She held up one finger, "Moment." She closed the door. Fiona waited. A few moments later the door reopened. Now, sporting jeans and a paint spattered sweatshirt, the woman waved Fiona in.

"I am Sophie, Sophie Sebastian. Maybe someday someone will want to see where *I* have lived."

"Thank you so much. I am Fiona Hedge." The apartment was small, but well served by windows. Fiona smiled inside, good light. As she entered into a hall to the main room she saw a tiny kitchen tucked in on the left and another smaller, closed door on the right. Fiona figured that was the bath. Straight back was a small living/sitting room filled with slouchy, slip-covered, student furnishings tucked into a bay window alcove overlooking the street. On each side were doors to what Fiona gathered would be the two bedrooms.

Her hostess led the way. The bedroom to the left held a full bed, in the only spot in the room that would accommodate it. A dresser was tucked below the windows. In the far corner there was a door to what could only be a tiny closet. Sophie led her to the other side where there was an even smaller bedroom tucked into the area next to the stairwell. "Would you like to take photos?"

"Oh yes, please, just a few." Fiona quickly snapped shots of the bedrooms, the view out the windows and the main room sitting area."

"Thank you. You have no idea how much this helps me."

"Was this place important to her?"

"Very much so. She was in love here."

Sophie nodded. "What were her paintings like?"

Fiona thought hard. How do you explain a painting or a painting style across language barriers? Her hand brushed the laptop hanging on her shoulder. Fiona looked down, "Do you have a moment?"

Sophie giggled. "Yes, since I *was* asleep."

"I'm so sorry."

"I'm not. Suddenly there is a romance in my apartment. That is a nice thought."

Fiona sat down and slid the laptop out of its case. She opened it and set it on the end table where they both could see the screen. She scrolled to the library of Caites paintings that Marvin had emailed her. Fiona began to select images to show Sophie. She picked the self-portraits, the picture of Thomas as a boy, holding his paint brush aloft, the picture of the bicycles at Lake Merritt, the painting of the row boat done in Emma's Mills era, two of the plein air landscapes. In all, she showed about fifteen images, moving on when Sophie had digested a particular picture, and nodded to go on. They didn't speak a word during this showing.

"She was good, very good. So, why was she not famous?"

"I'm not sure. She liked painting more than promotion, she was a female in the early Twentieth Century, she was disabled. It's hard to know."

"It scares me, you know, this talent, unrecognized. It is the fear of art school, that the art won't be big enough."

"I understand."

"Have you been to the school?"

"No, I'm here during Christmas, it's been closed."

"I am a graduate student. I have keys, would you like to see it?"

Fiona could hardly believe her ears. "I'd love to."

Sophie went to the bedroom closet and pulled out a coat. She wrestled her boots on at the door. "Come, I have some work to pick up. You can come along and see how the school looks. I understand there have been very few changes over the years," she snorted, "Except for the tuition." Sophie opened the door, and led the way down the stairs.

"When Emma attended, she complained that the work was all from copying old masters. Is that still true?"

"Not as much. The…" she struggled for the word, "curriculum, yes, it is much the same as many other art schools now. Not so much the copies of old paintings. Still at Beaux Arts, for the undergraduates it is still conservative. For me, I can do anything, so long as my advisors agree." They crossed the street diagonally and they were right there, on campus.

Sophie led Fiona to a side door. Inside the corridor, it was dim, the lights all turned off during the holiday but the layout was as Emma had described, a warren of classrooms connected by short halls, each looking out into a courtyard area. Fiona guessed where the east wing would be, and peeked in to the room where the class photos would have been taken. Otherwise, the atmosphere was very much like the art college which Fiona had attended—plain halls and classrooms set with dull still life displays, or with draped platforms awaiting the arrival of the model. The nicest feature was the courtyards, interwoven with the classes and studios. They passed a bulletin board in the hall, and Fiona laughed. There were the typical posters and ads for apartments, to sell bicycles, to share accommodations for the summer. And, typical of art students, the flyers and ads were little masterpieces in their own right. Fiona warmed to the smell of oil paints and solvents. She could picture Emma here, brush in one hand, cane in the other.

As a graduate student, Sophie had a small windowless studio to herself. Fiona followed her in, while Sophie flipped on the florescent lights. The walls were lined with drawings and small

210

rough studies for larger paintings. There were several on easels, luminous, almost ethereal portraits and interior scenes. The paintings had a delicate, almost spiritual feel to them.

"They feel religious."

"I use the old ways, egg tempera and glaze paintings. I want to show today through old eyes... maybe ultimately to show God in science."

"Wow. For you, classical instruction is an advantage."

"Your painter is making me think. Her work is not so delicate but still feels connected. I may rethink landscape."

"What you do is beautiful."

Sophie smiled. She nodded at Fiona's laptop, "As you know, beautiful is not enough. Something else must shine through." She picked up a small painting of an intimate interior and a palette box. "Your painter, comment s'appelle... Emma?"

"Yes, Emma Caites."

"When you finish your book, please send me one. I'd like to know how she ends up." Sophie grinned, "I think you have my address."

Fiona hesitated, "Some would think it has an unhappy ending. She died quite young."

"And you, what do you think?"

Fiona paused, "I don't know. She painted almost till she died. She was in great pain and suffered many losses, but she continued to look for, and find, beauty every day. I don't know. When is an artist's work finished?"

Sophie smiled, "Maybe now, with you... a better ending. Thank you for coming to my door today. Instead of sleeping, I have much to consider."

"Thank you. Now I can picture the little home where Emma found love, and the school where she grew as an artist."

Sophie led the way back to the Rue Bonaparte side of the campus, and locked the door behind them. Sophie reached out and shook Fiona's hand. "Good Luck."

"And to you, too." Fiona headed south to the Luxembourg Gardens, and Sophie went home to put new ideas into paint.

Fiona could hardly believe the events of the morning. She was surprised that she'd gone into a strange apartment building, and shocked at how she'd connected to Sophie. She could only imagine what Denise would say! She shook her head and decided to blame

211

the Parisian coffee.

Even with the unexpected wondrous events of the morning, it was still early. Fiona checked her watch. She'd figured that the walk to the park was just about two miles, plenty of time. She headed south on Bonaparte past St. Germain des Pres to St. Sulpice. Fiona got a little turned around at St. Sulpice, cut west and then south again to the Gardens. Fiona immediately understood the attraction for Emma. This was a huge and well used park. There were tennis courts, chess tables, sculptures and fountains, and there was a little lake which had been Emma's primary draw. Fiona was not prepared for the size and variety of the park. Emma had written to Wren extensively about Luxembourg Gardens. She marveled at how the Parisians, many with small apartments, would extend their living into this lovely green space. She loved to paint the children sailing toy boats across the pond. She painted the old men playing cards and chess. And she loved to lay down her paints and join the children watching the Grand Guignol, the traditional Parisian puppet shows. It was winter now. The formal gardens were nearly dormant, and aside from the dog walkers, the Gardens were quiet. But Fiona spent hours wandering the grounds. She could picture the lawns, green and tidy, the acres of formal flowers. She could almost hear the squeals of the children in response to the puppet antics—raucous scenes played out repeatedly, and which still delighted. She checked out the Medici fountain and the sculptures of French queens and noble women. She didn't take many photos, since this winter garden was not what Emma would have seen. But it was just what Fiona needed, a little open space in a lovely, but foreign city.

When the sun was slanted in the December sky, she grabbed a taxi for the ride to Bon Marche to pick up wine and chocolates for her dinner with Jeanne-Marie. She had naively expected a supermarket. Nothing prepared Fiona for the size and selection. After a long day, it was almost too much—too much choice, too much for the eyes. Eventually, she found the wine section, and chose a bottle of the same red wine that the waiter had given her with the onion soup on Christmas Eve. Then, asking directions, she found the confectioners and a perfect box of a dozen mixed truffles. Necessities secured, she wandered the store, finding every kind of food imaginable, accessories and clothing. It was the largest shopping emporium that Fiona had ever been in. This was entirely her own experience, since Bon Marche was not of Emma's time.

212

Emma had shopped at Les Halles, long since demolished and then recreated. Fiona had decided not to go to the new market, not to visit the paler, modern version of Emma's environs. Roaming the store, Fiona happened upon a fun display of pajamas. There, of all things, were the same colorful boomerang pajamas that Sophie had worn. Fiona sorted through the sizes and selected sets for Denise, Amanda, Jennifer and herself. She delighted in the silliness of it all, and found another taxi to take her back to the hotel.

Chapter Forty-Four

After a quick shower, Fiona dressed for dinner. She settled on an outfit that had become her Paris uniform—lined wool trousers, a turtleneck and a sweater vest. It wasn't dressy, but it was warm. To spice it up a bit, she donned an old-pawn Navajo necklace that was part of her standard image. She felt that the look was particularly American, the role she'd likely be playing this evening. The silver, coral and turquoise were a handsome counterpoint to her aubergine trousers and brown and mauve vest.

Fiona had packed some dressier clothing, but had opted repeatedly for the comfort of casual wools. She'd expected to take in a ballet or opera performance during her stay, but found herself so exhausted each evening that she was happy to spend the time quietly in her room with Emma's letters. Even tonight, though she was excited to meet again with Jeanne-Marie, part of her wished she could just curl up with Emma's romance.

Fiona noted that her clothes seemed to be hanging a little loose. Certainly that wasn't the result of croissants for breakfast every day. Fiona calculated her approximate mileage. She wanted to see Emma's Paris, so she'd been logging many miles on foot. She figured she'd walked eight to ten miles per day since arriving in Paris. Who would have expected to return from Europe *thinner*? Fiona resolved to keep up the momentum and walk Lake Merritt each day when she returned to Oakland. Walking gave her the head space she needed to sort out Emma's story. She pulled on her coat, and without hesitation, picked up the laptop. Jeanne-Marie wanted to fully understand why Fiona was in Paris and, as with Sophie, Fiona figured that a showing of Emma's paintings might best explain her quest.

She hailed a taxi in front of the hotel, and handed the driver a slip of paper—the address in Jeanne-Marie's neat handwriting. Jeanne-Marie lived in a small apartment building, not far from St. Augustin's. There was an antiquated buzzer system and Fiona held her breath, waiting to see whether the scratchy intercom could overcome their accents. She needn't have worried. In seconds, Jeanne-Marie flew into the lobby and escorted her back to the apartment.

There, in the aroma of what would prove to be an amazing dinner, she met Gaston, Jeanne-Marie's other half. Gaston was the musical director at St. Augustin's. It wasn't clear whether they were married. It seemed to Fiona that Jeanne-Marie had said she was married to a musician in New York. In any event, it didn't make a difference and it only amused Fiona that both of them worked for the church. Clearly the church in France was more laid back than anything in Fiona's experience. Gaston's English was not as good as Jeanne-Marie's, and much of what was said had to be translated. He had a good sense of humor though. Right after introductions, Gaston winked at her, and said, "Nice coat." Where she could, Fiona spoke French, but most of their topics were well beyond her conversational skills.

Fiona presented the gift of wine and chocolates, which Jeanne-Marie pointed out, would be perfect with dinner. Gaston nodded appreciatively at the bottle, and opened the wine to let it breathe. Jeanne-Marie had made a cassoulet and the aroma of garlic, onions, tomatoes and sage reminded Fiona that she'd missed lunch in order to roam around Luxembourg Gardens. Jeanne Marie explained that the cassoulet was special tonight because she'd made it with duck *and* sausage, though it took several tries in the translation and some quacking before Fiona caught the drift of "canard." Perhaps that was why it smelled so rich. Jeanne-Marie was trying to explain to Gaston why Fiona had come to Paris. This seemed like exactly the right time to bring out the laptop, and as Fiona followed Jeanne-Marie's tortured re-telling of the Emma Caites tale, the images appeared on the screen. As soon as Fiona began to show the paintings, the atmosphere changed. Both Jeanne-Marie and Gaston were mesmerized by the parade of images on the screen. The slide show helped illustrate her quest, showing that this was truly the work of an undiscovered talent. Now, they understood.

They most loved the self-portraits, but the plein air landscapes and the paintings of Thomas also won their hearts. At times they spoke to each other, pointing out the subtleties of texture and light. Fiona could barely follow along, but she could tell that these were appreciative and knowledgeable eyes. Suddenly Emma was not merely an unknown artist. She was a sensitive painter whose work spoke to them. After viewing about thirty paintings, Jeanne-Marie suddenly looked up, and *remembered dinner!*

She quickly took the cassoulet out of the oven and removed the lid. A bouquet of aromas filled the room. They ate their meal in a dining niche off the kitchen. The table was simply but elegantly laid, white dishes with red and gold linen napkins. In the center of the small table were three small poinsettias, their pots bound together with a broad, gold ribbon. Jeanne-Marie put the cassoulet on the sideboard near the table with a serving spoon, and then fetched their salads from the kitchen.

"We'll have our salads first, in the American style," she announced. They were a simple mixture of frisée, baby endive and arugula. Across the top there were several thinly shaved slices of red onion, crumbled French feta and pan-toasted pecans. Gaston motioned for Fiona to be seated at the end, as the couple took their places at the table.

Fiona waited. Even though she was starving, she didn't know if her Catholic hosts intended to say grace. Instead, Gaston lifted his glass in a toast, and in heavily accented English said, "Great paintings, new friends, *nice coat.*" As the laughter faded, they all started in on their salads.

"Mmmm, C'est bon," Fiona gestured with her fork, "The dressing, is it walnut oil?"

Jeanne-Marie smiled, "Oui, with just a touch of Dijon and balsamic."

"It's perfect."

Gaston put his arm around Jeanne-Marie, "I knew her before New York but when she came back she could now cook."

Jeanne-Marie laughed, "It's true. I was not very French here, but there, I had to learn. It's not like here, where on every corner is a wonderful restaurant. If I wanted the taste of home, I had to make it."

"Well, you certainly learned well. I've been dining in Paris for almost a week now, and this is… merveilleux."

"My mother had to learn to use email, to save me. It was too much, always calling her for some recipe."

"America is not so bleak as you think. My friends and I get together to cook splendid meals regularly."

"Not only pizza? We hear Americans eat pizza." Gaston smiled.

"Well, sometimes pizza," Fiona tipped her head and thought of Jennifer. "But good food, too."

Gaston said something that Fiona missed. Jeanne-Marie translated, "He says you live in the San Francisco Bay Area, that's not like living in the rest of America. With so many French living there, the food has to be better." She reached over and served up the cassoulet. Gaston went to the kitchen and brought back a breadboard with a chewy peasant bread and fresh butter.

Fiona took her first bite of the succulent bean mixture, and closed her eyes. "The herbs are wonderful and the beans, so tender, they have taken on the flavor of the broth, it is superb." Another bite had Fiona shaking her head in appreciation. She looked up at her hosts, "With your inspiration I will make this for my friends when I get home."

Gaston and Jeanne-Marie both beamed. It was the perfect compliment. They ate in silence for a few moments, then Gaston piped in with a question—the same question that had plagued Fiona ever since she found the painting of her apartment.

"And why is she not famous?"

Fiona thought about her answer, as she took another piece of the chewy bread. "I don't know. Many reasons. Her gender, the times, her disability. Later, she had a child out of wedlock and may have wanted to be discreet." Fiona shrugged, and buttered her bread. Jeanne-Marie translated, complete with a French shrug.

Gaston leaned forward, "Would the child have mattered so much?"

"It's hard to say, but the country was not so liberal then about illegitimacy…"

Again, Jeanne-Marie translated. Gaston put down his fork, and rapidly rattled off something in French. She turned to Fiona, "He asks how you found her, how you became aware of her work?"

Fiona explained about finding the first painting of her apartment and of the subsequent search.

Gaston's eyes widened. "And for this, you came to Paris?"

Fiona hesitated, "Mostly, yes."

Gaston pushed the envelope of his English, haltingly, "This is so… American, to do *the other*. We French, we do our work and enjoy living. What is this desire to do everything?"

"That's what Jeanne-Marie asked me," chuckled Fiona. "It's curiosity at first. Then, once the story unfolds, you do it for the story. And now, I do it for Emma."

"But you are an accountant, no?" Gaston was searching for understanding. Jeanne-Marie stood to gather the dishes.

"Yes."

217

"And this is not enough?" He looked at her earnestly.

"No, I guess not."

Gaston sighed, "Jeanne-Marie has a husband, Michel, in New York. He is French, like me, a musician. It is all he does. He is a good person, my friend, *aussi*. But jazz is all. So much, that there is not enough of him for Jeanne-Marie, too. She was too alone, and came home. And now, she is with me."

Jeanne Marie was blushing. "Yes," she added, "This French *single purpose* is a burden too."

Gaston looked at Fiona and Jeanne-Marie, "Maybe for your Emma, painting was enough."

"Excuse me?"

"Just the painting. Maybe it was enough. Perhaps she didn't care for the fame, maybe it was enough, only to paint."

Jeanne-Marie brought in the dessert. "Like Michel's jazz," she added.

Fiona felt numb. She looked at the plate in front of her, pears poached in wine. They were beautiful, sliced thin and then fanned out over the plate. Jeanne-Marie served some crème fraiche alongside the pear, then grated just a hint of nutmeg over the top. As a final touch, she placed one of the chocolate truffles on the edge of the plate.

Fiona shook her head, "But nobody does just one thing." She gestured at her hostess, "Jeanne-Marie works at the church, but here, she is an artist in the kitchen. Look at that dessert. And most of the French speak English. No one does just one thing."

"Except Michel," said Jeanne-Marie, resignation in her voice.

Fiona didn't like the image of an Emma so limited. In her letters there was philosophy and humor, she enjoyed politics. Fiona didn't want her Emma to be some painting idiot-savant. She kept shaking her head.

"Maybe…" And Jeanne-Marie's voice was a little sad here, "Maybe, it's not that they can do only one thing, it's that they only do what is important to them."

Gaston reached over again, and touched her, "I think dessert *is* important." Jeanne-Marie looked up at him and laughed.

With the somber mood broken, Fiona nodded, and picked up her fork. The pear was tender, just on the short edge of sweet, with a creamy finish and the merest shadow of nutmeg. It was quintessentially French, a dessert that left her palate clear, unlike an

American sugar rush. At the end, though, she popped the tiny truffle into her mouth. The perfect end to a perfect meal.

Gaston spoke and Jeanne-Marie translated, "It troubles him that she might not have cared about recognition. In one way, it speaks to pure art, but it also might be arrogance. He says he will have to think about these things." Gaston was becoming caught up in the Emma mystique.

"With Michel, he could be lost in his music, not arrogance," defended Jeanne-Marie.

The questions pushed Fiona harder. Her brow furrowed, "I need to look deeper in her letters. It's been a mystery all along—why isn't she famous. Maybe you're right, maybe fame didn't matter."

Gaston asked if there were more paintings, so Fiona retrieved the laptop and showed them the remainder of the slideshow.

"What of her Paris paintings?" asked Jeanne-Marie.

"Mostly she sold them. She was very proud that she could support herself during school with her work."

"So Paris has Emma Caites, too?"

"I guess, if you could find her."

"It makes me happy to know her work might still be here. What did she paint?"

"Luxembourg Gardens and its people, Pont Neuf, Notre Dame. I only know from the letters. We have no paintings from the Paris period." The three fell into sated, silent reflection.

It was late. Fiona thanked her hosts, who called for a taxi. It had been a wonderful evening, even if it disturbed Fiona a bit about Emma. She and Jeanne-Marie exchanged addresses. Fiona invited both of them to visit California, *The Promised Land* for the French. Fiona told them again what an amazing meal it had been and that she intended to recreate it for her friends back home, to demonstrate how the Parisians really ate. When the taxi arrived, Fiona thanked them once again for everything, right back to the rescue at Galleries Lafayette. They all embraced and Fiona climbed into the taxi wondering how she could compress all this for her next email report home.

Chapter Forty-Five

From: fionahedge@yahoo.com
Subject: Paris Impressions
Date: December 26, 2007 11:58 PM
To: artantikmarv@sbcglobal.net,ohamandakins@aol.com,
norminisstormin@aol.com, jennsullymills@gmail.com,
thomascaites@mindspring.com

So, Emma and Pierre meet at La Palette after the end of the day. She is so nervous that she is trembling. By the end of this day she ultimately sends three letters to Wren. Wren is her confidante, her sounding board and perhaps, her conscience. Pierre is also anxious, but he is a patient and loving man. He sees this, this unexpected shake up, as a possible opening to make his feelings known. We know this because as soon as Pierre takes a seat at the table, he pours his heart out to her. Our Emma reports every detail of her encounter to her friend by letter. Emma is dazed by the revelation. In a letter only earlier this day had she examined her feelings for Pierre, revealing that perhaps she enjoyed his attentions more than just as a friend. Now, confronted with Pierre's sincere outpouring of unrestrained affection, Emma is confounded. Every prior prospective suitor had been dragged to her mother's house by his mother's apron strings. Her only acknowledged attraction had been the family fortune. Since her illness she'd been regularly reminded that she could not expect love or children in her life, that no one would want her. Emma has no frame of reference for this earnestness. She has concealed her fortune to protect herself. But otherwise, with no expectations, Emma has only just been herself without guile or artifice.

She looks at Pierre unreservedly for the first time. He is tall and slight of build with sandy blond hair and steady hazel eyes. He has a square Dutch jaw, a Roman aquiline nose, perfect teeth set off against olive skin and a ready laugh. He has large hands with broad palms and then long narrow fingers. He has big feet. He is an odd mix of French and Dutch. She imagines him as a gothic scribe. Emma realizes that she finds him beautiful.

Petrified of physical intimacy and especially of revealing her defects, she cannot find words for her feelings. For awhile they sit quietly, their tea growing cold. Finally, Pierre reaches over and takes her hand. "I know I am no catch for an American of such talent. I am slow, I am not as schooled in history and culture, and it is likely that my mediocre skills will land me a life-long sinecure as a wine merchant. But if you could look beyond that, my feelings are pure and good. I have come to care deeply for you this year."

Emma is shocked. He is insecure about his position! She snorts at the joke of it and then when he recoils, she is desperate to explain. She leans forward, takes his face in her hands and kisses him lightly on the lower edge of his jaw.

"No one has ever wanted me. I am stunned and I am very afraid."

"Afraid? Afraid of what?" He gripped both her hands earnestly.

"That you will discover the ugliness of me, of my infirmities. That you'll come to know my shortcomings and then all will be lost, love and friendship. Friendships are all that I have."

"How can you say that? You have talent and beauty, intelligence, poise. Your gifts outshine everyone in the school."

Emma sat upright and looked directly in his eyes. "I am an orphan cripple. My devoted grandparents, who raised me, are dead. My own family rejected me out of revulsion for my frailties. They are effectively dead to me. I know too well the value of belonging... of friendship. It is all we really have." To her shame, tears filled her eyes and spilled down her cheeks.

It was Pierre's turn to be taken aback. He regarded her with a new understanding dawning. Still holding her hands, he said, "I can't imagine sharing life and becoming evermore intimate, with someone who is not a friend." He cradled her face in his hands and wiped away the tears with his thumbs. "Perhaps we can learn to belong to each other." He slid over on his seat, till she was sitting directly facing him, and he gathered her to him, wrapping his long arms around her and gently rocking her.

While the Parisians may be comfortable living out the dramas of their lives in public, this openness was more than either Emma or Pierre could bear.

After a bit he whispered in her ear, "We should go."

Wordlessly she pulled on her jacket, took up her cane, and pulled some francs from her pocket to cover the tab. Together they stepped out into the night. He turned and kissed her. His arms enveloped her and held her in the cool evening. Where to go? Where to go? For the first time, Emma was shy about bringing him to her hotel room. She wanted privacy, but not an expectation of physical intimacy. Her small hotel room dominated by a bed was too suggestive for her modesty. Yet, Pierre shared a crowded student apartment with four others. Where to go? Emma reached into her pocket and felt the key, the key to her new home. While completely empty, it was hers. Emma swallowed hard at the gravity of her action, took his hand, and led the way to Rue Visconti. Pierre followed, without question. They climbed the stairs, hand in hand.

In the dim hallway Emma turned the key and opened the door to her small retreat, their footsteps echoing into the empty room. Her hands searched the wall by the door, and finally finding the switch, she flipped on the light.

Pierre winced at the sudden brightness, "What's this?"

"This is my new home. I rented it this afternoon."

Pierre surveyed the apartment. Like a cat, he walked its perimeters and checked each room.

He turned and nodded approval, "Emma, it's perfect. School's right across the street! You have your own studio space. It's incredible." He threw his arms around her, this time in a congratulatory embrace. Then he lifted her up and swung her round in the empty room till she was dizzy. He stopped and steadied her. Then he kissed her again, passionately, his hands skimming down her sides, resting finally on her narrow waist.

Emma panicked and pushed away. All of the warnings of her life echoed in her ears, the dangers of intimacy and the peril of pregnancy. "I can't do this. I cannot risk pregnancy!"

Peter hesitated. He nodded and then, "But we can touch each other. Please each other."

Emma, who knew nothing of passion, pressed her forehead to his chest and considered this. He lifted her chin and they kissed again, and her compliance gave way to her consent.

She reports in her last letter regarding that day that they "spent the night in an unfurnished apartment, touching and exploring, pleasing, kissing and talking." She is amazed at the sensation and pleasure of it. In the dark and in his embrace, Emma doesn't give a second thought to her impairments. They are whole together. No one had ever communicated what it was she was missing, what it was her world had expected her to do without. Pierre opened the door to passion, to the stirrings of new feelings and wonder.

In the morning they awoke in each other's arms. Stiff from hard floors, they got up groaning and laughing. They dressed in rumpled clothes and headed to La Palette for breakfast. It alarmed Emma that, with even the smallest caress, the touching of fingertips or his hand on her shoulder, she'd catch her breath, transported to the tender ecstasies of the previous night.

Today, though, was critique day, the final judgment of a year of instruction. Their displays were ready. They were nervous, but preoccupied with new connections. Later that night, Pierre held his ticket on a night train home for the summer. On a lesser day, Emma might have lamented the now imminent departure. That day though, there was too much fullness to anticipate the loss, too much busy to reflect.

The protocol for the critique is uniform. It is a public event. Each of the major professors, painting, drawing and design/classics tours the room with their comments and criticisms. Then the floor is opened for student input, with any rebuttal or comment by the individual student in question. Then, reviewing their notes, the professors announce their conclusions. Though the written grades will follow by post, the students will know at the critique whether their grade will allow them to move up to the next level, or, in some cases, even to return in the fall to continue. Both Pierre and Emma were confident that they would progress to the second year classes, but instructor comments were crucial.

223

Emma's display was near the last to be critiqued in her class. The judgments thus far had been stern, but constructive. As she explained to Wren, the students were "wincing, but not cringing." Student participation had warmed up, and Emma was impressed at the thoughtfulness of the comments they made, not necessarily complimentary, but solid observations. She braced for the instructors' comments on her work. The design instructor commented that her arrangements sometimes lacked in cohesion and that she could focus on ugliness that was exaggerated for impact. This was a fair comment, as he was focusing on those drawings from M. Duprès' class, where that had been precisely her objective. In her work outside of class, he said her design was strong and showed a confidence unusual in a first year student. The painting instructor jumped in, with compliments on light and color, primarily on her outdoor work. As he had for most of the students, he commented that Emma's museum studies were competent, but static. Copying in the Louvre was their least favorite assignment. The instructors were challenged to comment on the life studies by the female students, because they had been done outside class, as the women were barred from life drawing studies at school. The professors had to judge solely from the drawings and canvases without having seen the actual models. For the other female students the comments had been, at best, perfunctory. But here, with Emma, M. Duprès began to get his digs in. Her figures were exaggerated, crude and unnatural. They showed a basic artistic immaturity and an unfamiliarity with the human figure which was typical, and ultimately dispositive of women's art. Her undisciplined approach was acceptable for tourist canvases but would never amount to actual artistic merit. As for the nocturne paintings, he said that she suffered from impressionistic plagiarism in a loose and unprincipled style that discredited the school. He decried that this student (Emma) clearly had some raw, native talent, but it was wasted on the vulgarity of an untrainable mind. Emma was dumbfounded. She had not expected praise from Duprès, but neither had she expected this. Were she not riding high on the intensity of her new connection to Pierre,

224

she would have been distraught. No other student had been so excoriated. Even the painting instructor looked alarmed at the vehemence of Duprès' spitting critique. After that, the students looked at their feet, and shifted about, but no one would comment on Emma's display.

It was Emma's turn. She rose and stated simply that she'd learned a great deal that year, that while she bridled some with the classical restrictions, she'd become more accurate and more sensitive to the subtleties in the masters. She said that her painting instructor had been invaluable in aiding her in new approaches to color. She defended her life studies by saying that it was a shame that the women in the class were forced by the rules of the day to endeavor life drawing on their own, without instruction, but that even there she'd learned and improved, perhaps more so than under the tutelage of some instructors. Her fellow students gasped at her bold retort.

In their conclusions, it was clearly a two to one split. Had Duprès carried the day, Emma could not have returned to Beaux Arts. The other instructors stated that she had shown significant improvement over the year, and that she should certainly be given the opportunity to continue to hone her skills. Duprès looked livid. He spat that the shortcomings of her gender and the deformities of her (and there he paused before continuing) character, made her incompatible with serious art instruction. A pall settled over the students. This was not a critique, it was open warfare. They glanced sideways at Emma, whose jaw was set, but who otherwise looked resolute in her stance. The remaining displays were critiqued without incident. In all, from her class of thirty, only one student was prevented from continuing and two were held back from advancing in painting. Emma was advanced in all classes, but had been unmistakably singled out for the harshest treatment of all students in their group. She had prevailed, but she had made an enemy. When the professors cleared the room, her friends rushed to her side. The class was full of the tension of it, and some students slunk out to tell the tale in other classes. The critiques had run long.

It was well past lunch and students still had to disassemble their displays and vacate class space before the end of the day. It was easy for Emma. Fueled by anger she just marched her works across the street and up to her little apartment. Simone, anxious for her friend, followed along, cheering Emma on and filling the air with friendly chat. Emma longed to find Pierre, but the door to that studio was still closed. Nobody would dare disturb ongoing critiques. By four o'clock, Emma had broken down her display and vacated the year's work. She helped Simone with hers then went to the administrative offices to change her address. There, even the clerks had heard of the dressing down she'd received in critique. As one of the few female students, Emma was known to all and was particularly the underdog for the office staff. Despite the sting of the criticisms, Emma was buoyed by the heartfelt encouragement she was receiving from all quarters.

At the end of an exhausting day, and particularly after a night of little sleep, she was done in. She retreated to La Palette for comfort and chocolate. When she stepped in the door, half the school was there, all basking in success or licking the wounds of the day. She scanned the restaurant for Pierre, with no luck. Others, noticing her arrival, began to stand. Several began to clap. Within a minute the entire restaurant, even the waiters, who of course knew the students and had heard everything, all stood in an ovation for Emma. The pressures of the day finally snapped and Emma began to cry. She was immediately surrounded by well-wishers, embraced by her best friends, and led to a table where her standard fare, café au lait and a pain au chocolat, magically appeared. Simone stepped in and served as her buffer and their core group of weekend painters took the seats at the table. It was safe. Emma was no academic miracle but she was recognized and well loved at her school. No one much liked M. Duprès and his conduct that day, especially in so public a forum as the year-end critique, was denounced universally. That Emma had stood up to him, without anger and retaining her dignity, placed her well with everyone.

226

Where was Pierre? Emma knew that his critique had run long. She also knew he had to clear out from his apartment as well as from the school. She'd wanted to give him the key to her apartment so he could store there over the summer. Still, she couldn't believe he'd get on his train without seeing her, not after the night before. And though their usual pattern was to meet at La Palette, she really hoped for a few minutes together, alone. Apparently, this post-critique fete at La Palette was a long-standing tradition for the students of Beaux Arts. And after weeks of preparation, this last day of school was the unwinding, for good or for bad; students could at last relax.

Finally at about six, Pierre came in. He slid onto the bench next to Emma. He looked harried. He'd heard about the critique and was worried about her. He'd been to her hotel, tried at the apartment. Under the table his hand squeezed hers. Emma was thankful for both his outreach, and his discretion. Everything was happening so quickly. In hours, he'd be on his way home. Emma felt she'd need the whole summer to grasp just the past 24 hours.

"So, did you decide I could store that painting at your place this summer?"

Emma looked up at him, understanding that this was a bid for privacy. "Sure, I thought you'd forgotten."

"No, just been too busy. I hate to tear you from the party, but I have to leave tonight, could we move it now?"

Their friends all groaned at the table, "Pierre, you just got here." "Emma, don't go, just give him the keys."

"I would but he's not been there, I must go. I'll be back." The two sidled out of the crowded table and made their way out. They hurried up the street to the apartment. They were no sooner in the door but Pierre took her in his arms. He kissed her face, her forehead, her hairline. She pulled him close, ran her hands down his back. He lifted her and set her on the drain board in the kitchen and pulled her snug up to him. She followed his lead and wrapped her legs around him. They pressed their torsos close, pressed their cheeks together and held tight, whispering through gasping breath.

"I heard. I thought I'd die from the pain if it. I can't believe

227

he'd do that to you. By all accounts, you were magnificent."

She tilted her head back and kissed his neck under the chin. "I was stunned. I couldn't have stood it but for new strength, found just yesterday... last night... this morning." She kissed him again. He held her tight and shook his head.

"I don't see how I can go. I don't know how I could stay."

"Of course, you will go. Your father is relying on you. I'll be here, waiting for your return. We'll write. Pierre, will you write to me?"

"Pieter."

"What?"

"It's my given name. It's the name I'm called by everyone who loves me. Call me Pieter."

She kissed him again. "Will you write, Pieter?"

"Every day on paper. Every minute in my heart. Emma, I am so happy but so sad it took so long. Just when I'm leaving."

"I'm so happy it happened at all. We can wait. It's just the summer."

"I want you."

"Good, then I'm assured you'll return."

There was a knock on the door and they both started. Emma cleared her throat, and slid down from the drain board. She smoothed her dress and then stepped to the door and opened it. Outside, Simone and Emile were there with several bottles of wine. The others could be heard coming up the stairs.

Pieter sighed, "I'll run and get the painting. I'll be right back." He slipped out just as the others came in.

The tiny flat filled with about fifteen art students. Emma's little apartment was a big hit with her friends. They were surprised that the place was unfurnished, except for Emma's artwork stacked in the little studio room.

"I only found it yesterday," she defended.

"Yeah, I heard you've been busy," mugged Joseph.

Simone was babbling excitedly about taking Emma to the Marche des Puces to furnish it. "Maybe you could even trade paintings for stuff."

Emile smirked, "She already does, she trades them for money." The others laughed along with him. Georges opened the cupboard and found it empty, no glasses. He opened a bottle with his pocket knife, took a swig and passed it around.

He held up his knife to reveal an attached folding corkscrew and winked. "Toujours Francais!"

"Don't go far with that. We'll be needing it," added Jean Luc, tipping the bottle back. Emma helped herself to a gulp of the wine, passed it on and realized, mortified, that this was her first party.

Later, she reported to Wren how strange, she is happy here, a vacant apartment, no dishes, no chairs but her friends are laughing, voices raised to be heard over the lively din, some standing, some sprawled on the floor. No comparison, she ventures, for the high style of the wife in the diplomatic service, but an animated jovial event, nonetheless. Her friends were wildly plotting the most grueling and appropriate revenges against M. Duprès. Simone waved her arms talking curtains and tables and laughing that at least Emma has art. On cue, Jean Luc had found some nails in the walls and he hung several of her paintings up, haphazardly. Pieter returned with one of his Nocturnes and a sac of cheeses and bread. He was toasted by the rowdy crew, who pressed him with wine. Pieter raised the bottle, getting everyone's attention.

"To our hostess, who shares all that she has, and who battles dragons fearlessly for our benefit and for honor." A cheer rose by all, and the bottle made the rounds again, as Georges opened yet another. Isabelle spread the cheeses and bread on the counter where they were devoured in minutes.

Pieter slipped back to Emma and brushed her palm with his fingertips. "My train...."

"I know."

His lips touched her forehead, "Write."

Emma nodded and leaned discreetly into his warmth for just a moment. Pieter called out and waved goodbye to the group. Then he was gone.

The party kept up until the wine and the energy ran low. Emma cleaned up after the last of the stragglers, throwing the trash into the kitchen sink.

Finally, exhausted, she headed back to the Hotel Angleterre for her last night there.

—And in the same vein, I must close for the night. The story carries me but Paris (and bed) beckons and there's more to see tomorrow. Good night.

Fiona

Chapter Forty-Six

From: fionahedge@yahoo.com
Subject: Paris Impressions
Date: December 27, 2007 10:32 AM
To: artantikmarv@sbcglobal.net, ohamandakins@aol.com,
norminisstormin@aol.com, jennsullymills@gmail.com,
thomascaites@mindspring.com

I'm going to take a few moments this morning to dash out
more of the Emma story before going out to my last day in
Paris. I could stay a month. I will surely be back, though on
my own account. I wish I had time to search out Pieter, in
Holland. I have to remind myself that this is not really his
story. It'll be a bit faster now. The letters thin out a bit. I think a
lot of Emma's writing energies that summer went to Pieter.
(Too bad we didn't get his papers.) Also, Wren has her baby
and her letters slow down a little, too. I'm not sure what to do
today. Paris has a famous flea market, which Emma
frequented to furnish her apartment, but that's not exactly a
winter attraction. She also loved the cemeteries. I'm torn
between Paris and following Emma and her story.

Emma was happy that summer. She painted, and sold her
work at an amazing rate. The streets were full of American
tourists who bought her paintings and were treated to Emma's
generous tips on the best spots of the 'real' Paris. Their
encounters make her wonder who she really is. Is she
French, as the tourists first think when they encounter her? Or
is she still deeply American? And then, in her quiet moments
she wonders if someday, she'll adapt to a new life in a new
country. She sells for the same prices as other students, but a
theme develops, one that continued into her Oakland days,
that her prices were too low. There's no rancor in the debate,
but I wonder if Emma's work doesn't undercut the market a
little. The artists around her chide her to increase her prices
so as not to crowd them. It may be a self-esteem question for
her and also that ultimately, Emma has the confidence of an

inheritance. In any event, she more than covers expenses that summer and accumulates some savings. She rarely mentions her fall-back money to Wren, but frequently mentions that she is more than covering expenses. Perhaps its freedom negates her mother's comments that even a crippled spinster couldn't expect to be supported.

Emma idled away her long summer evenings scrounging to furnish her apartment. She immediately bought a full bed and a good mattress with linens. Though the bed is an antique picked up cheap at the flea market, she spares no expense on the mattress, on the theory that her back and hip required good support. Then she spends the summer meandering Paris looking for furnishings. By August, the little apartment is furnished and homey. Her artwork peppers the walls. Emma was playing house. She points out to Wren that she has enough furnishings in storage in Oakland for a whole house. It's good furniture too, custom Arts and Crafts originals made for her grandparents. While she loves it, with all its memories, Emma has as much emotionally invested in the eclectic mix of fun she pulls together from the Paris flea markets. This apartment is the first home she has made for herself. I wonder if, in the back of her head, it's a home for Pieter, too. She mentions that she visited a Parisian doctor, for assistance with female issues, and is prepared in the event her relationship with Pieter becomes more serious. So, I am sure that Pieter figures into her upbeat mood.

Emma tells Wren an illuminating story about the building superintendent, one she probably didn't share with Pieter. One day a minor plumbing problem sent her down to his unit. He followed her back up, and on entering the apartment he is stunned by the artwork. Shaking his head he looks very unhappy. Emma queries him and he admits that when he first rented to her, she had paid in cash, in wrinkled bills. He'd assumed that she was a prostitute and he'd been looking forward to the day when she might not be able to make rent. Now that he could see that she was an artist, and a good one at that, the prospect of taking the rent out in trade seemed unlikely, and not what he'd expected.

We don't have Pieter's letters, which is interesting because Emma did save Wren's from the same period. So we have to guess at what's up with Pieter, based on what Emma tells Wren. We know that Pieter writes almost daily. He fills her in on rhythms and details of his life at home, his work in his father's business and his remorse that there's no time, or support, in the mix for him to paint at home. He loves his home life, and catches up on practical jokes and silly stuff with his sisters. They clamor for him to draw, and to his mother's chagrin, he does little sketches and caricatures on demand. He had returned home with his paintings, which his father noted were very good, better than his own had been. Even his mother had to acknowledge that Pieter showed artistic talent and promise. Pieter surmises that his mother is not pleased that art school has found so responsive a student. The message of her own past is not lost on her—after all, her husband left his country, religion and family to marry her. She teases him, only partly in jest, that art, or some other dalliance, will steal her beloved son from her and that he will remain in France.

Pieter works six days a week in town. He knows the work, he's been helping since childhood, but he finds it deadly boring. The only good news is that he can take breaks during the day, in which to write Emma. He sends her long romantic letters, punctuated with illustrations—pictures of the wine racked in the warehouse, little portraits of his sisters, engaged in various household tasks, the view out his window, anything to bring Emma closer. Emma comes to know the tiniest details of his life, how one sister carefully trims the fat off her meat and another likes double portions of jam, how Holland's summers can be as hot as Paris, but twice as humid, how important it is to store wine at the correct angle and to handle it with care so as not to bruise its flavor. Since Pieter picks up the mail for home and business, no one in his family is even aware of his ample correspondence. He calls her his secret life. Only the postal clerk comments and he silences her with a smile and a wink. Sundays are Pieter's heaven. It is his one free day and he usually packs up a big picnic lunch to take

233

the sisters out for a day in the sun. He brings his tablet and pastels and captures the Dutch countryside, often adorned with the flying blond braids of wild sisters. His mother wonders aloud that he rarely includes his old friends on these events, or even a girl from town. Pieter just rolls his eyes. Hidden in these stories, Emma notes to Wren, is the fact that Pieter has not told his family that there is someone special in Paris. A little of her old fears linger.

The heat of mid-summer fades and August leans into September when the students will return. Emma has pulled strings with the office clerks at school, and has been reassigned to a new drawing class. She will not have M. Duprès scowling over her. Pieter has secured his old apartment and roommates, and will arrive on September 2nd. Emma can hardly wait. Pressed by their friends, Emma planned a big party for the first weekend back, and does invitations in pastels for the event. She tells Wren the picture on the invitation shows the sitting room of her home, just to show she finally has furniture! The enclosed invitation shows an airy, light-filled space, rendered in an impressionist style, its walls shoulder to shoulder in paintings. The colors are bright, yellows and greens, dotted with bits of red. A wooden table decorated with flowers is surrounded with colorfully painted chairs. Yellow curtains wave in the breeze of the open windows above a red settee. The invitation looks like a Van Gogh interior.

There are no letters for the first two weeks of September and I feel cheated! Emma reunites with Pieter and has the party without me! I guess she was busy. The letters resume in mid-September, by which time Emma and Pieter are an established couple and the party is described summarily as a grand success. Emma does discuss Pieter, but the letters are not so different than those of the previous year. Her ardor has not dampened her appetite for painting and art. She still is the driving force behind the core group of friends and they spend the better part of weekends painting plein air. Now that she has a kitchen, the picnics are richer, tastier and cheaper. One wonders if packing lunch for a lover isn't also a basic incentive to upgrade the culinary fare. Her new drawing instructor, M. Gauthier, is a gem. Emma's drawing perspective and layout work improves markedly under the eye of guidance without judgment. He also agrees to review the life drawings done by the women at the school, to provide pointers, even though he does not actually supervise the sessions. Since her apartment has heat, Emma's becomes the studio for the unofficial women's life drawing class. There are ribald jokes about what goes on, and the models, both men and women, are in on the fun. They launch rumors that circulate throughout the school, each wilder than the next. With smug satisfaction, Emma notes to Wren that, whatever the reputation, the women now compete qualitatively with the life studies done by their male colleagues. As usual with Emma, it is the work that is the yardstick of success.

Pieter lives in his crowded, shared apartment about six blocks from the school. Weekends he usually spends at Emma's. While Emma is the metronome that sets the pace, Pieter insists on continuing the lazy Sunday tempo he has established in his summer. While Emma resists, she comes to enjoy their quiet Sunday mornings. It is a time for sleeping in, sweet loving, newspaper reading, tender talks with coffee and breakfast in bed. Emma blooms with the attention. But it's clear that the question of the long term gnaws in her head, because she repeatedly wrestles with who she is, and where she's from. Our Emma was struggling to find her sense of place in a world where she forges all of her connections. She shared that pull with her friend in the intimate stories she chooses to reveal.

"One Sunday morning, we sipped our coffee with the sunshine streaming in around us in bed. Pieter had been telling me stories of home and in a lull, I asked, 'What is it to be Dutch?'
Pieter paused, 'That's difficult to answer because I am also French. You want to know Dutch, but I can only answer you in French.'
'But, you identify more with Dutch?' I pressed.
'I do. What is Dutch, hmmm? It is thrifty. It is knowing that

235

the elements can turn on you. It is knowing that you hang on by your fingernails to a sliver of land and build it up, literally saving it from the sea. It is finding beauty in it day to day, in your work, your family, your place. The Dutch are industrious, they have to be. But they also love art and flowers.'

'Family is part of it?'

'Very much so. Family and history.' He lifted my face towards his, 'So, let's turn this question. What is it to be American?'

I leaned back on the pillow and thought about my own history. 'The best and the worst of it?'

'Yes, though that's not entirely fair, I didn't give the worst of the Dutch'

'I think for the Americans it may be the same thing—the best and the worst. I think being American is about being able to look forward without looking back at all.'

'At all?' He did not look like he believed me.

'For some. My ancestors came from England. They did not look back. They were farmers, then merchants, then manufacturers. Then, when the family was quite well off, my grandfather did it again. He came to California against the wishes of family and started all over. He was successful and rich in his own right, never looking back.'

'This is not Dutch.' Pieter laughed, 'When you fight so hard to steal land from the sea, you don't leave it so easily.'

'But,' I protested, 'You have Dutch who came to America, New York was settled by Dutch.'

'Not Dutch my girl,' Pieter leaned over and kissed me, 'Those were budding Americans.'"

Emma confided to Wren that Pieter was so deeply tied to home and family that she had accepted that any life with him would have to be in Holland. Any other result would be taking a fish out of water. She speculated that it was feasible, since her ties to Oakland were so tenuous. Only memories held her to California, her parents and siblings, "still burned by the inheritance," had made it clear that their relations with Emma were over. (Maybe Thomas can shed some light on this issue.)

236

As winter stole the light from the days, the art students grumbled at the inevitable return to boring still life drawings and paintings. Emma loved the life drawings and longed to do full paintings of nudes. The other women students recoiled at the idea, it was too controversial. Emma began doing studies of Pieter, pencil and charcoal drawings mostly. They both agreed that they were some of her best drawings, but that she could never show them at school, and neither could he show drawings of her. Posing for each other became one of their favorite seductions and they joked that the fire would be out if they could ever finish a drawing.

Emma wanted to do more nocturne studies, this time of Notre Dame, and once some snow fell, she wanted to paint the espaliered apple trees at Luxembourg Gardens. She loved how their naked twisted convoluted branches caught the snow and shone in the moonlight. Pieter reluctantly acquiesced to revisit the chilly nightly painting, but these dark studies actually suited his style even more than hers. The paintings were stunning. At the short critique in December, even their professors were entranced by their shadowy, undulating world of Paris nights. The critique results were glowing for both of them. Their fellow students admired the works, but thought the couple had become the vampires of L'Écôle des Beaux Arts. Despite his occasional complaints that Emma was all about the art, Pieter flourished with the inspiration. As they moved into spring, it became a toss up whose work was better. One day, while painting at one of their regular stations at Pont Neuf, the couple was approached by a dealer who wanted to carry their work in his gallery. It was the ultimate compliment for an art student, but risky because of how it might be received at school. Pieter wrote to his father for advice, who asked Pieter to send one of the canvases in question. The reply was amazing. "Son, this is a work of such sensitivity and beauty that even your mother wept when she saw it. We are awed."

The only wrinkle that I can see in this idyllic arena was Emma's awareness that Pieter didn't include any mention of her to his family. With summer approaching, Emma wanted to

237

visit him at home. This wasn't possible unless Pieter began introducing the idea to his parents and in particular his mother. Pieter resisted Emma's urgings, for fear that any hint of romance in Paris would end his parental support, and he intimated so to Emma. Secretly he probably feared his mother's reaction to Emma's disability. Pieter didn't want to rock the boat, either with Emma or his parents, so he resolutely held his tongue.

Critique was coming, but neither Emma nor Pieter had any concern over their accomplishments. Their year's work had been stellar. They were the acknowledged leaders in their class and in the school. They'd decided to hold off on the gallery connection until after critique, and Emma would manage their artistic affairs through the summer, including the gallery representation. This year's end was not so dramatic as the year before, but found a more secure and happy Emma. Her summer would be in Paris again, and also in Provence, where she planned to travel with Simone. Pieter was headed home to the wine business, but not without having impressed both his parents with his talent and prospects in art. When they parted for the summer, it was with the solid comfort of an established couple. Emma was deeply in love and it had only enriched her artistic capacity. Pieter's talent too had burgeoned. Emma found a new confidence in his steady hazel eyes. At its core I think the strength in that confidence came from Emma.

—On that happy note I'm off to see a little more of Paris. I'll try to read at lunch and get more story to you tonight. In the meantime, Thomas, what were the terms of Emma's inheritance? I think it figures deeply into her self image.

Fiona

238

Chapter Forty-Seven

From: thomascaites@mindspring.com
Subject: Paris Impressions
Date: December 27, 2007 10:00 AM
To: fionahedge@yahoo.com, artantikmarv@sbcglobal.net, ohamandakins@aol.com, norminisstormin@aol.com, jennsullymills@gmail.com,

Fiona,
I think I have two of Peter's paintings. Both are nocturnes, one of a stone bridge (I assume Pont Neuf) and the other is of pruned trees in the snow. My mother never mentioned Pieter; she said she'd bought the picture of the trees in Paris. I didn't notice till now that the signatures on the two were the same.

The story of the inheritance is understandable, but very sad. My great grandparents were concerned that, without independent funds, my mother would be the victim of the narrow whims of her family. My great grandparents did not discuss their estate with their only daughter, my grandmother, so it came as a complete surprise to the family when my great grandfather died. They left all of the business assets, the company the business accounts, inventory etc., to my grandmother. She and my grandfather had effectively been running the store for a decade at the time of my great-grandfather's death, so that wasn't unusual. They left everything else to my mother. That was their house, furnishings, artwork, and personal accounts and investments. It amounted to just over half their net worth. My grandmother and family were livid. They tried everything they could to get my mother to waive her interests under the will. She refused. They contemplated a will contest, but if they lost, the will made it clear they would forfeit whatever they had inherited to my mother, so they didn't actually sue. My grandmother's opinion was that my mother had used her influence to steal what rightly should have gone to my grandmother. There was no affection in that mother-daughter relationship. My great-grandparents had good reason to skip a generation, and they did provide a good living to their daughter, but their reasons were not accepted. When my mother wouldn't cooperate, there was an ugly scene which effectively terminated any contact between my mother and anyone in the family. I think she died without another word to any of them. I learned of the estate matters from Aunt Henrietta (whom you call Wren) after my mother died.

Years later, after the war and my uncle's death, we learned that my mother's family had lost everything in the crash and the Depression. Because of her inherent financial conservatism, my mother had been very careful with her money in the twenties. She invested in government securities and what would now be considered growing technology stocks (mostly telephone company and telephone equipment companies). She may be one of the few who not only survived the Depression intact, but afterwards actually ended up ahead. Wren said that after the Depression my mother lived frugally partly out of habit, partly because she was proud of supporting herself and partly to keep a low profile. Mom was concerned that if family knew she still had money they'd be after her, and she didn't want them to get their hands on me. It also made it easier to blend in the arts community if she wasn't perceived as independently wealthy. There were continuing hurts there for many years. I don't know if Mom ever recovered. After all, most of these stories came to me from Henrietta after Mom died. I never knew she had family or money and my inheritance came as a complete shock. Since Mom rarely drew on her grandparents' estate funds, and since she was an astute investor, the estate was enormous by the time my mother passed. Mother was right though; after she died, her sister approached me, long lost relative and all, sniffing about for some share of their grandparents' estate.

Thomas

Chapter Forty-Eight

Fiona flipped down the lid on the laptop and slipped it into its carrying case. It was her last full day in Paris. She wanted to make the most of it, even though it was hard to drag herself away from Emma's letters and the unfolding story. She slipped on her coat and pulled the laptop strap over her head. With the new information about their nocturne paintings, she was tempted to head back to the Luxembourg Gardens to have another look at the apple trees. They were pruned to act almost like a fence, but without their leaves in winter they looked tortured.

Again, Fiona marveled at how there was something she had actually seen, and yet missed, though it was in plain view. Through Emma's eyes, the same scene was beautiful, enough so to steal back into the park at night to paint it in the winter cold. But Fiona was loathe to retrace her steps, and since she'd have Pieter's painting to look at, she decided not to go back. She was excited to see Pieter's two paintings, but would have preferred there'd been Paris works by Emma in that mix.

She was a little jealous of Marvin's getting to inventory Thomas' collection. Fiona was still kicking herself that despite spending over an hour in Thomas' office, she'd failed to connect with even one of Emma's paintings. Also waiting at home were the new paintings that Marvin had found. Fiona realized that she was a little homesick, and she was also exhausted. Between her daytime excursions, reading Emma's letters, her email reports and the research and documentation for the biography, she was worn out. Still, she was especially thankful for Jenn's organizational charts. She'd spent hours filling in the details of her reading, the references, dates and the topics. As she went, it made all the information instantly accessible through the sorting parameters. With that ready info, her notes were enormously complete, and the actual biography was almost writing itself as she went along. Now she just had to sort through her own preferences to decide what last bits of Emma's Paris she wanted to drink in today.

There were dozens of museums she'd like to see, but those weren't on Emma's list, so they'd have to wait for another trip. Emma loved the flea market, so Fiona decided to keep it on a back

241

burner, in case there was time. She also loved the cemeteries, and while that's not exactly a winter event, the Paris cemeteries have incredible history. Emma had been taken with the amount of sculpture included on the gravesites. The cemeteries, while not exactly parks, were peaceful and beautiful oases in the busy city. Fiona was not so taken with the concept of the famous dead—she didn't need to do the Jim Morrison pilgrimage, which obviously wouldn't have been an Emma event. But a reflective walk along the aisles of history might be just right on this last day. Fiona pulled out her guidebooks and decided to visit Père Lachaise. It was a famous and venerable cemetery, and one noted for its elegant headstones and sculptures.

Fiona grabbed a taxi. Père Lachaise was on the metro line, but at this late date, she didn't want to start with Metro maps and buses. The day was cool, crisp and bright. The cemetery was beautiful, a small stone city for the dead. Fiona didn't want to study the stories of those buried, she just wanted to ramble and bask in the impressions of the sculptures. She knew Emma had some favorites, she'd described them to Wren, so Fiona was going to just walk the aisles, and enjoy as it unfolded.

It was a good walk. Fiona had picked the wrong way to approach it, and found herself walking uphill. But the day was nice, so she just unbuttoned her coat and kept up the pace. Even without searching the ones Emma mentioned, Père Lachaise was full of wonderful surprises. Fiona specifically wanted to see the grave of Theodore Gericault, the famous painter of Raft of Medusa, which had been Emma's first Louvre painting assignment. Emma also loved the grave of Francois Vincent Raspail, which she reminded Wren they'd seen together. Fiona didn't get a description, just that it was hauntingly beautiful, an odd portrayal for funerary sculpture. In spite of these goals, Fiona kept getting sidetracked. Fiona liked the sculpture of Mme. Lardin de Musset, obviously a writer of some sort, a kindly looking woman sitting up with a book in her lap. She loved the mysterious tomb of Felix Faure, with a sculpture of a distinguished man on his deathbed, slightly turned with his arm outstretched on the empty side of the bed. Fiona was sure there was a story there and vowed she'd come back another time for her own research. She snapped a few photos.

She turned a corner, and found Theodore Gericault. Fiona understood immediately why Emma liked it. Across the top of the tombstone, the artist is reclining in bed with his palette in one hand and brush extended in the other. The sculpted face is dramatic, with deep set eyes, high cheekbones and a long face offset by an elegant bald head topped with a cap. Below, on the pedestal in low relief, is a depiction of the famous painting. Emma must have loved to visit here, view the painting she'd known so well and the strangely beautiful portrayal of the young man who'd painted it. Fiona took a dozen photos of this elegant tomb, in part because of its complex beauty and in part because it was from Emma's Paris. Fiona continued, awed by the *who's who* of names. She turned just past Chopin's tomb, and disoriented, headed back towards the entry of the cemetery. While she groaned at being directionally challenged, the diversion brought her to the tomb of Camille Pissarro, the early Impressionist painter. Near there, was a bust of an unknown, Jacob Robles, with a sad face and a bony finger pressed gently to his lips. Fiona loved the evocative gesture, and knew that M. Robles would stay in her mind for some time. Another photo for the group back home. She ran across the tomb for the ancient lovers, Héloise and Abelard. By their dates, it was obvious that these tortured souls' remains had been relocated to the more-recent Père Lachaise. Fiona wondered at what would shuffle the celebrity dead around France, from cemetery to cemetery. Whatever happened to the concept of the quiet repose of a final resting place? She shook her head. Plus ça change, plus c'est la même chose.

Fiona wanted to avoid the famed, perpetual crowd at Jim Morrison's tomb, so she scouted ahead and circled around along the perimeter, where she saw a lovely sculpture at the grave of Georges Rodenbach. In it the decedent is breaking free of the stone of his tomb and reaching out with a naked arm to extend a rose. This place was full of stories. Still avoiding the Morrison crowd, she turned right, and found what she knew immediately must be the tomb of Francois Raspail. This was the one Emma and Wren had seen together. It was beautiful. Outside the tomb she found the form of a woman, fully shrouded in draped cloth except for one arm reaching up to the grated window of the tomb. Fiona paused at this eloquent statement of mourning. The achingly beautiful sculpture captured the loss; it spoke to Emma and her friend, and was just as poignant now, eighty years later. She pulled out the camera again so she could share it. Fiona, lost in thought, wandered noting the names she recognized. Ingres, Corot (with an amazingly lifelike bust),

Daumier. The tomb of Rene Lalique had a crucifixion scene in etched glass, making Fiona smirk. Even in death we promote our product.

Fiona made her way to the back end of the cemetery, where she found a tomb topped with an unnerving life sized sculpture of a man, just shot dead, his top hat dropped at his side. She didn't know what Victor Noir's story was, but wondered at the surviving family who would permanently enshrine the victim in the worst moment of his worst day. Relief came, just steps away, with the resting place for Maroun-Khadra; exquisitely rendered in white stone was a life-sized sculpture of a woman in bed, peacefully nursing her newborn. Here the sculpture was so quietly personal that just taking photos felt invasive. Fiona felt out of her league in French history. Some of the most poignant memorials were for names she did not recognize.

Fiona realized she was getting hungry and tired. She could take the back-entry out of the cemetery, but that would put her in unfamiliar territory. Instead, she looped around on the north side. There, was the tomb of Sarah Bernhardt, which she'd missed on the way in. Fiona hadn't even realized she was French! The woman had lived a long illustrious life, fully and with verve. Fiona thought about Emma, trapped in a body that gave out long before her spirit, but painting all the way. To make up ground, Fiona headed again for the perimeter, but stopped to see the bust of Balzac. A bit further along she found the combined tombs of Croce-Spinelli and Sivel. She didn't know the story of these two men, but whatever their fate, they'd clearly met it together; they lay side by side naked but for a loose covering waist-down, hand in hand. Again she stopped to take several pictures, wondering if this wasn't the gay version of Heloise and Abelard. She hurried past the tomb of Georges Seurat towards the entrance, but then stopped and giggled that they hadn't somehow made his marker more, well, pointillist. Fiona was a little punchy, tired and hungry. She checked her watch, and was surprised to see she'd been there nearly six hours. She hailed a taxi, and headed for her home-base, La Palette.

Hungry, but edgy, Fiona didn't have an appetite for anything specific. Finally she ordered Emma's favorite comfort food, café au lait and a pain du chocolat. When the waiter served her, she looked up and asked him what the secret of Parisian coffee was.

He looked flustered at first, then motioned for her to wait, "Un moment," and disappeared into the kitchen. Fiona flipped open her laptop and resumed reading the letters. She'd left off this morning, in the fall of Emma's last year in Paris. Wren, pregnant with her second child and with the first toddler in tow, had come to visit Emma in Paris for a week. Her post-visit letters nostalgically revealed how together they'd toured the museums, the parks, and of course, Père Lachaise. Wren met Pieter, and in her usual discreet way gave her nod of approval. Emma had taken time to paint a portrait of Lytton, Wren's little towheaded boy. She'd also persuaded Wren to pose for two quick portraits, one clothed and one nude.

The head waiter, her favorite, approached with her regular waiter just behind him.

"Excuse me madame, you have questions about our coffee?" Fiona looked up and said she hadn't meant to make a big deal of it.

"If you could follow me, I will explain." He motioned for her to follow. Fiona snapped the laptop closed and left it with her things at the table. The waiter nodded that they'd watch her things. She followed the head-waiter back to the kitchen, where there was a station, devoted only to coffee. He then proceeded to give her an education on the processes and nuances of Parisian coffee. He explained the machinery, the proper grind, the correct and critical temperature of the water. Fiona felt overwhelmed. She asked questions—how would you do this at home? Was the equipment any different? The waiter nodded.

"If the grind is good and the water is good, you can have good coffee with the press-pot." He tapped a single serving glass coffee pot. "If you want the espresso and the steamed milk, then you must buy the machine."

Fiona nodded, thanking him profusely. She returned to her seat to savor the last few bites, and sips, with a new appreciation. She glanced at her watch again. There might be time to slip out to the Marche des Puces. It would make a long day, but Fiona didn't want the adventure to end. She tipped generously and few moments later, climbed into a taxi and zoomed off to one of Paris' best amusements.

The famous flea market was where dealers found new homes for Paris' cast-off goods. If ever a place demonstrated that one man's junk is another's treasure, this was it. There was everything from antiques—real antiques, much older than the average American fare, to the kind of household items found in Norm's shop. The market was home to a handful of permanent dealers, while others had lesser stalls set up. Fiona pulled her laptop and purse in tight to her torso. This was *the* place for pickpockets. Even though it was late in the day, the flea market was still abuzz with energy. Fiona would have thought the winter weather would slow it down, but apparently Parisians were made of stronger stuff than Californians. It was a riot of colors and textures. There were vintage clothes, dishes, furnishings and cheap plastic household goods; some in original packaging, showing that these were overstocks, or worse. She was dizzy with it. She could hear the customers dickering in French. She laughed, remembering Norm and her original purchase of Emma's painting. Inside one of the permanent shops, were racks of old paintings but nothing of the quality to which she'd become accustomed. Emma Caites had clearly spoiled her. On a table at the back there was a collection of miscellaneous items, old lamps, a spittoon (Fiona wouldn't even touch it!) and various metal items. There, amongst the shoe scrapers and mechanical apple-peelers was a lovely simple little bronze sculpture of a mother and infant. Avoiding the spittoon, Fiona reached for it. Barely six inches tall, it still had some heft and Fiona thought about its weight in her luggage. But it was lovely. She turned it over, and saw that is was a signed original. She did the conversion in her head on the price. It was only twenty-seven dollars. *Sold.* It was now hers, or maybe Marvin's, she wasn't sure yet. She found the shopkeeper, and held it out with her money. He eyed the piece, as if there was some mistake, but shook his head and honored the deal. He wrapped the piece in *Le Monde* and put it in a plastic bag. The transaction took only a minute, and with no words spoken, Fiona was relieved.

In the next stall, there were bolt ends of lovely French fabrics. Only a yard or two apiece, they had little value except for pillows and such, but what pillows. Fiona dug through the display pulling out fabrics to match her furniture, or Amanda's or just really nice cloth. She brought her armload of goodies to the counter. She thought of Amanda at the estate sales.

The saleswoman tallied the total on a piece of scrap paper and then announced, "Soixante euros."

Fiona heard her and did the conversion. *Too high.* Her first inclination was to thin the bundle, return some of the lesser choices. Instead though she looked the clerk in the eye and said, "Quarante."

The clerk looked at Fiona, then at the stack of fabrics she'd already measured and folded, then back at Fiona, "Cinquante."

Fiona nodded and handed over the cash, almost giddy with excitement, her first *intentional* barter. She could feel her heartbeat in her temples. She could never tell, because no one would understand. Surely Amanda the wheeler-dealer wouldn't understand this, Fiona's triumph.

The clerk wrapped the stack of remnants in tissue paper and slid them into a bag, "Merci." Fiona nodded and took up the handles of the sturdy bag. It was more than she could stand. She tucked her little bronze into the larger bag, and meandered through the flea market. She didn't think her heart could manage another purchase.

It was dark outside. Fiona was exhausted. She was ready to pack it in for the day, but wanted just a little something solid for supper. She thought of the onion soup at La Palette. A corner table, a bowl of soup, the perfect end to a week in Paris. Fiona hailed a taxi. She piled into her favorite warm little corner table at the back. Her waiter nodded and brought over a menu.

"No, merci," she said, not needing the menu. "Ce soir je veut la soupe." The waiter nodded. He brought a glass of red wine and a cheese board with crusty bread. It looked like heaven to Fiona. She pulled out the laptop, and opened to where she'd left off. In a few minutes, the waiter brought the steaming bowl of soup, and hesitated at her table. Fiona looked up.

"You always read, what work is it that you are always so diligent?" He slid the soup before her.

"I'm writing a book. This is part of my research, to read these letters." She tipped the laptop so he could see Emma's steady square handwriting." He squinted at the letter on the screen, nodded and said, "The date, 1927?"

"Yes, an art student at Beaux Arts in 1927."

He nodded appreciatively again. "Enjoy your dinner and your research." Fiona pulled the laptop back so she could read and eat. After a while the waiter came back, took away her dishes, and poured another glass of wine. Fiona just kept reading. Occasionally she glanced at her watch, but mostly she was glued to the screen.

Her waiter began sweeping up and wiping down the tables for the night. By now, the restaurant was nearly empty. He glanced over at the American customer, who had stayed quite late. At her table, Fiona sat in the glow of her computer screen, with her face in her hands, weeping.

Chapter Forty-Nine

From: fionahedge@yahoo.com
Subject: Paris Impressions
Date: December 28, 2007 11:58 AM
To: artantikmarv@sbcglobal.net, ohamandakins@aol.com, norminisstormin@aol.com, jennsullymills@gmail.com, thomascaites@mindspring.com

This is a tough report. It covers a long period, and is a veritable roller coaster of emotions. Perhaps I identify too easily with Emma. It's a little like reading a war novel; you already know how it comes out at the end, but that doesn't ease the bumps along the way.

Our Emma had a marvelous second summer in France, so much so that she felt a twinge of guilt at not missing Pieter more. They had parted intact, though Emma was a little peeved that Pieter still hadn't mentioned her to his family. There are fewer letters to Wren this summer, I think because Emma spent a good deal of time traveling, so the correspondence rhythms were interrupted. Wren was pregnant again, which surprised Emma, and in a later letter Wren confided that it had surprised them too. The pregnancy came at a hard time, since they were scheduled to relocate from the Orient to Greece that autumn and it usually fell to the diplomat's wife to arrange and oversee the move. By then, Wren would be too far along to be of much help and she could feel the clucking of the other diplomat hens. Emma sensed a little loneliness where Wren had few female friends and no family nearby with whom to share the joys and fears of new motherhood. One of the downsides of being the wife of a diplomat was that she always lived in a foreign place, a foreign culture. Since they moved so frequently, the wives never were able to connect in a lasting way, and they retreated to formality to preserve sanity. Emma found this sad, and said so, because that very defense mechanism mirrored the distant formality of Wren's family.

So Emma wrote and reported dutifully the gritty details of a Paris summer. It was hot. The real Parisians all seemed to flee to points north for the summer, leaving the city on a skeleton staff, at the whims of the tourists. Her little apartment stayed cool enough, so long as she left the windows wide open and the curtains flailing in the breeze. Emma contacted the art dealer who'd sought her and Pieter out in the spring. Gallerie Caron agreed to take their work, though its terms were a little heavy handed. M. Caron came to the apartment to select the paintings he'd take, and to set prices with Emma. Since the gallery would be taking 60%, Emma wondered what difference her input made, but was glad to learn from the process. This was why she could sell so much more cheaply on the street, and still make money. M. Caron tried to discourage her "street" transactions, pointing out that they undercut the more lucrative gallery market and exposed her to possible robbery, but Emma just laughed. After that though, she was a little more careful with how much money she carried with her but she wondered to Wren whether thieves would consider 60% enough to qualify in their ranks. Caron took almost all of Emma's paintings and all of Pieter's that he'd authorized her to sell. They'd disagreed, since Emma wanted him to keep the largest nocturne from the Luxembourg Gardens. Pieter, though, wanted to show his parents that there was an income in art, and so listed everything he didn't take home for his family. Emma's revenge was that she insisted on setting the price on that one piece very high. It was the best of the lot, and she picked a price at which she was sure it wouldn't sell. Emma had no such attachments to her own work and put it all in the hopper. Within ten days, M. Caron contacted her and asked whether there could be additional paintings added during the summer. Thereafter, the only impediment to Emma's sales was the rate at which the oil paint would dry. Emma restocked her goods three times in July alone. The gallery prices were much higher than Emma's standard fare but in the end, Emma made less on them than her street sales. Nonetheless, from a career building point of view, a steady relationship with a gallery was wonderful for a new artist. Several times that summer, M.

Caron mailed Pieter healthy checks for goods sold. Emma wondered at their reception back in Friesland, and if Pieter even shared the information with his parents. It's not clear whether Pieter maintained his previous summer's writing frequency. We only know that Emma mentioned him less to Wren. This may well have been because the routine details of an established lover's summer are probably less pressing than the previous summer, when she'd been confiding the urgency of new love.

In early August Emma and Simone headed for Provence. Simone had family in the area, so they kept their costs low. Emma's paintings soared with the fresh air and plein air opportunities. The light reminded her of home, golden California light. For the first time since she'd come to France, Emma was homesick. She painted like a fiend. Simone humorously scribbled in the margins one of Emma's letters to Wren to tell her friend to ease up, that her health would suffer if she didn't rest more in the summer. If it was a strain, you couldn't tell. A photo tucked into Wren's letter showed a robust Emma, tanned and smiling standing under a tree with a field of lavender in the background. Emma was so impressed with the beauty of the area, and at how it spoke to her specifically, that she shipped a landscape to Wren. As usual, her paintings sold quickly, and she feared she'd have no Provence paintings available for posterity at all unless she gave some to friends. She shipped several canvases back to the Gallery Caron, which begged for more of Provence. Emma wasn't inclined to agree, since she paid the shipping and then lost out on the gallery cut. Local sales suited her just fine. Simone convinced her to pick the time of day she wanted to paint and then to spend some time in town, near a café, painting "little scenes" with her other canvases displayed around her. It was the perfect sales approach. Rarely did a day pass when Emma didn't sell as many canvases as she'd painted that day. Emma was thrilled that Simone was picking up on some of the marketing tips that Emma had been espousing for a year, though it appears Simone's motives were as driven by town socializing as by art. Simone painted too, but she also visited with relatives and chatted with the waiters in the cafés. They stayed with Simone's aunt and uncle. After gently quizzing them about what they loved about their home, Emma did a small series of paintings specifically for them. They were entranced. Simone's whole family was won over, and offers for the following summer rolled in. At the end of August, renewed by the sun, good food and country air, Emma and Simone headed back to Paris.

Back in her apartment, Emma settled into her Paris routines. She delivered a selection of Provence paintings to Gallerie Caron, and noted that all of Pieter's paintings, except the winter painting of the Luxembourg Gardens, had sold. Her own selection in the Gallerie was much diminished. M. Caron fawningly wrote her a check for her works, but the sum seemed slim in comparison to the number of canvases delivered throughout the season. Emma took the check, but requested an accounting. M. Caron looked offended and made a great commotion about his expenses incurred in framing and handling the Provence works. His theatrics troubled her, made her suspicious. Emma made note to Wren that she'd not to deliver any more paintings until after receipt of the accounting. Emma hoped Caron had been honest with Pieter.

Emma did not know the exact date of Pieter's return. She was eager to see him, to share her summer and its adventures. Now in Paris the void was bigger and in one of her rare intimate moments, she revealed to Wren that she missed "his touch, his smell, and the smooth feeling of skin on skin, she missed their dreamy Sunday mornings in the sun, silly talk while marketing at Les Halles and the fervor of undressing one another with cold hands after long nights painting outdoors."

In his absence she planned a party. She and Simone made up the invitations with Provence images in pastel, with lavender sprigs pressed into the fold for the fragrance of it. Emma loved that their friends came to her place to celebrate the return to school, indeed for most of their events, and she planned a Provencal peasant feast for the event. She and

Simone had been developing the menu all summer, with every new taste from Simone's relatives, or from Simone's constant beaus, the waiters at the cafés. As summer closed, their friends migrated home to Paris, invariably stopping by Emma's to see what was up. She passed out invitations from a basket on the table, and everyone planned to attend. Emma took one of the invitations, and a little framed pastel of Provence, to the building superintendent, a little insurance for the party. She urged him to come early, so there would still be food.

Finally, with only two days to spare, Pieter was scheduled to return. Emma was delighted and met him at the station with a taxi. Pieter was cool, his face clouded over and pinched. He turned so Emma could not embrace him and nodded towards a young blond woman, a half step behind him, who appeared to be his traveling companion. He introduced them. Lisette, a new student at Beaux Arts, was from Leeuwarden, and was the daughter of a friend of his mother. Emma was presented casually as a friend from school. She was wounded. Whatever was up, she didn't like it. He could have warned in his letter, this was rude and dismissive. Was Lisette some new love interest? It didn't seem so. Indeed, Pieter was as dismissive to Lisette as he was to Emma. Why was Emma given the cold shoulder? Obviously, whatever the situation, Emma remained the secret, the unmentioned part of Pieter's Paris education. Emma fell into step behind the other two and let Pieter take the lead. When their goods were loaded and Pieter and Lisette slid into the cab, Emma stepped back and waved. Pieter sat forward, his face slack with shock, then almost protesting, but Emma turned away and secured her own taxi for the ride home. Emma didn't know if she was more angry or injured. She described the events almost cinematically to Wren in a letter written from La Palette, where she'd gone immediately upon arrival home. Pieter could find her here, or maybe she'd buy some time to cool off first. It was one thing to be kept a secret at his home, another entirely for him to bring that chill here to Paris.

Pieter came by that evening. Things were icy. Pieter

explained that his mother had thrown he and Lisette together at the last moment. He could not have warned ahead. He felt that Lisette was a liability, or worse, his mother's spy. Emma countered that there'd be no need of spies and intrigue if he just honestly shared with his family that he had a girlfriend at school. How was he going to manage his little secret with all of their friends? Did he expect them to all pretend as well? Pieter was distraught. His cheeks wet with tears he spoke of his shame that he needed his parents' support to continue school. They held the purse strings. His mother, who while acknowledging his talent, was not happy with the idea of an artist son. She'd cringed this summer, each time a check arrived from Gallerie Caron, and had castigated him that he couldn't expect to live and raise a family on such meager stipends. Clearly she'd expected him to wash out early and now his growing gifts threatened her plans for his future. Pieter begged for time to work with her. Emma was sympathetic, but guarded. She explained that with school starting the next day, word would be out about the party. She would not pretend in her own home. If Lisette came, Pieter should stay away. It was his choice.

They parted that evening with barely so much as a quick hug. Lisette was staying in Pieter's apartment until her lodgings were secured. He could not stay late, for to do so would rouse suspicions. Emma nodded and steered him to the door. It was a hollow homecoming for both of them. Emma slept alone that night and cried.

There was little time to waste in weeping. The next morning was the start of her third year. Advanced students jumped immediately into the projects of the day; there was an expectation that the upper level students were ready to get to work upon arrival. Emma was. The air was filled with the buzz of kinship and reconnection. Many of Emma's associates asked openly if last year's "first day" party had become tradition. Emma just nodded. She and Simone rushed to Emma's at the end of the last class and finished assembling the foods and drink. There was food for thirty or forty. Drink for more. The table was piled high with fruit and cheese, and terrines of steaming peasant stews. By six, already students were filing up the stairs. The building superintendent shook his head, "Artists!" but he came early, laughed and filled his belly. There would be no problem with the landlord.

Almost everyone came, even some of the professors. The event spilled out into the hall and Emma's neighbors joined in. One had an accordion, and began to play and students danced in the halls outside Emma's door. It was bedlam, but fun, spirited bedlam. In the hubbub, few noticed the elegant wisp of a blond who climbed the steps and presented the hostess with an abundant bouquet of flowers. Emma embraced her and introduced her around. Lisette struggled to keep up; her French was not up to the challenges of this clamor. Emma's tears could easily have been mistaken for outpouring of overwhelming emotion at the joyous and wonderful warm homecoming. She spent her time pouring; wine flowed and the evening's silliness followed. Emile stood on a chair and denounced the degenerates who deconstructed the human form with abstraction. Simone laughed, pulled him down and kissed him into silence. Over the din, students earnestly confided summer romances or undertook to articulate their artistic goals for the new year. Georges loudly renounced the use of black. Isabelle, who'd moved heavily into sculpture that summer, sat on the settee with a first year student and drunkenly questioned the reductionism of two dimensional art. Everyone laughed and danced and drank. Echoing from time to time was the refrain, "Where is Pierre?" The party wound down very late.

Simone stayed, and though thoroughly drunk, helped Emma clean up the worst of the mess. The superintendent, bless his heart, came up at midnight and carried down the bulk of the trash, even though the party was still in full swing. Emma made a note to do something special for him. By two, only stragglers remained, and when Emma recruited them to help clean up, it sent most of them scurrying home. By three, she and Simone slid into bed, exhausted. Only Emma felt the full brunt of Pieter's absence.

In the morning, Emma dragged herself out of bed and set out for class. She left Simone snoring. Most of the students were there, though some looked pretty rough. Emma's letter that night to Wren jokingly described the ragged crew of shaky artists whose training would be incomplete if it didn't include drink and debauchery. Lisette stopped her in the hall and thanked her profusely for the invitation. The young woman was responding with such genuine warmth, Emma could not fault her for the rift in her own heart. Emma responded that she was happy to make a new student, especially a foreign student, feel welcome, since she knew the feeling of foreignness so well herself. That day Emma poured her flagging energy into the work. Her drawing instructor, himself a little green, took the class outdoors for some quick studies along the Seine. It may have been a first for the school, but (aside from the bright sun) the fresh air offered relief to many bedraggled artists in training. At one point at lunch, Emma saw Pieter ahead of her in the hall. She did not quicken her step to catch him and instead turned to take another exit rather than see him on the way out. The day didn't end soon enough. Emma made her way home and immediately to bed. She'd intended to reflect and mourn her differences with Pieter, but was so exhausted she quickly succumbed to sleep. The next morning she dashed off a letter to Wren over coffee at La Palette and headed back to school.

Emma enjoyed school. She couldn't help it. She buried herself in the task at hand and it filled her. In painting the professor was lecturing about new ways to combine colors to show qualities of light. Though intuitively Emma had used many of the new techniques, she marveled at the multi-layered complexity of the craft. In the back of her head she thought of the European guild systems, apprenticeship programs lasting years that, after years of near slavery, slowly taught the intricacies of the craft of painting. Emma noted that she was still learning and it suited her. On her palette she mixed the paints according to formula and experimented on paper with the new combinations. It made her want to run out to Pont Neuf, and try it out on a favorite subject. The thought of Pont Neuf, without Pieter, caught her breath, but she pushed on with the color experimentation. Emma confessed to Wren that her friends were beginning to wonder what was up. Pierre had not come to the party. They were not seen together and he was seen several times with that new blond girl. Emma didn't herself know what to think so she just kept mixing and applying paint. She didn't know what she'd say if she did discuss it with friends, she didn't know where she and Pieter stood. She only knew that there was a smallness in Pieter's vision that she wouldn't agree to share. She had painted the golden light of Provence. Her vision, her appreciation of open air and space, her loving, these could not be reduced to small secrets and indiscretions. This was Pieter's problem. The class finished and Emma wiped her brushes clean. She stepped out quickly, thinking that the days were still long enough that she could stretch some canvases and paint at Pont Neuf to catch the late light on the bridge. Emma hurried home.

When she let herself in, Pieter was sitting at the table. Without speaking, Emma stepped into the kitchen area and put on water for tea. She quartered, cored and peeled an apple and set it out on a board with cheese. The water boiled and she filled the strainer with loose tea, suspended it in the pot and poured the boiling water. Still in silence she placed two cups on the table and then returned with the teapot. She sat down, leaning her cane against the table between them. After a bit, she poured two cups of tea. Pieter watched her, but when she sat down, he looked down at his hands. She studied him in silence.

"I told her everything."

Emma nodded.

"I should have done it before. Yesterday she told me how gracious you were, what a marvelous party. I felt small."

Emma swallowed. It wasn't what she'd thought. He'd told Lisette. Lisette was not the problem. She was just the problem of the moment.

"It's okay now. I'm sorry." Pieter was crying. Emma was crying too.

She took him in her arms and held him, both of them weeping, but only Emma knew that their tears were for

256

different reasons.

In her letters, Emma divulged every nuance, every detail, to Wren. Emma knew that this was not the final showdown. She also knew she wanted the relationship. She wanted Pieter. She wanted his warm embrace and their place in their circle of friends. But she could never fully have Pieter as long as she was a secret. In this, Pieter hadn't opened the secret. He'd only recruited another to keep the silence. Emma loved him, but was pained at his weakness. Pieter spent the night and after the gentle sweetness of reunion, they resumed the way it was before. But not entirely.

Emma was elated. Wren was coming. With the relocation to Europe and Wren's difficult pregnancy, she was coming on ahead of her husband for medical care in Paris before she joined him in Athens. If the doctors weren't satisfied, Wren and Lytton might even stay until the baby was born. Guiltily, Emma longed for just enough illness to warrant a lengthy stay. In addition to Emma, Wren had a good friend stationed in Paris, who'd put her up in the embassy and assist with coordinating top notch care. Emma's letters could barely contain her excitement at her friend's impending visit. This was her first American visitor. Wren was family. Mostly they spent their time together in quiet pursuits, because of Wren's condition. Emma painted Lytton, who warmed to her immediately. For the first time in her life, Emma connected with a child and she understood Wren's aching love for this sweet little boy. Pieter joined them and they spent long evenings laughing and exchanging stories. Pieter wanted to know about Emma, her grandparents, her exploits at school, and Wren obliged him. Wren's French was not as facile as Emma's and they giggled through halting conjugations and endless translations.

Emma took Wren to Père Lachaise and they both marveled at the sensitive eloquent sculptures that seemed too beautiful to grace a grave, making sorrow permanent. They shopped and played, ate and talked. It was like old times and both bloomed with it. Emma's tender pains of September melted with the solace of a true friend. Wren's own aching loneliness abated. Emma painted two portraits of Wren, one at the table in the sitting room with their never ending pot of tea in front of her, and the other nude, pregnant and curled in the sun on the daybed in Emma's studio. (I think Jordan has at least one of these paintings.) Who knows whether French medicine was the cure, but Wren was fully recovered in less than three weeks. They were three full and fabulous weeks. Pieter was jealous of the restorative powers of that visit. His tender attentions for over a month had not restored Emma to her former resilience, but Wren did.

Lisette joined in their lively evenings, and Wren loved her. In summing her up, Wren said that Lisette was a gentle soul whose primary artistic talent was to make those around her feel whole and happy. Emma had fretted terribly at Lisette's lagging artistic skills, but Wren helped her to see that even a year at Beaux Arts would be wonderful for Lisette, but that her real talents ultimately would be home and hearth. Both Wren and Emma painted Lisette. Wren, who'd not painted since Mills decided to return to it as soon as having the baby would permit. Pieter's appreciation for Emma amplified, as he saw her now through Wren's eyes. Since Pieter's frame of reference was always family, seeing Emma as part of Wren's family opened his eyes to more of her spirit. October was a healing month. It was, and led to, some of the sweetest times Pieter and Emma ever shared.

With heavy hearts they waved goodbye to Wren at the end of the month. Emma's later letters acknowledged how entranced she was with Wren's luminous, taut, round beauty. Other than avoiding pregnancy, she'd never given it much thought. Here with her dearest friend positively glowing with it, and with sweet little Lytton as proof of positive outcome, Emma had to rethink her revulsion. It was based on fear. Since childhood, she explained, doctors had warned her, and she had expanded the concept universally. For the first time, secure in her love for Pieter and observing Wren's fullness in motherhood, those ominous warnings held loss for her. She confided to her friend that it pained her, that she could never

258

know the fulfillment of bearing and raising a child with her lover. Worse, the flip side of it took her breath away. With her, Pieter would never know it either. Between the lines of Emma's even squared script I feel an awakening, connected then to a deep mourning.

Wren wrote to Emma about Pieter shortly after her departure. She warned that Pieter's strength was also his weakness. He was loving and soft and hated to disappoint. Wren told Emma not to pursue the relationship if she couldn't live with a wine merchant. Pieter, she said, was too sweet to succeed fully as an artist. He would always be torn trying to please, and so would have difficulty blazing his own trail. Emma responded that all this was true, and more.

November brought short days and rain. Emma, willing to paint in cold or snow, really hated the rain. She did a series of interiors, her apartment, Lisette's and finally a series of paintings inside La Palette. Pieter loved the restaurant series. He tried too, but couldn't capture the simultaneous serenity at the tables and the bustle of the waiters. Emma took intimate views and seized the feeling of La Palette. The proprietor was astounded and purchased most of the paintings before anyone else could. Pieter expressed his continuing amazement at her talent, and at how she constantly explored new ways to see and show her favorite subjects.

The depth of Pieter's commitment to Emma grew. He began spending all his time at her place, reveling in their tiny moments of domestic bliss. A shared pot of tea, a simple dinner, Pieter could become passionate with the smallest of tender exchanges. With sales a little slowed by the November rains, they took pains to economize, yet to eat and live without losing the artistic flair of it. They shopped at the farmer's market at Les Halles, and experimented with foods they'd never eaten. Emma cooked and Pieter cleaned up. Pieter, ever Dutch, brought home flowers for their table. Emma took pains to find the perfect wine. Their work in and out of class glowed with the new energy. Emma had never been happier. It was exhilarating. She was the focus of

Pieter's attentions. Never before had anyone been so entirely with her, so present. They modeled for one another and were left weak with desire.

In the strength of this more profound loving, Pieter began to mention Emma in his letters home. This prompted inquiries from his mother, to which he responded, "She is beautiful and talented. She has a gentle nature and boundless energy and enthusiasm for art. She is American, but speaks French fluently without accent." He did not say that she was crippled. Partly, Pieter did not see Emma that way. Her limitations were not part of his conscious view of her. But he knew his mother too well that she'd look for any reason to reject Emma, so he kept his counsel on the subject. Emma felt validated for the first time. His honesty with his parents was the most heartfelt gift he could ever give her. In early December one of their friends, Emile, was practicing his photographic skills at the school. He took some lovely shots of the students in studio classes, one of which caught both Pieter's and Emma's eyes. Without communicating, they each bought several prints of a particular shot. In it, Emma stands next to her easel listening intently to the instructor, while two easels down, Pieter stands gazing unabashedly at Emma. Both of them look lovely in the photo, so Pieter sent a copy home to his parents, thinking it a romantic introduction to his beloved. Neither Pieter nor Emma noticed her cane hanging from the edge of her easel in the photo—but Pieter's mother did. She wrote inquiring about the injury that had led to the cane. Pieter responded with the truth, the childhood illness and that it had left her with a limp and a cane. He then filled the letter at length with stories of her beauty, her natural leadership and compassion. Pieter could not see how there could be any objection to Emma, given the breadth of her positive qualities.

His mother responded with an odd letter. It discussed the history of tulips in Holland. Over the centuries the Dutch had always admired when a tulip would "break" that is, when it would spontaneously begin to bloom with a blaze of new color, different from how it was originally bred. A white tulip could suddenly bloom with a flash of red, or yellow. This beautiful anomaly had made this rarity a treasure in Dutch culture. Only recently, his mother reported, was it learned through science that the break was caused by a virus, carried by a peach tree beetle.

Pieter received the letter and was overjoyed. He believed that his mother's letter signified her acceptance of Emma, infirmity and all. Indeed it seemed to express that her talents and other forms of beauty were in part the result of her illness, God's gift to release these other qualities. Pieter believed he'd won his mother over. He translated the letter to Emma and they rejoiced. Emma felt accepted by his family. Like teenagers, they made plans for a marriage that neither of them had ever thought possible. Pieter longed for his parents to meet her. It was the answer to his prayers. Emma felt on the precipice of a happiness that she'd always been told was not for her. In Pieter she felt whole. Since she had known him, she'd known that Pieter was a product of family and that without his family's blessing, no long term relationship was possible. She hadn't imagined any family would love or accept her. Pieter wrote his parents, thanking his mother for the lovely letter and analogy. He said that he wanted them to meet Emma and suggested that he'd love to bring her home for a visit over the Christmas holidays so they could meet her. These were deliriously happy weeks. They painted, made marriage plans, made love, and lay whispering in each other's arms.

Finally, his mother's reply arrived. Pieter picked up his mail, and opened it at the table while Emma made their tea. Pieter read it, his face draining of color. Before she could set the tea down, Pieter threw the letter onto the table. Cursing, he stormed out of the apartment. Emma didn't understand. She picked up the letter. It was short and neatly written, but entirely in Dutch. She waited for hours for Pieter to return. Finally, in desperation, she took the letter to Lisette. Lisette read the letter and put her head down on the table and wept.

She looked up at Emma, tears streaming down her cheeks and said, "He's lost to you." Lisette stood and found a piece of

261

paper and then laboriously wrote out the translation from Dutch to French. She handed it to Emma, who read:

Dearest Son,
I regret that I was not so clear with you in my last letter. Obviously you read it with your romantic French side rather than through your pragmatic Dutch roots. I am sure that you have sincere feelings for your lovely American. Yes, from the photo she is beautiful. She is also a cripple. All of her talent will not help her to be what you need in a woman. You will need a wife and hopefully a mother for your children. A career in art will barely provide for you with an industrious family. It cannot provide for the extra services to make up for half of a woman. And so—if she is talented—are you prepared to live on a wife's creativity? To cook and clean so that she can paint?
I fear your creative energies have been abducted by your feelings for this girl. Your father and I have decided you should return immediately to Leeuwarden. You may study here, or, if you prefer, take up a position in your father's firm. Enclosed are sufficient funds for your trip home. It is the last funding we will provide. I am sure you will return rather than to live off of your American friend. I know that this news will come hard to you. It is not our intent to cause you pain. I thought you would understand the Dutch ending of the broken tulip saga. Recognizing now that the break is an illness, one that threatens the productivity and health of the tulip crop, we Dutch now cull them. I feel for your losses. Return quickly son, you are much loved and needed.
Mother and Father

Emma is dazed. It is everything she was raised to believe. She is defective and undesirable. He is lost to her. She could never ask that he give up his family for her, indeed it is in large part his love and connection to family that she has found attractive in him. Emma can barely speak, or breathe. She thanks Lisette, takes the letter and translation and returns to her little apartment. Our Emma cannot bear it, this little home that sang with happiness just hours ago. Pieter has not returned. Emma packs her clothing and turns to look at the apartment. She says goodbye to her studio, the paintings, the furniture. The rent is paid through the end of December, but Emma is not prepared to remain in Paris alone. She does not want to continue at school. She takes Pieter's painting of Pont Neuf down from its nail on the wall. She leaves the rest. At the end of his mother's original letter on the table she writes, "Adieu, Mon Amour, Emma." She leaves her keys on the letter.

Emma immediately books her passage home. She stops at the Gallerie Caron to give them an address in Oakland and buys Pieter's painting of the Luxembourg Gardens, which she ships to the States. Sobbing she makes her way to the train station to begin the journey home. We know that Emma never sees or communicates with Pieter again.

—I am coming home too. This story has broken my heart and I want nothing more than to be among dear friends to recover. Paris has been wonderful and horrible. Thomas, I hope this doesn't break your heart.

Marvin, remember to pick me up in San Francisco. I'm supposed to arrive at 3:45, flight 1897.

Fiona

Fiona was exhausted. On the flight she'd read Emma's exodus letters. Not much there but pain and self-doubt. In her heart Emma had no question but that the end result would have been the same. After all, she had never even been able to win over her own mother, whose view of her condition exactly mirrored that of Pieter's mother. But part of Emma yearned for Pieter and his love, which she knew that, while weak, was genuine. Part of her wished she could have settled for less, even if only to have the romance last through school. Emma wished she could be less intense, less demanding of everyone around her, even herself. But that didn't seem to be who she was. Fiona ached for her. Just as she'd been jealous of the force of her loving earlier, Fiona could see that the fall from it was equally as painful as its presence was passionate. Fiona felt like her own life had been in black and white compared to Emma's Technicolor.

Fiona rarely slept in the air, and this trip was no exception. She tried to organize the week ahead, juggling work, which would be backed up already, with her need to reconnect with friends. Though she'd really only been gone a week, it felt like months. Fiona had the odd sense of living two lives simultaneously. Running through the events in Paris, she was caught up in the profound reality of Emma in her life. Fiona felt that her experiences of Pieter, Simone and Wren were as real as that of Sophie and Jeanne-Marie. Stepping on the plane was the same kind of reality check as stepping out into the sunshine after a particularly engaging matinee. Were it not for the current angst in Emma's life, Fiona wasn't sure she'd be so pleased to be shaking herself free and returning to her own life. It was hypnotic.

Real life offered peanuts and warm cola, a plastic wrapped chicken salad sandwich somewhere over a vast gray body of water. Paris was definitely over; Fiona was in culinary shock. Emma's own return trip to Oakland, including the time she spent with friends in New York, took her five weeks. By the time she returned, the immediate crush of grieving was gone, but Emma was left deeply depressed. Fiona was pleased to be coming home to a full plate, since the busy routines of work would help her get out of Emma's head and redefine her own boundaries.

Fiona planned a weekend trip to meet Jordan. She could hardly wait to see the new paintings and, in particular, to see Pieter's Pont Neuf and his nocturne from Luxembourg Gardens. She wanted to quiz Jordan about Emma's painting from Provence.

Fiona was curious, and a little concerned, about the impact the story would have on Thomas. She tried to think how she'd feel if someone revealed to her the intimate details of her own mother's life. Parents are fixtures in the lives of their children, their dreams and aspirations buried under years of responsibility. It made Fiona think about Denise. That was a minefield of trouble, but mostly, Fiona realized, it was Denise's trouble. Fiona felt that the revelations of Paris would help her weather whatever storm came from *that* direction.

Already Fiona was planning a themed dinner to recreate the true Parisian dinner she'd enjoyed with Jeanne-Marie Baptiste and Gaston. It would be simple, elegant, hearty and, most of all, genuine. It would be the perfect solace for the damp, dark and rainy winter months ahead in Oakland. Fiona was relieved that she'd sent the email reports back each day. Though she wondered how they might have been received, she was glad she wouldn't have to recount all that she'd learned at a future dinner event. It felt too much like gossip. Now with everyone on the same page, they could move together into Emma's future. Fiona marveled at how painfully intricate Emma's story was. Who she was, and how she handled who she would become, made increasing sense in light of the triumphs, challenges and injuries of her past. Emma was deliciously human, warm and flawed. Despite her challenges, she remained amazingly self-possessed, especially in her artistic talents and pursuits. The more she learned about Emma, the more Fiona was impressed with her grandparents and the prescience of their concerns. They helped her to develop her talents, and gave her the skills needed for a young woman with her challenges. Certainly there must have been the temptation to coddle her but that hadn't happened. In their love, her grandparents had reinforced Emma by building her curiosity and her internal aesthetic foundations.

Had Fiona done as well with Denise? She didn't think so. Denise was just a little younger than Emma had been in Paris, and she was clearly not handling the transition to adulthood with nearly the grace that Emma had. It might merely be a matter of necessity. Denise could afford the indulgences and occasional pettiness of a normal young woman. She had family, a husband and a network of friends to fall back on. Emma, at twenty-seven, was entirely on her own. Any family connections she had, she had built. Now, Fiona was eager to find out how Emma landed on home turf, after her escape from Paris.

The inane, in-flight movie was droning on. Fiona tried to update her notes and read more of the letters, but the light was dim and the battery on the laptop was low. Fiona eventually nodded off and dreamed briefly about the colors and displays at Bon Marche. She woke feeling pressure in her ears, and her head filled with the images of dancing boomerang pajamas. Fiona was almost home. Exhausted, she hoped Marvin would be waiting. All she wanted now was to collapse into her own bed. She wondered whether the group had made plans for New Years. Another holiday. Another celebration opportunity. Fiona wondered if she could get her act together with the cassoulet in time. The plane touched down, then bumped to a rolling stop under a gray and foreboding sky. She gathered her things, and stood in the narrow aisle with the others as she waited her turn to finally be home.

Marvin honked and pulled up just as she exited the terminal. Short of grabbing a cab, she'd never enjoyed such service. He hopped out of the car, and put her suitcase into his hatchback—grateful she'd followed Jenn's advice to ship her purchases. She kept the laptop strapped over her shoulder, armed with it as she had been for most of Paris.

"Welcome home, you've had quite the trip." Marvin gave her a welcoming hug. "We've all really missed you." He stepped back and surveyed her appearance, "Damn girl, you look good, and that's a *great* coat!"

Chapter Fifty-One

Fiona checked her watch. She just couldn't seem to wrap her head around time. This jet lag was no joke. It was only four in the afternoon, but she ached for a nap to set her straight. She had to collect Amanda and Norm before seven, for New Years with Thomas and his wife in Berkeley. Fiona was looking forward to finally meeting Ardley, even if Marvin feared interference. Fiona missed Jenn, who was still back home with her family for the holidays. This ensemble endeavor felt too much like family to leave anyone out. The rest of them were unattached, and Fiona wondered at the probability of that. Were they an odd bunch, or was this just the new American reality? She yawned, and looked down at her files, realizing she'd been sitting for thirty minutes with no progress in her work. She might as well pack it in. Though it flew in the face of all the jet lag advice, Fiona closed the file and slipped upstairs to her bedroom for a quick nap.

The alarm buzzed, and for a moment Fiona had that Paris feeling of not knowing exactly where she was. She looked at the clock, 6:15. She was home and it was New Years Eve. Fiona rubbed the sleep from her eyes, reluctantly scraped herself out of bed, splashed her face with water and deftly applied a touch of make-up. She pulled a turtleneck over her head, careful not to muss the work she'd just done, and finished up with her lipstick. With a pair of burgundy wool trousers and a vest, Fiona was in her Paris uniform, and ready for a cold evening out. Fiona pulled on her coat, scarf and mittens. She left her hat at home, not because it wasn't nippy, but because she didn't want to deal with post-hat-hair on this evening out. She chuckled at her own vanity.

Fiona drove to Norm's shop. Amanda and Norm had some retail project underway—it had been a big secret, so Fiona was eager to see what those two had cooked up over the holiday. It was dark already when she parked. The display windows had been covered over with craft paper and though some light peeked through, the interior was obscured. Norm's shop was in an older building, one with stucco walls and early art-deco tile, in black, teal and pumpkin around the entry, at the ends of each store facade and around the long line of store-front windows. There were broad, angled tile window sills, which was not a regular retail look. It made the storefront feel more homey and open than most. The building had four stores in it; Norm's, a beauty supply place, selling natural braids and fake nails, a small neighborhood realtor and a Bikram yoga studio. Fiona wondered at the eclectic mix of clientele needed to keep these disparate shops afloat in this funny neighborhood. There were apartments above, with the same tile trim and window sills, only scaled down. Mercifully, the building had survived the years without major renovations. The store's entrance, also covered with craft paper, was a wide oak door with the original beveled glass windows. Fiona was glad that the original entry was also still intact. Most retail shops of this vintage had long since 'upgraded' to the ubiquitous and soulless aluminum/glass portal. Fiona took off a mitten and rapped at the glass with a bare knuckle. She could hear voices and music inside.

As Amanda opened the door, a bell hanging on its interior announced her arrival. Fiona suddenly remembered the sound from her first visit, when she'd bought the painting.

Blocking the door, Amanda stuck her head out, "We tried to get it done, but we're just not ready. It's your choice, you can come in and see it in progress or you can wait a couple more days." Fiona weighed the options. She knew that they wanted the *surprise factor*, but her curiosity was killing her. This was the tacky little store where she'd first found Emma Caites, where it had all started.

Fiona paused, "Amanda, I know you wanted to surprise me, and if that's important, I'll gladly wait. But I'd love to be a part of this too, so, go talk to Norm, I'll wait outside."

"You're a sweetie, I'll be right back." Amanda disappeared, leaving Fiona standing in the cold. She pulled her mitten back on and was glad for her coat. Moments later, the door swung wide open. Amanda and Norm stood there with the same silly grin pasted on their faces. "Okay, come on in."

Fiona stepped inside and was floored by the bright, cheerful interior. It seemed much bigger than she remembered. Sure, there were still things to be done, but the place *shone*. The dust was gone, the floors, previously just dark with grunge, had been polished to a deep terrazzo glow. The walls and ceiling had been painted—the ceiling and two walls an eggshell almond and the remaining two in a deeper pumpkin to contrast with the tile sills on the windows. A row of new display racks held the vintage clothing, cleaned and hung on matching hangers with colored size-markers. On one side, against an almond wall, there was a huge armoire, with a two-toned, teal and pumpkin distressed paint finish, set behind a matching table. In the armoire and on the table stood rows of crisply ironed and folded quilts and table linens in neat stacks. Near the entry sat Norm's old cashier's counter, repainted in a clean deep teal, with a brightly polished brass cash register ready for check out. A lighted glass extension of the counter contained a spare but lively array of colorful costume jewelry, clunky necklaces and bangles, displayed on vintage silk and Viyella scarves. The end of the glass counter was graced with a hanging rack of forties and fifties handbags. A bank of cubed shelves now made up the back wall of the shop, again, painted in the eggshell solid teal. The shelves were adorned with dishes, salt and peppers, teapots and knick-knacks. The paintings, (not Emma's), the ones on which they'd practiced their cleaning skills, hung well-framed, behind the register and across the top of the cube shelves. Vintage furniture filled in the open spaces that also served as more display for the lamps, vases, antique toys and other décor items. On the wall behind the jewelry area, a pumpkin painted corkboard sported a collection of vintage aprons festively tacked in rows. Even with the boxes and packing materials on the floor and in the corners, the effect was stunning. Fiona stood in the center of the shop turning slowly with her mouth open.

"She can't even speak," Norm laughed, "This might be a first!"

"Well?" Amanda prompted, "What do you think?"

"I can't believe it, you guys. It's gorgeous; it's upscale and vintage at the same time. Where did you get all this stuff?"

"It was all here," Amanda laughed. "Oh, I added the linens, but everything else—except the clothing racks, was here already. We just had to unclutter and reveal it."

"You wouldn't believe the things she made me do," moaned Norm, melodramatically. His face revealed the truth. He was thrilled at the transformation.

"How did you do all this, in what... a week?"

"Amanda's high school students—she called them up, and we paid a small army, who worked like dogs. You should have seen them; they're crazy about her." Norm was beaming at Amanda.

"Well, there are *some* advantages to being a teacher. Most of what we did was clean up and cosmetic, but we never could have done it without the kids. Norm's even going to hire a couple of them for weekend coverage."

"It's tremendous! But all this must have cost a fortune."

"Nope, she bet me she could do it for less than $1,500 in materials. We went over that a bit, but only because she showed me the light fixtures, and I had to have them. Then, about $700 for the kids'. It was a complete commercial makeover for less than $3,000. Hell, I'd already made that on eBay sales," Norm boasted.

Fiona looked up at the ceiling. Two huge illuminated alabaster bowls hung in the center, surrounded by eyeball can-lights along the perimeters, washing the walls with warm light.

"Aren't they great?" Amanda caught her looking up at the lights. "I found them all for a song on Craigslist. They came from a restaurant that went belly-up." Fiona still couldn't believe the transformation.

Amanda rattled on. "It's too bad we missed the Holidays, but we'll be open next weekend. I've got an *in* with someone at the Tribune who'll do a little piece on the transformation, and then we'll hold off on advertising till next month and do it up big for Valentine's."

Norm piped in, "Plus sales are still perking along on eBay. That'll keep us busy for awhile. We still have a bunch more that needs cleaning up, so as inventory depletes, we'll be ready to restock. You wouldn't believe how much we donated or tossed. I even had to rent a Dumpster."

"I think that with just my regular estate routes and Norm's regular purchasing patterns," she elbowed him, "but a little pickier, we'll be able to keep fully stocked on both the eBay and the retail sides."

"You guys, this is amazing. Has Marvin seen it?"

"Not yet, we wouldn't let him come. When we have our grand opening, he and Jennifer will see it for the first time then."

"I'll do dinner for it," volunteered Fiona.

"Yeah, you have something *special* in mind?" Amanda was acutely aware of the culinary pressure.

"I want to duplicate a dinner I had in Paris."

Norm laughed, "You're on. You know I wouldn't turn that down."

Amanda looked at her watch, "We've got to get going to Thomas'." She pulled on her jacket, while handing Norm his.

"Okay, let's move out."

Norm nodded her way and teased, "She's like a drill sergeant, but she gets it done."

Fiona chuckled at the interaction. Clearly the two of them had found a working rhythm, and as usual, Amanda was in command. Fiona saw how easily Norm fell into step, just as she had over the years. Fiona felt it explained Amanda's teaching success over the years with the toughest classes. And still, everyone loved her along the way.

They climbed into the car with Amanda and Norm still chattering about the shop.

"She wanted to paint it pink! Can you imagine?" Norm was railing.

"Not just pink, pink and creamy yellow. Those colors go so well with a lot of the vintage and retro stuff."

"Yeah, but I'd have to sit all day in a pink shop!"

Fiona interrupted, "So how *did* you settle on the colors?"

Amanda jumped in, "We couldn't agree, so we took it from the tile, you know, on the exterior. The tile window sills already wrapped into the shop, so we just went with it."

"I thought she was nuts when she started painting that armoire with those two colors, but when she sanded through, revealing a little of the contrast, it was just perfect. The kids were helping, and when they saw it, they went crazy."

The two were high as kites. Fiona smiled to herself as they babbled on. She turned her attention to the traffic—she was always wary on New Year's Eve, especially so tonight, as she wound her way up through the narrow streets and into the Berkeley Hills.

"Has *anyone* met Ardley yet?"

"I have," Norm called back. "I met her the day I went to see the old car. She's a little shy, but very nice. Once she got talking, she forgot to be shy."

Fiona made the final turn and pulled up in front the house. "What did you two talk about?"

"Oh, I was telling her what a cute kid Thomas was. He was dying of embarrassment, but Ardley loved it. She told me how much he resembled their girls. She showed pictures from when they were little. One of them looks just like him, and of course, a bit like Emma."

They trooped up to the front door, and Norm rang the bell.

Thomas answered, with Marvin and Ardley in tow. Ardley was a small, compact woman with short cropped, almost silver hair. She had intense dark eyes, which Fiona immediately recognized as resembling Emma's. She wondered if Thomas had ever made the connection.

"Come in, come in," Thomas intoned, "We were just discussing the exhibit. Marvin and Art Bradley have some wonderful ideas for the organization and layout." Thomas took their coats, and then turned to Fiona and Amanda, "Amanda, Fiona, this is my wife, and life partner, Ardley."

Fiona extended her hand, but Ardley stepped up and embraced her warmly.

"I've read every word of your emails. It's meant so much to me, to have Emma come alive in our home after all these years. It seems we've missed so much. I cannot thank you enough for this gift."

Fiona stepped back and held Ardley's hands. "It's been a gift for everyone. Emma seems to have come to all of us, in ways we each needed her."

Ardley hugged her again and then turned to Amanda. "And Norman has told us so much about you, the energy behind his rejuvenation!" She reached out, and hugged her too.

"Aw, Norm keeps me busy." Amanda was uncharacteristically shy.

"It certainly does seem to be working in all directions." Ardley turned, gave Norm a hug, and then waved them all in to the living room. Marvin handed them sake cups and then poured the warm sake, the perfect thing to take off the chill.

Fiona looked around to get a feeling of the room. It was large and open, with low, modern furnishings. Two matching sofas, in a heavy earth-toned tweedy silk, sat perpendicular to each other and separated the seating area from a grand piano they passed as they entered. Opposite was a loveseat in a rich coordinating chestnut leather, with a matching chair and ottoman. The walls were cream colored, with elegantly mounted tribal carvings, subtly lit from above. The back wall was done in a coarse grass cloth, its expanse broken by several restrained abstracts—variations on a theme of lighting and form. All were signed by the younger Caites. In the center was a roughly carved coffee table, which looked African or Indonesian. The total effect was serene and confident.

They seated themselves in the living room as Thomas returned to the topic of the exhibit. "Arthur and Marvin have put together some good ideas. Mostly we wanted to avoid the static, straight chronological approach. Since we have so many paintings we can mix it up a little. We want to generally follow chronology, by decade but overlap a bit to show stylistic development themes that flow from one period to the next. We have some from the early twenties, mom's Mills period, but nothing from France."

"Not quite, we'll have three portraits and possibly a landscape," Fiona interjected.

Thomas' eyebrows arched even higher, "Really, you found paintings in France?"

"No, but Jordan has some that Emma did when Wren visited Paris. I'll be picking them up in a few weeks."

"Do you know what they are?"

"Two portraits of Wren, a portrait of her son as a toddler and maybe a lavender landscape from Provence."

Marvin nodded, "They'll fit in nicely with the Mills works, especially with the Wren connection."

Thomas nodded, "Then in the late twenties and into the thirties we have the early Oakland paintings, I know Arthur wants to call it the Depression Years, but I'm having trouble with that because… well, it's when I was born."

Norm chuckled, "I think he means capital D Depression, no reflection on you, Thomas."

"The paintings in that time frame seem intimate. She saw the world in small focus, maybe because of financial and childcare restrictions." Marvin was beginning to piece together the sense of who Emma was as it came through the works.

Fiona added, "Well, later in the forties, when things picked up, the commissions began to shape her work, and that didn't always reflect the Emma view."

"At some level, all artists have to do what pays the rent," Thomas continued, "I know sometimes she hated those house paintings, especially if she didn't like the people."

"That's a quote I'd love to put on the wall," Marvin laughed as he circulated and refilled the sake cups. Ardley came in with a huge tray of exquisite sushi. There were plates and condiments, wasabi, ginger and soy, already on the table. She returned with two big bowls, one empty and one with steaming edamame; soybeans in their shells.

Norm looked up at Fiona with panic in his eyes. Fiona couldn't help but smile—finally, food that stymied Norm. But Ardley was one step ahead of her, and without disturbing the flow of the conversation, she took the seat next to Norm, and quietly introduced him to the new foods. She showed him how to pop the beans out of their pods and then, drew him into a discussion of sushi and its taste components. She explained the wasabi heat and the fresh edge of the ginger. She showed him how to mix the wasabi and soy into a dipping sauce for the sushi that would help meet his tastes and tolerance for hot. Fiona instantly loved her. She had correctly sized him up, and positioned herself to make her guest comfortable. In minutes Norm went from tentatively sampling and tasting to extolling the flavors and combinations to the others. Fiona met Amanda's eyes, and they both nodded. Ardley was a keeper.

"Good thing Norm's here, the sushi looked so pretty, I didn't want to be the first to disturb it," Amanda joked.

Norm looked up, "With a food guide like Ardley, exotic goes beyond just presentation." They all laughed and reached for their own plates.

Marvin jumped right back into the exhibit, "I get really excited at the change in Emma's work in the late forties and into the fifties. While I was always attracted to the Arts and Crafts and plein air paintings, she really breaks loose here with the music paintings and abstracts."

Fiona looked up from her appetizer, "Music paintings? Are these the jazz pieces?"

Thomas said, "As usual, Fiona's way ahead of us. She's had the letters."

"Yes, but I didn't know there were any surviving paintings. I can hardly wait to see them."

"We could do a slideshow," Ardley suggested.

"Well, maybe several. To really do it, we need Fiona to give us a biographical report for each period." Marvin turned to Fiona, "I'm sorry it falls to you, but you *are* the biographer."

"First I need to go see Jordan and spend a little organizational time with Jennifer. And next weekend I think we have a grand opening to attend, with a Parisian dinner to follow at my house."

"The shop's ready?" Marvin was agog, "You barely started on it!"

"You can't believe what a trooper this woman is," Norman

274

nodded at Amanda, "It's amazing!"

"It really is," Fiona added, "I was only gone for a week, but it looks like professionals have been at it for months. They've done a beautiful job on it." She turned to Norm, "So when is the grand opening?"

Amanda and Norm looked at each other.

Amanda grinned, "Whadya think Norm, you got anything happening Saturday night?"

"Works for me. We can open Saturday, and our event can be... about six?"

"And then my place for dinner after." Fiona popped another piece of sushi into her mouth.

Marvin looked around, "There being no dissent, the event is scheduled."

Thomas looked at Fiona, "Dinner will be a little odd for me, a bit of a homecoming."

Ardley picked up the now empty tray, and put her arm around her husband. "Doesn't Fiona live in the apartment where you grew up?"

"Yes. I'm afraid that that happy accident led to me trudging all over his life, poor man." Then Fiona added, a little softer, "I've been worried about the invasiveness of all of this. Emotionally it's been a roller coaster for me and I can only imagine how it has been for you, Thomas."

"I'm doing much better with it than I would have imagined." Thomas wrapped his arm around his wife, "I've had great support."

"It's actually brought us closer together," Ardley added. "I didn't know what a block it had been for him. And now, through your telling, I find myself loving and grieving for a woman I never met but who helped shaped my adult life in many ways."

"It's true," Marvin said, "I was hovering over my computer all through the holiday, waiting for my daily Emma fix. You've brought her to life in a way I didn't expect."

Ardley stood and motioned them all into the dining room, and the conversation followed.

Thomas sidestepped into the kitchen and came out with a large, steaming cast-iron bowl, holding it by a built-in metal handle. He placed it at one of the place settings. Ardley followed with another cauldron and in a few moments the two had ferried out an iron bowl for each setting.

275

Ardley opened a drawer in the sideboard, "We have traditional Western flatware if anyone wants it, but the Japanese way works well for anyone willing to try." Norm put his hand up, surprisingly, so did Thomas.

He turned to Norm, "I love that Ardley immerses herself in other traditions but I hate to give up the comfort of a known tool. I'm a serious fork man." Ardley groaned, but it was all in fun. She grabbed a stack of forks and spoons and laid them in the center of the table as Thomas distributed tall frosted glasses of beer to each of their guests.

"It's true. I love peasant and tribal traditions. There's a continuity of form and purpose in folk traditions that transcends other cultural barriers. This evening we are trying a traditional Japanese peasant-style meal and it's great with rice beer." Fiona looked down at the rich broth, topped with fresh sliced scallions. The aroma was heavenly.

Thomas stood at the head of the table and lifted his glass, "I want to thank Fiona for her sensitivity and perseverance. I want to dedicate the New Year to the success of this group in all its ventures, and to Emma Caites."

"Seconded," clamored Marvin.

"To new friendships and family," added Norman.

"To reinventing ourselves and discovering what's really important at the core," said Ardley, glancing coyly at Thomas.

"To learning new skills and applying old skills to new challenges," smiled Amanda.

Everyone paused, looking at Fiona. She thought for a moment and then finished up the toast, "To any dedication to a discipline, and to the greater human understanding that comes out of it."

The room was quiet for just a moment then Norm added, "And to a lot more good times *and* good food." Everyone touched glasses, laughed and tipped them back to enjoy the cold beer. Fiona dipped her ceramic spoon in the broth to sample. It was crisp round and light, with just a hint of ginger and that sea taste that comes with kelp. Ardley was right—the beer was the perfect compliment. Fiona glanced across the table, and caught Marvin engaged in the same analysis. He looked up, saw her, and they laughed. Food was its own language.

"Ardley, this is incredible. It's both light and hearty at the same time." Fiona remarked.

"Thank you. It's a traditional New Years dinner, though not usually the Western New Year." Norm had his fork and spoon in hand, as did Thomas.

Amanda was savoring the chicken. "How do you get the chicken to keep its texture?" she asked.

Ardley looked caught. Sheepishly she admitted, "I cheat a little. I marinate and cook it separately, and add it back in at the end. My way is not traditional, but I don't like that gray, boiled chicken look or texture."

Norm looked up, "Ardley's giving away her secrets but unfortunately, Jenn's not here to catalogue them for us!"

"That girl *is* an absolute delight," exclaimed Marvin, "She's curious, competent and game for anything new."

"It's the red hair, you know, a genetic thing." muttered Amanda.

Fiona howled. "Red hair is it? Does it have to be natural, or can I dye it?"

"Usually it has to be natural but in Norm's case we've decided he can have honorary redhead status."

"And who is the *we*, who decided this?" Fiona pushed.

"Well, Jenn and I of course. We're the redheads, so we decide,"

Norm chuckled, "Hey, I'll take it. Any honorary status I can get at this age is a good thing."

Mugging, Marv piped in, "Does this mean I get honorary *blond* status?"

"Who'd want it?" Thomas quipped.

"Hey," Marvin retorted, with feigned injury, "Not all of us get the dignity of a full head of silver hair."

Fiona noted that Thomas had joined in the riffing, and smiled to herself. Thomas officially belonged now, a member of the tribe. She yawned and realized the jet lag was getting the better of her. Quietly, she said to Ardley, "You have achieved the kitchen magic of making the meal authentic but still interpretive."

"I love that this group is so into food,' she replied, "In fact, I like how everyone has a connection with the tiny, wonderful details of living, making everything a celebration. I don't know how you pulled together such an eclectic bunch." The others were still laughing and debating the funny stereotypes behind hair color.

Fiona nodded and rolled her eyes. "I didn't, Emma did. The only ones who even knew each other before this were Amanda and I. The rest just happened."

"I really loved how you wove Emma's tale into your emails."

"Thanks, Ardley."

"Will you be able to get the book written in time for the show?"

"It's going to be tight. Though I'm doing a lot as I go with the research, March and April are set for finalizing and editing. Arthur Bradley has offered to help and Mills has connections with academic publishers. Once Arthur gives the approval they'll print. I understand Marvin, Thomas and Arthur are already almost finished photographing the paintings. I have to see them all, and then Arthur and I will select from the catalogue which ones will go into the book. It's a complicated endeavor. I still have my own work, so it's going to be a busy spring."

"Let me know if there's anything I can do to help."

"I appreciate that, and I do have Jenn. That kid is really a miracle worker."

Ardley glanced around at the group, "I get that, I can't wait to meet her. Did you get to enjoy Paris at all, or was it just research?"

"I loved it and the research actually enriched it. It was incredible seeing Paris simultaneously with 1920's eyes and 2007 eyes. Without the framework, without the quest, I never would have gone. I feel it's transformed me."

"It came through in your stories, a little like giving birth."

"Hmm, giving birth, being born, sort of wrapped together."

"That way for us too, as readers, especially for Thomas. I know you were concerned about him but this whole process, particularly the story, has been tremendous for him, and for us too."

Fiona reached out and took her hand, "There isn't anything you could have said to give me more confidence in this project than that."

In the background they could hear that the conversation had moved on to a discussion of the transformation of Norm's shop. Marvin was especially intrigued, "You've spent under three thousand? What did you say your square footage was?"

"Marvin, you're just jealous. Inside you're champing at the bit to start your own gallery. So, why don't you just do it?" Thomas had hit the nail on the head.

"It's not so easy. I have eight years in with this gallery. A partnership is a lot like a marriage; it's hard just to give up on it."

"And like a bad marriage, you usually stay *way* too long," Amanda jumped right in after Thomas.

278

"We'll see. I have a partnership meeting this week, and we'll look at the '07 numbers. I'm sure my partners will see straight from the spreadsheet just how valuable my contributions are."

"Of course, you've already run the numbers, right?"

"Yes, Amanda, I have and they look very good for me."

"Look out Marvin, when she gets that tone, she already knows where she's going." Norman knew from experience.

Amanda sighed and looked directly at Marvin, "Sweetie, I've been there. When you're already counting on your fingers behind your back, you're really just counting the days. I know, you're hoping against hope that some bright light will go on and they'll suddenly realize your worth. The good news is that *you* do." She reached across the table, and squeezed his hand. "When you're ready, let us know. The transformational talents of Amanda and Norm are at your service." She bowed her head.

Marvin nodded enthusiastically.

"We're here for you too!" announced Ardley.

"Me too, well... not in March or April," joined Fiona, with a yawn.

"Why, what's up then?" Marvin asked.

"Gotta finish the book."

"Girl has her priorities right," Marvin beamed back at Fiona.

Ardley looked around the table at the empty bowls, stood up and started to collect them. Thomas stepped in to help.

"Tonight's dessert is a surprise, brought to you by Marvin. A New Year's special," declared Thomas.

"Not a surprise so much, but I wanted to bring champagne, and then one thing led to another, and this dessert seemed the perfect complement. It's an anise-flavored crème brulée with almond biscotti. See if you can figure out why I chose it."

Thomas was already placing the champagne flutes on the table. Marvin stepped into the kitchen, and retrieved a tray of white ramekins with perfect, golden, caramelized tops, and a bowl of biscotti, while Ardley set out spoons. Then, Marvin fetched two bottles of champagne and deftly opened both, without the overly dramatic pop and filled each glass. He smiled, looked directly at Fiona and Amanda and said, "Analyze away ladies." The gauntlet had been thrown down before them.

Amanda reached for a ramekin and a spoon. Fiona sipped her champagne, and smiled. She understood even before she tasted the dessert. Then she too reached for the tray. The others followed suit.

"Wow, this is smooth," Amanda tapped the glassy brulée skin and took a second delicate spoonful of the creamy mixture. "The anise is so light… mmmm. It's perfect."

"Now sip the champagne," suggested Fiona. Amanda raised her glass.

"Oh my god, it's almond! It's incredible!" Amanda took a bite of the biscotti, "Marvin, what a combo. All the tastes are subtle but blended they're wild."

Fiona broke into a wide smile, and then tapped into her own brulée cup, so did Marvin. "What champagne is this? Where'd you find it?" demanded Ardley.

"It's a little California vineyard, down south, Wilson Creek. It was served at a friend's wedding. We had it outdoors in a garden where anise was growing. The mix of aromas was intoxicating. I knew that day I'd have to mix them together."

Thomas reached out, and refreshed their glasses. Norm sat in silence as he scraped the cup clean and washed the last of his biscotti down with a sip of champagne.

Ardley reached out to touch Thomas's hand. "He wasn't kidding," she turned to the others. "He came back after your Christmas dinner and said that this group spoke food as a secret language."

"*Happy New Year* everyone! This will be a year of magic." Fiona had tears in her eyes. All glasses raised again, a quiet clinking of glasses as they drained the last of the champagne.

"Thomas, I'd hoped to see some paintings tonight, but I'm exhausted. Would it be okay if I came sometime this week? I'd like to do it before I see Jordan." Fiona yawned again.

"Absolutely, just call to make sure someone's here. Either one of us can show you the pieces."

"What's up with you, sleepyhead?" Amanda wasn't used to seeing Fiona so wiped out.

"Jet lag. I just can't get my head on straight. I'm dragging during the day, then wide awake in the middle of the night."

"It'd be fine with me if we pack up a bit early. I'm exhausted from the week," Norm volunteered, "I haven't worked this hard in decades."

Amanda jumped up to clear the dessert dishes, and Marvin joined her. She turned to him, "If you'll give me a lift home later, we can let these two sleepyheads slip away early."

"Sure," Marv looked up at Fiona, "Go on, we promise we won't have too much fun without you."

"Yeah," Ardley added, "We'll just be looking at paintings and discussing *your* future."

Fiona was torn and exhausted, but hated to miss anything. She looked up at Norm, who really did look spent. "Okay partner, let's pack it in."

Everyone exchanged hugs and kisses at the door, while Thomas handed them their coats. Fiona pulled hers on and buckled its belt.

"That's a lovely coat, Fiona. Where did you get it?" Ardley reached out to touch the fabric.

Fiona beamed and twirled, "Oh it's a little something I picked up in Paris." Everyone laughed, but Fiona knew they'd laugh a lot harder when they got the whole story. She reached into her voluminous purse and pulled out a wrapped box, which she handed to Amanda.

"Good night, everyone. Come on Norm, let's go home. We'll see you all next week for the Grand Opening!" The two headed out into the night.

Chapter Fifty-Two

Later, her ears still ringing with the echoes of ideas and plans, Amanda slipped into her apartment, finally ready for bed. It had been a full evening. Amanda was thrilled at Fiona's reaction to the shop. Now that Amanda was immersed in Emma's story, she felt more connected with her paintings. The show-and-tell slides at the end of the evening were an especially sweet exhibit preview. Amanda could now see why Fiona had bonded so quickly with her first little painting. And driving home with Marvin had been an unexpected opportunity for Amanda to urge him to pursue his own gallery. She felt she brought a marketing perspective that was different than the rest of the group, and she hoped he was listening.

As she got ready for bed, Amanda remembered the package from Fiona. After retrieving it from the living room, she sat on the bed and ripped open the wrapping. It was a pair of goofy pajamas, covered in a cool retro pattern of boomerangs. Amanda laughed out loud. She stripped out of her nightshirt, donned her new pajamas, and climbed back into bed.

Chapter Fifty-Three

Amanda was waiting, impatiently, by the door. "Come on, come on. We can pull this all together afterwards."

In fact, things really were already pretty much together. Fiona set the oven timer to reheat the cassoulet in time for the dinner. As promised, the menu was the duplicate of her Paris dinner with Jeanne-Marie and Gaston. Fiona had been emailing Paris all week for recipes, tips and final touches. From her side of the ocean, Jeanne-Marie was captivated by the Emma story, and wanted regular updates. She was particularly impressed with the plans for the exhibit. To Jeanne-Marie, Fiona's biographical adventure epitomized the difference between the French and the American experience, in art and in life. She wrote that she was flattered at Fiona's recreation of the Paris cassoulet. Jeanne-Marie emailed all her Bay Area, French friends and directed Fiona on a veritable treasure hunt of shopping, since the ingredients all had to be authentic. Fiona was meeting an entire cast of French enthusiasts, most of whom had already heard the Emma story. The chef at La Note—the only one Jeanne-Marie trusted to locate the best duck had already marked her calendar for Emma's opening. Fiona grinned that the exhibit already had a built-in French contingent.

"Fiona, this is Norm's night, so let's move it." Amanda was beyond impatient. Fiona, now feeling a little guilty, grabbed her coat and headed out the door, behind an exasperated Amanda. It was already dark, but not terribly cold. Not a bad night for an opening. Checking her watch, Fiona saw that they were still pretty early. To her great delight, Norm was treating this as though it were a *gallery* opening, and not just a remodeled thrift shop. She loved the enthusiasm and the build up. Amanda's friend from the Tribune would be there, and they'd be serving the traditional gallery fare of cheap white wine, cubed cheese and crackers with grapes and strawberries.

"I want to be sure to get there before Marvin," explained Amanda, "I want to get a look at his face when he first sees the transformation."

"Has he ever been there before?"

"Years ago, when he was bottom feeding, like me. Norm wants

to impress him, and well… I do, too."

"Really Amanda, there's no need to be nervous, the place is gorgeous."

"Norm wants to win Marvin over. There's a yoga studio in the building that's probably going under. Norm wants Marvin to get it for his gallery."

"You guys should cool it. Marv's situation isn't good but I don't see any indication that he's ready to jump ship. Besides, it's not exactly a good economy for launching a new gallery. I mean, if a yoga place can't cut it, would a new gallery?"

Amanda shrugged, "Well, it *is* Bikram yoga. The only reason it's going under is the price of energy."

Fiona just looked puzzled.

"Oh for God's sake Fiona, you know, the yoga freaks who work-out at a hundred plus degrees or something. I thought you'd know about it, now that you're a jock." Fiona pulled up to the store. The lights were ablaze and the windows had a festive glow.

Fiona paused before getting out of the car, "Look, I'm not a jock. I just decided to start walking in the morning. I thought I'd keep it up after Paris, besides, what do I know from Bikram?"

"Me neither, really, but it's just that Norm thinks the space may become available and that it'd work for Marvin."

Once inside, they could see that the store was packed. Norm greeted them at the door, grinning ear to ear. There was music in the background, but you could hardly hear it over the din. It looked like the whole neighborhood had come to check out his new digs. Amanda scanned the crowd for her reporter friend and found her talking to a few of Norm's neighbors. She wasn't hard to find— Cheryl was statuesque, with skin the color of mocha. She wore her hair snugged to her head in cornrows and dangling beads. In her brick color damask caftan, she had the presence of a runway model. Cheryl spotted Amanda, and pulled her aside.

"I thought you were joking, but this will be a great little story. All the neighbors are excited, it's a great 'Oakland revitalized' piece. And that Norm is as cute as a button. I took some pictures. I'm going to try to get my editor interested. He'll really like the *eBay* angle, you know, *Old Guy, Bricks and Sticks Store Gets New Life with Internet Boost*. Who'd have thought a thrift store opening could bring out such a crowd?" Cheryl popped some cheese and grapes into her mouth.

"That's *vintage*, hon. *Thrift* is history."

Amanda took Cheryl's arm, and led her around the store, giving her an animated tour, pointing out the merchandise and remodeling highlights. Fiona was speechless. Amanda could really work a room and Norm was going to get a little feature story that would certainly help with marketing. She inched her way back through the crowd to Norm, and gave him the reporter scoop.

Norm had noticed Amanda's sales-pitch, too. "Really? I talked to her but I thought the story angle was Amanda's idea of a joke."

Fiona cocked her head to the side, "Norm, I've *never* known Amanda to joke about marketing."

He nodded, "That girl could push you off a cliff and convince you it was flying."

"Seen any of the gang, yet?"

"Yeah, Jenn is over in the corner rummaging through 1940s bakelite bangles. I told her *no sales* tonight but she's determined. I saw Thomas and Ardley drive by looking for a parking spot, and Marvin called to say he'd be a bit late." The bell jingled and Norm turned to greet more well-wishers, by name. This was old home week for him.

Fiona waited for the entry-way to clear, "What did Jenn say when she came in?"

"She was floored. Her reaction alone made it all worthwhile. She walked around and didn't say anything for awhile, and then finally she said, 'Norm, this is a place *I* would shop at!'"

"You can be proud, Norm. You two have totally transformed this place."

"I know, I am really, but I have to give Amanda most of the credit. She's fearless."

"So," Fiona waved her hand at the crowd, "Are they just neighbors, or would these folks actually shop here?"

"It's a mix but there is some real retail interest. Some of my bottom-feeders were in earlier, but they didn't seem too pleased," he grinned.

The door's bell tinkled again and Thomas and Ardley stepped in. Norm gave Thomas a bear hug, and then a daintier embrace for Ardley.

Thomas nodded at the crowd, "Quite a turn-out Norm. Did you expect this?"

"*I* didn't, but Amanda did. She kept telling me it would be packed but I didn't believe her. She insisted that we buy tons of refreshments from Costco, and now they're almost gone."

Fiona stepped aside to give way to a group leaving. One woman called out, "I'll be back tomorrow Norm. I see some things I really want!"

Norm smiled and replied, "I'll be here. And I want to hear your suggestions!" Thomas and Ardley followed Fiona's lead, stepping inside to check out the goods.

Fiona turned to Norm. "What kind of advertising did you do?"

"We ran an ad in the Tribune and then a bunch of little teaser ads on Craigslist. I wish I could tell what brought them in. We didn't think about tracking the results."

A few more customers left, many thanking Norm on the way out, as though the locals had a stake in the improvements, a pride of place in the neighborhood. Norm beamed at the recognition, and in the glow of his connection to his neighbors and customers. He turned back to Fiona, "Who'd have thought that my neighbors would turn out like this? I don't know what to say."

Fiona reached out and took his hand, "I saw the new sign. Was it always the store's name?"

"*Lily's*? Yeah. I named it after my wife when we first married. Some years ago, just after she passed, a big truck hit the sign. The city wouldn't let me replace it with the same kind of sign, because of the overhang. I never had the heart to get a new one. Amanda made me do it, pulled strings to do it. Like it?"

"I love it, and I love the story. What did Amanda say?"

"She likes the name, says it sounds retro. Then I showed her pictures of the old sign, said we had to do it just like that. I'm thinking Lily would like it, so I'm pleased."

"Norm," another little old lady swooped in and took his hand. "It's such a pleasure to see the store looking good again. Good for the whole neighborhood. Lily would've loved it." Fiona backed away and let Norm connect with his clientele. She turned and saw Amanda still earnestly chatting with Cheryl. Jenn stood with them, gesticulating. Fiona's curiosity got the better of her. She wove her way through the crowd, and sidled up to the trio just as Amanda was explaining the connection between Norm and the Emma Caites exhibit.

Cheryl didn't miss a beat, "I think Arthur has something there. It's not a big part of the story but the Emma Caites discovery is a part of her story too. I hope you'll pursue that as a part of the exhibit," she nodded to Jennifer. "Go ahead, put this young lady on it, and I'll see to it that the whole affair gets the attention it deserves. I like the angle. Digging for Oakland history, right here at home."

"What's this?" Fiona couldn't help but nose in.

Amanda explained, "Arthur Bradley thinks we should do a side exhibit at Emma's show about how she was rediscovered. He likes the serendipity of it. He's suggested that Jennifer put that together, perhaps for extra credit, then she would have an Art History exhibit of her own under her belt. She'll have to interview us and put the story out, not so hard since she's already in the thick of it. Cheryl thinks the idea has legs."

Fiona furrowed her brow. "But that would be about us."

Amanda turned to Cheryl, "And here's your hurdle, when the greater good comes up against the shy." Cheryl shrugged and pursed her lips.

"It's not about shy," Fiona protested, "It's that it really should be about Emma."

Cheryl focused her attention directly on Fiona, "It's a great idea. It's about context and framing. Without it, you'll just have a good show that's seventy years late. With it you bring your audience on the journey, an exploration. It's everyone's dream, you know, Antiques Road Show. A woman finds a painting and it leads to a quest."

Fiona looked dubious, "I think as a group, we'll have to discuss it. I am not entirely comfortable with making the search part of the event."

"We've done it already," chimed Jennifer. "We thought you might have trouble with it, but the support is unanimous. We think it makes Emma's story more personal, more accessible."

Fiona swallowed hard. "Even Thomas is on board?"

"Yup. And Ardley, too." Jennifer reached out and gave Fiona a reassuring hug. "Don't worry. It's a small part of the larger whole and the focus will stay on Emma."

"And, it's great marketing," added Amanda. Fiona looked at her friends and saw that the decision had already been made. It felt a little like an ambush, and that came with a measure of panic. Part of her was pleased that it caught Amanda's interest. She'd felt awkward about not bringing her friend more into the center of the

Emma quest. Marketing was just up Amanda's alley. Still, Fiona was nervous about featuring in the exhibit, and that part she knew was about shyness.

Now, Cheryl jumped in, "And good for the book sales, with the *story within a story*, it'll give reviewers an easy in."

"I'm not putting it in the book," Fiona blurted, "The book is about Emma."

"Of course, but the back story will already be out there. It makes the whole package more doable if you give interviews and do readings."

Fiona shuddered. This was *way* beyond her comfort zone. Just finishing the book felt daunting. Just thinking about public appearances made her squirm.

Amanda saw it. "None of this is anything she needs to deal with now. It's hard enough juggling a full work load and one life, let alone two lives and writing the book too!"

But Cheryl pressed. She put her arm around Fiona and lowered her voice to an almost seductive tone, "Fiona, I've only read your Paris emails to Amanda but if the flavor of the book is like the reports, it goes way beyond an academic biography of an obscure painter. It's a crossover book. It speaks to a larger audience. It's got it all. Personal growth, overcoming obstacles, physical disability, finding one's way in an artistic discipline, and a woman holding her own in the art world in the 1920s." She smiled broadly, "And, it has heart."

Fiona held her breath. The pressure was too much, and it wasn't about Emma. She looked up at Cheryl. "I'm just writing *Emma's* story. I'm sure many people will see larger themes but that's not mine to say. I just write how Emma lived it. That has to be enough for me, or else it turns into fiction." Even still, Fiona felt herself wavering under Cheryl's charms.

Thomas walked up behind her, just as she said it. He put his arm around Fiona, and turned to the women assembled, "It's why I knew Fiona was the right writer for the task. Her sensitivity lets my mother shine through without any particular lens. Don't mess with her, ladies, she's the real thing." He gave Fiona an extra squeeze and added, "I'm not sure why, but Norm wanted me to tell you Marvin's on his way in."

Jenn inhaled, "Oooh, thanks for the heads up. We want to see his face when he sees the store!"

"Oh, is that what this is. Well, mission control reports that he's parked and approaching ground zero."

Fiona and Jenn headed to the front, where they could catch a good view of Marvin as he entered. Fiona wished it was a little less crowded, so Marvin could scan the store better from the door. She said so to Jenn.

"Don't worry. He'll catch it all as the crowd thins out. This is good because the turn out is so impressive." Fiona caught sight of Marvin's blond mop crossing the sidewalk. His face was in a knot. Something was wrong. The door opened and Marvin stood just inside, surveying the scene with his mouth agape. Whatever was bothering him on the way in melted from view. Fiona caught Norm's anxious eye. This debut was important to him. This brought him from junk to vintage, and Marvin's approval meant a lot.

Marvin turned to Norm, "I can't believe it. It's not even the same place. Norm, it's beautiful."

Norm returned the compliment with a hug. "You could do this too. Me and Amanda will help, anytime you're ready."

Marvin's face clouded over again. "I may just have to take you up on that." Then he smiled, "If it turned out like this, it might just be a blessing." Marvin reached out for Norm's elbow and said, "Okay Norm, show me around." Norm gave the tour, with all the details of the remodel, the inventory, the Dumpster, the lighting, the color disputes. It was like doing stand-up, a running monologue about his personal process of letting go of junk while opening up to retail. Norm had Marvin in stitches, exactly what Marvin needed. Fiona relaxed. She gave Jenn's hand a squeeze, and said, "Tell Amanda Marvin approves."

Fiona loved that there were splinter factions in the group, even if they did plot against her. She loved the way their different combinations came together and worked on projects, and then reconfigured for the next event. It was like a minuet, coming together, then changing partners.

Amanda came up beside her, "Something's up with Marv."

"Yeah, I saw that."

"Well, let's keep tonight light and fun. We'll be here if he needs us but let him lead."

Fiona winced at the dance analogy, plucked straight from her thoughts. "Light and fun, is that what you planned for me?"

Amanda squinched up her face, "Sorry about that. Cheryl can be pushy but her heart is good. She did wonders for Norm on this and her input guarantees a good turnout for the exhibit too. She's an Oakland native and the city's biggest booster."

"I like her, but I'm just having trouble with marketing *us*. It just feels a little crass, everything as marketing. I don't see Emma that way."

"And you won't have to, because we'll take care of that. As I pointed out to her, we can even market your genuine and shy sincerity. Got your back, babe."

Fiona nodded towards Cheryl, "Invite her to the dinner, would you? She could be a good addition to the team."

After a pause she added, "Amanda, have you heard from Denise?"

"A quick call over Christmas, looking for you. Boy, was she shocked when I said you were in Paris!"

"I've left her half a dozen messages since I got back, and no response."

"Let it go for now. If we don't hear soon, I'll give her a call."

The advertised end-time for the opening was approaching, and the crowd spontaneously began to thin. Fiona checked her watch, and was relieved that she'd pre-set her oven. Dinner would be perfectly timed. Amanda formally introduced Cheryl to Norm, who enthusiastically embraced the much taller woman, spinning her around in time to the music. Fiona marveled at his light-footed nimbleness.

"Woman, anytime you want any fancy vintage gewgaws, you just come on by!"

Quickly recovering, Cheryl whistled, "Man's got moves! I sure will, Norm. It's so good to see sparks of life in Oakland retail. There's life in this old town yet!"

Amanda interjected, "Cheryl, can you join us for a celebratory dinner?" The two conferred on the arrangements.

With the event winding down, Jenn was pawing at Norm. "I know it was a no-sales event but, now that it's over, can I *please* get some things?

"Okey-dokey, kiddo. What do you want?"

Jenn led him over to her cache of goodies, stashed in one of the drawers at the cashier's counter—she was taking no chances. Fiona reached out and touched Ardley's hand. "I'm going to slip out and get things ready for dinner. I figure Thomas knows the way there."

Ardley laughed. "We'll see you in a few minutes." Fiona started to retreat when Marvin interrupted her.

"You need any help?"

"Probably not, but you can keep me company."

Taking their own cars, they headed out to set-up for dinner.

Fiona got there first. The oven had just switched off and the cassoulet was piping hot. The salads were ready, and Fiona quickly assembled another for Cheryl.

Marvin rang the bell and she called out that it was unlocked. He came into the kitchen, bearing flowers, an incredible assortment of whites and greens. There were chrysanthemums and lilies in white, three varieties of eucalyptus sprays, hydrangeas. It was full and lush, but with the quiet dignity of a winter bouquet.

Fiona looked up, "You're such a sweetie." She took the flowers and arranged them in a clear, square depression block vase which she placed on the sideboard.

"It's going to be tight in this dining room," she moaned.

"Yeah, but you won't get any complaints. To criticize would be to criticize Emma Caites, wouldn't it?" Marvin smiled.

"Hmmm. Never thought of that, I guess right now I could get away with a lot. This will be an interesting homecoming for Thomas." Fiona looked up again at Marvin, who was rearranging the place settings to add one for Cheryl. "You okay?"

He waved his hand. "Oh, rough day. Things are not going so well at the gallery."

"What happened to your meeting with the spreadsheets?"

He shrugged, "It appears that the facts don't matter."

"I hate when that happens."

Marvin sighed, "I guess I'll just have to wait it out, but it has become so corrosive to work where I always seem to be the odd man out."

"You know, we all decided that you need to go it on your own, set up your own gallery."

"Yeah, I gathered that. I really do appreciate the vote of confidence but it's dicey timing. The economy's not doing so well, and what with this being the post-Christmas season. Remember, my area is antiques. That requires cash on the barrel-head. It's an expensive prospect to start up a gallery."

Fiona put her hand on his shoulder, "Well, just so you know, they're out there scouting locations for you."

Marvin laughed, "Have they found anything good?"

"They're hoping the yoga studio by Norm's will fail."

"The Bikram? Yeah. I'll bet the heating bills are killing them."

Fiona paused, "How come everyone knows about that but me?"

"Silly woman," Marvin patted her on the cheek, "I'm gay. I know *all* the trends."

Fiona laughed.

Marvin nodded, "Really though, it's not a bad location. If things continue as they are, I might just consider it."

"Your partners would have to buy you out. If you get to that, I can do business valuations. I'd be happy to look at your books and to give an opinion."

Marvin kissed her smack on the forehead. "You are such a gem. I really don't know what I'd do if I hadn't happened into this bunch." The doorbell rang and Marvin turned to get it.

It was Norm, Amanda, Jenn and Cheryl. In they trooped, as jubilant victors. Laughter and chatter filled the air. Jenn's arms were laden with vintage bangles. Cheryl, the newcomer, was babbling about the event like she'd invented it. She was using the word "we," which brought into question her journalistic objectivity. There was no doubt that Cheryl was on board. Amanda caught Fiona's eye, and winked. Norm was flush with triumph, or maybe it was hunger.

"Fiona, that smells incredible. What are we having?" Norm was certainly staying in character.

The doorbell rang again.

Marvin turned to her, "I'll get this underway. I think you have a little tour to give to Thomas and Ardley. Or maybe they have one for you." Fiona nodded in appreciation, and headed for the front entry.

She swung the door wide, "Welcome home."

Thomas smiled, "Yes, this *is* a little odd."

Fiona gestured them in. "Thomas, you can wander around and show Ardley your old digs if you like, or first, you might like to see the painting that started all this."

Thomas's eyes lit up, "Oh, yes please. We'd love to see the painting."

Fiona led the way upstairs. It was as good a way as any to make him feel at home.

"It's better in the early morning, when you recreate the lighting of the painting..." Fiona presented her first and most significant

Emma Caites treasure.

"Oh, I remember this one." Thomas stepped in close and then turned Ardley, "My mother loved this view in the morning. She made her coffee and would watch the sun come up from this spot. Ard, hon, come stand right here."

Husband and wife took turns, looking out the darkened window, with hands cupped against the glass against the light and then at the painting, nodding and pointing at the subtle lines or angles of light. Fiona wondered what it would be like to have a partner with whom you could share such an aesthetic connection. Watching Thomas, Fiona saw what it was that Emma had had with Pieter. Suddenly, she felt like she was intruding on a private moment.

Ardley turned to her, "It's exquisite." She took it in again, "Someday, if you don't mind, I'd like to come see it at dawn."

Fiona was touched. Ardley had linked into exactly the same way Fiona most loved the painting. "I would love to share it at dawn. It would be great to have someone appreciate exactly this feeling that the painting gives me."

Thomas headed out to the hall, "Ardley come and see. This was my room."

"If you two will excuse me, I have to check on dinner. Take your time, look around and enjoy." Fiona stepped back to let Thomas share the memories with his wife. She swallowed hard at the tenderness of it, and headed back down to the kitchen.

Marvin looked up and got the drift, "How long till we serve?"

"Can we give it a few minutes?"

"You got it." He continued opening another bottle of wine.

Where the upstairs had been quiet and intimate, downstairs was raucous and celebratory. Norm was toasting Amanda. Cheryl was toasting Oakland. And Amanda was toasting Emma Caites. Jenn was joining in on every toast. All this drinking with no food, Fiona shook her head. She quickly reached for the tray of cheese-leek tarts in the refrigerator and popped them into the microwave.

Marvin saw it and concurred, "Good idea, or this group is going to start to sing."

Fiona laughed. After the timer buzzed, she pulled the tarts out of the microwave and loaded another batch. The warmed ones went on a tray, and were scarfed up immediately by the hungry revelers.

"Ah, this is what we've been waiting for." Norm was savoring the tart. "This is our fringe-benefit of your trip to Paris."

293

Marvin grabbed one and took a nibble, tilted his head back, and nodded, "The leeks are incredible, they're almost sweet. And is this a goat cheese?"

"It's sheep's cheese. Not quite as much edge to it as goat cheese. I like the nuttiness of it with the smoothness of the leeks." Fiona reached over and took one from the tray.

Amanda helped herself to another, adding, "Well there's no shortage of nuttiness in this group. Did you see Jenn's arms?"

Tart in hand, Norm answered, "I think she bought every bangle in the store."

Jenn stepped up to the counter, and helped herself to two of the tarts. "Well I won't wear them all at once, except tonight. It's an easy way to carry them. Norm, I never saw them in the store before, or I'd have snapped them up then."

Fiona giggled, to no one in particular, "You ever notice how everyone always ends up in the kitchen? I'm refilling this tray, and this time it's going to make it into the living room." She reached into the microwave, just as Thomas and Ardley came in.

"What smells so good?" Ardley reached for a tart, as Marvin handed her a glass of wine. Thomas took two and Norm took another. Fiona sighed and gave up on the living room. If everyone wanted to convene in her tiny kitchen, it was fine with her.

"Fiona you have some really lovely paintings of my mom's. I love the one of me with the paint brush. Now I understand why Jennifer said she restored me."

"Thanks, I don't yet know how we'll be integrating all the works into the exhibit. Any thoughts on that, Marvin?"

"Well, I wish Arthur were here. Jenn and I have seen the general framework, and we have a pretty cohesive plan. Maybe at the next dinner I should do an exhibit slide show."

Norm joined in, "I'd love that. So when's the next dinner?"

"What that man won't do for food!" Amanda reached over and affectionately tousled Norm's hair.

Ever the diplomat, Marvin interceded. "I think Fiona has to set the next date. She's the one with the heaviest workload on this, just now."

"Yeah, I still have to interview Jordan. That's next weekend, then I'll integrate what I get from that into what I've already put together. I don't think I'll have time to get together again until maybe the first week in February."

"So let's plan for Groundhog Day," Jennifer offered. "What do you say Norm, you and I can do dinner at your place?"

Norm looked stunned. He was no cook.

"Come on Norm, I'll help. It'll be great." Amanda sidled up to him.

Norm looked back and forth at the two redheads. "Why not, we'll plan an appropriate groundhog feast."

"With that resolved, we'd best move on to tonight's menu. Now, if you'll all just wedge yourselves into Emma Caites' tiny dining room..." Fiona put the empty tart tray in the sink, and motioned to the dining room. "Since it's so tight, everyone just stay put and Marv and I will do the serving. We'll have to pass on the far side, but no one will starve."

"Excuse me. I know I'm coming to all this late, Fiona, but why is this *Emma Caites'* dining room?" Cheryl had missed out on the chapter one of the Emma quest.

Norm glanced at Fiona, and with a dismissive wave of his hands assured them "Don't worry, you two just bring the food, we'll bring the lady up to speed."

Fiona stepped into the kitchen where Marvin was already taking the salads out of the refrigerator. She reached for the dressing and gave it a good shake before dosing each one. She listened to the others recounting the tale, Amanda and Norm squawking about the original painting purchase, Thomas adding that this was the apartment where he'd grown up, and Jenn telling how she'd been working the library that day at Mills when Fiona had come in. Everyone had a part, and they were reeling Cheryl in—soon she'd have a part in it too. Fiona and Marvin passed out the salads, then took their seats.

"So, Fiona, I heard there's a story behind this particular menu, something to do with an authentic, French meal?" Thomas raised his wine glass to punctuate his inquiry.

Fiona recounted the social and culinary details of her Parisian dinner.

Amanda pressed for details, "But there's a missing piece to this story. Just how did you come to be invited into their home? What, were you soliciting on the streets of Paris for authentic, home-cooked food?"

Fiona had thought long and hard about this, just how much did she want to tell? She launched in with the tale, arriving in Paris just

295

when it snowed, her trip to Galleries Lafayette to buy mittens and a hat, and how she was enchanted by the store. Fiona noticed that her guests had finished their salads, and stood to collect their dishes. She continued with the story about the discovery of the coat, while she passed out the plates for the entrée and set out several baskets of sour peasant bread. She returned to the kitchen and brought out the cassoulet, placing it in the center of the table. She removed the lid releasing the aroma of roasted garlic, onions and thick chunks of duck floating amongst the chopped sausages with tomatoes and beans. Norm interrupted with a gasp, as the rich aromas wafted in his direction. Fiona handed Marvin the serving utensils as she continued telling her story. Fiona stopped for a moment to collect herself as she helped pass the steaming plates. Then she launched into the story of the coat purchase. Standing where the tiny dining room opened into the kitchen, she acted out the saga of her purchase. Nobody touched their food.

Here was this unassuming middle aged American playing tug-of-war over a coat, in the middle of the grandest mercantile palace of Paris. Fiona had them in stitches. The incongruous vision of their staid hostess, beet-faced and unhinged, and the grace of her French rescuer took the guests aback. That gentle woman was Jeanne-Marie, and this dinner was *her* recipe. By the time Fiona finished telling the story, she was as flushed and agitated as though it had just happened, giving her friends a glimpse of the panic, just under her shy reserved exterior. Marvin abruptly stood up, and without a word, threw his arms around her, while everyone applauded.

When they'd all settled back down, Marvin raised a glass for a toast. Every glass raised, and in his most solemn voice, Marvin tipped his head to Fiona and said, *"Nice Coat."* They all howled, then proceeded to attack the savory fare before them.

The cassoulet was perfect. The beans soft, but not mushy and the flavor of the sage and the broth infused into them. The duck was tender and fell cleanly from the bone, and the herbed sausage was the perfect counterpoint to the sage permeated broth. They fell into silence while they relished the hearty fare, broken only by quiet compliments on the textures and blended tastes. For such a simple meal, it was a great success. Thomas fetched another bottle of wine from the kitchen and kept the glasses full.

Fiona told them a little about Jeanne-Marie and Gaston, and their discussion about the difference between the French attitude of

296

specialization and the American can-do approach. Thomas added that it was a theme his mother returned to over and over—how Americans were hands-on, and wanted to engage themselves in the creative process. It was one of the reasons she taught painting classes. She liked the energy and enthusiasm of her students.

"Where did she teach?" Cheryl asked.

"Mostly here, downstairs in the garage. In good weather, mom and I would take the class off to the hills to paint outdoors. I always painted with the classes. Mom thought it was good advertising to have her little tyke along. I must have started painting when I was only three. I was in my fifties before I realized that it solved a day-care problem. I'd always assumed I was actually co-teaching."

Norm laughed. "Actually, you were pretty good. But your mom lost a few students along the way when they gave up because they couldn't paint as well as a toddler."

"I don't remember it, but my mother used to say that when I started school, I changed my drawings and paintings to match my peers. She was disappointed because I had good skills, but suddenly the work coming home from school looked like the typical stick drawings of the kids my age. I guess I didn't want to be different."

Norm put down his fork and changed the subject to something close to *his* heart, "That was incredible. Not bad for beans and franks. And now that I'm stuffed, I suppose you're going to say there's dessert."

Marvin stood and began collecting dishes. "Indeed, she's made poached pears, but Norman," he winked at the others, "There's always room for a little fruit."

Everyone laughed, nervously at first, unsure what to do with the double-entendre. Finally it just rolled, and the group was near tears.

Her tiny dining room wasn't big enough to contain all this. Fiona stepped into her little pantry where she'd precariously stacked the dessert plates, with the poached pears already sliced and splayed on them. Thankfully she'd made extras, both so she could pick the prettiest of the lot for serving, and in case Norm, Amanda or Jenn wanted seconds. She lined them up in the kitchen, poured a little of the warmed sauce on each, and added a generous dollop of crème fraiche. The final, crowning touch was the small chocolate truffle on each plate. There it was, Jeanne-Marie's Paris Dinner. She would be proud. Marvin helped her carry the desserts in, to the oohs and ahs of her guests.

297

Ardley turned to Thomas, "You weren't kidding. They've elevated good food and good friends to a high art."

Cheryl nodded, "I must've been living under a rock, because I've never been to a friends' dinner like this. Do you always do this?"

Amanda laughed, "It's turned into a tradition, it's because of Norm. He's so much fun to cook for, that we all just started to do it up!"

"I'll be happy to take credit for that," piped Norm.

"How do *I* join?" Cheryl pressed.

"Silly girl," Norm shook his head. "You already did."

When the last bite was eaten everyone stood. They chased Marvin and Fiona out of the kitchen, and taking turns, in her tiny kitchen, proceeded to do the dishes. It was boisterous, but since Fiona didn't hear anything breaking, she figured all was well.

Ardley stuck her head out and said, "Fiona, we're all missing the Emma updates from Paris. Now that you're back, will you still email us memos on her progress?" From inside the tiny kitchen there was resounding agreement.

"Sure. It'll be a good way for me to stay on track but don't expect anything until after I've interviewed Jordan."

She turned to Marvin, "Arthur Bradley has offered to edit the book, but I'd like someone in the group to preview it, would you do that?"

"Of course, I'd love to. Arthur and I don't want you to change your voice for this. We'll let the footnotes do the academic work. I'll read it, and Jenn can help assemble the footnotes and references. I'll probably have time to do it at the gallery. It's going to be a quiet spring."

"I wouldn't count on that," Fiona smiled.

Chapter Fifty-Four

Fiona disembarked with her carry-on, and headed out into the bright lights of the terminal. It was Jordan's idea to take the late Friday flight in, the only way, she had said, to avoid the traffic on the ride to Pasadena. Jordan said someone would meet her at arrivals, so she followed the crowd to the baggage carousel, where she found a uniformed driver with a discreet sign— "Hedge."

She identified herself to the driver, who took her bag and asked her to follow. He led her to a black, Town car and opened the rear door for her. She slid in across leather seats and belted herself in, while the driver loaded her bag in the trunk. This was a little more than she'd expected. The driver took his seat and turned to apologize for the Town car, "With only one passenger expected, they'd reserved the limo for a larger event." Fiona laughed nervously. She and her little overnight bag would have been ridiculous in a limo. Without another word the driver pulled out into light traffic through a soft rain. The only sound was the steady beat of the wipers on the windshield. Already Fiona was uncomfortable in the back seat; it seemed pretentious and unfriendly. Though she regularly did the accounting on large estates, she usually worked through an attorney, and never met the clients. This was a lifestyle she could recognize on a balance sheet but didn't actually contemplate. She thought for a minute or two on it, and realized that Thomas and Ardley could probably live like this if they wanted, but didn't. The formality seemed at odds with Jordan's warm charm on the telephone. The discomfort eased and Fiona began to wonder how the weekend would go with Jordan.

The car pulled into a landscaped, semi-circular drive to a new, Beaux Arts style building—one that looked to Fiona like a hotel. The driver opened her door and said that she was expected at the front desk. A doorman ushered her in, relieving the driver of her carry-on. From there, her bag was whisked away by a bellman, signaled by some secret, almost silent code. At the desk the attendant asked her name, and announced that Mrs. Montcolm was expecting her, just as another bellman arrived to show her the way. They proceeded up the elevator and down the hall; her escort pushed the doorbell and melted away once the door was opened, by what seemed to be yet *another* employee.

"Ms. Hedge, I am Eugene. Mrs. Montcolm knows you're here and is waiting for you. If there is anything you'll need while you're here, please let me know. Mrs. Montcolm is in the study." He then led her down several labyrinthine halls to a small, elegantly furnished study. At the entry to the study Eugene softly announced her arrival to an elderly woman seated at a desk near the door. Jordan Montcolm struggled a moment to rise, and leaning on the desk with one hand, reached out with the other, to take Fiona's.

"Fiona, I can't tell you how pleased I am that you came. We have so much to discuss. Forgive my familiarity, but after the emails you've sent, I feel that I know you and it's been a surprisingly lovely acquaintance."

Her warmth immediately set Fiona at ease. Jordan signaled her to have a seat. She sat in a burgundy leather loveseat with its back to a window. Jordan took up her cane and settled into a matching chair, flanking Fiona. Without a word, Eugene moved to the window to adjust the curtains. He retreated to the door, and looked up at Jordan.

"Thank you Eugene, could you check back with us in a few minutes? I'm sure Fiona would like to settle in just a bit." Fiona looked around at the study. It was a small room, warmly and comfortably furnished. The loveseat on which she sat faced into the room, bounded by two matching chairs, set up in a U, around a thick plate glass coffee table with a simple wrought iron frame. The chairs and loveseat had soft leather throw cushions in camel and navy, matching a mid-sized tribal rug in camel, navy and burgundy, visible through the table. At the door was an elegant secretary style desk, with a tall glass display cabinet. The walls were cream, except the one behind the secretary, which was done in a cream and camel grass cloth. There was one painting in the room, a Wayne Thiebaud, one of his newer delta landscapes. The desk's display case was filled with Chinese ceramics—bowls and small sculptures, which Fiona recognized, having seen similar items displayed in San Francisco's Asian Museum of Art. The desk was an antique, customized to accommodate a computer monitor tucked in on the left where originally there'd been nooks and little drawers, like those remaining on the right side. The desk was strewn with letters and notes. Leaning in a corner formed by the desk and the wall was a black cane with silver banding. Fiona strained to see it more closely. Over all, the room said, tasteful, casual elegance.

"This is a lovely study."

"Thank you. It's my favorite room in the entire suite. One of the few where I kept what I had from the old house." She laughed, "This is one of those fancy, high-end senior housing facilities. This room, *and* Eugene, are the remnants of my old life." Fiona noted the slight sag on one side of Jordan's face, and thought again about that cane.

She directed her attention to her hostess. Jordan was a tall, good looking woman, one who'd probably never been beautiful but had good bones. Short, swept back silver hair balanced gray deep-set eyes. She had a tall forehead and great cheekbones, but a slightly weak chin that made her appear vulnerable.

"Yes, I'll admit that I was a little intimidated on the way in, a well-manned fortress."

"I think my children would like to see a moat. I didn't pick this place, the kids did. They were in such a panic after my stroke that they swooped in and uprooted everything, sold the house, and stuck me in here. It's the *medical care for life* feature that sold them, socializing on site, and all that. Actually, I think my son fancies the place for himself. When I'm gone, I think he'll move in. By the time they relocated me here from rehab, I had actually recovered fairly well. Probably, I'd have been fine in the house," she sighed. "I can only hope they have the good sense to be sheepish about it, in their private moments." Fiona thought fleetingly about what Denise would do if something happened to her. She shuddered.

"I'll have to think about that. With my daughter, I'm not sure she'd even show up on Sundays."

Jordan smiled and nodded, "They either do what they think is best for you or nothing at all. I only just wished they'd asked me how *I* felt about it." She folded her hands very precisely in her lap, "Still, I can't complain. I live very well."

Eugene appeared with a tray bearing a teapot, fixings, cups and a plate of ginger snaps. He slid the tray onto the coffee table, and then poured the tea. He turned to Fiona, "I picked chamomile, so it won't keep you up."

She was really beginning to like this guy. "Thank you. It's a perfect way to unwind after the flight." With just the hint of a nod, Eugene made a quiet exit.

Fiona's curiosity couldn't wait, "I'm sorry, but I noticed the cane," she nodded towards the corner, "Wasn't that Emma's?"

Jordan glanced at the cane, "How astute that you noticed. Yes. My mother asked for it when Emma passed and used it in her later years. Now, since the stroke, I use it for stability. I can be a little wobbly, I'm afraid. But it pleases me every time I have to reach for it. There is history there."

"I couldn't have missed it. It's in every photo and every one of Emma's self portraits. Before I leave, I'd love a photo of you, seated and holding the cane, if you don't mind. It'll be part of the back-story to the exhibit."

"Back-story?"

"Yes, apparently everyone at Mills is taken with how Emma's story came to light and would like to do a small side exhibit on the effort to rediscover her. Perhaps without even knowing, you've been a huge piece of that effort."

Jordan paused letting the idea sink in, "I think it's a charming idea, clever marketing too. As long as it's discreet, I don't mind." Jordan put one hand to her cheek, and with her lip quivering added, "This process has been valuable to me, too. I loved Emma, and I've reconnected with that. Because you sent me my mother's correspondence, I've come together with *her* history as well. My mother was a wonderful woman, and she loved Emma like a sister. In some ways I think they made the losses in their lives bearable for each other." Tears welled in her eyes. She sipped her tea.

Fiona reached out and took her hand. It was alarmingly frail feeling and light as dry leaves. Fiona gave Jordan's hand a soft supportive squeeze. "Their relationship was life sustaining, through thick and thin, and usually from great distance. Over thirty years of regular correspondence, and that cut short only by death. They *rarely* make friends like that nowadays." After saying it, Fiona felt a pang. She didn't mean to shortchange Amanda, and their friendship had already gone on even longer.

Jordan's hand turned and enfolded Fiona's, "Well, if they do, we'll never know. Telephones, email, it seems to make our connections more and more ephemeral. There's little record. Even cremations limit what's left behind to track us."

That was it, exactly. Fiona thought of the decades, full living she'd shared with Amanda, through lost loves, family troubles and personal triumphs, as well as failures. Unlike Emma's elegant packets of ribbon tied letters, Fiona noted that there was no trail marking the richness of their friendship. Despite their otherwise modern lives, Emma and Wren had been positively nineteenth century in chronicling their lives, through letters.

"My friend Amanda and I have a friendship, I think as dear as Emma and Wren's, but there's nothing to attest to it. My daughter knows, but not wholly. I guess, like most people throughout history, we just quietly pass into oblivion."

"Unless you write, or paint or sculpt, in the old days even musical talents were ephemeral. My mother had trouble with that. She called it her 'Mills thing,' the feeling that she had an obligation to have been more, more than a good wife and mother, more than she had been."

"And she was a good friend. Let's not forget that. In fact, it's only because she *was* such a good friend that we finally get to fully explore Emma's talent. Good friends may be the unsung heroes of history."

Jordan leaned forward, "I think you may have something there. Have you ever read the correspondence between Abigail and John Adams?"

Fiona paused, "No, I didn't know there was such a collection."

"It was brought out a few years ago. Until I read it, Abigail was a footnote to me, you know, a bit of trivia, wife of the second President. But their correspondence shows her contribution, not just as a wife, but as a thinking being, a partner in a shared life dedicated to living and to the cause of an infant country. It's what made me rethink my mother and her Mills thing. Now I'm picking through Mum's letters, and finding many wonderful, lasting contributions. I don't know if they're universal enough to do what you're doing, but I am thankful for a new way of seeing. I wish I'd found this perspective before she died so I could have shared it with her. The thing is, those contributions were there, whether I dug them up or not. They made lives richer, better in the moment. For most of us, that's the limit, and the reward."

Fiona tipped back her head and sighed, "You know, my Emma Caites journey has really helped me to fill in gaps in my life. But it's bothered me some that suddenly *I* was the writer. I hadn't quite put my finger on it before, but I think it's because I'd been experiencing it as an ensemble effort. It's been Emma, and Thomas, Marvin, Norm, Amanda, Jenn, then Ardley and Cheryl, and now you."

"You know, you sound like Emma."

"How so?"

"She was forever telling us that family is who you collect. Sure there's blood family, but they're as often a curse as a treasure. She had no family. Her bond to Mum was more heartfelt family than anything since her grandparents. Her parents and siblings were horrific. But she regularly invited people into her life. Even in her down periods she built connections. Norman was one. He was just a kid, but she treated him special because she saw he had a good heart."

"You knew Norm?"

"Only just a bit. When I was at Mills, Norm was the skinny kid who worked at the framer's. He was very kind to Thomas, and Emma always remembered that."

"What did you mean, 'her down times'?"

"Emma had several periods of terrible depression in her life. Not that she was dour or anything, but life dealt her some hard blows, and she reeled from them. I don't know what she'd have done if she didn't have painting."

"What periods were they?"

"Well, some of this comes from Mum, since I was too little, but things were bleak when she came back from France. After a bit she filled the void from Pieter with friends, artists and art types. Emma was constantly rebuilding family, and she pulled together an amazing group of friends in the late twenties through early thirties. Oakland was an exciting place to be, part of the art world in the late twenties. Then she suffered a sort of dark period, a post-partum low, after Thomas but I'm not sure if it was actually a physical post-partum, or because she chose social isolation. Are you aware of this?"

"Yes, and I think it was a combination of things. I think she was also still grieving her friend, Florence. She was a big part of the art excitement in Oakland. Her death was a deep blow. Then of course, Emma also had her hands full with an infant."

Jordan closed her eyes nodding, "Yes, I'd forgotten about Florence. That was a deep loss. I think my mother was a little jealous of Florence, so I have to be cautious in how I assess her." She paused, leaned forward and opened her eyes, "But she died several years earlier, didn't she?"

"She died late in 1931, but I think Emma felt Florence's loss more acutely, after having Thomas, because of her isolation. Also, I think that Emma felt Florence's fate was tied to the social standing of women, as was her own when she was suddenly found herself an unwed mother. Florence had been an integral part of the Oakland Art Gallery. There were quiet rumors that she was romantically connected with its director, William Clapp." Fiona repositioned herself to face Jordan. She wasn't sure, but it seemed that she was holding back. Fiona continued, "What was clear was that in the twenties, Florence was an inspiration. She had a clear vision of the changing landscape in the arts. As a woman, she had to work behind the scenes, but her influence was tangible. Florence helped to put Oakland in the forefront of the art world and helped to make the Oakland Art Gallery one of the most avant-garde in California, maybe in the country. Emma had just returned from Paris, and she found her new friend to be a breath of fresh air. I think Florence felt the same way about Emma. It's all in the letters, but you have to read closely. Emma knew that your mother wasn't taken with the friendship."

"You've really done your homework." Jordan sipped her tea. "My mother was very guarded about any suggestion of impropriety. She was discreet and conservative, no fan of scandal. What did your research tell you about Florence?"

"Florence had divorced her husband in the late twenties and suffered health problems that resulted in a lot of time lost from work. The Gallery Board tried to get rid of her, despite her years of dedication. I guess they didn't like the divorce scandal either. Clapp protected her job, but she never got over the lack of loyalty from the Board. Florence died very young of heart trouble. Emma believed she died of a *broken* heart." Fiona leaned back and sighed, "I think it may be the reason Emma decided to drop out of her circle of art friends when she became pregnant. The parallels must have been scary—bright, talented young woman with health trouble cast aside when loyalty was no longer convenient."

Fiona shook her head in dismay. She leaned forward earnestly, "It became Emma's armor. She refused to be the object of scandal, even if it meant that she abandoned everything she knew, again, and started over. Still, I don't think she ever forgave the Gallery for the way her friend was treated. Florence was rejected for health problems and because of the scandal. These resonated deeply with Emma. As much as having Thomas brought a different kind of love into her life, it came with some sacrifices. From our modern perspective it's hard to know whether those sacrifices really were imposed by societal judgment, or whether they were self-imposed." Fiona looked up at Jordan, "It might have been shame."

Jordan defended, "They *were* very different times. A bastard child was not a career asset. A lesser soul wouldn't have survived intact. Remember too, that the pregnancy did serious damage to Emma's hip, so she had a long recovery to deal with, as well." She fingered the silver band on her cane. "Mum and I visited several times between thirty-five and thirty-seven. By the end of that period Emma had bounced back to her regular enthusiasm. That woman's excitement about art was positively infectious. Every time we came home my mother and I would go on a painting spree. In 1937 she was doing her diminutive "Intimates." They were stunning, have you seen any of them?"

"You mean the little studies?"

"Yes, she and Mum called them The Intimates. They captured the small personal moments in life. They were tiny paintings, just perfect for a little girl my age. I wish we'd collected some of them." Jordan chuckled, "Emma didn't want us to have them, because she wanted us to paint our own."

"What's tiny?"

"Six-by-six inches or maybe six-by-eight. They were lovely. They hooked me on a lifetime of art and collecting."

"What was it, you think, made them so special?"

"Oh, Fiona, they were *exquisite*. Petite, even diminutive scenes that were so ordinary, and yet so beautiful. She did a whole series of them, like shoes at the door. There were her shoes and Thomas' baby shoes, on the mat at the door. Sometime the door would be ajar, with the sunlight streaming in, she could always capture the warmth of the Oakland sun. Just the intimate design and layout of something so mundane became so stunning. I've never seen a shoe at a doorway since without those paintings flashing back to me. She did another set of gardening implements, a watering can, trowels and the like. I loved them. One was just a tin watering can, offset on the canvas, so the can's shadow was the central part of the image. It made you think of shadows in a new way, as a tangible central character in your visual field. I felt all these things, and I was only about ten." Jordan paused to catch her breath. Her whole being had perked up with the memory. Her eyes flashed as she continued, "Surprisingly, everything around me now qualified as possible art.

306

Because the paintings were small, and of simple subjects, they spoke to me, just a kid, in a particular way. Small. My world was worth painting. I loved it. I loved her. She'd paint the laundry hanging on the line, or the neighbor hanging it. She painted Thomas' tiny toys, or his colorful sand bucket and shovel. She painted coffee cups and spoons, sometimes with coffee still in them. You'd have a snack with her, and something about the table would catch her eye. Once she liked the way I'd bitten into my sandwich and she wouldn't let me finish it. She made me another, and then spent the afternoon painting a half-eaten, jam sandwich. I thought she was a little crazy, but wonderfully so."

"I've only seen a couple of these but I didn't know she'd painted so many. I wish we had more for the show. These are wonderful stories."

"Mum said The Intimates brought Emma out of her funk. I don't know causation but they certainly brightened my viewpoint. It's one of the reasons I've always loved Wayne Thiebaud." She nodded at the painting on the wall, "He has a similar sensibility, only bigger, for adults."

"And, at adult prices. Can you compare Emma with such a big name?"

"Fiona, she *was* good." Jordan looked at Fiona directly, "She was all that and more. I often wondered if having a toddler brought her viewpoint closer to the ground. You should tell Thomas that."

Fiona smiled broadly. Her mind flooded with images of tender smallnesses from Denise's early years. In the context of young motherhood, The Intimates made perfect sense.

Fiona pressed on, "Do you remember other times she was depressed?"

Jordan's face clouded over, "Mostly after her fall. It killed me to see her in such pain. She still painted some, but Fiona," now her eyes filled with tears, "I was actually relieved for her when she died, and I've always felt guilty feeling that way. But she couldn't be who she truly was, that way. She needed the drugs for the pain, but they dulled her down. She could barely get around and used a walker, but watching her move was excruciating. That hip was her undoing. When drugged, she had trouble painting, you know, fumbling with the brushes. She lost her feeling for the brushstrokes, and that only added to her frustration. Towards the end, she was doing tiny paintings again, but it was because her world had shrunk. She said

307

she didn't want disability to turn her into an Impressionist dabbler. My mother and I even argued about this."

"Your mother didn't understand?"

"It was a tough time for her. She and Dad never really recovered from my brother's death, and I had just married and moved away. The loss of her dearest friend was devastating. I think it made her feel old," she paused, "She couldn't put her own losses in perspective." For the first time that evening, Jordan was looking drawn and tired. She reached for the last cookie and reflectively nibbled at it.

Fiona's tea had gone cold. She glanced at her watch and realized this might be a strain on Jordan. "I think we've covered a lot this evening but it's late, and I've exhausted you. Perhaps we should start fresh in the morning."

Jordan looked up appreciatively. "Yes, I think that would be best." The older woman reached for the cane, and motioned for Fiona to follow.

"Let's not bother Eugene. I'm sure we can find your room in here *somewhere*." Then, leaning on Emma's cane, Jordan led the way, down the marble hall.

Chapter Fifty-Five

Fiona woke up and for the first time, realized she was in the loveliest room she'd ever occupied. Its pale yellow walls glowed in the early morning light. The curtains were a rough silk weave in cream and golden yellow, with a flowing jacquard vine pattern in pale gold. Along the vine stems were clusters of soft brown gingko leaf shapes. The duvet and shams in the same pattern also had rope piping in a gold raw silk. As a counterpoint to the delicate curvilinear florals, there was a separate set of pillows, now piled on the empty side of the bed, with a matching chair in pale yellow, gold and the same taupey brown, in subtle thin stripes arranged in bolder bands of alternating stripes, with an understated pattern of light gold squares in satin embroidery across the muted skinny stripes. Fiona reached for her glasses to get a closer look. The quiet colors sang. There were two paintings in the room—a winter landscape in off-whites, grays and taupes, and what looked like a midsummer harvest landscape of wheat fields under a crystalline sky in yellows, summer golds and pistachio greens. The bed was a carved-oak deco antique, French or Belgian, with a matching dresser and nightstands.

Fiona thought she could wake up in this room every day and never grow tired of the refined tonal arrangement of colors and subtle contrasting patterns. It felt like home. She slipped out of bed and found her valise waiting on the dresser. She pulled out her laptop, and retreated back to bed. There, propped in enough pillows for a queen, Fiona started tapping in the stories and her impressions of the night before. She was still fully engrossed almost an hour later when there was a soft knock at the door.

"Fiona?"

"Yes, come in."

Jordan poked her head in, "Ah, I see you're already hard at work. I hope you were comfortable?"

Fiona sat up. "Comfortable? It's the most beautiful, serene room I've ever seen. I love these fabrics. I feel like royalty."

Jordan's face beamed, "I designed this for my daughter. I had a wonderful time doing it. I'm thrilled you like it so."

"I see there's a little artist in all of us. You must feel very gratified by the result."

"Never more than right now. I'll admit my daughter is a bit spoiled. Her reaction was not quite as enthusiastic." She craned her neck a little, looking at the laptop. "Can I press upon you to show me how you're organizing your materials for writing?"

"Certainly," Fiona scooted over on the bed, and tilted the laptop towards her hostess. Without missing a beat, Jordan leaned her cane against the nightstand, and settled herself in.

Fiona tilted the screen so both could see, "Jenn set me up with this, she's such a whiz." Fiona ran through all her programs and systems, explaining how she'd built the Emma story with the tools. Jordan seemed to know all the right questions. They were still immersed when there was another soft rap at the door.

"Oh my," Jordan apologized, "I was supposed to ask you about coffee!"

Fiona laughed. "I'd love some. Come on in, Eugene."

Nervously, Eugene poked his head in the door. Seeing the two of them sprawled around the computer like teens at a pajama party, he laughed. "I should have known."

"I'm sorry, Eugene, I meant to come back down, but we got talking..."

"It's okay," he waved, "Shall I bring up a tray?"

"Please do," piped in Fiona, "I am really enjoying all this pampering." He closed the door as he left.

"We'll need an agenda for our day, or we'll fritter it away with idle chat."

Fiona laughed, "Nothing about *this* is idle or frippery. I'll need a few more hours of interview time, and of course, I'd love to see the paintings."

"Was last night an interview? I thought I was just reminiscing." Jordan smiled, "If you can interview on the fly, there's a wonderful exhibit of mid-century painters downtown just now, it's particularly interesting when you keep Emma's work in mind."

Eugene reappeared and put a tray on the nightstand. He passed Jordan a steaming cup of coffee and asked Fiona how she took hers.

"A little sugar is all, thanks." She turned to the laptop, "I'm setting up a quick slideshow, a preview of some of the paintings under consideration for the exhibit." Eugene prepared Fiona's cup and then carefully handed it over. Fiona turned the screen towards her two companions. The slide show, at four seconds per frame, would run for over seven minutes. Eugene joined the two women on the edge of the bed. Fiona sipped her coffee and watched their faces while Jordan and Eugene watched the screen, spellbound for the duration.

Jordan was the first to speak. "Fiona, it's going to be a tremendous show."

Eugene nodded, "This is a major undertaking. I didn't understand it was so comprehensive." He turned to Jordan, "Your paintings will fit right in to that early period."

"Would you set them up in the dining room, Eugene? We'll be down in a little bit."

Eugene thanked Fiona for the slide show, and slipped away.

"I agree with Eugene. He's actually very astute in art matters. I think you'll be pleased especially since, so far, your exhibit hasn't many portraits. This is an exciting project. Fiona, I'll certainly be there for the opening. Let's get this day moving." Jordan dashed down the last of her coffee, and reached for the cane. Fiona wondered whether she was seeing enthusiasm for the Caites' paintings or the power of coffee.

Fiona quickly showered and dressed. She could smell the bacon and followed her nose to the kitchen, where to her surprise, she found Jordan cooking up a small feast. Three places were set in the breakfast nook. Jordan served up the plates and Eugene carried them in. Fiona was beginning to enjoy watching the rhythms of their easy domesticity. Years of employment had softened into friendship, respect and companionship. Fiona sat down to an asparagus omelet with sautéed mushrooms, sprinkled with pecorino, melon slices, generous strips of bacon and another steaming mug of coffee. She was in heaven.

"I hope I haven't taken liberties with your cholesterol." Jordan smiled widely.

"Nope. Breakfast is the most important meal and I'm totally given over to the sumptuous."

"Thomas has mentioned your friends and their culinary adventures. It's inspired me. After the stroke, I pulled in for a bit and neglected cooking. That was not true to my nature. Food is always important in diplomacy. But when times are stressful, sometimes you forget that food is one of the gifts, like art."

Eugene laughed, "Fiona, just keep reminding her. I've enjoyed every minute."

Jordan laughed at that.

Fiona nodded, "What makes it easier is having an appreciative audience. Our group keeps me on my toes. So does Emma. I find myself trying to live in her shoes. In so many ways she lived for the direct experience, for the art. She also loved food and good times with friends. You see it in Paris—always throwing parties. You see it in Oakland in the late twenties and early thirties. Even during hard times Emma made sure that she could connect with friends, and she did it in part with great food." Fiona savored another bite of the asparagus omelet, the earthy grassy flavors against the salty edge of the sheep's cheese. "This," she pointed at her plate with her fork, "Would get you into the club."

Eugene nodded in agreement. Jordan bowed her head in gracious acknowledgment of the compliment.

Jordan tipped her head, "I can't speak to Paris, or to early Oakland, but Emma always made every visit an event. She didn't necessarily do fancy, but she did great food. She was a big fan of hearty soups with salads and great breads. When I heard you'd made a cassoulet, I wondered how you'd known that it was a favorite of Emma's."

"It was? I had no idea but I'm thrilled to hear it. I got the inspiration form a woman I met in Paris."

"Emma loved to make exotic, peasant foods whose ingredients were inexpensive, and where the result and the presentation were attractive. That was her frugal nature battling with her refined tastes. Since she was always hiding her balance-sheet background, she made efforts to entertain in a hearty way, without appearing to break the bank. A cassoulet in the midst of the Depression was a fancy way to serve beans. Whenever a friend was down and out, she'd throw a dinner and make sure to send enough leftovers home to feed the family."

Fiona nodded in acknowledgement, "In Paris, she was always entertaining."

"She never stopped but she felt she had a special obligation to her artist friends in the hard times of the thirties. Cassoulet, ratatouille, split pea soup, onion soup. All frugal, solid foods, served with style and fun. She always made everyone contribute a bit, an onion, a couple of carrots, work chopping vegetables, whatever they could provide. She practiced a sort of *Stone Soup* charity. She told my mother that the worst thing you could do for a friend, was everything. She told her friends that she'd learned it all in France, the country that'd fought a revolution over food, yet still insisted upon style, art and presentation."

"Did you get to participate in any of these meals?"

"Always... though a bit later in the thirties. Sometimes when my mother and I visited, I think the ingredients would get a little more exotic. She knew she didn't have to hide anything from us."

"Did you have a favorite, or a particularly memorable meal?"

Jordan leaned back in her chair. "Oh yes. My favorite wasn't just about the food. Emma threw a brunch for my birthday one year, while I was at Mills. It was amazing, a complete surprise. She gave me art supplies and invited my friends. She made an incredible meal, poached eggs on a wilted frisée salad with asparagus. She served it with an incredible bacon-mustard dressing. With a garnish of fresh fruit, it was the most elegant breakfast I'd ever seen. I never felt so sophisticated."

"She *was* generous of spirit."

"Yes, and in the most incredible ways. Mum said that she could have competed and won every artistic prize in the area. Most of the artists were struggling. Many talented painters had never sold a single painting! But Emma never competed and never even submitted for the WPA mural-work of the Depression. She didn't want to take any opportunities away from friends who needed them, needed the work. She couldn't justify it when she was not financially strapped herself, and since she never had difficulty selling her own work." Eugene stood and began to clear away the dishes.

"Why did you think that was? I mean even many of the renowned painters of the day, Society of Six, and all, had to hold day jobs. Why could Emma continue to sell?"

"My mother and I debated that. For one thing, she *was* a great talent. She also had a marketing sense that was stunning and a personal approach that was warm and genuine. Some folks bought from her because of the French credentials, and some just because they liked her so much. A weekend or holiday never went by when Emma wasn't painting plein air in some conspicuous place. She taught those classes, which built loyalty and a market at the same time. She was visible but not overwhelming, and she kept her prices reasonable, maybe a little too much so."

"When you say you and your mother debated it, did you hold widely different opinions?"

313

"Well, we *did* agree that her work was stellar. It was simply her view of the world, translated through light, color and plane with no ego attached. But my mother felt she under-priced, and thus, captured the market. I didn't think that was it. Even in the Depression, when there was no market, Emma made her way. Emma was always visible, and was very human and present. I always thought she could sell because she knew *how* to sell. She could work a crowd like nobody I'd ever seen. When Emma focused on you, you were the only person on the planet. Not many could resist that kind of intensity. And when she couldn't sell paintings, she sold classes. Emma sold *artistic vision*—after talking with her, people came away with a *new way of seeing.* I loved the story about the Paris cripple challenge, but it missed the point since the challenge didn't address the charisma issue. Pieter called that one right."

"Did you spend much time with Emma when you were at Mills?"

"Yes, Emma made growing up bearable. I'd been a diplomat brat. I was very well traveled, cultured, spoke several languages, though none of them well. You'd think I'd fit well at Mills. But I was very lonely and at that time, very insecure. I was tall and gawky. I'd moved about every three years of my life, and had never settled easily into having friends. Emma was always wonderful. I spent many weekends with her, sometimes painting, and sometimes just spending time with family. For Emma, painting was the cure for all ills. We'd head up into the Oakland hills on a beautiful day, paint and talk. I was homesick, and Emma filled in the gap. Just that bit of belonging translated into a confidence that helped me connect in school, and then socially."

Tears welled in Jordan's eyes. "When Lytton died, Emma was there, for both my mom and me." Fiona's heart ached at how some losses are never healed. She reached out and laid her hand on the older woman's forearm.

Eugene appeared and softly cleared his throat. "Anytime you ladies are ready, I've arranged the paintings in the dining room."

Fiona swallowed the last of her coffee. Following Eugene's lead, she stacked the dishes on the table and bussed them into the kitchen. After a moment, to collect herself, Jordan grasped her cane, and then led the way into the dining room.

There were a total of five paintings, three of them portraits and two landscapes. The closest, as Fiona entered, captured an animated Wren at tea in Emma's apartment. In it, Wren was sitting on the settee in front of the windows. Wearing a blue and red dress, with a blue shawl over her shoulders, she's framed by the closed windows and the yellow curtains. Wren is leaning forward intently, face flushed, holding a cup of tea in one hand and her other hand is open and spread, as though explaining some spatial relationship. There's a teapot on the table, and a bouquet of violets in a small vase. Next to her, on the settee, barely visible over the table, sits a little, blond boy, imitating the hand gesture, unbeknownst to his mother. Because she is so engaged, so animated, it is not a traditional portrait. If Fiona didn't know the story behind this painting, she'd have sworn this was taken from a photograph. In fact it was painted one afternoon, after a gallery excursion, and Wren couldn't sit still through the pose for all the excitement of it. The brush strokes are hurried, but the painting is fully rendered and round. Fiona wryly noted that all that speed, developed in Duprés' class, hadn't been wasted. Emma caught the essence of the moment, on the fly. The colors, red, blue and yellow are intense, and fun, with just that hint of the purple flowers in the foreground. With the table in front of her, you cannot tell that Wren is pregnant. It is a portrait of a bright, engaged young woman in the flower of youth.

"This is stunning. Your mother looks so present, so alive. I know from the letters that they'd been out looking at art, and during this sitting were debating the modern paintings of the day. Wren was especially taken with some of Picasso's work but Emma was not so impressed. The debate rings through the image." Fiona hesitated, "And look at that kid. I'm sure Emma loved that echo of his mother."

"My mum loved this portrait. It brought her immediately to the intensity of her discussions, her friendship with Emma. Because of this picture I learned all about Paris and the apartment, that trip. My brother always loved that he was included as that little footnote in the painting."

Fiona turned to Eugene, "You're right, this will fit beautifully into the exhibit. And it's perfect, the way that it fills in a piece of Paris—we have so little to show of that time period."

Fiona moved to the next canvas. It was another portrait, a nude of Wren, partially draped in that same blue shawl, curled with her feet tucked up under her, leaning back on a pile of pillows on the

315

bed. Here, she is visibly pregnant, one hand resting lightly on her taut belly, one full breast cradled against her arm and the other concealed by the draping. Her head is slightly tipped forward in a quiet contemplative posture. It is an intimate and revealing, elegant nude but in no way sexual. Fiona was taken by the stark honesty of the painting; stripped of sexuality and sentimentality, it becomes primarily a portrait. In lesser hands it would have descended to a cheesy Madonna. Here though, it portrays a reflective young woman, heavy with child but without pretense. It is exquisite, one the best of Emma's works Fiona has seen. Her usual brushstrokes are more subdued, almost with a Dutch-Vermeer quality. The sunlight is flooding in, playing across the bed—the colors are golden and warm.

Fiona turned to Jordan, her eyes brimming with tears, "This is so beautiful. It's so obvious how much she loved your mother."

"I know. I've always loved it. It made Mum a little uncomfortable, even though she knew it was beautiful. I've only displayed it publicly, since she passed. She never did know how to deal with it, so it was often kept in storage."

"That's a shame. It's so lovely."

"Well, Mum *was* a diplomat's wife," she chuckled, "Some things just won't do. Dad loved it, and he always wanted it up. So, they compromised and sometimes it hung in their bedroom. Mum said that until she brought this home, Dad had always been a little jealous of the time she spent with Emma. This cured him. It's not just that he got the painting. It was that he saw that they were on the same wavelength. Anyone who could capture this in my mother was special, was family."

Fiona moved down to the next piece. It was an odd shape, taller than it was wide, about thirty by fifteen inches. Fiona wondered if Emma specially stretched the canvas to capture the perspective. It was a portrait of Lytton, all two years of him, kneeling on the settee in front of the table. He is holding a teacup and saucer in his hands, outstretched in front of him, one in each hand as if offering some, and trying to keep the saucer and cup nestled. He has a broad smile, mouth slightly open. His blond hair is tousled, and the buttons on his sweater are misaligned, by one. It's a loving, sensitive and fun portrait of a two year-old's fresh enthusiasm. Again, the painting had a snapshot feel that was uncharacteristic of the time. It reminded Fiona of her painting of Thomas with the paintbrush. She remembered how this visit had changed Emma's thinking about children. This painting captured the little boy's freshness clearly, and again, without sentimentality, but with a grasp of the fun of the moment.

Fiona nodded, "Another winner."

The first landscape was a small nocturne of Pont Neuf on a foggy evening. The stone edges of the bridge, painted in grays and mauve, faded in and out of the silvery fog. A clear patch in the sky was indigo, with the cool light of just a couple of stars peeking through. It was ethereal and wispy. Emma's usual bold brushstrokes gave way here to a smoother, worked surface, catching the texture of the fog. Only the stones in the bridge felt solid with Emma's usual concrete grasp of form. It was small, but a deft rendering of the meeting of delicate translucence against the substantial geometry of the bridge, its arches and planes. The street lights piercing the fog on the topside of the bridge are the only warm elements in the painting.

The last painting was a large canvas full of sun and light. In it, women are harvesting fields of lavender, gathering the dry, late season lavender into large muslin sacks. Each woman has one side of the sack tied to her belt, the other held wide as she leans and cuts, stuffing the loose flower fronds into the bag. The fields themselves, with row upon wide row of lavender, were painted in the gray-green of the leaves and dotted with blue purple flowers, giving way into the distance to a purple haze. The fields are nestled into golden hills. In the foreground on the right several olive trees, in another dry silvery-green, framed the view. Fiona could see why Emma felt at home in Provence. The gold hills, the dry greens, it was the Bay Area resonating for her. With a golden sun saturating the day, it was enough to make Fiona homesick.

"So there it is. France. It so captures what we'd been missing. These are all incredible." Fiona sat on one of the dining room chairs and surveyed the paintings. "It makes me feel so much closer to her, having read the letters. Now, I see these things through her eyes."

"You must put them in the book. The book, if it flows like your emails, can be punctuated with color images to bring exactly that feeling home to the readers."

"I really haven't worked on the visual format of the book yet. I've been so caught up in finding the story."

"You should talk to Thomas. This book could be much more

than just a story, more than a coffee table catalogue."

"Well, Thomas *and* Marvin and Arthur. I think I mentioned that this is an ensemble effort."

"Well, maybe then, *I'll* join the ensemble and give Thomas a call, myself."

Fiona laughed, "Do that, he'll love it. Thomas has really had to let go of a lot for this to happen, but I think it's been good for him. He even started painting again."

"The cure for all ills," Jordan nodded, "His mother would be pleased."

The two women sat quietly, taking in the paintings. Fiona took advantage of the silence to broach one of the more difficult issues she needed to discuss.

"Jordan, I have some questions I need to ask. We've both read the letters but they don't flesh out the reasons for, or the impact of, Emma's exile after the pregnancy. What do you think about it?"

"Partly from what Mum told me, and then, much later, Emma was very frank with me about it. Except that she wouldn't reveal the identity of the father. You see, Emma was a very social person. She came back from France pretty broken, but soon was reconnecting. I don't really know much about the darker days. My mother was worried that she'd quietly pine away. But more importantly, she wasn't painting. But Emma *was* a survivor. She bounced back, looked up old Mills friends, and soon found a group of struggling artists, and artist wannabes. Emma lived in a tiny, little place in Adams Point. Mum said it made garret sound palatial." Jordan paused, took a deep breath and changed gears, "We have a lovely garden here, would you like to walk a bit?"

The women gathered their jackets, and threaded through the halls to the building's rear elevators. They came out into a sprawling back garden with cobbled paths and resting benches. Squinting into the full brightness of the day, Jordan gestured down a path flanked with lavender, pruned back into rounded cushions, for winter.

"There's really not much blooming now, but the air and sun will do us both good."

Fiona slowed, matching her pace to the older woman's.

"I've been rethinking Florence since we spoke last night. She was an important part of Emma's recovery, after Paris. I don't think my mother ever acknowledged the weight of that relationship. When Emma found Florence, they bonded immediately. Florence was well integrated into the Oakland art scene. When Emma arrived in 1928, Florence had been with The Oakland Art Gallery, for years. She knew the ins and outs, knew all the members of the Society of Six. The Gallery was on the cutting edge of the modern art of the day. It was one of the first galleries to show Negro Art, as it was called at the time. They showed art from Germany when the Germans were still persona non grata, after The Great War. For Florence, all that mattered was the quality of the art experience. The Oakland Art Gallery hosted the best annual Exhibit West of the Mississippi. Florence had a good eye; she and William Clapp kept that little gallery in the news, and in the know. As I said, my mother was a little jealous of her, even while, at the same time, she was relieved that Florence was helping Emma recover from Pieter.

Florence always considered Emma to be a top tier painter. She was enormously frustrated that Emma refused to exhibit, especially since Emma had European credentials and consistently sold. Florence always laughed that Emma was her only financially viable artist friend. So Florence made the introductions, and Emma made the friends. I guess today most of them would be considered listed, but second tier artists—even the Society of Six members were just weekend painters at the time. Mostly Emma and her painter friends got together for dinners, discussions and drink. They were a tight support group. Emma was discreet because hardly anyone else sold paintings, especially after The Crash."

"If they were all such good friends, why did Emma disappear with the pregnancy?"

"This was a mixed group, mostly married and many had small children. Most of the painters were men, though there were a couple of women, but they all socialized together. Emma had returned to her pre-Pieter role and expectations; she did not expect a relationship or marriage. She thought she had learned her lesson with Pieter and felt that it was enough just to belong to the group. Emma related to the men as painters, and to the women, well, as women. She moved through the group with a... sort of androgyny. Here she was, a beautiful woman and everyone pretending she was one of the guys. Florence had been part of her protection—as Florence's friend, Emma had instant recognition and safety. Remember that these were really hard times. The painters, if they were lucky, had day jobs. Money was tight for everyone, which was why those potluck dinners meant so much. It was a way to stretch the food, and throw in a little fun. Emma made sure to provide a few extra dishes to the mix. The least fortunate of the group that week would usually take the leftovers home. Often, they were all so hungry that there would be no leftovers. These get-togethers were also their primary source of entertainment."

"Wouldn't that be all the more reason to stick with the group when she needed the extra support?"

"When Florence died, Emma was devastated. Florence was too young to die. I guess she'd had rheumatic fever as a child; it weakened her heart and ultimately it killed her. By then Emma was well established in the group but without Florence, Emma was suddenly an unescorted woman. You have no reference point for how limiting that was in that time. Emma's grieving Florence didn't help. It made her more vulnerable—more feminine. Florence left a void that Emma ended up filling with impropriety. Hard times were also taking a toll on the marriages within the group. Sensitive artists did not take well to manual labor, or whatever they could get to put food on the table. Several of the wives were unhappy. Some took in laundry or did piece work to take up the slack. The men retreated to drink and anger. It's not surprising that Emma and Thomas's father found each other. It wasn't love so much as intimate comfort. But he was married, with small children. At first they were just painting but as they confided in each other, it became more, until finally it was a discreet affair. My mother knew and, needless to say, she did not approve."

"And the pregnancy blew the top off the discretion."

"Yes, and it was worse for Emma because she knew and admired his wife. She called her Clara—though I know that was not her name. Emma had broken an unwritten code; after convincing them all that she was merely a painter, she turned out to be a woman, after all." Jordan sighed and surveyed the gardens. She found her way to a bench overlooking a quiet fountain and parked herself gingerly, facing into the sun. Without a word, Fiona arranged herself on the bench, facing her hostess.

Jordan's story slowed, while choosing her words, "Emma knew she would never again be trusted by the wives, which meant she couldn't enjoy the painting camaraderie of the men in the group. As far as I know she never told anyone, except my mother, who Thomas's father was. She didn't want to break up the marriage. She didn't love him, not like with Pieter anyway. So when she began to show, Emma just disappeared from the group."

"Why didn't she terminate the pregnancy?"

"Oh my dear, it was not so easy then. It was dangerous and illegal. It was also common, but there was more to it. Emma longed for a love that couldn't be taken away. Ever since that Paris visit with my brother, the idea of a child had filled her heart. She was scared, but she persevered. She would never have planned it, but presented with the options, she chose the child."

"I don't buy this. Emma, one of the social organizers of their tribe for years, just drops out and they let her, nobody seeks her out?"

"Fiona, it was 1934, in the middle of The Depression. Illegitimacy was no small matter. Of course they found out, it was a small circle. They also figured out that the father was within their ranks and they promptly circled the wagons. Emma was on the outside, looking in. Unless she'd gone screaming to their doors, there would be no further mention of her. It was a quiet disgrace. To give you the feel of the time, even her landlady rejected her. They'd always been friendly, but when she discovered Emma's condition, she made it clear that Emma couldn't stay on after the baby was born. That's why Emma moved to your apartment with Thomas. In some ways, while having to relocate was difficult, the move itself was good. For the first time, Emma had enough space to take her grandparents furniture out of storage, and she really set about to create a home for herself and Thomas."

"So she had no further contact, ever?" Fiona was shaking her head in disbelief.

"Not really. She told me she never saw the father again. She discontinued contact with all the members of the group. She even changed framers—all the painters in town used Bosko's but Emma found Norm's uncle, and switched to him. Once, just after she'd moved to Wayne Street, she found a basket of hand-me-down baby clothes on her doorstep, with a thank you card, *from Clara*. That was it. For the second time, Emma abandoned her life to escape its losses. At that point her reticence to exhibit through regular channels became resolve. Emma was now fully on her own."

"It would really be the third time, if you count her birth family," Fiona brooded. She stood and walked around the fountain. She couldn't imagine the loss of it, juxtaposed with the joy of a new child, but faced with a life alone. She reflected on the poignant

321

paintings of Wren and her young son, the impact that that bonding had had on Emma. Emma couldn't contemplate a world in which she was worthy, yet she went out repeatedly, and constructed one. Fiona thought about Denise, the fragility of relationships, and she vowed to fix it somehow. She whirled back to Jordan, "Did it need to be so bleak?"

Jordan shrugged, "It just was, for a lot of people. With hindsight to the story, do you see any other good options? You take your hits, you move on." Jordan leaned back. "In a funny way, my Mum blamed Florence—in death Florence abandoned Emma." She shielded her eyes looking up at Fiona's pacing. "I think our lives kept us apart, and Mum suffered for not being able to be there for Emma. There was Florence—educated, artistic, connected and available. Her loss set Emma up for the affair. It's not that Mother didn't love Thomas, she did. But she saw the costs."

Jordan's hand absently caressed the smooth carved top of the cane. "You couldn't keep Emma down for long. Bounce back may be one of the advantages of low expectations."

Eugene appeared near the top of the garden. He caught Jordan's eye and tapped his left wrist as a signal. She looked up at Fiona, still pacing the cobbled walk, and waved him off. He nodded and retreated.

Fiona took her seat again, next to Jordan. "So what? She just decided to go it alone, to be alone her whole life?"

"Many do, Fiona. I don't know, but I think *you* might have. The power of parenthood has a strong pull. But, probably she didn't look at it that way. She simply chose the child. She'd rebuilt before, so she just chose to rebuild with Thomas in the picture. Who knew how much energy it would take, painting, mothering, keeping house and all the million other things that make up life?" Jordan laughed, "Maybe I'm talking about myself."

"Or *us*. I never realized when my ex moved out, how long and lonely it would be. I never regretted it. We were never a good match. But I never knew there wouldn't be any energy left over for me. Between work and Denise… well that was all there was. I've had a few good friends, especially Amanda, but beyond that there just wasn't any time."

"Any regrets?"

Fiona sat quietly. She shook her head, "Not really. I suppose I spoiled Denise some." She paused, "It's funny, we're not even speaking now, but in my heart I know it'll turn around. The core is solid. I just can't live for her now. She has to figure her own life out."

"That's how Emma felt, when Thomas was a teenager. They fought fiercely over college but Emma stuck to her guns, and endured the distance."

"What was the issue?"

"Thomas wanted to be an artist. He wanted to forego an education to just go out and paint but Emma wouldn't hear of it. She also wouldn't let him major in art."

"Odd, considering *her* training. Was he any good?"

"He was, and still is, amazingly talented. Fiona, it was just flat out sexist. She figured since he'd have to support a family, an art education for a man was an indulgence. To hear it, you'd have thought you were talking to *Pieter's* mother! Right down to holding the purse strings! Art was good enough for her, and she supported him, but she was adamant."

"So, how did she convince him?"

"Force of Nature, really. Mostly it was just the power of her personality. She believed, correctly, that part of his objection was financial. He didn't want to be a burden, and there she was, sitting on a family fortune. He had no idea there was money. So she told him his great-grandparents had left funds only for his education— for the education of any child of hers. She wasn't going to sit by and let it go to waste, and neither was he. Of course, if she'd told him how *much* money, he could have gone into art with no worries. But she didn't want him relying on old money. She felt it was important to be able to make one's own way."

Fiona laughed, shaking her head, "It's funny how you try to do the right thing, and then turn around, and encapsulate the same mistakes of your parents. I've come to realize that I was so determined to give Denise an easier life that I ended up not insisting on marketable skills. And now, within her marriage she's struggling with the same issues about earning a living that I'd had. But in my case, my mother *insisted* that I wouldn't need job skills because a man would support me."

Jordan joined in, "And my mother so regretted our vagabond, wayfaring ways in the diplomatic corps that she pushed me into a marriage with a wealthy businessman, only to have him travel the world, dragging his family in tow, and ultimately to become an ambassador on the appointment plan!"

They both saw the pain and the traps, and laughed. Fiona stood up again and reached out for Jordan's hand. "Let's go look again at those lovely paintings." Jordan smiled, and took Fiona's outstretched hand. Slowly they walked quietly back through the garden to Jordan's suite.

Back in the dining room, Fiona surveyed the line of paintings. They sang. This was Emma's Paris, Emma's France. People she loved, places she loved. These paintings were a critical bridge, showing the arc of Emma's growth. They were the youthful enthusiasm, the passion that later led to the calmer Intimates and the warm reflective paintings of Oakland. She pulled up a chair and sat with those images, in silence. She turned back to Jordan and noticed the winter light had waned, the afternoon having fled.

Fiona raised one eyebrow, "So, whose idea was architecture?"

"That was Thomas. He found an acceptable profession that had artistic expression built in."

"He's done very well with it. It hasn't exactly been a failure."

"I don't know if you would call it a happy accident but Emma would have been pleased if she'd lived to see it bloom. It came with costs though, costs and freedoms." Jordan extended her hands, as if to weigh the two.

"Now *that* sounds loaded. Care to Explain?"

"In every parent-child relationship there's a struggle for autonomy. In fairness, this would be a topic for Thomas." She sighed and continued obliquely, "Emma pushed him out, into life. I think she thought she had to. Even in her forties, Emma was very aware of her own mortality. Her hip continued to deteriorate; she was afraid. Because he didn't need her so much, it was also her first time in years to have an adult life, some privacy."

"What does that mean?" Fiona pressed.

"I think you know as well as I do; we're getting to Willie."

"I know, and I don't want ambiguity or vague allusions. The letters don't say much. I'm left with murmurings of inappropriate relationships, criminal activity, and a large and unusual bequest. I haven't really wanted to ask Thomas about it."

Jordan sighed, "I'm not sure what Thomas would even know." She looked at the ceiling, and interlaced her fingers over her knee. "This goes *way* back. Ever since Paris, Emma loved jazz. Back in that day, Oakland had a thriving Jazz and Blues scene. It was all over in West Oakland. Slim Jenkins had a place down there. It was considered to be a rough area at the time, but that was really just because the race laws concentrated most of the blacks there. During the war the minority population skyrocketed, mostly folks coming to work in the shipyards. Despite the hard times of the war, these were heady times in Oakland, prosperous and relatively flush." Jordan shifted her weight and turned to face Fiona.

"Starting when Thomas was about twelve, Emma would go out occasionally for music. Oakland really had incredible entertainment then, Sweet's Ballroom, Slim Jenkins' or Ali Baba's for big bands. Sweet's really was a ballroom for dancing, and that didn't hold much appeal for Emma." She smiled, remembering. "I tell you, those really were the days."

Fiona sat back enjoying Jordan's reminiscing and teased, "Well, I know *Emma* wasn't much for dancing."

Jordan's eyes flashed. "No, she preferred the smaller venues, where she could sit and enjoy the music, like Hambone Kelly's for jazz, Lu Watters or Turk Murphy. When I moved to Oakland, to go to Mills, sometimes she'd invite me to come along." She closed her eyes, "It was deliciously risqué, smoky and fun. Emma made me *swear* not to tell my mother. Sometimes we'd bring my friends from Mills, but Emma was very careful about that. They could only come if they smoked, *and* their parents knew it! I'm not sure how she managed that screening method, but it was hers."

"That shows some odd judgment, bringing impressionable young women out to jazz clubs. In retrospect, what do you think about all that?"

"Interesting point." Jordan lowered her eyes, "I thought about it a lot later, when *my* daughter was young. Being the mother of a daughter sure makes you think about those things. In some ways Emma was close to me because she identified at my level. Her life hadn't offered much license for fun. Maybe it was questionable, but I reveled in the part of our connection where she treated me like a peer."

"So when *did* Willie enter the scene?"

"Emma met Willie in the late forties, probably forty-seven. He played saxophone mostly, some other horns. She was a regular, where he played, and they became friends of sorts. He was a wonderful, gracious man, elegant and humble. One day she arrived at the club in the late afternoon and his sax was sitting out in the gleaming sun, leaning against a sandwich-board sign. A pair of freshly polished shoes were propped up, one on each side, like parentheses holding the sax upright. She asked him if she could paint it. It was perfectly Emma, one of her Intimates, and with *shoes* even! He thought, at first, she was kidding, or worse, maybe making fun. She pressed, and he relented. She *flew* home for her paints and came back in time to catch the image before the light changed. Willie watched her work, and was entranced. Things changed between them that day. He told me that, after she died. He said it was the day they fell in love. He thought she was a little crazy until he saw the image on canvas, saxophone, shoes and a sign that read, 'Showers, $2'. She loved painting that saxophone, and did it in every style, abstract, impressionist. She loved the reflections in the brass and the light glinting on it. Daylight, club light, you name it, she painted that sax."

"Why all the secrecy?"

Jordan regarded Fiona patiently over the top of her eyeglasses, "*Fiona*, think about it. Jazz, in the forties, in Oakland. Willie was black. That kind of thing just wasn't done. It could even have been dangerous for him."

Fiona sucked in her breath. Of course, she didn't put it together, it just hadn't occurred to her it could be that serious.

Jordan continued, "So they met in the late forties, and got to be good friends but I don't think it was romantic until forty-nine or fifty. She loved his language of music. He loved her language of light and color. She did not share this friendship with Thomas. He was already very jealous and protective when it came to men. She didn't think Thomas could handle it. She didn't tell me till fifty-two. I was visiting, and we went clubbing. Willie joined us at our table between sets, and the body language was a dead giveaway. By then they were comfortable, but discreet, adoring lovers. There was a tenderness in the way they respected each other that was heart-achingly sweet."

"True to Emma's way, though, there she was again, forbidden love." Fiona slumped in her chair.

"Yes, but there's no sadness in this, just caution. They made it work for them. She painted; he played. They came together at the intersection of their talents. Emma was enormously happy, being with Willie. And Willie was smitten with her. He was older, maybe ten years older than her. Theirs was such a gentle, mature love. Not that it wasn't passionate, Emma let on that it was, but that it wasn't urgent. They took it as it came."

"So, she pushed Thomas to go away to school, for that?" Fiona shook her head in disbelief.

"No, see, that's the problem, making such a simple, straight line equation of it. She was urging Thomas to develop a life, have friends, to network, as they call it now. By the time it had become a *relationship* with Willie, Thomas was almost ready for college—he started at Cal at seventeen. Emma was reserving time for herself. Time that he wasn't really spending with her anyway. What teenager wants to spend Friday and Saturday evenings with his mother? He didn't like her at the clubs for safety reasons, but she didn't let him dictate her free time."

"What did your mother think?"

Jordan sat back. "She was appalled. That's why there's so little of it in the letters. Once Mum expressed her position, Emma just kept it to herself."

"Was your mother prejudiced?"

"How do I answer that? As I said, they were different times. My mother was afraid Emma would get hurt again. Mum didn't understand why she couldn't find someone more... more socially acceptable. So, there was a little prejudice, showing around the edges. She did meet him, once, at the club. She admitted that he was charming and talented, but that's as far as she would go. She simply did not approve. Emma, of course, was disappointed but it wasn't the first time her heart led her into dicey territory."

"What were the veiled references to criminality?"

"I'm not sure, could just have been the inter-racial relationship, but later on, it was more likely the heroin."

Fiona's jaw dropped. "He provided her heroin?"

"Yes, but of course you understand that it was for the pain. Modern medicine, at that time, was just past blood-letting. Her hip was crumbling and there was nothing they could do to help her. So, Willie had his contacts in the music world and for Emma, money wasn't a problem, so they cautiously navigated dangerous waters to keep her comfortable. The drugs probably bought her five or so years of relief. After her fall, it was all she had."

"You said there were costs *and* freedoms?"

"You mean with Thomas? The freedoms were obvious. Discretion let Emma enjoy a love with Willie that was mutually satisfying and rich. The costs were high; time was limited. She wanted to enjoy her son, but he was at a stage in his life where he naturally pulled away. She couldn't fully share her life with him, and that added up to more distance. She knew time was short, but didn't want to alarm him." Jordan folded her hands in her lap, "Emma loved Thomas more than breathing, but she was determined to give *him* room to breathe."

"And she continued to paint, at this point?"

"As much as she could bear; the drugs dulled her, but made it possible. After her fall, Thomas wanted to swoop in and take charge. Emma would have none of it and that frustrated Thomas, but what he was offering was the same thing the medical establishment had been pushing for years, institutional care."

"What would have been so bad about professional care? The woman was in excruciating pain, she needed assistance."

"Institutional care would have meant the end of Willie. No nursing home was going to provide private visiting privileges to a black man. Not surprisingly, Emma opted for her own way."

Fiona dropped her face into her hands. This was as painful as she could have imagined. Once again, Emma was shortchanged by life. So much talent and love. Fiona felt dwarfed by the enormity of it.

Jordan saw her angst. "Fiona, it *is* a success story, all of it."

"You've got a funny concept of a happy ending."

"She painted almost to the end. She enjoyed a loving and rewarding relationship with Willie. She raised a wonderful son, and was proud of his talents and achievements, and she knew he'd be okay. How many of us can say that?"

Fiona raised her head and looked directly at Jordan. "Do you think she really killed herself?"

"I don't think it was her intent but I think it was inevitable, given the dosages she took. But that wouldn't have been her objective."

Fiona sighed. The late afternoon sun crept across the floor. They'd talked the entire day away and she was wrung out. She stood up again, and went to the Paris paintings.

"I really need to see some of the later works. It'll help put it in context."

"Fiona, I need to take a break, to rest a bit. Perhaps we should take an hour or so and then we'll go to dinner."

Fiona looked at her hostess, who once again had taken on the frail appearance of the previous evening. "I'm sorry, I've worn you

328

out."

"I've been waiting almost fifty years to tell this story, so a little fatigue is well worth it. I'll see you in an hour or so." Jordan stood, taking up her cane, and made her way back to her room, leaving Fiona with the paintings. Fiona realized that she, too, was exhausted and padded off to the guest room.

She woke up to a gentle tapping. She had dozed, reclining on the bed, replaying the photo gallery of Emma's paintings. Fiona couldn't reconcile that steady stream of robust and lovely images, springing from a life that held such pain and so many losses. She looked up to see Jordan rapping lightly on the open door.

"I hate to wake you, but you must see what Eugene has put together." Fiona glanced at her watch and was surprised to see that it was already seven.

"Oh my. I didn't mean to nod off like that. I hope I haven't spoiled any evening plans."

"You weren't the only one to drift off, but Eugene has saved the day. Come and see." Fiona sat up and slid off the edge of the bed. She closed her laptop, and followed Jordan.

Down the hall, in the nook off the kitchen, Eugene was setting places with plates, napkins and chopsticks. In the center of the table were dozens of white cardboard folded boxes with wire bails, enough Chinese food to feed a crowd.

"Eugene! How much do you think we can eat?" Fiona was agog at the total volume represented by the tidy army of white boxes.

"Well, I didn't know what you'd like," he countered, smiling, "so I just got a little of everything. We can always eat it as leftovers." He nodded at Jordan, "We often do that, she has quite the appetite for Asian cuisine."

Fiona quickly returned to her room, and washed her hands and face. The cool water woke her up and reset her sense of self. Fiona had noticed that Emma's emotionally wrenching stories often left her floating, feeling like she didn't exactly belong to herself, or to Emma's past.

She rejoined the others and sat down to the treasure hunt of tastes, sampling from one carton to another.

"Eugene, this is perfect," Jordan peered into yet another carton, "Ah, ginger shrimp, I knew it had to be in here somewhere. Their eyes met and Jordan grinned; Fiona realized that this was a regular treat.

"Mmm, cashews and snow peas, I don't know how you knew, but I was too tired to go out. Just the decisions posed by a menu would've worn me out." Fiona reached for another unopened surprise.

"This is Eugene's contribution to *our* family's traditions. When the kids were young, Eugene volunteered for the occasional evening of babysitting. The kids raved over it. We wondered why. One evening our plans were cancelled, and we returned home to find a festival of Chinese food. The kids were sprawled on the floor in front of the television, sampling all these wonderful treats. We joined in, and it became a tradition.

Eugene added, "With those kids, we only had one rule—they had to eat everything, so the parents wouldn't discover our secret."

Fiona surveyed the spread, "I certainly hope you've abandoned *that* rule."

"Nope, you'll have to stay till it's all gone!" Jordan laughed.

"Works for me. I love my room, so I may be here a while." Fiona reached for the garlic eggplant that Jordan had just discovered.

Eugene leaned back and furrowed his brow. "You know, we might just have a Gewurztraminer that would be good with this. He stood and went off to forage in the kitchen.

"That man is a gem."

"I don't know what I'd do without him. He's a link to my past and a connection to many of my aesthetic benchmarks. Like the wine, or the fact that he really likes Twentieth Century Art, or that he'd spoil my kids with Chinese food." Jordan set down her chopsticks, before continuing, "He lost his partner, back in the late-eighties, before my husband died, and we vowed he'd never want for a home, as long as we lived."

Fiona paused a moment to take this in. "Do you feel any affinity with Emma and her Willie?"

"Probably. But some people just are family. Emma didn't have that because she couldn't share Willie with Thomas. If I ever suggested putting Eugene out to pasture, my kids would have me institutionalized. You don't turn your back on family."

Fiona nodded. "How did Thomas react to the arrangements after Emma's fall?"

"Well, he didn't like it. I don't know if you knew this, but Willie's niece, Clarice, lived with Emma as a full-time caretaker.

330

Willie was around most of the time, but in deference to social convention, he never spent the night. Clarice had a salary and Willie never took a dime, even if he lost work taking care of her."

Eugene came back in with three wineglasses and the chilled white. He opened and poured.

"You visited during that time?"

"Yes, during a particularly rough spell. Willie had assured me it wasn't always bad, but on a bad day, she just upped the dose and was bleary. On a good day, Willie would set her up to paint, or the three of them would play cards or Scrabble. Willie even tried to teach Emma to read music. It never seemed to take. On the bad days, he'd sometimes sit and softly play his sax. One of the neighbors mentioned it after she passed."

"And Thomas?"

"He was a wreck. He couldn't help his mother and wasn't comfortable letting Willie do what he felt *he* should. He wasn't able to watch her suffering, so mostly he buried himself in school and then work. The time I came, I found him outside, leaning up against the wall, sobbing. Now, having been with my mother at the end, I understand."

Eugene joined in, "If you've ever loved someone and lost them that way—slowly, you know it can't be fixed. But if you can stick with it, you never question your love for them. It sounds like Thomas didn't come out of it with that reassurance."

"For most young people in their twenties, it's a time of pulling away from parents, and discovering who they're going to be. Thomas was yanked away from a life, which his mum had forced on him, and pushed into a world full of loss and pain. He tried his best and did as well as anyone could've asked."

"In hind-sight, do you think any good came of it?"

Jordan paused, "A funny thing happened. I resented it at first but it really did work out. There was a bit of a wedge between Mum and Emma. Partly Willie, partly some of the same frustration Thomas had. Mum was petrified of losing Emma and there was nothing she could do. Emma had always been her mainstay. Mum reached out to Thomas. There I was with Emma; I wrote, I called, we connected and there was my mother with Thomas. It was like we traded mothers for a bit there, and it worked out. I don't know what Thomas would've done after, without Mum, or she without him."

Fiona sipped her wine. Again, she thought of Denise, in her

twenties, and struggling to establish exactly that sense of self. She looked down at her glass, the wine was great. Eugene was right, it was the perfect accompaniment, especially with the spicier morsels. "This is really great. I may try doing this with the group."

"It's so good. It's not really even cheating."

Eugene laughed. "Jordan has told me about your group and the dinners. It almost sounds like you're keeping score."

"It's true," Fiona melodramatically put the back of her hand to her forehead, "You just don't understand the pressure. It is *enormous*."

They all laughed. Talking about food spurred a renewed round of peering into the little cartons and finding just the right taste, for the moment, but the servings were getting smaller.

Jordan added, "I can hardly wait for the show, I'm sure there'll be some kind of food extravaganza." She reached and poured more wine all around.

"Too much for me to contemplate right now. I have to get the book done and that's as far as my future range can absorb."

"What happened to Willie?" Both women turned to Eugene's question.

Jordan answered, in a measured way. "Well, Emma left him the controversial bequest. Enough for him to buy a house and live out his life comfortably. Forty thousand dollars for a Negro attendant in 1958 was an unusual and notable chunk. It forced Thomas to face the significance of their relationship, but well after he could be part of their shared life. That was difficult for him. In fact, though I understand *why*, the whole under-the-table nature of the relationship made it more difficult for everyone. Emma couldn't share the relationship publicly, so Willie was robbed of his rightful role as the grieving widower, and Thomas didn't get to experience his mother as a whole person with romantic connections of her own.

Fiona nodded her head, "I understand what you're saying, but how important could it be to be a widower?"

Eugene quickly interjected, "Don't underestimate the magnitude of an unrecognized loss. There's a social support system for grieving, but it's not available unless the relationship is acknowledged. You have to work hard to keep it in your heart because it can evaporate and leave you feeling crazy."

Fiona was taken aback by the intensity of his response. It came back to the sadness of it all. Everyone was shortchanged.

Jordan summed it up, "We're getting better. More and more we are dropping the barriers in loving. Emma and Willie weren't icons, just the victims of cultural stupidity. In that mix though, don't lose the importance on a personal level. They *were* a couple. She loved him as fully and openly as they could safely. His warmth and love shines through in her paintings. He's there. She used to revel in listening to him play. It's not all sadness."

"Maybe it was hardest for Thomas, as he was excluded from that rich fullness."

"I think so, but there were consolations. My mother stepped in, with Thomas. They were very close right up till she died. For him, it was an avenue to his mother. For her, I think it helped to heal the loss of my brother. And she taught him survival skills. My mother taught Thomas how to have money with dignity."

"I'm not sure what you mean?"

"Emma never prepared Thomas for the money; she trained him in frugality and self-reliance. Emma herself had never reconciled the connection with her grandparents' estate. The wealth, while a boon and a safety net, became a huge responsibility. It came to symbolize the loss of her nuclear family, a sort of... consolation prize. Emma was financially brilliant, but since the money was secret, she never shared those skills with Thomas. Mum was the understudy, to that task. When the time came, she filled in brilliantly. She taught him diplomacy and grace, while they pieced together Emma's strategies, and continued investing. Without Mum, Thomas would have been left to the wolves."

This struck Fiona as over the top. "Well, that's a little strong. Too much money is hardly a problem, and what wolves? In my experience, the doors are always open to wealth."

"Ah, yes, but not always the *right* doors. True to Emma's predictions, as soon as she passed, her family came out of the woodwork, sniffing about to see if there was anything in it for them. Emma's sister, the remaining twin, was on his doorstep within days of the obituary. There were new nieces and nephews, cousins to Thomas—instant family, if he wanted it. People, who hadn't cared one bit in almost forty years, suddenly became grieving family."

"Yes, I've seen a lot of that in my work. It *is* amazing. But how did they find out there was money?"

"A press release from Mills. $250,000 was a sizable endowment at the time; it was newsworthy, *Giant Bequest From Struggling*

Single Artist. Mum had a fit over that. She said it was just chumming-the-water. Sure enough, Thomas was beset with relatives, offers of financial guidance and demands that he share."

"Demands?"

"Well, when making nice didn't pan out, the sister threatened to contest the original distribution to Emma, from the grandparents. She pointed out that Thomas's own birth status was questionable, and that the bequest 'to that negro' was obviously the result of some kind of undue influence—essentially she threatened an ugly bit of public mudslinging."

"Poor Thomas."

Jordan paused a moment, reflecting, "So, my mother was needed, and she needed to be needed. She used to call me, or write, indignant about all the ugliness. She'd always had reservations about Emma's vehemence against contact with family, but *that* little episode drove home just how right Emma had been. Mom and Thomas became protectors of Willie, and that worked out well too, for all of them. I think Willie and Thomas reached a level of mutual appreciation, that wouldn't have happened, but for the sister. So, in an odd way it was a silver lining for the three of them. Mostly Mum buffered Thomas, and provided him with a sounding board. He'd been left with a legacy much like Emma's—an unexpected windfall that could never make up for the loss."

They sat in silence for a moment. Fiona wondered what Emma would've thought about how all this played out, then *and* now.

Eugene looked up, "I think we've done about as much damage to this spread as possible. Does anyone want tea?'

"I'd love some," Jordan began sealing the cartons. "We didn't do so badly, we managed to eat about two-thirds of it!"

"I'm not sure whether to be proud, or ashamed," Fiona rubbed her full belly, "All I know for sure was that it was *really* good. Just the ticket for a roller-coaster of a day." She helped seal and stack the now reduced army of white cartons.

Eugene turned to Fiona, "For someone who came to this venture by the coincidence of a painting, you seem in tune with the story and its emotional rhythms. Do you feel it's taken a lot out of you?"

"Some, but not nearly as much as it gives back. I've come to love Emma and I've built a whole new family of friends in the process."

Eugene came back and sat down with the teapot and cups. "We

334

could do dessert. I could whip up a cold zabaglione and biscotti."

"Oh, *God* no." Fiona insisted, "I would burst. But thank you anyway. I'll take a rain-check, because it sounds really good. And I'm always open to stealing a new dessert idea"

"Eugene brought up an interesting point." Jordan put honey in her steaming cup and stirred it slowly, "I'm at an age where I no longer believe in coincidence and it always seems the universe steps up to fix things, though on its own perverse schedule," She turned to Fiona, "Do you ever wonder how you got into all this?"

"I really try *not* to be the story."

"Yes, but it has to have been a big change for you. Do you wonder how, or *why me*?"

"Here we go," Eugene exhorted. "Why is it that everyone over eighty suddenly sees the hand of God in *everything*."

Jordan smirked, "You can see we've had this conversation before."

Fiona paused, "Well, it's not like it isn't important, but the work has to speak first, not a deeper meaning. Like, when Emma painted, surely you see more peeking through than paint. There are landscapes that laugh or weep, but it's the work, not the hidden meanings that need to be the driving force. It's all an exploration."

"That's why those hidden meanings often remain hidden." Jordan smiled.

"Not so much, it seems they're always visible, but we have to be receptive. The Paris painting of your brother, Lytton; since I saw it this morning, I can't help but feel that the painting is the manifestation of Thomas's conception. Thomas became possible because of the love Emma felt, years before, for *your* mother and her son. Look at that painting; it's the truth shining through. Is that the hand of God? This year I needed to find something in my life that made it bigger than the sum of its parts. I found an old painting. Is that the hand of God? I can't answer that question. But I can tell you it's the work. It's about getting to it everyday, and peeling back the layers wherever you find them. You may not even see the bigger picture, but it's there and that's enough. I now know more about Emma Caites than I do about any other person. Through that lens though, I'm beginning to see others. I don't know if Emma's story is universal, I just find it compelling so I pursue it. It's changed me. Maybe it will change things for others, too. That's not my call to make."

Eugene poked Jordan in the arm. "I think that sums it up. It's about the mundane *and* the hand of God. They're the same."

Jordan shook her head, "Not so easy, we'll have this conversation again. You see, there's that thing she just said, about the lens. We all see the same thing, just through different lenses. Fiona has been seeing the sadness and suffering in Emma's life, maybe more than Emma did. That's another lens. Deeper meanings may come about because of the different lenses."

"Yes, but you've been disabusing me of the suffering view, I'm coming around."

"Wait a minute." Eugene was intent now, "If the meanings are as diverse as there are perspectives, you undermine your view of God in the process. One event can't mean everything to everyone."

Jordan hesitated, "Well... I'll have to think about that. Eugene do we have any of that shortbread left?"

Fiona giggled at that, "That's what I like about you two. You'll never let philosophy get in the way of dessert."

Eugene grinned broadly, "Yup, and more of the ginger snaps, too."

Fiona leaned forward conspiratorially, "Now you're talking. Bring em' on!"

Eugene set the plate in the center of the table, and poured more tea all the way around. Fiona continued, "There's a portrait of a black musician that Thomas has, but I don't see it as one of the selected works. I don't know if Thomas and Marvin didn't pick it because of artistic reasons, or for some other reason. If it's Willie, shouldn't it be included, and the saxophones too?" She turned to Jordan, "I may need your help on this."

"You've got it, of course. What do you propose?"

"I'll write up what I have so far, particularly from this weekend's discussions. I'll ask him if there isn't a portrait, since it's central to finding wholeness in Emma's story. Without including Willie, we have an artist, successful in art, but unable to form lasting meaningful relationships. Willie is a resolution. If there's resistance, I'll want you to jump in."

"Done."

"Women!"

"And what's that supposed to mean?" Jordan feigned offense.

"Bad enough that you're usually already a step ahead, but damn, you even plot ahead."

336

Fiona smiled at him sweetly, "Nice work if you can get it."

"Well, I'm exhausted, it's late, and I'm outgunned." Eugene stood and collected the empty plate. "Fiona, what time is your flight tomorrow?"

"Eleven a.m. *If* you let me leave without finishing the Chinese food."

"So we need to get you there by ten, Ladies. I'll be doing wake up calls at seven. Sleep well. Fiona, it has been a pleasure. I hope we'll see you again."

"Well, you'll be coming to the Opening, correct?

"Yes, of course."

"So, I'll see you then, and tomorrow morning, of course."

Eugene bowed his head, and then, took his leave. Suddenly the evening was over. Fiona looked at the kitchen clock and was shocked to see it was almost midnight. "Wow, do you realize we've been talking for the entire day!"

"I know. It's been exhilarating, and exhausting. Fiona, I can't tell you what a relief this has been for me. My mother told me this would happen that some day; I'd have to tell Emma's story. I didn't know if it would happen in my lifetime. I think you're the perfect person to be entrusted with this and that's what I meant about the hand of God, when the right things just come together."

"Well, that and just luck."

"Whatever it is, it works for me. And I'm sure for Thomas. He needs this too."

Fiona paused. "Jordan, I have an odd question, not about Emma. I'm just curious you and your brother both have unusual names. Is there something to that?"

Jordan nodded. "It's a southern thing, from my dad's family. You give a girl child her mother's maiden name, and the boy child, if not named for dad, gets his father's mother's maiden name. It's not a tradition that I continued, but it was important for dad."

Fiona threw her head back and howled.

"What was that for?"

"I'm so happy *my* family didn't share your tradition. It would have been tough to grow up with the first name of *Grunzig*."

Now it was Jordan's turn to laugh. "Fiona, I love your perspective. I agree with Eugene, you have to come back."

"Once I finish this book, in a heartbeat. I've had a wonderful time, too."

Jordan gave her a tremendous hug, "Goodnight then, I'll see you early."

The next morning slipped by too quickly. They had a lovely light breakfast, followed by a quick tour of Jordan's other art works. She seemed to have everything, more Thiebaud, a Diebenkorn and a varied collection of early California plein air painters. Martinez, one each of Arthur and Lucia Matthews, Rolo Peters, Grandville, Bischoff, Lauritz, Wendt and others. Fiona was dizzy at the parade of talent, pieces that should be in museums. She took quiet satisfaction that Emma hung proudly on walls with her more acknowledged contemporaries, and that her work was on par. She took some quick photos of Emma's paintings, for Marvin, and they discussed how and to whom they should be shipped for the Exhibit. She asked Jordan to pose, with the cane across her lap, in her study and took several wonderful shots that captured the warmth and dignity of this woman, whom Emma had loved. Too quickly, it was time to go, and with hugs all around, Fiona stepped into the Town Car for the trip back to LAX.

Chapter Fifty-Six

From: ardleycaites@mindspring.com
Subject: Re: Jordan Interview/Emma Update
Date: January 25, 2008 9:58 PM
To: fionahedge@yahoo.com

Fiona,
I am awestruck. I can't fully grasp the enormity of your task and I marvel at the thoughtful sensitivity you bring to the undertaking. If ever I question the delicacy of your efforts, I need only look to Thomas. Some of this has been tender for him, yet your unfolding of Emma's story has brought him new insights and ways to appreciate her. I am afraid that over the years he has bought into the dark and tragic, the disability, the drug abuse, the socially challenging relationship with Willie, without looking to the best part. Now he sees his mother as striving always to make the best of it, to find love and to find relief in ways that freed her creativity, even if others might not understand her ways. Emma was fiercely independent because she had to be to protect her decisions. This new perspective has brought Thomas peace. It has given him a way to love her anew, without judgment. In that peace there is great beauty and the opportunity for Thomas to explore the things he shared with his mother, to find a better connection with her and with the best parts of himself. I am grateful, on both of our behalf. Don't become discouraged, the work is incredible.
Ardley

From: ohamandakins@aol.com
Subject: Re: Jordan Interview/Emma Update
Date: January 27, 2008 2:05 PM
To: fionahedge@yahoo.com

Hey Fi,

It's going really well. The buzz from the group is phenomenal after that last update. We can see the story coming to a close and we're jubilant and sad at the same time. Jenn says she's helping with the academic stuff—don't let it get in the way, cause what you're doing has heart. I sent a copy to Cheryl, she's nuts about it. She's reveling in the story being so Oakland. She knows she can't spread it around, but as soon as there's a working draft of the full book, we need to get it to her. She thinks there's a synergy between the exhibit and the book that will put Emma on the map. She wants a saxophonist at the opening, jazz, art and pathos. I agree.

If you get a chance, give Marv a call. He's really getting grilled at the gallery and could use some support. Norm and Jenn are excited about the Groundhog Day dinner. They don't want any help with it. I'm getting vibes, are you? Keep up the great work. See you then.

oxo
Amanda

From: artantikmarv@sbcglobal.net
Subject: Re: Jordan Interview/Emma Update
Date: January 30, 2008 5:47 PM
To: fionahedge@yahoo.com

Fiona,

Sorry I'm so slow about responding. That last update was wonderful but surprising. You'll want to cross-reference with Thomas and the letters. Perhaps it speaks more to my mood than anything, but I'm having a little trouble with this heroin addicted, pain ravaged happy ending. In the end, I know you'll check your facts and go with what's faithful to Emma. The others aren't bothered a bit and Cheryl is entranced. She is researching Oakland's jazz days for photos to add to the exhibit.

Things on my end continue to be tense. We're in the post-holiday lull and the mood is grim. Despite leading in sales, antiques on hand are now treated as a capital albatross. You'd think I was stealing food out of the mouths of children. I'm lying very low on the Emma front, as that would blow sky-high under current conditions. Let me know what the read is from Thomas, I'm curious and will consider anti-depressants if I'm wrong! Don't despair if the story is more dire than Jordan felt—the tragic artist story is always good for sales. Look at the bright side! You've really got to talk to Art Bradley. He'll breathe new life into you when you hear of his exhibit plans.

Keep at it Babe, you're in the trenches for us all. Love, Marvin

Chapter Fifty-Seven

The feeling of this was so different from the last time she'd met with Thomas at Bateau Ivre. Fiona made the hard right into the parking lot, remembering how nervous she'd been that first time meeting Emma's son. This time, he called and wanted to meet without the group. Fiona was pleased. She needed to ask some additional questions, but was hesitant to push the matter until she knew how he'd digested her last report. Ardley's email helped, but Fiona wanted him to be comfortable with the story without having to sacrifice any of Emma's authenticity. Thomas calling her was a good sign. Fiona thought how much easier it would be to do a biography of someone truly historical, without anyone left alive who had a stake in the game. She laughed out loud when she realized that she was musing over the relative challenges facing biographers, and realizing that she was placing herself in that club. Jeanne-Marie's comment rang in her ears, "Accountant-writer who focuses on art biography." Maybe there was something to it.

She found a space in the back, clear of any other cars, and parked precisely between the lines, backing up and pulling forward till she was satisfied. She grabbed her purse, slung it over her shoulder and headed inside. Thomas was already seated at the same table where they'd first met. He stood and wrapped her in a huge hug, and then just held her. Fiona curled her arms around him—all that warmth, it was like hugging her dad. Thomas leaned back and looked at her curiously.

"Are you getting *smaller*?"

"Oh, just a bit, it's from all the walking that started in Paris. It's keeping me sane now. I walk fast and ponder the problems with presenting the story."

"I haven't seen any problems, really, I'm completely entranced. So sit, I've ordered a cheese plate and wine."

They both sat and pulled their chairs up close so they could hear over the buzz of the card-reading, backgammon playing, late afternoon crowd. The waitress came by with a generous spread of cheeses, pear slices and a fresh baguette. She set down two glasses and opened a bottle of pinot noir. Thomas tasted and approved, and she whisked away, leaving them their privacy.

"I'm not kidding. I am very pleased with the progress of your reports. I'm hoping the actual text of the book can keep that very personal feeling." Fiona, I've neglected my mother. You have come in the nick of time to reclaim her, and give her back to all of us."

"My biggest concern is that it be true to *her*." Fiona spread some goat's brie over a slice of pear. "It's academic but I hope it still reads like a story. But is it true to who she was, or is it who we want her to have been? I'm clear on it up through the fifties, because I can triangulate with her letters. By the early fifties, she does not share everything with Wren in the letters, and after her fall, the letters slow considerably."

Thomas sucked in his breath. "I'm hoping to lean on you for clarity here. I was not as present, at that time, as I should have been."

"The letters indicate that there was some friction between you and your mother. Jordan said I should ask you about it, and about college and architecture."

Thomas shrugged. "Normal growing up stuff, I think. My mother wanted me to have a career, a profession. Given our lives, it seemed awfully white collar and somewhat hypocritical to me. I was also worried about the expense."

"So, you *didn't* know about the money?"

"Not a clue. I had a wild-eyed vision that I would become a painter and provide for both of us, as she had. But she was busy pushing me out of the nest. I resented it."

"Jordan thought that this was a big area of dispute." Fiona refilled their glasses.

"It seemed so at the time. I felt pushed away." His eyes met Fiona's, and he smiled broadly. "Since then I've raised two girls of my own and their young adulthood was a minefield by comparison. Looking back, it's easy to see that my mom was just watching out for me. I didn't make it easy for her."

"*That,* I understand. I'm in the middle of it with Denise and I know I have to just let it unfold."

He cleared his throat, "It wasn't especially traumatic but it was significant. It cost me dearly." Seeing Fiona's puzzled expression, Thomas explained, "Our clock was ticking. I lost precious time being a normal young man. It took me a long time to understand the last few years of my mother's life." The loss registered on his face. "Maybe Jordan can help with that, the part where I wasn't paying attention."

"Jordan's been wonderful, and she was in constant contact with Emma, right through to the end, by telephone, but I'm worried about substituting her optimism for Emma's disposition. Jordan loved her and is vested in a rosy view of the last few years. No one wants to face bleak."

Thomas sat silently, reflecting for a moment. "She continued painting and for me, that's always been an indication that Mom was making the best of it. Painting was finding the beauty in one's world, whatever its size." He fingered the cloth napkin, running his fingertips along the edge of the folded hem. "I tried not to know what was going on in her life. I didn't approve."

"Of what?"

"The drugs. Willie. Funny that I clung so tight to conventions, I certainly wasn't raised that way."

"Well, it was the fifties. How much did you know about her drug use?"

"It was obvious sometimes. She'd be totally out of it, or heavy-lidded and slurry." He paused, "Even I had to admit though, it was better than the pain. I understood, but at the same time, I didn't. Watching the pain was worse, so I gave the whole thing a wide berth. I'm just glad I didn't know it was heroin. That might've made me try to do something about it."

"How was her work, her painting?"

"Oh, Jesus, Fiona, sometimes it was brilliant. Then sometimes it was muddled. You could tell when she was in bad shape." He sipped his wine. "I told myself I'd step in when her quality of life deteriorated. *I* measured that by her paintings. It's what Mom would've called a *reasonable measurement*." He stopped and spread some cheese on a slice of pear.

"She did a series she called *Light Breaking* in… I think it was '57. They were stunning. Abstract, but cognizant. Studies of reflections in strong light on common objects. I thought they were brilliant. I've never been able to find any of them. My mother wasn't stoned; she was coping. We *did* have some incredible discussions about the relationship between breaking light and mathematics, and about the similarities in fractionating light frequencies and jazz. She was enormously present. Trapped in that broken body, she was as sharp as ever. I couldn't fault it. On the good days, I loved and admired her more then than at any other time in my life." His voice caught. "On a bad day, she could barely handle a paint brush, or even talk. And she had contempt for that."

"If she'd failed that *reasonable measurement* test, what could you have done?"

Thomas dropped his head, "I don't know. I had contingency plans. Institutional nursing care, I guess. I'd worked the numbers. I figured I could afford it. I didn't know she had money."

"Would something like that have made a difference?"

Thomas tilted his head back. "In hindsight, her arrangements surpassed anything I'd conjured up. She was home. Clarice was an incredible caretaker, and Willie did everything and anything with a level of loving I tried not to notice. Some days I'd visit, and we'd all just sit and listen to Willie play. It soothed her in a way that I couldn't." Thomas emptied his glass. "His playing... it soothed us all."

"And Willie, what did you feel about him?"

"I'm ashamed. I can't explain it. It was 1957. Willie was black. My mother loved him dearly, more dearly than I ever knew. I'd never had to compete for her affections before that and I didn't handle it very well." Tears spilled out, and Thomas covered his face.

Fiona reached out and took his hand. "Nobody does this as well as they'd like. I know I didn't with *my* mother, and without most of the issues you had."

Thomas lifted his head, but faced her obliquely, "After she'd died, I came to truly appreciate Willie. Even to love him. And I became so angry that I didn't get there earlier, when I could have appreciated and loved them together. It would have meant the world to me to have seen my mother loved and loving someone. The times were small-minded, but I learned."

Fiona finally cut to the chase. "So, my problem is that I have two competing views. The addict-artist with the tragic and sordid ending, or the winding down and culmination of a life that was fully lived. Which would *you* choose?"

Thomas looked as if she'd slapped him. "That's the lack of clarity I mentioned. I'm not sure."

"But Thomas, I'm sure you have an opinion?"

"Fiona, before all this, I had bought into the tragic view. But was it shame, survivor guilt, racial guilt, Oedipal love? You name it, I've considered it. Your emails from Paris, and with what I learned about Willie after my mother passed, it now looks like she was fully

345

realized. I am both relieved and humbled. I shouldn't have judged her, just loved her, and yet, I refused to take her at face-value. Sometimes the straight line really *is* the shortest distance between two points. My mother was never dishonest, just discreet. Willie loved her more fully than I could at the time." Tears flowed freely again, down his cheeks.

"How did you find out the true nature of their relationship?"

"After Mom died, my aunt became a nightmare. She threatened to turn my mother's estate into a public circus. I found out that there were plenty of loaded issues to fight over. There was my illegitimacy and the bequest to Willie. Both were… well, non-standard, embarrassing. Suddenly I was on an even footing with Willie. I realized I had to protect him. He wanted to reject the bequest and just walk away. He was grieving and he was a mess. That bequest was my mother's wish; I had to convince him to accept it. How many people would walk away from such a gift?"

"So, you think your mother's life wasn't a tragedy, after all?"

"Not in how she acted. She was dealt a lousy hand, but she played it well."

"And Willie?"

Thomas turned his face away from her. "Loving, loyal, talented, humble, centered, gentle, genuine, he was more than I was at the time. In spite of the barriers, he was her life-partner in ways that we can't measure today."

"So, you wouldn't object to his portrait and the saxophone paintings being included in the exhibit *and* the book?"

"I called Art Bradley the minute I finished your report. How my mother lived her life is the biggest part of it. The art is a reflection of the rest of it."

"Well, that tells me what I needed to know. I think am pretty clear on this." Fiona sighed. She poured the last of the wine into their glasses.

"But there's more. Remember, *I* called you to meet."

"Oh yeah. But I don't know, this is pretty fundamental stuff. What else could there be?"

"It's about my mother's collection. When you asked me before, I wasn't entirely clear.'

"How so?"

"I told you my mother didn't leave me many paintings, and that's true. She left me five. But I am not solely responsible for accumulating the collection. It was Willie's quest first."

"She gave him some of her paintings?"

"A few, but after she died, it was Willie who set out to collect her work. It was Willie's idea. He wanted, very much, to surround himself with what had been *her*. Then, when he died, he left me his collection of my mother's work—well over a hundred paintings."

"Oh my God."

"And I continued on from there. Willie has to be given credit. The core of it is his collection, *his* vision. It was a measure of his love, for her."

"Of course." She shook her head. "Oh, wow..." Now Fiona's eyes brimmed with tears. "Do you know which are from Willie's collection?"

"Absolutely."

"And *that's* why you called me?"

"Yes. I had to tell you."

Fiona looked down at the table. This certainly supported Willie's devotion and their connection. Emma *was* complete. She found love her own way. She didn't descend into desperate addiction; she coped. She continued to be herself, with those who loved her until the very end of her life. For Fiona, this was enough.

"I'll talk to Art about the accreditation. Willie will be honored. This makes all the difference. Thank you."

This time, Thomas reached over for *her* hand. "No, thank *you*, Fiona"

"Again and always, an ensemble effort." She nodded.

Thomas squeezed her hand tightly, "You have no idea how much this has meant."

"To me, too."

"And it means I can now let go of some of the paintings."

"Pardon me?" Fiona furrowed her brow.

Thomas leaned forward, "I've been obsessively collecting, following in Willie's footsteps. But you were right. I need to share her to fully appreciate her. Fiona, I've been hoarding against a world that I felt couldn't recognize her value. You've proved they can. If this book and exhibit are as good as I expect, I'll be able to pass on some of her work."

Fiona cleared her throat. "Well, first step, you need to pick some pieces that are of stellar quality, universal pieces and you need to selectively donate to quality museums. That shouldn't be too hard after the exhibit. My personal favorite would be the Oakland Museum. After all these years, it's about time."

Thomas nodded, "A good start."

"Then, of course, once her name is out there, and you're ready, you'll need a gallery you can trust to slowly sell the pieces that you don't need to keep. Oddly enough, I have just the person in mind for such a task."

Thomas tipped his head back, mouth slightly open as he realized the sheer poetry of what Fiona was about to suggest.

Chapter Fifty-Eight

Fiona was ready to knock off early for the day. She wanted time for a quick walk around Lake Merritt before heading over to Norm's for *Groundhog Day* dinner. With her regular work schedule and writing on top of it, Fiona was trying to pace herself. She'd never undertaken anything this complex before, and the pressure to produce something genuine and accurate was intense. Walking helped. Lost in thought, she jumped when the phone rang.

Without even waiting for a *hello*, Marvin jumped in. "Hey babe, what do you think about dropping by my place this afternoon before our dinner plans?"

Fiona could tell by the tone of his voice he was at work, with an audience. "Sure *honey*, what time?"

"Well, I'm headed home now, I have something there I'd like to show you."

Fiona stifled a giggle as she realized Marvin was making it sound like she was his date. She wondered whether the gallery phones had caller id. His partners would surely be surprised if they checked up on him and found out he was flirting with a woman. "Sure, I was just shutting down a little early, I'll head right over. Any hints?"

"What, and give away my secrets? You know better than that." The phone clicked.

Fiona smiled, setting the handset in its cradle. She shut down the computer and stood up, stretching. Her walk would have to wait.

Before Fiona had a chance to knock, the door swung open. "So, what's big the rush?" She pecked Marvin on the cheek as he closed the door behind her.

"Paintings my dear, paintings. I got seven of them."

"*Seven*? Anything really good?"

"Nothing I'd hold the presses for. They're good, but investment grade. Well, I should withhold judgment till you've seen them. Sometimes you have an eye for what's under the grime." Marvin led the way to the basement. The paintings were leaning face out along the center wall. True to his concerns, they were pretty filthy. Fiona studied them, quickly surveying the lot, and then looking intently at each in turn.

"Someone must have stored these in a furnace room. They're awfully sooty." She paused, "Mostly they're good though, representative pieces for the period, but none of them speak to me specifically. I do like that little landscape, the one of the dry streambed, but it's not as good as some of mine already. Where do you think that is, Temescal?"

"I think Tilden Park, far side of the lake. Look at the rocks." Fiona nodded at his assessment.

"The rest of these are interesting. Cityscapes and harbor views. They're late forties, Emma exploring West Oakland. She spent time there because of the clubs, and maybe because of Willie—painting his world. That counts for something. This is before Oakland was a big port town, so the harbor views seem more quaint than industrial."

Marvin whistled. "You've sure learned a lot. That's gallery sales talk." Fiona smiled and curtsied.

"But you're not crazy about them?"

"Maybe the streambed, but I am really spoiled now. I've seen the best."

"That was my take on it, very marketable, but lacking the personal touch."

"They're better than the house portraits, but something is missing. Maybe a cleaning will make the difference."

"I hope not," Marvin confided. "I don't want to fall in love with every painting. It just makes it harder to contemplate selling them."

"Good point. Unless we get Norm into it, cleaning will have to wait. I'm up to my ears writing, so I need Jenn for footnotes and research. Do you think we'll need them ready by June?"

"I think we'll need a little lag time after the show. It's running June through August. I think we should shoot for late July. But we can't call on Norm. He's been swamped with the shop. It's really hopping. I think Valentine's Day is going to make up for missing the holidays." Marvin sighed and his face was all in a knot again.

Fiona studied Marvin. The last few times she'd seen him, he'd been unhappy to the point that his whole body projected *tense*. "You're wound up like a top again. What is it?"

"Oh," he waved his hand, "Just office politics. It'll pass."

"Marvin, I know it's none of my business, but things haven't been good there since we met. It isn't getting any better and it's wearing on you."

Marvin plopped down into the desk chair in the middle of the room. "They want to cut my hours and stop paying for my acquisition search time. It effectively turns me into a sales clerk. If I continue on my own, I subsidize them with *my* time. If I don't, I won't be contributing to the creative vision and look of the gallery. There won't be any antiques, so antiques sales won't be in the bottom line." He sighed again.

"Get out, dude. Force them to buy you out while your efforts still show in the numbers. They just want to grind them down so they can starve you out."

"No, it's just that everybody's nervous about the economy."

Fiona shook her head. "Don't believe that for a second. I've seen your numbers. Your sales have *increased* in recent months. Face it Marv, you're already history, all they're doing now is running out the clock, getting your numbers down. This isn't about business. I see it all the time—squabbling over estates that leave operating businesses. Jump now, while the trend is in your favor."

"And do what, Fiona?"

"Open a gallery. *Your* gallery. And you know it. You've got the contacts and the vision." Fiona sat on the desk facing him. "Just what do you think is going to happen when the show opens and your name is associated with a successful Caites retrospective?"

"Yeah, I've been dreading that. Isn't that ironic, something I've wanted for so long, and I'm dreading it even though it'll prove I was right. But they'll take it as if I'd been holding out on them."

"And have you thought of how you planned on marketing the Caites paintings? It will be a little awkward, don't you think, competition with the gallery, unless you cut them in on it."

"It's not as easy as you think."

"It's easier. Talk to Thomas."

"I don't want to hit him up for financing. This whole Emma adventure has been the best thing for me, like family. I don't want to spoil it."

"I'm not talking financing, I'm talking inventory. *Talk to Thomas*. The retrospective is going to create demand for Caites paintings. Come on, she's a female, early Twentieth Century California artist. The only markets that aren't soft now are the burgeoning regional art markets. Emma's paintings are going to land into a perfect market. We've got some, and Thomas has a bunch. He's interested in selling, but doesn't want to be directly

351

involved. He'll need a gallery he can trust." Fiona smiled winningly, "And I'll let you sell my book."

Marvin snorted. Some of the tension drained out of his face. "Just that easy, eh?"

"Yes, and no. Opening the gallery will be the easy part and you've got friends who'll help. But you'll probably have to sue to get your share out of your partners. That'll be the hard part. Do you have any savings to tide you over?"

"Some, I've been tucking it away."

"Marvin, it's doable. I've been running various scenarios, even collecting the names of attorneys. And you know, the Bikram's not doing so *hot*." Fiona winked.

That was it, Marvin let loose and really howled. "That poor little business. Battered by energy prices and the *evil eye* of all my friends. I gather then that you've *all* discussed this?"

"Yup."

Marvin laughed again. "I can't be offended. I should, but I just can't. Okay, I'll talk to Thomas."

"There may be another problem. The Bikrams aren't out yet and the building owner is a real pain-in-the-ass."

"Is that going to be a problem?" Marvin cringed.

"Well, the problem is… Norm. He'd be your landlord." Fiona grinned.

"What?"

"Yup, he owns the building."

"Where his shop is?"

"Yup, and the Bikram. He and his wife bought it back in the early fifties, lived upstairs for many years. He's very particular about his tenants. I could give you a recommendation."

Marvin stood up and enveloped Fiona in a big hug. "This doesn't mean I'll do it, but it sure is wonderful to have friends who'll scheme for you." For the first time in weeks he dropped his shoulders, and his face relaxed into a real smile. "Let's get on the road. I'm dying to see what Norman and Jenn have put together for Groundhog Day."

"On these," Fiona gestured at the paintings, "Maybe if it doesn't tax your cash flow, you should do this lot on your own. I think you'll be needing inventory."

"You don't need to do that, a deal's a deal."

"But I don't mind. My money's a little tight and we're all betting on the same horse. If this flies, I'll be getting a return on the book."

Marvin shook his head in disbelief. "We'll talk. There's a lot to sort out before it's all settled. Let's go eat."

Marvin and Fiona pulled up to Norman's, fashionably late. Inside, there was a heated debate going on between Norm, Thomas and Jenn about the proper protocol for the language and format for the identification tags on museum artwork. Jenn was taking the conservative museum approach, supporting the existing nomenclature. Thomas was arguing for more flexibility, to give more information on provenance and significance of a piece, and Norman was fuming over the tiny type size and the cryptic and ridiculous limitations. Norman wanted the artists to explain their works, especially abstracts. Jenn argued vehemently that that was a curator's decision and role. Marvin and Fiona looked at one another, and laughed. Thomas was trying to get Jenn to accept a non-standard collection designation, one that would give Willie credit for his role in starting the Caites collection. Jenn was trying to argue the matter—that that information should be provided separately. Fiona stepped in, and ended the argument.

She turned to Thomas, "Aren't you lending the pieces for the show?"

"Of course, that's not a question."

Fiona jumped right back, "But it should be. If, as the donor, you want a particular designation, you make the loan of the piece conditional on the designations. End of story."

Jenn's jaw dropped. "You can't go undermining the canons to satisfy every donor's whim!"

Thomas laughed, "I think we just did."

Norm jumped on the bandwagon, "And make sure the type is big enough, the seniors shouldn't have to bring three sets of specs just to see a show."

Marvin pointed his thumb at Norm and winked at Jenn, "Yeah, what *he* said."

Ardley couldn't resist, "Don't you think it interesting that the youngest person in the group is arguing the most conservative, even stuffy, position?"

Amanda had been silent up to now, "Yeah kid, loosen up."

Norman took the opportunity to set out the appetizers.

Amanda eyed the rolled mystery-bites. "What's this?"

Norm grinned, "Jenn calls them endive-surprise, with a French accent, so it sorta rhymes! Try them. Some have cheese, some salmon and some fancy ham."

"Prosciutto," Jenn corrected.

The group descended on the hors d'oeuvre, with a round of appreciative murmurs.

Amanda, ever practical, demanded, "But how are we supposed to know which is which?"

Norm wagged his finger at her. "Ah, that's the surprise, silly." He reached into the refrigerator and pulled out several bottles of an Oregon Pinot Grigio. As he poured he looked up at the assembled group. "I've been really busy at the shop, kinda lost track of the project. Where do things stand?"

Jenn stepped up to the counter and popped another appetizer, while reaching for a wine glass. "Fiona is writing like a maniac. I edit and compile her footnotes as she finishes each section. Arthur is breathing down our necks for the book. He's an odd duck, but really knows what he's doing. Marvin has emailed scans of all the paintings and Thomas's family photos. That at least is keeping Arthur busy creating the exhibit catalogue. He's having a great time doing it and being involved. The Mills Board is ecstatic with the project. Everyone feels like they have a hand in rescuing a talented Mills Alumnus from obscurity. I think Marvin is set to assemble the selected paintings and photos for the book, as we get it moving further along."

Amanda raised her eyebrows, and looked at Fiona. "Who put the kid in charge?" Jennifer beamed.

"Don't rock the boat." Fiona looked exhausted. "Between work and the book, I barely know what day it is.

"Anything else?" Norm was leading the way.

"Looks like we'll be going on tour." All eyes turned to Marvin. "Arthur was at an academic conference and he mentioned the project. There's a good deal of excitement about the prospect of introducing a new California artist. A museum in Pasadena has expressed interest and one in San Diego. Mills will sponsor, so the insurance and logistics are covered. Emma may be touring through the end of the year. It'll be up to us, and Jenn, whether her part of the exhibit will tour too."

"Ooh, kid, go for it, it'll be a real feather in your cap." Norm proudly put his arm around Jenn and gave her a squeeze.

It was Amanda's turn. "Jenn and I finished reviewing the

paintings which are appropriate for note cards. We've created the print-ready files and sent them out. We'll proof the advance sheets, and then they'll be back from the printers in mid-May. And the posters will be ready at the same time. We're going to give Mary Cassatt a run for her Impressionist money."

Thomas turned to Norm, "Any news on our other project?"

Norm shrugged. "I gave them till the fifth to pay December's rent, and get current by the fifteenth. So, we'll see. I'm not going to push any more than that. They've still got eight years left on their lease."

Marvin's ears perked up on that. "Is this Bikram?"

"Yeah, they're falling further and further behind." Norm looked nervously at Marvin.

Marvin blushed and bowed his head "Yeah, Fiona told me you're all planning my future. I'm not on board yet, but I'm flattered and intrigued. Things *have* been really rough lately." Amanda gave him a reassuring hug.

"Okey-dokey, I think this calls for a toast," Norman raised his glass. "To Emma Caites, and the blessings she's given us all."

Glasses tapped, and for just a bit, the group managed a moment of quiet reflection. It didn't last though.

Ardley broke the silence, "Since there's a tradition for Openings, like a rehearsal the night before, Thomas and I have booked Chez Panisse for that evening, so don't any of you make other plans. And make sure everyone reserves it, that includes Arthur Bradley and Cheryl, and anyone else connected with this crew."

"We'll have to alert Jordan and Eugene. I've already invited them to the opening," inserted Fiona, "It wouldn't be complete without them."

Jennifer leaned forward, "Fiona, I saw the photos. Does Jordan really use Emma's cane?"

Fiona nodded, "That's why I took the photo that way. Seeing it almost made me shiver. To me, it seemed like such a big part of Emma, in her paintings, and her life. Jordan has the same feeling for it."

Thomas nodded, "The photo brought me back, too." There was another lull in the conversation.

"Well, it looks like it's time for me and Jenn to hustle a bit. The menu is Salade Niçoise, with marinated barbecued flank steak and…" Norm shook his head and looked up at Jenn, "Kid, what are

355

we calling the fries?"

Jennifer laughed, "They're pommes frites."

"Oh yeah, the pum frits. We've got to step outside to deep-fry and grill. I'm sure you all have plenty to discuss." Norm nodded knowingly at Thomas. "We'll just be a few minutes." He and Jenn stood, and slipped out the door.

Thomas and Ardley went directly to Marvin. Fiona could hear Thomas urging Marvin to consider opening a gallery in which he would be the exclusive dealer of the Caites collection. It was the perfect entreaty to a man whose creative efforts had been overlooked and belittled for so long.

Amanda came over and gave Fiona a hug. "You look great, but I hope the weight loss isn't stress over the book."

"Naw, you know me. It's my Parisian conversion to jock. I've been walking every day. It helps to beat the stress and organize my thoughts. What's new with you?"

"Busy. School of course, but Norm and I have been prepping for Valentine's Day. We're actually struggling to keep stocked ahead of sales. Cheryl's publicity has really put the shop on the map. Not that I'm complaining. It's really tacky to complain about success. Do you think Marvin will go for the gallery?"

"I don't know, but I sure hope so. His partners are eating him alive. My fingers are crossed." Without a word, the two of them started straightening up—picking up the wine glasses and wiping kitchen counters. Marvin and the Caites had retreated to the living room.

Amanda wiped the crumbs from the counter, into the sink, and ran them down the drain. "So, Fi, any word from Denise?"

Fiona shook her head. I've left two more messages, but I won't leave any more. I don't know what's up with her. I wrestle between respecting her boundaries and wondering whether I've abandoned her."

"I'll give her a call, if you like."

"Let's let it go till after Valentine's. It's a new marriage and I definitely don't want to get in the middle of that. You know, we used to do Valentine's up big."

Amanda nodded, "Maybe just a card or something. Hey, you can send her one of the Emma Caites cards and see if she notices."

"Oh, I like that. Jenn can help me print one up. Hmm, maybe the picture of Thomas with the paintbrush, it's obviously our kitchen."

Fiona reached into the cupboard for the plates, and started setting the table. Amanda followed suit with the flatware.

"So why did Norm and Jenn need to go outside to cook?" Amanda queried.

"Barbecue and deep-fryer."

"I get the grill part, but the deep fryer?"

Fiona shrugged, "Norm said something earlier about there not being 220 wiring in the house, only the workshop."

"Oh. Okay. Do you think they need help?"

"Well, actually I thought we'd discreetly partake of the gallery conversation."

Amanda nodded, "Yeah, that sounds like way more fun. It'd be great, now that I spend so much time at the shop, I'd get to see him more." The two women filled their wineglasses and wandered into the living room.

Thomas was seated in a big armchair, with Ardley delicately perched on the upholstered arm, leaning forward. Thomas was leading the conversation, "So, absent any exhibit recognition, cleaned up and framed well, what do you think Mom's paintings are worth, retail?"

"It'll vary, but low end I'd say $2,500 each, if they're presented well. And the book will help."

"And if the exhibit *does* make a difference?

"Well, then she becomes listed and that definitely increases the value. Perhaps three times the minimum, even as much as ten times. But that's pushing it."

"So you could swing it if you sold three paintings a month, not to mention whatever else you carried. Marvin, you've *got* to do this. What do you think about carrying my work as well?" Ardley reached over and took Thomas's hand in hers.

Amanda caught the turn and winked at Fiona. First, the general discussion and then the assumption. The last question assumed proprietorship. Classic sales tactic. Fiona had sensed it was going well, but Amanda confirmed it.

Marvin answered sincerely, "Of course, any combination helps. The mother-son angle would be a nice, exclusive touch. You know it's like Wayne Thiebaud, his son had a gallery in Sacramento with his work."

Amanda added, "If you do this, it should start during the show. I'm sure Cheryl would have an interest in the *Oakland artist* angle,

357

and you'd get some free press. I can't tell you what her pieces have done for Norm's shop."

"*Okay* everybody, I am seriously considering it. I may be nutty, but I can't stand where I am much longer. I don't want to think about it anymore tonight, it already feels like my head will explode." But Marvin was smiling. "And you know, Bikram will have to fail first."

"Oh, they're failing. They'd close the doors today, except they're afraid Norm will go after them for the balance of the lease." Everyone looked at Amanda. She shrugged. "Well, they're neighbors, you know, people talk. And to them I'm just a part-time clerk in the shop next door."

There was a slam at the back screen-door. Fiona went to see if she could help. Norm was wrangling several large platters full of food. The aroma was intoxicating. Fiona relieved him of one of the platters and placed it on the table.

Norm juggled the remaining platters to the table. "Oh sweetie thanks for setting the table." Jennifer came in right behind him with a big bowl of steaming-hot fries. She set them down and immediately began taking salads from the fridge, and setting them out at each place. The pommes frites smelled incredible. Fiona reviewed the fare. On a bed of greens there were a number of seared tuna filets, rolled in sesame seeds. The flank steak, also rare, was heavy with garlic and soy sauce. The third platter held marinated grilled vegetables, onions, asparagus, red and yellow peppers and Japanese eggplant. Jennifer set to carving both the tuna and the flank steak into thin slices. She laid tuna slices over each of the salads, added olives and dressed the salads. All in all it was a colorful and delightful spread. Norm called everybody in for dinner.

"Wow Norm, this is incredible." Marvin *was* impressed.

"It's beautiful." Jennifer grinned wildly, *oddly*. Fiona noted it, but didn't know what that was about.

Thomas and Ardley joined them, and everyone found their seats. It was getting late, and they were all starved. Fiona was amazed at the dinner, the appetizers and the presentation. Norman had outdone himself. The friends set upon the food with vigor.

"So, Norm," Thomas was casual but serious, "What do you think it would take to convert that yoga studio into a gallery?"

"Not much, especially if you could get my friend Amanda involved. She's a whiz. Mats cover the hardwood floors, so they should be in good condition. The mirrors would have to come down, and that'll tear up the walls some. Lighting, some drywall, paint and minimal, high-end furnishings. Galleries are often sparse."

Amanda stood and took a small bow. "That means we get to do *another* opening?" Her enthusiasm was contagious.

"But with better cheese, this time. We're talking art." Fiona grinned. Ardley laughed and almost inhaled her bite of tuna. Amanda stuck her tongue out at Fiona. Marvin was holding one of the fries, looking at it quizzically.

Thomas reached for a second helping of the grilled vegetables, "These are wonderful, Norman, what was the marinade?"

"Sesame oil, soy sauce and some light olive oil," Norm turned to Jennifer, "Anything else?"

"Just a little garlic," she smiled. Fiona noted that same edge.

Amanda planted one of the fries in her mouth, "These are really good. Fries aren't easy."

"Pommes frites," answered Jenn, staring down at her plate.

"Check out the tuna in the Salade Niçoise," Ardley remarked, "It's got ginger in there with the sesame seeds. Norman, Jenn, there's a lovely balance to this meal." Fiona considered the spread. It far exceeded her expectations, and she felt guilty that she'd short-changed them in her culinary estimation.

The cooks looked at each other with broad smiles. "Thanks, Ardley," almost in unison. Norm continued, "We tried to do French, with a twist."

Marvin seemed lost in reflection. He was pondering his plate, moving his fries around with his fork. Fiona felt for him, it'd been a tough day, even if the outcome was hopeful. She figured he must be exhausted. Marvin excused himself, and pushed his chair back. "I just need some air." He headed out the back door.

Everyone looked at each other. Thomas looked at Ardley, "Did I push too hard?"

"I don't think so, hon, but it's not going to be an easy transition for him." She looked up at the others, "We need to be gentle and accept any decision he makes."

"Too bad, I did so like the pushy part." Amanda grinned. They all laughed, and then immediately felt guilty.

"Should I check on him?" Fiona didn't know quite what to do.

Thomas looked certain, "Just give him a few minutes."

Quietly, they picked at their food, hoping Marvin was alright.

Moments later, a strange gulping howling sound erupted from the back.

"That's it. I'm going." Fiona threw down her napkin and hurried out the back door. She found Marvin in the workshop, leaning on the worktable, shaking, making the strangest strained, almost sobbing sounds.

"Marv, Marv, are you alright?" she put her hands on his shoulders.

He turned, and there were tears streaming down his cheeks, but, as he gulped for air, it was clear that Marvin was convulsed with laughter.

Fiona was stunned. She didn't understand. The others had rushed out and were grouped around the door to the workshop. "Marv, what is it? Are you okay?"

Still shaking and unable to speak, Marvin pointed to the worktable. Finally, he reached out and picked up several small, white bags with small golden arches printed across them. The bags were strewn across the work surface—*McDonald's* bags.

Fiona didn't immediately understand, but her friends did and the laughter was contagious. Then *she* got it. Those perfect pommes frites were Mickey-Dee's. Fiona was gripped with the most infectious laugh she'd ever known. She turned, and everyone, Norm and Jenn included were gasping, convulsed with laughter. Ardley was laughing so hard she'd slid down to the floor, quaking. Thomas was leaning on the wall of the workshop. Jenn, gripped in giggles, slid down, and joined Ardley on the floor. They put their arms around each other and laughed with abandon.

Amanda caught her breath first, "Jeez, you two, that would have been such a waste if Marvin hadn't caught you. This is the best."

Marvin recovered, "Okay, everyone inside, let's eat."

Slowly, the crew pulled itself together, and headed back. When they could keep straight faces, Norm tried to explain, "The rest of it *is* authentic…" but it spurred a round of giggles. Poor Jenn was laughing so hard she was crying. She'd never been part of such a prank, and it had rolled out beautifully. None of them could look each other. Finally, Norm stood up and put some music on, which helped to settle them considerably. They finished the meal with light conversation and jokes. Norman pulled out a pie from Fatapples, and set dessert plates on the table. Amanda did the honors, and the party drowned its giggles in generous slices of blueberry pie and whipped cream.

Norman turned the music up loud, and they all did the dishes to Bonnie Raitt, dancing and singing along. At the end, they were deliriously exhausted. Everyone left bonded and giggly. Nobody doubted for a second that Marvin would be opening a gallery next to Lily's.

Chapter Fifty-Nine

Laden with two large bags, Fiona pushed awkwardly at the buzzer for Amanda's apartment. Opening the door, Amanda hooted and grabbed one of the bags, "You weren't kidding. You think the three of us can eat all this?"

"So maybe there's leftovers. What of it?"

"My, aren't we wild in our old age. It's just as well though, looks like *you* haven't eaten in weeks." Amanda reached over and pinched her cheek.

Fiona shot her a hard look, perhaps unfairly, but she was getting tired of fielding comments about her weight. Nothing had changed, except the walking, and she was loving it. But, after a flash, she thought the better of her irritation. As her best friend for over forty years, Fiona figured Amanda had nudging rights. Since she'd been working so hard these past few weeks, Fiona realized that she'd been under pressure, and a bit crabby.

She started to unpack the little white boxes from the bags. Amanda had already set the table. Jenn bounced in to help.

"Geez, that smells good. I'm starving."

Amanda came back from the kitchen with three cold beers, popped off the caps and deftly poured them into tall pilsner glasses.

"What are we celebrating tonight?" Jenn pulled out her chair, and tucked her legs under like a pretzel.

"Surviving Valentine's Day!" exclaimed Amanda.

"Really, was it so bad?"

"Not bad, just busy." The circles under her eyes attested to the long hours. "We struggled just to keep up. Norm was a real trooper, and even *he* was amazed at the response. We've changed our goals for stocking and taking another look at our pricing. In all the pandemonium we had to stop from time to time and remind ourselves it was a good thing. We did more for Valentine's than Norm did all last year. He's really excited. He catches on quick too. He's starting to think of really great marketing ideas."

Jenn nodded, "That guy is mind-blowing. He resists just a little at first but in the end he's more open than most people *my* age. Whatever it is he's got, we should bottle it."

"That'll be the next project." Fiona sat and reached for the first of the boxes. She was reproducing Eugene's dinner. It was an easy solution to an impossible schedule.

"Any other celebrations?" Amanda raised her glass for a toast.

Jenn glanced at Fiona, "I'm not supposed to tell you this, but the first section of the book is great." She turned and gave Fiona her full attention, "Arthur is amazed. He says it's academically up to par with anything Mills has ever published. With the photos and paintings included, Fiona, it really is impressive. Marv is positively raving. I think they're reconfiguring parts of the Exhibit to match the organization of the text."

Fiona blushed, "They're an easy audience."

"It doesn't hurt that Emma is such a sympathetic character. She's got all the genuine warmth of a Mary Cassatt, all the intrigue and independence of a Frida Kahlo, without the thorns or bad eyebrows."

Amanda almost spit out her beer. "Who said *that*?"

Jenn shrugged, "Arthur, why?"

"Wow, from behind closed doors the art world can be catty."

Fiona joined in, "Any small group can look lofty from the outside, but close up, people are all the same. Warts and all. Women in the arts get particularly harsh judgment."

"Emma seemed to leave all that by the wayside. If she rejected the judgments, she excluded the company. In some ways it cut her off, but in others it preserved the *her*, of her." Fiona leaned forward, "I haven't decided whether it worked. It didn't buy fame, but creatively, she marched on to her own drummer."

"Have you tried the cashew chicken, it's really great with the garlic eggplant." Amanda reached for another box.

"Do you think she was happy?" Jenn looked serious.

Fiona paused before replying. "I think she was fulfilled. I'm not sure what happy means." As she said it, she questioned what happy really meant, even for her.

Jenn needed more, "Okay, here's what I mean. Does her relationship with Willie at the end change your view of her mental state? Without Willie, would the story be different?"

Amanda was intrigued by where this was going, "You mean does Willie give us the *happily-ever-after* ending?"

Reaching for the ginger snap peas and peppers, Jenn giggled, "You've sure got a funny idea of happily-ever-after."

"Look, I've really struggled with this," Fiona admitted. "I like

Thomas's position that her continued engagement in painting, in light and form, was enough. But even *I* have to admit that after her earlier problems, it was a relief to know that she was capable of a full satisfying relationship. I'm happy for her that she found that sweetness."

Now Amanda was following closely, "Would you have asked that question of a male artist? After all, weren't a lot of the artists of the day—the Society of Six and all, confirmed bachelors? And some of them drunks, at that."

Jenn kept pursuing, "Fiona, are you judging Emma by a higher standard? Maybe one reserved for women?" She was serious, and Fiona balked, realizing the possibility that there was something to it.

"I was relieved that her story wasn't the sordid, *addict-artist dies in squalor* ending."

Amanda chuckled and put her hand on Jenn's forearm, "Fiona's never been a big fan of squalor." They both laughed.

Fiona cleared her throat, and emptied the last of the bok choy and mushrooms onto her rice, "The point isn't that she succeeded in romance, it's that she was able to have adult relationships. Her friendship with Wren is equally as telling. Her connections with Thomas and with Jordan, to me, they indicate a caring person, someone who reaches out and connects. And yes, to me it makes a difference. Lord knows there were plenty of artists out there, who are self-centered jerks or curmudgeons. I wanted more for, and from, Emma. It's not that she's female, it's that she's *my* artist, and it's part of what *I* value."

"Yup, you picked good. From that first day in Norm's shop to now, you picked good." Amanda had a big grin on her face. "And it's worked out good for all of us."

"It *has* been a wonderful experience. The writing's been hard, but it's helped me wind it all up. Hey, I have *this* woman," Fiona put her arms around her dearest friend, "To thank for all of it. She dragged me out to those God-awful shops and estate sales and I found treasure." Fiona gave her a loud kiss on the forehead.

"Aw, shucks, now pass the Kung Pao chicken." Amanda smiled at Jenn. "Don't we have *more* good news? Didn't you bring proofs?"

"I sure did. Can we clear the table some?"

"Yeah, I'm stuffed anyway." Amanda gobbled down the last of the Kung Pao. All three of them busied themselves clearing the table of dishes and those lovely, little white boxes.

Amanda had to admit, "We did some serious damage. I'm surprised that we could eat so much." With the table now clear, Amanda opened three more beers while Jenn pulled out the proofs. In all, she'd selected about thirty paintings to print on note cards. Fiona was surprised at how clear and luminescent they were—very close to capturing the light of the originals. The women pored over the tiny prints, oohing and ahing at the results.

"They're great, but what's our objective here?" Fiona asked.

"Well, they market in plastic sleeves of six selections, either two or four of each card. We need to figure out how group them." Jenn looked to Amanda for her marketing expertise.

Fiona leaned back to watch the pro at work. She was struck with the memory of Emma's painting of three women around a table. Here they were, *life imitating art*. While Amanda and Jenn shuffled and reshuffled the cards into different combinations, Fiona made a mental note to talk to Marvin about that painting.

Finally they settled on four sets with twenty-four cards per set. Jenn broke down the actual costs and Amanda worked out the pricing. Fiona was fascinated. Emma was being commoditized. The cards *would* be great sellers. They decided that after this run they could be made available to galleries everywhere—the franchising of talent. It was all a big package, the Exhibit, the book, the catalogue and now the cards. Without rancor, Fiona marveled that they *weren't* including t-shirts and embroidered baseball caps. Even Wayne Thiebaud had t-shirts; she wondered, did Diebenkorn? Art was a funny world. Museum stores, web sites and catalogues were big business and subsidized museum operations. Half attending to the busy tones of her friends, Fiona drained the last of her beer in a silent toast; *Welcome to success Emma, this may be what it looks like.*

Chapter Sixty

Fiona stepped out onto her porch and emptied the mailbox of its contents. It was a beautiful day. She stopped for a moment to tip her face up to the sun. She'd been so buried these past few weeks that her only forays outside were for the mail and her daily trek around the lake. Amanda had even dropped by to bring groceries. But now, she was beginning to see an end in sight. Easter had come and gone without a break. She didn't initiate anything with the group because she felt she had nothing new to report, and the pressure was on for completing the text. Arthur understood that she had to see to the needs of her existing clients, getting their estate tax returns out, but from time to time at their meetings, he'd tap his watch, to remind her that they would not make the show if the book wasn't submitted for publication by May first. Allowing time for editing, Fiona's deadline would be a week or two before that. Everyone was pressing, *would the book be ready*? Fiona was grateful that Arthur had been such a gentle advisor.

She walked back inside, sorting through the mail. There were two postal package pick-up slips mixed in with the usual bills. Fiona cursed under her breath—she'd have to make the trip to the West Grand station. She'd been home the entire time and wondered why didn't the mail carrier just ring the bell? Usually these slips meant an attorney or client had sent oversize packages of documents for review. The prospect of two such tasks, waiting for her, felt especially daunting under the current schedule. She sighed. For the first time in her life, Fiona was rolling out of bed and jumping into her work, in her pajamas, robe and slippers. She slipped into a pair of jeans and a sweater, and checked the time. If she zipped down to the post office now, she'd be back by two o'clock. Then she could assess the work load and reschedule to accommodate.

Of course, at the post office, there was a line. Fiona waited patiently, rolling her current writing conundrum over and over in her head. She knew that there were specific formulas for academic biographies. However, they could be awkward, and she'd been breaking the rules lately, trying to make the flow of the story smoother. Jenn protested that Fiona had become a footnote abuser. Inside, Fiona wondered if the art curator training wasn't making that girl just a tad… anal. She'd mentioned it to Amanda, who'd just keeled over in peals of laughter. Fiona didn't appreciate the joke.

At the counter, the clerk took the slips and disappeared into the back. She reappeared with a cart containing two huge boxes. "Just bring the cart back, you'll need it." Fiona thanked her, but groaned to herself. If these were work related documents, it would be a setback of huge proportions. She looked at the top package and noted Jordan's address. Fiona thought that there must be some kind of mistake, Jordan had been instructed specifically to ship to Arthur, at Mills. Sending paintings to Fiona created a problem with the protocol for insurance and logistics. But at least *that* box wasn't more work. Once at the car, she wrestled Jordan's package into the back. It was heavy. The second box was from France. That wasn't work either. Fiona's curiosity was killing her, but, after returning the cart to the clerk, she made herself wait, taking the packages home without opening them.

Fiona heaved the boxes upstairs and into the living room. She grabbed a pair of scissors, but hesitated for a moment—deciding which to open first? She opted for Jordan's, the larger and heavier of the two. She snipped the stringed packaging tape and peeled back the flaps of the carton. There was a note on the top, and the goods below were swathed in tissue paper and buried in packing peanuts. The note said,

Eugene found these leftovers in the storage space.
I'm thinking you'll put them to good use.
Love, Jordan

Fiona dug through the paper to three wrapped large bundles. Ripping open the first she found yards and yards of the subtle striped fabric from the guest room at Jordan's. The other soft bundle contained the rich, soft yellow silk fabric, which had been the duvet cover and the curtains. Fiona sunk down into the sofa, in awe. She could hardly wait to redo her bedroom to claim that same sumptuous quiet luxury. Never in her life could she remember receiving such a personal, opulent gift. *Leftovers!* Immediately she was juggling her schedule for time to redo the room. She knew it would have to wait till after the book, but would definitely happen before the opening. The last bundle, well wrapped in plastic bags, was a gallon of the eggshell finish paint, in soft yellow. Fiona

367

giggled with the pleasure of it. She couldn't wait to show Jordan the results.

Fiona was so excited that she almost forgot the second package. Remembering, she forced herself to neatly wrap up Jordan's goodies and return them to the carton before cutting into the securely taped package from France. The return address confirmed that this lighter box came from Jeanne-Marie and Gaston. The box was partially crushed so Fiona took extra care in opening it. Inside was a letter, again on top of well cushioned and wrapped goods.

Fiona,

Your trip and emails have inspired us. Gaston is composing new music and I have been trying new recipes. Gaston will tell you he appreciates the results. I have also been combing the thrift stores and flea markets. For a long time, much junk but no success. Now I have found three Emma paintings. I have kept one, as it is of a location that Gaston and I have loved for many years. But these two will have more meaning for you. I send them for your collection. I hope it's not too late for the exhibit. We are saving up for a trip to California. It was our luck that we met a wonderful American in Paris.

Love,

Jeanne-Marie and Gaston

Fiona sat with the letter in her hands and tears in her eyes. There was such depth to the wealth of experience Emma had brought into her life. The paintings themselves didn't even matter. It was the connections. Gingerly she lifted the first canvas and unpeeled the bubble wrap. It was a small piece, a plein air portrait of a painter, outdoors on a beautiful spring day. A serious young man, with sandy hair and a roman nose was standing, pictured waist-up, in front of an easel, brush aloft, staring intently at a subject in the distance. Behind him a line of fruit trees were just coming into bloom. The painting had been dashed off, with rough brush strokes, quite possibly without the subject's knowledge. The sun caught his hair, and highlighted his high cheekbones. It captured the vigor of youth and the sincerity of the young artist's approach. This was *Emma's* Pieter. Fiona gasped. It was lovely. Just a simple portrait to most, but to her it was a missing link of Paris. Her eye followed the golden light, the brush strokes, the deft embrace of his slight build,

368

his long fingers on the brush, all caught in an instant. This was a painter's version of a snap shot. Fiona knew that this *had* to go into the Exhibit.

She reached in for the next painting. It was a winter nocturne, painted at Luxembourg Gardens. It was similar to the painting of Pieter with the espaliered fruit trees, but from a different angle. Emma caught the trees running lengthwise, the hedge line receding away from the viewer. The dark limbs, in arching loops and twisted angles contrasted with a light dusting of snow on the ground. Against the almost bluish snow, the darker limbs cut the field into elegant geometric shapes. Where the branches were flat and horizontal, they bore caps of snow, clinging to their tops. The scene was illuminated by the light of a full moon—obvious, but not visible in the painting—and by a line of street lights, behind the dark perimeter fence, running at an angle in the distance. The colors were somber, but the view was light-hearted, with an odd angled slice of the snowy garden challenging the viewers' assumption about the night. It was stunning. Fiona drew in her breath slowly. She could not believe the bounty of her universe. This painting also needed to be included in the exhibit. She reached for the phone to dial Marvin's number.

Chapter Sixty-One

Arthur Bradley rang the bell, fidgeting nervously at the door. His lanky frame tilted, weighed down on one side by his briefcase. He hadn't called in advance—not knowing what he could have said on the phone. There was no answer. Anxiously, he pressed the button again. He set the briefcase down, clasped his hands together, and waited.

Finally, Fiona swung the door open, eyes widening when she saw who it was. "Why, Mister Bradley... what a surprise." Clearly it was. Fiona was dressed in a T-shirt and jeans with her hair piled high on her head, wrapped in a towel.

Despite teaching for over forty years at a women's college, Arthur Bradley had never become accustomed to the rituals of female grooming. He couldn't imagine why a grown woman would be towel-turbaned in the middle of the afternoon. He blushed.

"Come on in," she invited. "I'll be just a minute."

He followed her in and stood awkwardly for a moment in the living room while she ran upstairs. Realizing he'd left his briefcase on the porch, he stepped out to retrieve it, and as he bent over to pick it up, the door swung shut behind him. His fear was confirmed when he reached down to turn the knob. *Locked.* He couldn't bear the idea of ringing the bell and stood, briefcase in hand, trying to decide whether to simply wait or flee.

He was still debating his next move when the door opened, and a confused Fiona peeked out. Her hair was damp, but combed neatly, she'd donned a cotton pullover.

"Well *there* you are."

Arthur Bradley blushed again. This time it was clear that she'd noticed, making him blush even more.

"Well, I guess you'd best come in, again. Would you like some tea?"

"Yes, please, if it's not too much trouble."

"No, of course not. I was just going to make myself a pot." She retreated to the kitchen to put on water. He followed her as far as the dining room, and seeing the table and chairs, set himself down for the duration. While she busied herself with the tea, he reached down into the briefcase and pulled out more than a few stacks of paper and a file folder, which he arranged neatly in front of him. All told, it added up to almost three reams of paper, separated into tidy piles.

Fiona brought the tea service in on a tray. Seeing the state of the table she retreated to the kitchen, and returned carrying only the two cups.

"Would you like sugar or cream?"

"No, thank you, black is fine."

She placed a cup in front of Arthur and held hers as she sat down across from him at the paper-covered table.

Art Bradley, apparently satisfied with his organization, sat straight as he addressed Fiona, "I want you to know how impressed I am with this. It is a monumental effort."

"What is it?"

Bradley had thought that self-evident, but replied, "Why, it's the manuscript."

"*My* manuscript? Surely it's not *this* big. I've never actually seen it printed."

"This is it. It's in the edit format and I made the print a little bigger. I've also separated it into functional segments, corresponding loosely with decades. And thank you for getting it to me in advance of the deadline. Almost no one does that. This stack here," he patted the largest stack of paper, "These are the footnotes."

Fiona looked on.

"It's very impressive. I certainly never expected this level of scholarship, or involvement."

"Thank you. I had a lot of help."

They sat quietly for a moment, surveying the array of paper on the dining room table.

Fiona sensed some discomfort from Arthur and broke the silence. "Is it *too* long?"

"Well... not exactly. It's academic."

"Yes. I thought that was, in part, the objective. It is, after all, an academic press."

Bradley laid his hand again on the footnotes. "I must say again, I am particularly impressed with this."

"Thank you..." Now, it was Fiona who was uncomfortable.

He picked up the footnotes, and flipped through them. "You, see, the heart of it is in here."

"Is that good?"

"Of course. You truly captured it. Not an easy feat for any

scholastic endeavor. With the accompanying exhibit materials, this is an exhaustive and sensitive approach to the art and times of Emma Caites." He smiled.

"Thank you." It was clear now that Arthur Bradley had something to say, but was avoiding saying it.

"If this were the Master's or Doctoral thesis by any Mills student, I would be proud to publish it. Honored."

Fiona couldn't sit quietly any longer, "Mister Bradley, is there a *problem* with the manuscript?"

"It's academic."

"Yes, you said that already."

He paused nervously, "Normally, that would be precisely what I'd be looking for."

Fiona leaned forward, as if that could get her closer to his meaning. "But not in *this* case?"

"Exactly. Thank you." Bradley relaxed a little now that Fiona seemed to understand. With his hand still on the footnotes pages, he sipped his tea.

"Mister Bradley, what exactly is it you want me to do?"

The question seemed to surprise him. "Why, fix it, of course."

"And *what* do you think is wrong with it?"

"It's academic." He saw Fiona's eyes narrow as he searched for the words, "It could be more. It's… inside-out."

"Inside-out?"

"The story is here," he patted the footnotes stack again. Then he waived his hand dismissively at the rest, "*These* should be the footnotes." Fiona hung in the silence. Arthur Bradley began to wonder if he'd offended her.

"Are you asking me to re-write it?"

He nodded.

"The *whole* book?"

He glanced over at her and noted her color draining away. "Well it's really a reworking that's needed. You've buried the story in the dates and influences. The footnotes, though, are lovely. They really sing. You've really got the story *there*."

"Mister Bradley, there's only…"

"Arthur, please. Call me Arthur." He smiled warmly.

"There's no time. There's just over a month to the exhibit. It's still got to be edited and printed."

"There's plenty of time to do it right. There always is."

372

"Mister..." She caught his glance, "Arthur, I've just spent three months writing it. How do you expect me to re-write it in three weeks?"

"Fiona, it'll be fine. But it has to be the best you can give. This just isn't that." She looked despondent. He'd thought there for a bit that she understood. He continued "Your research is done and the bones are good. You just need to turn it right-side-out." She was near tears. Arthur Bradley had *never* been good with emotional women.

"What is it, exactly, that you mean by that? I don't understand." Shaking her head, she challenged, "Inside-out, right-side-out, speak English. What the hell do you mean?"

Bradley was flummoxed. "You know Emma well. Maybe *too* well. Sometimes you tell the story of Oakland, or the times, but forget Emma."

"It's all there." Fiona was defensive, "I think I tell it all. Show me what you mean."

Bradley hadn't come to pin her to the wall. He was sorry that it was going so badly. He reached out, grabbed one of the stacks, and opened it randomly. He scanned the page, on which the text discussed the dynamics of Depression era art employment, particularly during the 1937 double dip period. At the end of the passage there was a footnote. Arthur Bradley handed her the page. "Read this section."

Fiona complied. She looked up, "So?"

"What's the footnote number?

Fiona scanned the text again, "137."

Arthur Bradley hoisted the hefty footnote section and flipped through its pages. He found 137, and handed it to Fiona. "Okay, read the footnote."

She skimmed through the reference. It explained Emma's reticence to exhibit, and apply for WPA jobs, quoting letters to Wren in which Emma lamented the plight of her fellow artists. Bradley saw her soften. She looked up and met his eyes.

"Which one of those passages tells you more about Emma?"

Her shoulders slumped. She sighed.

"It's like that throughout. Academic. And yet the footnotes tell a wonderful story."

Fiona flipped randomly to another page of the text and tracked it through to a footnote. She shook her head. Arthur Bradley sat quietly and watched her work the process through several times.

Wilted, she looked up, "Okay. Inside-out."

"It's okay, Fiona. Like I said, the work is done, just flip it."

She looked sapped. "How am I supposed to do all this?"

"You've already done it. Start with the footnotes, let them lead you. Much of what is your current text will become your footnote material." Arthur went on to discuss the plans for the exhibit, how each section would emphasize a phase in Emma's life, but that some threads would carry through, show her styles changing and growing. His excitement was infectious. Fiona sat nodding, understanding the exhibit's visual approach.

"For the exhibit, the paintings and some of the other items *are* the story. Emma's biography is the footnote. You can flip that, too—use particular paintings to illustrate events or trends in her life. You've already written it, Fiona, if you just look at what you've done. This is more of a reshuffling to make it less..." He couldn't find the word.

"Academic. Yeah, I get it." She continued rifling through the pages, "Can I keep these?"

"Sure. Of course you have all this on your computer."

"Yeah, but holding it, moving it around helps."

He nodded. "Me, too."

"Arthur, how do you know I can do this?"

He sat a moment, thinking, then reached across to the file folder on the table. He opened it up and removed another, smaller stack of papers. Fiona glanced over at the emails she'd written from Paris. He held them out to her.

"Because I've read these."

Chapter Sixty-Two

From: thomascaites@mindspring.com
Subject: Progress Update—New Paintings
Date: April 12, 2008 3:40 PM
To: artantikmarv@sbcglobal.net

Marvin.

Can you get the name and contact information for Fiona's friends in Paris? Maybe on the pretext that we need the info for insurance or for Jenn's Exhibit? Ardley and I want to give them tickets to come to the opening, but we want it to be a surprise for Fiona. Can you wrangle it? We think it'd be fishy coming from us.

Thanks,
Thomas

From: artantikmarv@sbcglobal.net
Subject: Progress Update—New Paintings
Date: April 12, 2008 6:15 PM
To: ohamandakins@aol.com, norminisstormin@aol.com, jennsullymills@gmail.com, thomascaites@mindspring.com, cheryl@oaklandtrib.com

Hey All,

We need to find a way to get together soon that does not burden Fiona. As you may have noticed, the woman has been inundated with the Emma Caites writing and her own regular work. Jenn would like to take photos of the group for her part of the exhibit. I slipped over to Fiona's today to pick up two more paintings, sent by her friends in Paris. If Norman can get them cleaned up in a jiffy, I'll get them framed and photographed. (I'll email you all photos once they're taken.)

They are gorgeous and absolutely necessary for the exhibit. If we hurry, we'll get them into the catalogue too. I'm missing seeing you all and can't wait for another dinner. Jenn, are you up to giving me a hand? (Without the fast food this time?)

Fiona's Paris friend, Jeanne Marie (the lady of the coat), found and sent these two Paris canvases. They're both stunning, but the one that really fills in the gaps is a plein air painting of Pieter, painting. (Say that fast three times.) It's wonderful to see Pieter, especially through Emma's eyes. Better, I think, than a photograph. You'll love them.

Fiona's last ditch deadline is May 1. I think she'll wrap it up earlier, but so as not to pressure, can we schedule dinner, my place for May 3? Hang in there. We'll have plenty to talk about then.

Marvin

Chapter Sixty-Three

Amanda swung by to pick up Fiona for Marvin's dinner. They hadn't talked much over the previous month because Fiona was so busy finishing up on the book. As best Amanda knew, the manuscript was now finished. She buzzed at the front door, surprised that Fiona wasn't her usual punctual self, ready at the starting-gate. Fiona answered, with her hair tied back in a kerchief and paint freckled over her face. The living room was strewn with piles from her bedroom.

"Geez, I'm sorry. I'll be ready in a flash, just cleaning up. These things always seem to take longer than you think."

"Just what *are* you doing?" Amanda didn't think of Fiona as someone who'd just launch into a painting project, especially solo. She took a long look at her friend, who'd gone through some kind of transformation in the past few months. Since Christmas it looked like Fiona had dropped twenty-plus pounds. She had a bit of a tan, which looked goofy, almost theatrical, with the pale yellow freckles. While obviously excited over painting, Fiona's face still looked tired and drawn, as it had the night of the Chinese food-fest.

"I'm redoing my bedroom. It's my *post Emma* project. Come see."

Amanda followed her upstairs into the main bedroom. Fiona had just finished painting it the soft warm yellow, leaving the existing white trim. Amanda considered herself to be an expert painter, and tried not to be *too* obvious inspecting her friend's paint job. She was surprised and impressed that it was so well done, and that the cutting-in was so crisp. Well, what did she expect from an accountant?

"Looks great, Fi. Really great. Whatever inspired you?"

"It's a gift from Jordan. She sent me the same materials used in that amazing guest room of hers. I've been sewing curtains and bed linens too. I'm hoping to be finished by next weekend." Amanda peeked into Fiona's spare bedroom and saw the sewing stuff spread all over. She stepped in, and fingered some really lovely fabrics draped over the bed.

"Wow, it's quite the endeavor. I'd have helped if you'd asked."

"I know, but I thought you'd be caught up at the shop, what with

377

Mother's Day coming, and all. Besides, I really didn't expect to get so deep into it. It just kind of happened." Fiona peeled off her kerchief. "I was afraid there'd be a let-down, and since Jordan had sent these things, I just jumped into it. I'm a little sorry I didn't rest up a bit more first, but I'm really happy with how it's turning out."

"Yeah, well you're starting out with the best. Look at these fabrics. They're gorgeous. With these new talents, we'll be calling on you for an upcoming gallery renovation."

"Really? Anytime. Is there something I should know?"

"Nope, I'll save it for Marv, it's his deal."

Fiona turned back to her room, "I'm glad you like it. I'm really thrilled. I figured I ought to treat myself for Mother's Day, I don't really expect any other acknowledgement." Fiona lowered her gaze, avoiding eye contact.

"No word at all?"

"Nada."

"Did you send that card at Valentine's?"

"I did. So now it's up to her."

Amanda's heart ached for her friend. She'd done the right thing undertaking the project, another sign that under it all, Fiona was really doing well. She glanced at her watch.

"Best wash up. We don't want to be the *sabot* in the works."

Fiona nodded and headed into the bathroom. Amanda heard a laugh, and figured her friend had just encountered the decorator freckles. A few minutes later, Fiona emerged looking more like her old self, crisp, freckle-free and made up. Fiona grabbed a cardigan and pulled it on.

"Okay, let's roll. Is there anything I'm supposed to bring?"

"Nope the pleasure of our presence is all that's required." The two of them trooped out to the car.

"Do we need to pick up Norm?"

"Nope, he'll come a little later. He's got to close-up the shop."

"I feel like I've been underwater for months. Between tax season and the manuscript, I've been a prisoner of my undertakings."

"So, you finished up okay and on time?"

"*Just* under the wire. Losing those two weeks because of Arthur's big changes and redoing whole sections almost killed me. But it's complete, and I'm satisfied. With the photos and paintings, it's going to be a beautiful book. I just hope they can get it printed on time."

Amanda stopped and embraced her when they got to the car. "I'm so proud of you, of everything you've done." Fiona returned the hug, and the two of them just stood for a moment, enfolded in each others' arms, renewing forty years of connection. They untangled, and Amanda unlocked the car doors.

"So, who's coming tonight?"

"Just the core group. Cheryl's at a wedding and Arthur is too busy formatting." Fiona winced.

"Don't feel bad, you did your stint, we're all doing ours in turn."

Fiona nodded, "I guess that's fair. I'm worried about Jenn. A lot of this falls to her shoulders, and right at exam time."

"Are you kidding? That kid is *queen of the campus*. They're so thrilled with her, she can do no wrong. If she feels she needs some kind of accommodation, she'll get it."

Amanda maneuvered through traffic and took the exit to Marvin's. As usual, there was no parking, but the night was warm and still light out. They ended up parking several blocks away and enjoyed the walk in.

Marvin's front door was wide open, and music blaring from inside—*Talking Heads*. Amanda and Fiona looked at each other, knocked on the open door, and entered without further fanfare. Jenn was dancing in the kitchen, putting the last garnish on the salad. She jumped when they came in.

"Where's Marvin?" asked Amanda.

"He's outside. He's got a roast on the barbecue, with the rotisserie. He's been running in and out for better part of an hour. I swear, if he keeps opening that lid, it'll *never* get done!" Both of the women laughed. Jenn was growing into herself, organized and never short on words.

Marvin appeared at the kitchen door. "There they are. The *Mother of Merchandising* and the *Queen of the Day*." He hugged them each. "I hear incredible things about the new manuscript. Arthur is in love. I even saw him smile."

Jenn laughed, "He's really much looser, once he gets to know you."

Marvin grinned. He reached for an open bottle of Pinot Grigio, and poured two glasses. "Okay girl, what do we have for appetizers? These two look like they need sustenance."

Jenn feigned defense, "Oh the abuse I have to take!" She leaned over and pulled a cookie sheet out of the oven. "We've got ham and cheese in puff pastry."

"That's prosciutto to you," countered Marvin.

"Bless you," she countered, and the two of them giggled at some inside joke. Jenn took two steps to the counter and deftly slid the savory pastries onto a serving tray. Marvin grabbed the tray and waltzed towards the living room.

He stopped at the threshold, and turned back to Jenn. "Come on kiddo. Everything's under control here. Grab some paper napkins everyone, we're going casual this evening."

Marvin led the conversation, "Things are perking right along. Arthur expects to ship to the printer in a day or so. It looks good for printing by opening day. Fiona, he really is pleased. He won't share it with anyone at this point. Says he wants it to be a surprise. And the catalogue is already in the printing pipeline."

Jenn added, "This has really been a boost for him, and for the school. It's like they're all proud to be hosting the return of a long lost alumnus. It just keeps getting better. Arthur and the Dean are patting each other on the back for discovering you, Fiona."

"I'm just relieved to have it finished. I'll just wait to see where it goes from here." Fiona sounded as tired as she looked.

"And what about *your* exhibit Jenn, how's that shaping up?" Amanda seemed to have a handle on what was current.

"Just some photos of the group, left to go. Oh Fiona thanks for the great shots of Jordan. I'm sorry Arthur isn't here, I'd like to include him too. I can't help but remember him that day, wandering around the Mill's basements with that ring of skeleton keys."

Fiona yelped with the memory of that image. She'd completely forgotten their dusty, filthy basement search. "See if you can get him to pose down there, holding the key ring."

Jenn nodded appreciatively. "I'll try. It'd be a fun approach."

Amanda looked at Marvin. "So, aren't you the one with the *big* news?"

Marvin nodded. "That may be. I've signed a lease with Norm for the gallery space. The poor Bikram people have fled. It's a little scary, but I'll be the exclusive dealer of the Caites collection. I'll also be handling Thomas's paintings, some antiquities, religious artifacts and whatever else I can find. My attorney sent a settlement demand letter to the partners and we're waiting for their reply. Of course, in the meantime they've locked me out, but I'm rolling with it. They haven't yet put together the Caites angle. I wish I could be there when they do. All that aside, I start renovations next week, and once school is out, Amanda will be helping. Our goal is to open simultaneously with, or maybe just after, the Mills exhibit."

"I'll help, as soon as exams are finished, if you'll have me." Jennifer's enthusiasm was contagious.

"And, you've got me too," piped in Fiona, "It'll be great publicity if we can work simultaneous openings."

A buzzer sounded from the kitchen and Marvin jumped up to tend his barbecue. Fiona followed him outside. Amanda chatted with Jenn, and then followed them down to the barbecue a few minutes later.

"God, that smells good. I'm starved." Amanda inhaled deeply.

Marvin opened the lid of the barbecue, turned off the rotisserie and inserted a thermometer into the roast. He read the result and nodded with satisfaction, "Another ten minutes should do it."

"I hope everyone arrives in time." Amanda winked.

"Well," he said, "Timing's not critical, it needs to sit another ten minutes before carving, and I'm going pretty rare to start. So we'll be fine." He looked up at Fiona. "How are you doing?"

"Tired, but good. I'm still recovering."

"You're looking great, but I can see you're a little worn." Marvin looked concerned.

"I'm fine, really. It's just been a major undertaking. It's the biggest thing I've ever done."

"Just so's you're okay."

Fiona nodded. "Marvin, you remember that early acquisition, a painting of three women at a table?"

"Yeah, wasn't much to start with, but it cleaned up beautifully. Why do you ask?"

"I'd like to give it to Jenn. She's done so much and that painting reminds me of the times we, Jenn, Amanda and me, have brainstormed this whole thing into being." Amanda nodded in agreement.

"Done."

"Is it in the Exhibit?"

"Yes. We didn't have much portraiture, so we slid it in."

"Can we just switch the Exhibit tags?"

"Huh?"

"You know, so the tag will read, *from the collection of Jennifer Sullivan.*"

"Oh, that's rich. Yeah, I'll check with Arthur, but I like that. We'll do it just before the rehearsal run-through." Marvin nodded, "Sweet. I love it."

"I'm really thrilled, you know, about your gallery."

Marvin gave Fiona a hug. "I'm petrified, but it feels like the best thing I've ever done."

Amanda smiled, "Marv, you know you've got a ton of support. Just tell us what you need."

"Yeah, I know. It's really wonderful. It's all fallen together." Marvin checked the thermometer.

"Hello, are you down here?" It was Thomas. He came down the back steps. "It's good to see you all. Fiona, I think I can speak for everyone when I say we've missed you. You appear unscathed by the writing experience. How do you feel?"

"Pretty good. And satisfied."

"You should be. You've brought my mother to life in a way I can hardly express." He turned to Marvin. "And this man is going to reintroduce her to the world. I am so pleased." Thomas inhaled deeply, "Smells great, by the way. I was sent to ask about timing."

"Just about finished, on the table in about twenty minutes. Thirty tops. In a bit, Jenn will need to turn on the flame under the beans."

"Is Norm here yet?" asked Amanda.

"Oh yes," Thomas laughed, "He's been regaling us all with retail stories. He's trying to convince us that there's enough foot traffic for the gallery."

"Well, maybe the other way around," Amanda declared. "The gallery will bring the traffic."

"Yeah, a gallery like this has to be a destination location. That neighborhood alone won't support it." Marvin had clearly thought it out.

"The gallery might help *his* sales, Fiona said smugly. "But don't tell him I said so. If he has to work any harder, he might retire."

Thomas joined her in that assessment, nodding to Amanda, "You two are so funny. You know it's in poor form to whine about success, especially in a downturn."

"I'm just hoping it's contagious." Marvin's brow furrowed deeply.

"I'll deliver the bean message to Jennifer. But Marv, you have nothing to worry about. I have a really good feeling about this." Thomas turned and headed up the stairs to the kitchen.

Fiona put her arm around Marvin, "He's right you know." Marvin smiled and lifted the lid on the barbecue, revealing a lovely bacon wrapped roast.

Amanda inhaled, "Mmmm, do you need a plate for that?"

"Yes. Could you grab one"

"Sure. Be right back" She went inside to where Jenn and Ardley were setting the table. Without a word, Jenn handed Amanda a serving platter.

Amanda laughed, "Kid, you need to buy a lottery ticket." She flew back down the stairs. "Well, is it done yet?" She playfully shoved the dish at him.

Marvin shot her a look before probing the roast one last time. He unplugged the rotisserie, and slid the roast off the long skewer onto the waiting platter. "Voilà!" The party now headed indoors.

"Fiona, I hear you're redoing your bedroom." Ardley called across the kitchen.

Fiona grinned sheepishly, "Yup." She felt shy about discussing her bedroom décor, but in this group, design discussion seemed completely natural.

"I have a chaise lounge that needs reupholstering, want it?"

Fiona tipped her head, mentally calculating her fabric "Yeah, maybe, if it's not too big."

"I can reupholster it for you." Norm offered. "Lily and I used to do that in the shop." Fiona beamed, and gave Norm a quick hug. Amanda saw that contented look and relaxed. She knew that all was well with her friend.

Marvin carved the roast while Amanda put the potatoes in a serving bowl. Jennifer finished up the beans and dressed them with a bacon vinaigrette sauce. A large green salad graced the center of the table. In a flash, the group was seated and ogling the fare.

"Wow, garlic and rosemary potatoes. Hmmm, my favorite." Amanda spooned a generous helping. Marvin had arranged the roast slices with the medium pieces on one side and the rare on the other. Fiona speared several of the rare slices and passed the platter on.

Marvin poured a lovely, full cabernet and offered a toast, "To Emma Caites, and all the wonderful things she's made possible."

The conversation steered towards Marvin's gallery and the Mills opening. Marvin announced that Arthur had called him that morning to say that, with just a few finishing touches, the book would be ready for the printer Monday. Arthur was determined to be ready.

On one side of the table, Norm, Fiona, Ardley and Jenn were debating the layout and color scheme for Marvin's gallery. Amanda winced. She remembered Marvin's comment about women and decorating. Every now and again, Jenn discreetly stepped back to take photos of the group. She seemed to know exactly what she wanted, and thankfully, never asked anyone to pose. Marvin and Thomas were quietly discussing the perennial Emma question. Why wasn't she more famous? Amanda saw Fiona look up and scowl.

Marvin continued, "She clearly had the talent, she was well financed and had connections. Even with her distance from the social side of the arts community, I don't understand why..."

Not quite under her breath, Fiona interrupted, "Yeah? Well, *you* try it."

There clearly was an unfamiliar edge to her voice that, even in hushed tones, caught everyone's ear.

"I'm sorry, what was that?" Marvin turned to Fiona.

A lull in the conversation caught the wave, and suddenly everyone was listening for Fiona's answer.

"Just that you all think it's so easy. Why didn't she just get famous? None of you have any idea how hard it was to do what she did. Just you try it and you'll see why she wasn't in the limelight." There was an edge in her friend's voice that made Amanda sit up and take notice.

Marvin was sincerely taken aback by Fiona's tone. "What exactly do you mean?"

Fiona sighed, "It's one of the toughest jobs out there. I know, and apparently I didn't even do such a good job of it. But being a single mom takes everything you have and more. The proof is in the pudding, and Thomas is the result," she nodded in his direction, "Emma *was* a monumental success."

Norm nervously took another serving of beans, and thinking again, more potatoes.

"Well, sure, but..."

Fiona didn't let Marvin finish. "*No buts!* She was an artist. Most who try can't make a living doing just that, *and* she had a kid during times that weren't forgiving of her status *and* she integrated it all into a life that was lived fully, *and* yielded phenomenal results. Her talent shines through. Her son, maybe her greatest endeavor, is a well-adjusted, loving and talented man." Fiona's voice caught for just a second, betraying her, "She *earned* their way, and didn't rely

384

on her inheritance. She continued to paint, making a living all through the depression, when many failed and left the field. She refused to apply for government WPA positions that sustained many artists, because she didn't want to take bread out of the mouths of others when she knew she had funds. She painted, quietly promoted herself, sold her own works, taught and she did it all with a physical handicap." Fiona was on a roll, "She didn't mean to turn her back on relationships or on fame. She just didn't have time. And all the while, her art continued to evolve. She grew. Right up until she died, her art was the most important expression of who she was. You guys don't get it. It's not an academic question. She was totally amazing. Norman said it once, 'She did it with her head held high.'"

Silence reigned.

Then, Ardley started it. She started clapping, softly. Amanda followed, then Jenn and Norm.

Thomas was crying. He leaned over and put his arms around Fiona. *"Thank you."* She embraced him back.

Marvin swallowed and recovered, "And that will be the mission and the motto of the gallery. I humbly stand corrected." He bowed to Fiona. By the end everyone was applauding, including Fiona.

As the applause faded, Norman sighed, "Well, I'm glad we got that squared away. Could someone *please* pass the roast?" The tension shattered, they all laughed.

The conversation returned to its lighter notes. There was a discussion on the best colors for gallery walls, neutrals or white. Ardley requested to come see Fiona's new color scheme. She wanted to get some insight into Jordan before she arrived. Marvin made arrangements to pick up the chaise. Under the table, Amanda found Fiona's hand and gave it a squeeze. Fiona's homily had become the galvanizing and calibrating event of the day. Now, more than ever, they were all on the same page.

Marv served a quick, light desert of sorbet and biscotti. Shortly thereafter, the conversation slowed, and yawns started to punctuate the evening. The event wound down early, not consciously, but perhaps out of group exhaustion.

Amanda and a tired Fiona were the first to leave. In the quiet car ride home Amanda gave Fiona one of her highest accolades. "Ya did good, girl. You set him straight. Hell, you set all of us straight. Do I still have to read the book, or was that the Cliff notes?"

Fiona laughed. "I know it was a little over the top. I'm just getting tired of the question."

"Really, you were fine. And anyway, how often does dinner come with applause?" She paused, "On a more serious note," Fiona leaned forward, and Amanda continued, "Do you have somewhere to sleep in that mess of a house of yours? Do you need a place to crash tonight?"

Fiona laughed, "Naw, I'm fine. I can stand my *own* squalor."

Chapter Sixty-Four

Fiona rolled over and savored her Sunday-morning, sleeping-in dreaminess. The smell of fresh paint reminded her of what she'd finished the night before, and she opened her eyes. She was in the room of her dreams. Basking in the completion of Jordan's gift made Fiona feel like a queen. From the duvet and matching curtains to the contrasting pillows, the room was an exploration of *elegant subtle*. For her, every detail made the room more serene, more luxurious. Never in her life had Fiona treated herself to something so personal, so intimately hers. It would be complete as soon as Norm finished upholstering the chaise lounge and she picked the right artwork. All that would have to wait until the end of the Exhibit, but even the contemplation of it brought satisfaction.

She sprung out of bed, *just* to open and tie back the curtains. She then slipped back under the covers and propped herself up on the pillows. She admired the drape of the fabric, the way it gathered, spilled down, and puddled on the floor. Other than paintings, no material possession had given her such pleasure since... and here she laughed, since the coat. What was she becoming? Fiona glanced over at the alarm clock and noticed that it was already well past ten. *Such languor.* If she got up now she could walk Lake Merritt and still get the day underway by noon. She had to clean up the guest room, the victim of her sewing frenzy. Tomorrow, it was back to regular work, but even that felt full of the promise of comfortable rhythms. Fiona felt content. Reluctantly, she slid out of bed, and thoroughly enjoyed making it—smoothing the duvet and placing the pillows just so.

Fiona pulled on her sweats, and was headed out the door when the phone rang.

"Yup?"

"Mom?"

"*Denise.*" Fiona was dazed.

"That's a funny way to answer the phone."

"I thought it might be Amanda."

"Happy Mother's Day!"

Fiona had completely forgotten. "Well thanks, sweetie." There was a long awkward moment, so she added, "So, how ya doing?"

"I finally found a job."

"Well that's great. What kind of job?"

"It's in Redwood City."

Fiona stopped. This was huge. Redwood City was just across the Bay, and definitely *not* in Texas. "Congratulations. That'll be a change. Are you pleased?" Fiona didn't ask about Tom.

"I read about your artist and, you know, the exhibit."

"Where did you read that?"

"It's in the Mills Alumnae magazine. There's a whole story about the discovery of this forgotten artist." She paused, "Mom, did *you* write a book?"

"Yeah, I guess I did. It's a long story."

"Really, a book?"

"Yup. There's still some tread on these old tires, you know."

"I'm just surprised. It's cool. *Incredible*, even. You don't expect to leave home and have your mom become a published author in the next breath."

"Well it was a little more than a breath, and you knew I was researching *Emma Caites*."

"I just thought you were obsessed."

"I was. But it was a good thing. Are you in Redwood City now?"

"Not yet. That's a long story too. I'm scheduled to start in mid-June, but I'll be flying in the morning your Exhibit opens. I didn't want to miss it."

Fiona noticed the first person singular. "Thanks sweetie, it's important to me. Email me your flight info and I'll pick you up."

"Don't you want to know what's up?"

"I'm dying to know, but I figure you'll tell me when you're good and ready. Some things don't change." Denise giggled at that.

"I really miss you Mom, I'll tell you everything when I see you."

"It's your call, Denise."

"So, you'll give me a private tour of your artist's exhibit?"

"You got it, kiddo. Anything else?"

"No, that's all. It's great to hear you."

"I love you Bunny." Fiona thought she heard a hint of a sob at the mention of their old pet name.

"I love you too, mum. Happy Mother's Day."

"It is *now*. I'm really glad you called." Fiona was having trouble keeping her *own* voice even.

"Things are still kinda weird here, but I'm sorting it out. For now

388

it's enough that I'll see you for your opening. I gotta go, okay?" Fiona heard her voice quaver.

"Hang in there. I love you. Call if you need anything."

"Okay. Love ya mum."

"I love you, too." The phone clicked.

Fiona immediately dialed Amanda. When she answered, Fiona wasted no time with pleasantries, "Denise called! She's moving back to the Bay Area. She got a job... of some kind. But not a word about Tom. She called for *Mother's Day*."

"Holy shit! You okay?"

"Yeah, just a little stunned."

"When is she coming?"

"She's flying in for the Opening at Mills."

"Shit, Fi. That's amazing. Is she okay?"

"She sounds shaky, but okay. Didn't want to go into it on the phone. But, she called."

"Oh, Fiona, you've got to call her back. The big event is really the rehearsal the night before." There was a long pause. Fiona didn't respond. "Fiona?"

"Yeah, I'm here. Just thinking. We'll leave it like this. The rehearsal event is really for us, for the core group. She's not a part of that."

"Wow, Fiona. What are you going to do now?"

"I'm heading out for my walk around the lake. Wanna join me?"

Chapter Sixty-Five

Arthur Bradley and Marvin stood like gargoyles at the door to the Mills Gallery. Fiona and Amanda waltzed up in the warmth of the early evening. Some of the Mills people were already there; the librarian who'd helped Fiona and Jenn in their early search, the Dean, and Fiona recognized some of the Board Members who'd presided at Fiona and Jenn's presentation. Jenn was talking to the Dean, who stepped forward to shake Fiona's hand when she saw her.

"We are all so excited. Most of us read the galleys, before the book went to the printer. It's wonderful. Fiona, this is such a big event for Mills."

"I'm happy to be a part of it, too. It probably wouldn't have happened if Mills hadn't given me Jennifer. She's been my right arm, all along." She turned to Jenn, "I almost forgot, did we get the books back from the printer?"

Jenn nodded, "Everything arrived the day before yesterday. Fiona, the book is *gorgeous*."

"Are there copies of the book for the group?"

"For exhibit sponsorship there are one hundred promotional copies. We've already distributed copies to the Dean, the Board and two each to the two galleries down south. Tomorrow we'll be giving two to the Oakland Museum and we expect to dole out another twenty copies to various Northern California museums. Even then, there are plenty for our group, and then some."

Amanda approached Marvin, "Hey, we got all these bigwigs here, ya gonna let us in to see?"

"You're early. And nobody gets in till *everyone* is here." Fiona joined them.

Amanda pressed further, "Nobody?"

"Well, we let Cheryl in this morning," Arthur admitted, "but that was for an official, exclusive press tour. Her review will be in tonight's paper. And Fiona, we made those little *changes* you requested."

"With the exhibit tags?"

"Yes." Keeping Jenn in sight, he lowered his voice, "Jenn helped hang the show, but after she left, we made the switch."

"I can hardly wait." Fiona stretched up to a very tall Arthur and kissed him on the chin. He blushed.

Arthur recovered, "We've finalized the details for the Emma Caites Way tour in Southern California—those two museums. They'd like to know whether the author can be available for each of those openings."

"Sure, do *I* have to speak?"

"Not if you don't want to, you can just do it as a book-signing event if you'd prefer. They'd like a short address on how you came to the project, you know, found an old painting and all. I'll give you their contacts, and you can take it from there."

Norman came strolling up the sidewalk, clearly enjoying the warm, summer evening.

"This is a beautiful campus. Who'd think this little gem is tucked into East Oakland." Amanda reached over and gave him a big hug.

"There's Jordan." Fiona saw Jordan and Eugene making their way to the gallery. She waved. Jordan was leaning on her cane, busy pointing out the sights. Eugene saw Fiona and steered Jordan towards the group. They were intercepted by the Dean, who recognized Jordan from the photos. She had seen the alumnus opportunity coming up the walk. Fiona soon joined them, and gave Jordan and Eugene hugs. Norm saw Jordan, and walked over to connect.

Fiona turned to Jenn and said, "This is going to get out of hand, I'll need your help with introductions, will you recognize everyone?"

She nodded. "No problemo."

A limo pulled up and Thomas stepped out, and taking his wife's hand, he assisted her out. Two trim middle aged women disembarked behind them. They turned and faced the group, and both Jenn and Fiona broke into a laugh.

Jenn was the first to call it, "Thomas's daughters. And just take a look at those eyebrows!" The shorter of the two was a dead ringer for Emma Caites. The group just stood agape, then Norman turned from Jordan, and his jaw dropped. Thomas had hardly mentioned it. Maybe he didn't even see it.

Amanda sidled up to Fiona. "Get a load of that. It's like she's here. Come back for her own show." They both had goose bumps. Two more unfolded from the limo. Fiona looked and strained and looked again.

"*Oh my God*. It's Jeanne-Marie and Gaston!" Fiona set off for the limo, at a run.

Norm looked at Amanda, "Look at her go. Did you know she could do that?" Amanda just threw her head back and laughed.

Fiona reached Jeanne-Marie and threw her arms around her. "I can't believe it. How did you get here?" Jeanne Marie pointed to Thomas, "He sent for me, the *cassoulet lady*. And I would not have missed this for the world."

Gaston laughed at the total surprise, and gave Fiona a big hug. "Si maigre! What happened to you?" Fiona didn't catch the French.

They gathered at the gallery entrance, exchanging introductions and hugs, creating a confusing knot of bodies. It was as though everyone had forgotten the exhibit entirely. Arthur was looking overwhelmed.

Marvin stepped up, cleared his throat and announced, "Mills College, Arthur Bradley and the Emma Caites crew welcome you all to this preview of *The Emma Caites Way*, a retrospective collection of a fine, and until now, under-appreciated artist from Oakland and Mills College." Arthur swung open the doors, letting them in.

There shouldn't have been any surprises for Fiona. She knew the story better than anyone. As she joked later, she'd written the book, but the exhibit was beyond her expectations. It was a tribute to Emma, her art, to her life. In the vestibule of the Gallery hung the photo of Emma as a young Mills student in a drama production, fearlessly facing the camera. Next to it was a reproduction of her Mills application, complete with the story about her beloved grandmother. Near the entry to the main hall was the original of the Emma Caites Way painting class poster. Turning left into a separate room, in Jenn's exhibit, was Fiona's first painting—the apartment and a corresponding photo of the view out her window. They hung with the story of her discovering the painting and an introduction, one by one, to everyone who'd made the unfolding of Emma's story possible.

Fiona proceeded straight ahead, into the main exhibit. Above the entry were the words from the Emma Caites Way poster, about her French training and American can-do attitude. As she entered the hall, Fiona gasped. The center of the room was taken up with Emma's post-war car. Behind it were the paintings which included the car, her self-portrait and several others. Nearby, stacked and tied in their ribbons, behind Plexiglas, were all of Wren's letters, neatly and lovingly bundled by Emma. On an adjacent wall was an interactive computer display where visitors could search and read Emma's correspondence to Wren. The walls were lined with paintings, grouped mostly by decade, though occasionally by theme. Dotted between were photos: Emma at Mills, Emma's school photos in Paris, Emma painting in the hills of Oakland, Emma with her friend Florence, Emma and Thomas. A chronicle of her life.

One short wall held a collection of tiny canvases, The Intimates, with a photo of Jordan and the transcribed quote from her interview. The late 1930s and '40s were dominated by incredible landscapes of Oakland and the surrounding hills. Grouped together, they were a breathtaking tribute to Emma's love for her home. Mixed in were portraits, house paintings, paintings of Lake Merritt, the boatyards and the estuary. Punctuating the passage of years were Emma's annual self-portraits and paintings of Thomas, chronicling his childhood. Fiona had a hard time taking it all in. A group of Emma's Intimates silently explored the world through Emma's eyes. Fiona found one of Thomas's daughters, spellbound, standing before one of Emma's self-portraits that could easily have been a mirror.

She turned to Fiona, her eyes brimmed with tears, "They never told us. We never even looked at the paintings or photos before."

Later, Jeanne-Marie found Fiona in front of the painting of Willie's shoes and saxophone. "Your artist, she is incredible. All this is amazing." Behind her, Gaston nodded. The musical paintings had found a special place in his heart.

Norm and Jordan, arm in arm, examined The Intimates, marveling at how, even on so small a canvas, Emma's signature brushstrokes boldly carved the edges of light and dark. Eugene and Marvin quietly discussed the abstracts of the musical 1950s, the light reflections and the ever-present saxophone.

The Dean approached Fiona, "Did you know how big, how incredible this exhibit was going to be?" Fiona could only shake her head. She had explored it in bits, stories and images over months. Nothing had prepared even *her* for the totality of the experience.

Fiona grabbed Amanda as she passed by. "It's impossible to do this all at once. It's something you have to keep coming back to. You just can't absorb it all."

Thomas and Ardley, hand in hand, walked through the years,

Thomas quietly sharing the stories of his childhood, some for the first time.

Marvin, Jenn and Arthur were beaming. *They* were the artists tonight, the conductors of this symphony. They'd seen it come together. They were the ones who understood its total impact. They marveled at the effect it had on the participants. Jenn pointed out that this spellbound group was *more* prepared for the experience than the general public would be. She wanted to see the difference in tomorrow's crowd.

When it looked like Jenn wasn't actually going to finish making the rounds, Arthur led her over to the painting of the three women. The whole gallery heard Jenn's astonished response when she saw the tag designating the painting as *loaned from the collection of Jennifer Sullivan*. She cried and, if only for a moment, Fiona was glad to have knocked her off her cool. But that same surprise hit Fiona in the France section, when she stood back to admire the Lavender Gatherers, she noticed *her* name on the Museum tag. She cried, too. She found Jordan to thank her. Jordan simply responded with a wide smile, "Don't be silly, that painting matches your bedroom perfectly."

After an hour of wandering, looking and touching, Thomas announced that the restaurant was expecting them. Quietly, everyone filed out in small groups, a bit dazed, as though they'd just heard a long and moving eulogy. Outside, they winced at the sunlight; they'd been away in a strange world so intently they expected to disembark into the night.

Outside, Thomas gave directions to Chez Panisse, for the few who didn't know the way. They climbed into their cars, not wanting to leave, but also needing to shake it off, and to reclaim their own senses. Over and over, Fiona heard it, "I'm coming back."

In the car, everyone was quiet. Jenn seemed to be enjoying the stupor.

Finally Amanda turned to Fiona, "*Jesus*, I hope Mills printed enough books. No one is going to leave without one." Fiona knew her friend was back to her regular self. Back to marketing.

At the restaurant, Thomas had reserved the entire upstairs for the event. The center tables had been piled high with platters of incredible food, and Gaston's eyes were wide with the cornucopia. *Not* what he'd expected of American food.

Norman saw his reaction, and slapped him on the back.

"Welcome to the gang, young man, I think you'll come to enjoy it." It turned out that Jordan and both of Thomas's daughters spoke fluent French, so Gaston and Jeanne-Marie were in wonderful hands. Fiona could only register a small amount of the food offered. There were trays of roasted Cornish hens, a roast leg of rosemary lamb, garlic mashed potatoes, mounds of salad, corn, grilled baby vegetables, terrines of soup, loaves of crusty bread and much more. More food than Fiona could have imagined. There was a table of wines and Thomas took it upon himself to pour for everyone as they entered. Ardley helped lead the way, and following her example, the guests began to pile plates high with the rich and sumptuous fare. Still, everyone spoke of the exhibit in hushed tones, like they'd been in church.

There was consensus—the exhibit went beyond the art of it. It placed Emma at the leading edge of her century, and illuminated her art and the times in a way rarely achieved by any gallery. Cheryl soon joined them and passed out copies of the Tribune, with her glowing reviews of both the exhibit *and* the book. Fiona was stunned. It was overwhelming.

Tomorrow she'd pick up Denise and she'd get to bring her to the official opening. It all felt more like induction into a cult than a passing artistic event. Thomas took Cheryl's review, and stood up holding the newspaper.

"*This* calls for a toast." He paused a moment to compose himself, "Over these last few months there have been numerous toasts to my mother. Tonight, with this," lifting the newspaper, "Emma Caites finally achieves the recognition she always deserved. She takes wing and flies. The toast I offer tonight is not to my mother. I especially wanted to thank Fiona, but when I look around, I clearly see that it's not enough. So, tonight I want to toast all of us. Here's to our vision, our love, and our ability to connect with each other in amazing ways and to achieve incredible feats of staggering beauty." Thomas's eyes swept the room, taking in the assembled champions of Emma Caites.

"And so…" raising his glass, "To *all* of us."

Acknowledgements

This book would never have made it to press
without the contributions and assistance of an entire village
of well-wishers, confidantes, editors and supporters.

I'd like to credit the editorial assistance of Rick Edwards,
Keith Walters and Elizabeth Bernstein, the unending emotional
and cheerleading support of my family and friends, especially
Patricia, Keith and Kelly, Andrée, Leigh, Jane (all the way from
Toronto), Bruce, Suzie & Paul, all the folks on the farm in Two
Rock, and those faithful and patient serial readers in Copper
Harbor who sustained me in the early phases of the
NaNoWriMo challenge. And thank you to NaNoWriMo
for getting me off my duff to do this.

A.V. Walters was born in Canada, to American parents.
(And after thirty years in California, she no longer says 'eh'
at the end of her sentences.) She spent her last years there
at a chicken farm in Sonoma County and began writing.
Now fully recovered, she's returned to her home state
of Michigan, where, it turns out, she belongs.

Her second novel, ***The Gift of Guylaine Claire***, a nod to her
Canadian roots, is also available from Two Rock Press.